THE VAMPIRE COALITION

THE COMPLETE COLLECTION

ETHAN'S MATE

RORY'S MATE

NATHAN'S MATE

LIAM'S MATE

DARIC'S MATE

J. S. SCOTT

The Vampire Coalition: The Complete Collection Boxed Set
(Ethan's Mate, Rory's Mate, Nathan's Mate, Liam's Mate,
Daric's Mate)
By J. S. Scott

Copyright © 2013 by J. S. Scott

Includes:
Ethan's Mate - Book One Copyright © 2012 by J. S. Scott
Rory's Mate - Book Two Copyright © 2012 by J. S. Scott
Nathan's Mate - Book Three Copyright © 2012 by J. S. Scott
Liam's Mate - Book Four Copyright © 2012 by J. S. Scott
Daric's Mate - Book Five Copyright © 2013 by J. S. Scott

ISBN: 978-1-939962-37-9 (Print)
ISBN: 978-1-939962-00-3 (eBook)

CONTENTS

ETHAN'S MATE

BOOK ONE

THE VAMPIRE COALITION

PROLOGUE

Being a vampire was a lonely existence. Ethan Hale had walked the earth for the last five hundred years, surviving by stealth and by hiding his true nature, knowing that humans were not yet ready to accept and welcome the existence of vampires. The world had changed over the centuries. But not enough…

There were others of his kind, but vampires were solitary creatures, trusting no one, walking alone. While they might socialize occasionally, and his kind could call upon another of their brethren for help, they never stayed very long in the company of others. He had three brothers that he would give his own life for, however, in the end, they all dwelt alone.

The only hope of relief from his lonely existence was to find his soul-bonded mate. That life changing event had never occurred for Ethan and he had wandered for centuries without a soul.

Ethan and his three brothers fought the good fight, and popular vampire myths were often a topic of jokes among his brethren. Vampires were not "made," they were born. Living, breathing, flesh and blood with extraordinary powers and, yes, a need for blood to survive. The only thing that they lacked was a soul. Their soul-bonded mate held that tightly inside of her own, keeping it safe and protecting it until the day that it would be transferred to her vampire in a mating ceremony as ancient as the vampire species.

Vampires were *not* the monsters of lore, however, there were times when self-policing was necessary, which meant that Ethan, his three brothers and several others of his brethren had to unite to defeat a *fallen* that had given in to bloodlust. Killing aimlessly was against the code of the vampire. If one of his kind became too frenzied while feeding and killed, the lust for a blood kill would become permanent, making them beyond redemption. They would become a *fallen*, and immediate extermination of fallen vampires was the only hope of survival for his kind. Human detection would mean the destruction of his entire species. Although the vampires might laugh at the incorrect lore and the misunderstanding of true vampires, humans would see them as evil abominations that needed to be hunted and extinguished.

Vampires did not kill indiscriminately. They took blood when they needed it and left the human donor with no memory of the incident.

And their one true mate? That was no myth, that was real, but finding one's mate could not be rushed, as Ethan and his brothers had discovered over the last several hundred years of waiting. All vampires were born male, their female counterpart a human with a genetic difference. The human female mate was born with her soul combined with that of her vampire mate, a genetic mutation that meant that she had to call her mate to her, before he lost his life force. Female mates did not live beyond their thirtieth year unless they became bonded with their vampire.

Ethan was among the oldest of his kind who had yet to find his mate. Had she already passed, failing to call him to her? Had he not heard her call? It had been so long for him that he had stopped waiting. A vampire lost his ability and desire to have sex after the age of one hundred and it had been over four hundred years for Ethan. He had stopped believing that she awaited him or that she was yet to be born. He had accepted it, but it didn't stop the yearning and loneliness that were now a part of his existence.

His brothers, who were also unmated, had similar thoughts - it was those thoughts which had driven them all to work for The Vampire Coalition. They were all past the age for mating and had to accept that, for them, a mate was no longer a possibility. Perhaps he and his brothers would not have mates, but they could preserve their species for those that could. Mated vampires were happy, contented, living a life that was complete and filled with joy. Ethan and his brothers wanted their breed to continue its existence on this earth. It was what they lived for, their cause, a ray of light and hope for ones who lived in darkness. If they had nothing else to live for, they could remain in that ray of light by preserving the future for others of their kind. If they didn't have The Coalition and their goals, they knew it was possible to become the *hunted* instead of the *hunter*.

CHAPTER 1

ome to me. I need you.

Ethan Hale sat up in bed, his heart pumping, sweat dripping from his body so profusely that it saturated his bedding. He was panting as if he had just battled a dozen *fallen*.

I'm dying. My life force is draining away. Come to me.

The voice was weak and soft in his mind, a faint whisper with a female softness that sent a shiver down his spine. He recognized the voice of his mate from pure instinct, a certainty that had nothing to do with logic.

Another seeks me, but he is not you. Please come to me... before it is too late.

"Who seeks you? And why? Help me find you." He spoke aloud, although it was not necessary. He sought her in his mind, trying to reach her through the weak psychic connection. Something was... wrong. She sounded distant, depleted. It was still day...long before the sun would set and the connection was fragile.

Ethan tried to rise, but it wasn't possible. Nothing could pull him from his day sleep except his mate, but he couldn't function before twilight. He fought and struggled, frustration and anger driving him. He couldn't rise. Damn it! He couldn't rise! His body refused to cooperate and his mind was sluggish.

Nothing drove a vampire like the need of his mate. It was feral. Animalistic. Instinct. The need to protect his woman, to shelter her from all harm ripped through his useless body. Her pain and her need became his, and there was nothing worse than not being able to protect his mate. The instinct was there already and they had not even bonded.

I don't know who seeks and stalks me, but it is not you. I feel the evil. I'm growing weak. You must come to me.

Ethan's heart nearly exploded from his chest while he fought the seductive call of his day sleep. "Tell me how? Please." His voice was desperate now as he clenched the wet sheets, trying to feel her essence. It was so elusive, barely there, but he had to reach it.

Please find me…

Her voice floated away lightly, fading to… nothingness. The connection was completely severed.

Ethan felt himself being dragged back into his day sleep. He resisted, tearing at the sheets, pounding the bed. But the day sleep was relentless, pulling him into a dark abyss.

"Nooooo!!" His cry was an anguished howl as the darkness consumed him.

Brianna Cole woke with a frightened cry. Her eyes popped open and she had an immediate awareness of her surroundings. I'm home. In my own bed. Her heart pounding and her breath shallow, she sat up and looked around her bedroom.

"Nothing here," she whispered as she shivered and rubbed her arms to warm herself, despite the warmth of her bedroom.

She was always cold these days. Since she had been suddenly struck down with a rare and mysterious form of leukemia six months ago, she was constantly chilled to the bone.

Brianna was just grateful to be in her own home. Although her family and friends had objected, she had obstinately stuck to her guns and remained in her own house where she felt at peace. She hadn't been able to return to her job as a social worker, and more often than not, she was in the hospital getting a transfusion or some other experimental treatment. When she wasn't being poked and examined like a lab specimen, she needed to be home. It was the only thing that kept her level and sane in a world that had been turned upside down by her illness.

Brianna knew she was dying. She didn't need a team of experts to tell her that she was slowly fading away. She could feel the weakness, the slow draining of her spirit.

But I connected with him today! I called him.

She shook her head as the notion popped into her head involuntarily. Connected? What in the hell did that mean? Yet somehow she knew it was significant, that calling him meant something.

Brianna sighed as she pulled herself out of bed and rose to her feet. Stretching lightly, she cursed her weak and aching body as she made her way into the kitchen, her hungry feline tangling around her feet. She picked up Mr. Wiggins, named after a wonderful old gentleman she had worked with who couldn't keep the cat, and stroked him, enjoying the soft feel of his fur against her cheek.

"I'm just not ready to die yet, Wiggs," she told him softly as she continued to rub her cheek against his fur. "I don't feel like I'm supposed to die."

It was denial. She hadn't yet made it to the acceptance stage of her impending death and maybe she never would. It seemed like she had been stuck in the denial stage since her mysterious illness had struck. If she didn't hurry up, she would probably never make it through the stages of anger, bargaining, depression and acceptance. It seemed like she had been stuck in denial since the day her illness had been diagnosed.

She dropped Wiggs to the floor lightly and dug through her cupboard for the cat food. She filled the bowl and set it on the floor.

Wiggs, who was plump to begin with, devoured the meal like he hadn't eaten in weeks.

She raised an eyebrow. "Greedy little devil." Wiggs eyed her briefly with a look she could have sworn was kitty disdain before returning to his gluttony.

Brianna sighed as she plopped onto a stool at the breakfast bar and watched Wiggs make a pig of himself. She was still tired, but filled with a restlessness that she knew would never let her sleep. Truthfully, she didn't want to sleep anymore. Tomorrow she would be back in the hospital for another transfusion and she wanted to enjoy her one day of freedom.

She needed to call her mother and let her know she was still among the living. Maybe that was a bad expression to use with Mom. Brianna decided she would just check in and leave out the black humor that didn't usually go over well with her concerned parent. She'd just let her mom know that she was doing fine. If she didn't, her mother would come running over to check on her.

Denial! Denial! Denial!

As Brianna headed for the shower, she decided she really didn't care if she lived out the rest of her short life in that particular stage. If she only had a limited time in this world, she would enjoy it in any stage she damn well pleased.

She stopped in the bedroom to gather a clean pair of jeans and a shirt, frowning as she caught a glance at her reflection in the mirror over the dresser.

It had been several months since they had tried their last effort at chemo, so her blonde hair covered her head in a short, spiky style, but her face looked haunted and old. Dark circles framed her green eyes like she hadn't slept in days, whereas the truth was that she slept most of the day. And night.

But nights haunted her. She felt a yearning for… something. And then there were the night terrors, a time where she felt something evil lurking in the shadows. It might be the fear of her impending demise, but she didn't think so. She was still in denial after all and it felt more like a dark presence and impending doom. Every night the unknown entity felt closer, more suffocating. Every night it kept her awake longer, making her shiver under several blankets.

Brianna slammed the drawer, angry with herself for giving in to the fear. She would fight the darkness. If she could fight leukemia, she could damn well shake off this feeling that threatened to consume her after darkness had fallen.

As she determinedly made her way to the bathroom for a nice hot shower, she decided that she would enjoy every moment she had left and leave the darkness behind.

She marched into the bathroom, dropping her clothes on the vanity and stripped, knowing she made that promise to herself every day and it always worked... until the sun went down.

Ethan literally exploded out of his day sleep, angry and determined to find his mate. His eyes were wild and feral as he dressed himself and tried not to choke on the emotions flooding him.

Mine!

His mate was in danger. Ethan felt the tingle of awareness in every cell of his body and he was experiencing the need to protect, the need to kill anything or anyone that threatened his mate.

He just wished someone had warned him about the intensity of the mating emotions. His feelings had always been lukewarm...until now. Now... he was bursting with unbridled emotions, controlled by them, overwhelmed by them.

Sucking in an uneven breath, he tried to gain control of the raging feelings boiling inside of him.

Get a grip, vampire. Think. You can't save her if you can't function.

Shit...how was he supposed to function when his world had been turned upside down by one tiny, weak voice in his head?

He grabbed his cell phone and called his three brothers with a brief explanation.

They popped in, literally, moments later.

Nathan arrived first with his usual flare. There was nothing subtle about the oldest Hale brother. He was there in a flash of light so bright that it hurt Ethan's light-sensitive eyes.

Ethan glared at him, knowing his eldest brother was perfectly capable of showing up with a little less flare. Nathan was powerful and could control the flash, but when he was emotionally charged… he didn't bother.

Rory arrived without the flash, but was suddenly present with nothing more than a light popping noise that would never be heard by human ears. It was only evident to vampires because of their highly-developed hearing ability.

Liam…arrived like Liam. He faded in softly and without making a sound.

Rory and Liam were twins, and almost impossible to identify from just a glance. All of the brothers were similar in general appearance. Muscular. Tall. Dark hair and the signature brown vampire eyes. And at the moment, somewhat frightening in their unity and intensity.

"Has she answered?" Nathan demanded in his booming, low voice.

Ethan clenched his fists, feeling helpless and frustrated. "No. Nothing."

"She's probably not sleeping yet." Liam answered quietly, always the voice of reason in the terrifying quartet.

"I can't wait," Ethan decided as he paced the floor, his body tense, his emotions barely in check. "She's weak and in some sort of danger. I don't know exactly what. I have to find her."

"What can we do?" Rory queried gruffly, knowing his brother was in pain. Rory was generally the cheerful one, but he didn't appear quite certain on how to deal with Ethan in his current condition. None of the brothers were used to seeing Ethan in any kind of emotional chaos.

"I need to know that she isn't in danger from a fallen. She talked about being sought by another. Something evil. Find out if there's anything going on with our brethren or another that might cause them to seek her out." He struggled to think rationally as he added, "Anything out of the ordinary."

"Done," Nathan answered. "I'll investigate the possibility of it being a fallen, while Liam and Rory check with the others." He motioned to his two brothers who nodded once in agreement. As the eldest of the four, Nathan was good at giving orders. It often caused conflict between the brothers, but not now, not when they needed to come together to help Ethan.

"I'll try to reach her, try to find her. I'll call you." And just like that, Ethan disappeared without a sound, leaving no evidence that he had ever been present.

The three brothers were silent for a moment, each beginning to absorb the significance of what was happening to Ethan.

Liam was the first to speak, stating nervously, "He can't fail."

"Ethan won't fail," Nathan replied sternly.

"If he does…he won't survive." Rory voiced what the other two brothers could not, and did not, want to say.

"Then let's make sure that he doesn't fail," Nathan demanded and he flashed away, the others following seconds later.

CHAPTER 2

Ethan stood in the heart of the city, a place where most normal people feared to walk alone after darkness had fallen. He had fed well, knowing that he needed to be at full strength for whatever lies ahead.

Any creatures in the area, human or otherwise, fled as he stalked down an alley. It was as if they could feel his anger and frustration. He was dangerous. There might be some mad, bad creatures in this part of the city, of both the immortal and human variety, but nothing could compare to a vampire seeking his mate, especially when said mate was in danger.

Come to me.

Ethan stopped, his heart pumping, his adrenaline on overload. "Talk to me. Help me find you."

The connection was a little stronger this time.

He took a deep breath and opened his senses, trying to find her essence.

I don't know how.

"Just keep talking to me," he demanded as he moved steadily north, following her psychic trail.

I'm... afraid. I know I shouldn't be, but I am.

Ethan's heart ached as he heard the vulnerability, something he had a feeling this woman normally wouldn't admit to. "Of what?" He gentled his thoughts, trying to send her comfort.

Ethan knew he was drawing nearer and her spirit was stronger. He continued to travel faster than a human eye could detect, trying to zero in on her location.

There's something evil here. I know it sounds… gothic… but I can't explain it any other way. Even my cat, Mr. Wiggins, is huddling under the covers with me. His fur is standing up on end.

He was close, so very close. "Hold tight. I'll be there soon." Ethan changed direction slightly and asked with an amused smile. "You have a cat named Mr. Wiggins?"

Don't laugh at my cat. I'll have you know he is named after a very distinguished man. Wiggs is a very dedicated companion.

"I'm not laughing." Actually, he was, but he wasn't about to tell her that. Her indignant reply amused and delighted him.

You're laughing. I can feel it. Who are you?

Ethan sobered as he felt her anxiety. "I'm here to help. I would never harm you."

I believe you. I'm not sure why… but I do. What's happening to me?

The connection was strong and Ethan floated down to the window of her house, finding it easily as the connection strengthened even more. He flashed himself into her bedroom and immediately felt the sense of evil that was stalking her. He braced to confront it but as soon as he'd flashed into the bedroom the presence seemed to flee, completely and totally, leaving only the essence of his mate.

"I'm here now. Everything will be all right. You're safe."

It's gone. Thank you. I'm so tired…

Her voice trailed off and the connection broke. She slept the sleep of the innocent.

Ethan moved soundlessly to the side of the bed, looking down to get his first glimpse of his mate. His heart ached, beating in a wild rhythm as he saw her light blonde hair peeking out from a mound of blankets. She was beautiful and more precious to him than anything he had ever coveted in his entire existence. She was the one who held his soul and his future sanity in her fragile hands.

She looked so...delicate. Ethan glimpsed the dark markings around her eyes, taking in her slight weight, and the worry lines around her mouth, present even in her sleep.

He reached forward to touch her temple lightly. It was rude to invade her thoughts, but he wanted to know what caused her angelic appearance to be marred with worry.

Whatever was worrying his mate would soon be gone. He'd make certain of it.

Pain seized his body and he grunted as his fingers found and sought a mind connection. *She's sick. She's dying.* He felt the pain of her treatments, the torture her body had been through. She had fought bravely... but she was losing the battle.

He watched as her other memories sprang forth, most of them happy. At least she had led a peaceful life until the mysterious illness had hit her. He removed his hand, reluctant to invade too much into her thoughts without her permission.

Dying. Dying? *That* was so not going to happen. Ethan knew exactly what she was dying from, and it wasn't the rare blood disease her doctors had diagnosed. She needed to bond with her mate. She was twenty-eight years old. Almost twenty-nine. Damn it! Why hadn't he heard her sooner?

Ethan's gaze caught a picture on her nightstand. His mate was in the photo along with her mother, and either a friend or a sister, someone he hadn't picked up in the memories he had seen. He smiled, noticing she looked vibrant and happy in the image, the three women hugging each other and smiling.

He stroked her hair and kissed her on the forehead. He could touch her while she was sleeping without consequence. But the moment they touched consciously...

Ethan flinched. How in the hell could he mate with her when she was this fragile? The vampire mating and bonding process was rough. The mating was volatile and he would be engulfed with primitive instincts, completely wild. Once the vows were spoken and marks were joined, there was no turning back.

Damn it…he needed time, and time was something that this woman didn't have a lot of, judging by her frail appearance. The bond between mates was instinctual but he still wanted to get to know her. She would be frightened at discovering the truth of her existence, and she had to go into the bonding willingly.

Ethan left the bedroom and pulled out his cell phone. He called his brothers to see if they had dug up any information. Although vampires were psychic and could draw each other's attention through their minds, only mates could actually hold a conversation easily. With anyone else it was easier to just pick up a phone.

Nathan was the only one with any information. He had heard a rumor about some of the *fallen* who were stalking mates. They were picking the as yet unprotected mates who hadn't bonded.

Ethan slammed his phone back into his pocket. *The bastards! They were preying on the weak. Mates who didn't know who they were yet! Mates who didn't know that they guarded the soul of a vampire!*

Although drinking from another born vampire was poison to a *fallen*, taking blood from a mate who had not yet called her vampire to her was powerful. The blood of a vampire's mate was more potent than a normal human's and its power would absorb in the *fallen's* system, making them stronger. If a *fallen* got close enough to a vampire's mate, they could smell her, sense her. Ethan shuddered at how close the son of a bitch had been to his woman.

Just as he was about to head back to the bedroom to look in on his mate, he felt an uneasy twinge that made the hair at the back of his neck stand on end.

"Come on you bastard, show yourself," he whispered, his voice full of malice. "I'll show you your own asshole."

The *fallen* appeared in front of him and it was not a pretty sight. *Fallen* looked more demon than man with their glowing red eyes and hairless, sunken faces. *Fallen* could never get enough blood to regain their former appearance.

Ethan didn't know this *fallen* from its former life, but it didn't matter. He would have killed the bastard anyway. Occasionally, he felt a twinge of remorse and sorrow if he had known the former vampire before he had to slay a *fallen*. Right now, he wanted to tear this one's head off just for being in close proximity to his mate.

The *fallen* landed the first blow, raking razor-sharp claws over Ethan's face. But Ethan struck hard and fast, pulling a knife from a sheath at his waist as he struck the grotesque figure in the chest, sending it flying across the room.

He might not have time to conjure all of his fighting equipment… but he could improvise.

The figure bounced back, striking at Ethan's chest with its claws, but Ethan rotated away with barely a scratch.

The *fallen* tried to stalk Ethan, who wasn't in the mood to play. He was a vampire protecting his mate and he didn't feel like doing anything but destroying the threat. He struck hard and fast, landing blow after blow with his knife as he kicked and weakened his foe.

Ethan took a claw to his back as he spun around, trying to take the creature off balance.

Ethan didn't have a full set of claws, but he had a knife and fury on his side.

The battle raged on as the creature tired and Ethan got his chance. He pinned the *fallen* into the wall, slamming its left arm over his head as he plunged his knife deep, rupturing the heart of the evil bastard that was stalking his mate.

Rupturing the heart of a *fallen* was the only way to permanently vanquish it. While killing a vampire required beheading, bleeding dry, or prolonged exposure to the sun, it was necessary to annihilate the heart of a *fallen* to ensure its demise.

Ethan watched without a twinge of remorse as he muttered sarcastically, "Have a good afterlife, asshole." He knew there was no real afterlife for the *fallen*. They wandered aimlessly, absolutely harmless and constantly tortured, for eternity, in another realm. He hoped the bastard enjoyed it, having no pity for any being that would have torn his woman to shreds.

The *fallen* dissolved until it was nothing but a pile of ash on the carpet.

Ethan heard a gasp and instinctively whirled to defend himself, still in fight mode. It took him only a few seconds to realize that the exclamation had come from his mate.

She stood at the bedroom door, complete horror evident on her face. He felt her fear and he didn't like it. She should never be afraid of him.

Okay… maybe she had a slight reason to be afraid. His eyes were still wild from battle, his clothing covered in blood…and the living room looked like a war zone.

He shrugged. It was pretty much a normal situation for him, but it was obviously making his mate hyperventilate.

Ethan quickly flipped his hand and the living room righted itself in seconds. With another sweep he changed his clothing and cleaned the blood from his body, new clothing appearing in moments. He couldn't immediately heal his scratches, but they would disappear soon enough.

Okay….everything good now? Ethan reached for his mate with his mind… but she didn't answer. She just continued to stare at him with an appalled look on her face.

Damn. Didn't work! Ethan thought she would feel better if he cleaned up, but it just seemed to freak her out more. Oh hell… he didn't know how to act around a woman anymore. Or a human who didn't know his nature! It had been four hundred years for Christ's sake! He guessed that perhaps he should hide a few of his abilities until she calmed down.

He started toward her, asking gruffly, "Are you all right?"

You just did your personal grooming in seconds with your magic. The woman is human. She's probably not exactly okay with that.

Ethan cursed himself as he tried to think of a way to approach her without scaring her. Magic was as normal as breathing in his world.

It was difficult for him to remember that she was human and not used to anything that couldn't be explained by logic.

"Please don't be afraid. I'm here to help. The demon is gone. Remember me?" Ethan tried to activate her subconscious memory as his mind reached for hers.

Her mouth moved but no words came out. His eyes pinned hers and held them steady. "Remember me," he ordered softly.

Brianna shook herself, but her eyes were glued to his. He held her captive with his gaze, and she couldn't look away. "The evil is gone," she whispered in a trembling voice.

Ethan nodded. "Yes."

Brianna slid down the wall as though her legs wouldn't hold her. Her gaze didn't leave his as she asked in an agonized voice, "What's happening to me?"

Ethan released her eyes with a sigh. *She remembered. Everything!* And she obviously wasn't handling it all that well.

CHAPTER 3

Brianna buried her face in her hands, trying to make it all go away. Was she losing her mind along with her body? Her whole being was shaken and she wasn't sure anything would ever be right again. The only thing that made sense is if everything she had seen in the last several minutes had all been a horrible nightmare.

Please be a bad dream. Let me wake up and find out this was just a nightmare. I'll open my eyes and I'll be in bed. The blood-covered guy will be gone.

She uncovered her face. *Nope. No change. He's still here.* She sighed, deciding that obviously he wasn't going anywhere and she needed to understand, whether she wanted to or not.

"Who are you? *What* are you?" She was stunned, but after the initial shock she realized she wasn't really afraid of this man. They had spoken to each other while asleep. *This* man was her savior. She remembered it now and knew he had protected her from the evil that had been lurking around her.

"I wish I had more time to prepare you, but you must realize that there is something happening that can't be explained by logic, and you have very little time." He paused and met her eyes. "I'm a vampire. The demon that was stalking you was a *fallen*, a vampire lost to evil."

Oh, God. Brianna groaned and covered her face, breaking away from his eyes. In some strange way… it made sense… and *that* terrified her. But she couldn't deny they had spoken in her dreams, not to mention the horrific scene that had just played out before her eyes. *Oh, hell. I'm dying. What does it matter whether or not this is logical?*

"Good guy or bad guy?"

Ethan shrugged. "Better than him." Ethan gestured at the carpet where the *fallen* had dissolved.

She rolled her eyes. "Name?"

"Ethan. Ethan Hale."

"Ethan." She tested it on her tongue. His name was familiar. It was as though she knew him somehow. "I'm Brianna. Brianna Cole."

"Brianna." He breathed her name softly.

"I'm not afraid of you, Ethan. And after what just happened I sure as hell should be. Why is that?"

He answered her gently. "You know me. Subconsciously…you know me. Your life is ending so you're feeling with your senses right now instead of logic. You know that you're my mate."

She choked. "Mate? Me? I'm nobody's mate."

"You are, Brianna. You're my mate. My other half. Keeper of my soul," he answered her, his voice husky.

She looked for some sort of sign that this was a farce, but the guy was completely serious. "I don't even know you. Furthermore, I'm dying. That's a pretty lousy mate to have. I think you got screwed. I come with a pretty quick expiration date." She attempted to make light of his comments, but somewhere in her heart she actually *did* feel drawn to him.

"You aren't dying from a rare form of leukemia, Brianna. You're ill because you are not yet united with your mate. Your life force is fading," he explained patiently. He walked over and sat next to her on the floor, across from her so that he could see her eyes. "Somewhere on your body you wear my mark. My family mark is a dragon."

He held out his left arm. On his forearm was the perfect tattoo of a small dragon. It was fierce, multicolored and very detailed considering it was only about the size of a half dollar. "Oh shit." Brianna felt her heart flutter and her stomach drop. She had an identical marking on her right hip.

The mark had appeared when she had turned eighteen. One morning... it was just...there. She had never mentioned it to anyone. She rationalized it by saying she must have done it on her birthday. It was one of those rare occasions where she had partied with alcohol when she had been underage and had gotten roaring drunk.

"You have it?" It was a rhetorical question that Ethan already knew the answer to, but he asked her anyway.

"Yes." She could barely speak. This was all too strange. All too unbelievable.

"Don't be afraid, Brianna. We were created for each other. This isn't the way it is usually done. Generally I would meet you. Get to know you. Let you at least get used to me before I dropped this bomb on you. But you have little time. I think you sense that." His voice was urgent and worried.

"I do." She answered without hesitation. She did know it. She felt it. "I wish that we could have had more time together."

"We have forever. But it has to start soon." His voice was coaxing.

"Ethan... what part of 'I'm dying' did you not understand?" She was getting frustrated.

"We can mate, Brianna. You won't die. You will be with me for eternity."

"I can't mate with you! I don't even *know* you." But something inside of her wanted to. Would it be such a sacrifice to mate with a man who made her insides quiver without even touching her? He was the most handsome, compelling man she had ever met and something inside of her yearned for him, was reaching for him.

Besides, her other alternative was dying. Soon!

Yep. Tough choice! I either believe his story and mate with the gorgeous man, or die an agonizing death. It was sort of a no-brainer.

Ethan reached toward her and took her hand in his gently, as though afraid she would shatter, and she felt a jolt of energy go through her body. Just the light touch of his hand was electrifying. "Then know me, Brianna. Open your mind and know me."

He placed her hand on his temple and her mind flooded with Ethan. *Ethan as a young man! Ethan with his brothers! Ethan's thoughts. Ethan's battles! Ethan's emotions.* She was utterly and completely consumed by Ethan.

CHAPTER 4

Ethan was in hell. One touch of her hand on his body brought his senses roaring to life.

His body burned, demanding immediate gratification. He ground his teeth and tried to ignore the burning desire to take her. She was his. He needed to possess her, own her. He wanted to consume her and to be buried in her scent, her body, her mind.

His cock was hard and heavy. It had been a long time since he had felt that particular sensation, but never had he burned like this. He had been with women before he had succumbed to his involuntary impotence at the age of one hundred, but it had been normal desire and sex. This was more like a maniac's obsession.

She would feel it too, even in her fragile state. It was normal for mates. She wouldn't be dealing with the same frenzied desire as his, but her desire to mate would be there. Her desire to be satiated would be unrelenting...and it would drive him completely mad.

Once they were mated the intense desire and possessiveness would remain... but the frenzied craziness would subside. Once she was his. Once she belonged to him.

He let out an involuntary groan, trying to stifle it, let her have as much time as she needed to know him. She heard and pulled her hand back.

She said nothing, but her eyes spoke volumes. He could see her desire for him and he couldn't breathe, couldn't speak, his own need raging out of control.

Finally, she spoke hesitantly. "Can I make it through the mating… the bonding?" Though unsure, she didn't sound fearful and Ethan was touched by her courage. She was willing to try. This tiny woman had more courage than some of the members of The Coalition.

"We need to build up your strength. I won't lie to you, Brianna. It's… difficult. Once the vow is spoken and our marks are joined, every feral and carnal instinct I have to dominate you will rule me. It's something I can't overcome." He pulled her close and cradled her against him.

"I want to try. I'm not ready to die. How do we build up my strength? I have to drink your blood, don't I? I saw it in your mind." She answered matter-of-factly, but he could tell that she was hesitant.

"We have to exchange blood, but I can make it easier for you."

"How?"

"Like this." He lowered his mouth to hers.

The touch of his mouth on hers sent Brianna into a tailspin. Her senses whirled as his mouth took hers in a demanding assault. His tongue teased the seam of her lips and she opened to him willingly. His embrace possessed her, branding her whole body with fire. She lifted her arms around his neck and ran her hands through the rich texture of his silky hair.

His hands moved possessively over her body, leaving a trail of fire wherever he touched.

Ethan lifted her into his arms, never breaking contact with her mouth as he continued his relentless embrace. He carried her to the bed and lowered her gently to the sheets.

He took his mouth from hers and waved his hand. Instantly, her clothing disappeared. She was left lying naked and vulnerable as he stared down at her intensely.

"Ethan!" She squealed as she dove for the cover of the bed linens. "You can't do that!"

He quirked his brow and gave her a wicked grin. "I just did."

"I want my clothes back," she demanded with embarrassment as she cowered below the sheets.

He slid onto the bed beside her and lifted the sheets from her body. "And you will get them back... eventually." She saw his dark and passionate gaze before his mouth again lowered to hers.

She wanted to search for a covering. She was body conscious and she was too skinny right now, underweight from her illness, unattractive.

As his hand made its way to her breast, circling and teasing her nipple, she forgot about the covering. Oh God... his hands felt so good on her body.

"Don't think, Brianna. Just feel," he whispered in a graveled voice as his mouth left hers to lave her ear and the side of her neck.

How could she do anything else? His mouth continued to kiss and nip her face and neck while his hands teased her breasts mercilessly. His fingers made circular patterns on her skin as they slid slowly over her stomach. They moved in a lazy pattern that was driving her insane. She felt like she was on fire. Was this his vampire magic or the magic of his touch alone?

She felt his meandering fingers go lower and started stroking between her thighs, over the light curls, and she lost her breath.

"Open for me, Brianna," he demanded in a soft, seductive voice.

She complied immediately, needing to feel his touch, wanting those wicked fingers. His strokes were persistent, teasing through the wet, slick dew.

She moaned, grinding her hips up to meet his fingers. She needed more.

As though he sensed her need, he slid his finger up to the place begging for his attention, making slow circles on the sensitive bud.

The glide of his fingers brought her higher and higher, making her desperate.

"Ethan!" She cried his name as she squirmed beneath his ministrations.

His fingers slid slowly into her empty channel and her tight walls clenched around them tightly.

"You're so hot, wet and tight." She felt Ethan shudder as he began a slow rhythm that made her want more… more… it was too much… more. His breath was coming hard and fast, as though he were trying to get control.

His mouth devoured hers and he thrust his tongue in rhythm with his fingers.

His pace increased, his thumb sliding against her tender flesh while his fingers continued his in-and-out submersion, perfectly matched to his relentless tongue devouring her mouth.

Brianna felt lost. She had surrendered control and all she could do was feel the demands of her body. She had to orgasm. Her whole being was centered on her burning flesh, begging for climax.

Her release hit her hard and fast, wracking her with deep, unending spasms. Her channel clenched and unclenched around Ethan's fingers and she heard him groan as he dragged his mouth from hers, his breath coming in pants.

He nuzzled her neck, stroking his tongue along the vein. She barely felt his fangs sink into her neck as wave after wave of pleasure took control. Her whole body ignited as he drank from her, filling her with erotic pleasure, heightening her orgasm to an almost painful intensity.

As he sipped from her neck, he guided her mouth to his shoulder, nicking his skin. Instinctively, she latched her mouth onto his hot flesh, feeling moisture under her tongue. She lapped, taking his blood into her body mindlessly as she continued to lose every sane thought in her brain. The taste of him was like an aphrodisiac, flooding her with more erotic sensations. He tasted like Ethan, and he was intoxicating.

She felt him release her neck and he ran a finger over the punctures lightly.

As she slowly came down from her erotic high, Ethan pulled her away from his shoulder wound and swiped his finger over the cut. It stopped bleeding, but the cut was still there.

She lay in his arms, satiated and breathless, realizing that at some point Ethan must have dissolved his shirt and slit his shoulder.

She had ingested his blood…and she had relished it. At that moment all she had wanted was to share every part of Ethan.

As she recovered her senses she realized that some of her aches and pains were gone. Had her body filled out a little? Brianna felt a strength pouring through her that she hadn't felt since her illness.

"I feel stronger, Ethan." As she pulled back to look at his face, her euphoria over her improved physical condition fled when she glimpsed his sweating, flushed face and wild, dark eyes. Alarmed and concerned, she whispered, "Ethan, talk to me. Are you okay?"

He was trembling and his eyes caressed her naked body with a hunger that was anything but normal.

Brianna pulled the covers over her nudity and grabbed his face with both hands, forcing him to meet her eyes. "Ethan, talk to me. Tell me that you're okay," she demanded, her voice filled with anxiety.

He stared into her eyes and drew a deep breath. He let it out shakily as he answered slowly, "I'm fine, Brianna."

"You are not fine." She kept her hands on his head, forcing him to meet her eyes. He lifted one of her hands from his face and kissed the palm.

"You're my mate, Brianna," he answered in a low, tortured voice. "It's difficult not to take you."

"Then take me, Ethan. Or let me help you." Her hand slipped down to his jeans, stroking his erect shaft over the cotton material. She could feel the immense size and hardness of him and she wanted him desperately. She wanted him inside her, stretching her, filling her.

"No!" Ethan gripped her wrist gently and moved her hand away. "Not now, Brianna. You're not strong enough. Vampires are extremely sexual creatures with their mates."

"Then why did you do that?"

He kissed her softly on the forehead. "To make it easier for you, love." He shot her a devious grin. "It was easier, wasn't it?"

"Oh, Ethan," she sighed, not knowing whether to be exasperated or amused. She carefully wrapped a sheet around her body and snuggled into his chest. His arms came around her protectively, sheltering her. She felt so... safe.

She absorbed the feeling, enjoying the moment... until her peace was disturbed in a rather startling manner.

CHAPTER 5

"Hello!" A cheerful, deep voice emanating from the end of her bed made Brianna jump. If Ethan hadn't held her steady in his arms, she would have been five feet in the air.

Her eyes shot to the end of the bed. Three very large men stood there, all with varying expressions.

The one speaking was smiling.

One was brooding.

The other wore a dreamy expression.

The fact that they all looked suspiciously like the man lying beside her couldn't be a coincidence. She had seen these men in Ethan's memories. Rory, Liam and Nathan! His brothers! Although she couldn't tell which one was which, she assumed the cheerful one and the dreamy one were the twins. All of them looked alike, but those two were nearly identical in appearance.

"What are you two doing?" The cheerful one. "We're Ethan's brothers. I'm Rory. This is Nathan." He motioned to the brooding one. "And that's Liam." He waved a hand at the lost looking one.

Ethan didn't answer but she could see him getting red in the face and he was clenching his jaw. How did you smooth over the fact that they had popped into her bedroom uninvited? "Ethan and I... we were just... we... we were just talking and getting to know each other." Okay...she knew it sounded lame as she stuttered the words. For God's sake... they were in bed and she was completely naked. What the hell was she supposed to say?

"Oh, that's good. But I really hoped you were... oof!" Rory bent over as Liam slammed his elbow into his gut. Liam shot Rory a sharp glance as Nathan just smirked, a wicked expression on his face.

Brianna shot a nervous glance at Ethan. His jaw was clenching harder as he rumbled. "Get... the... hell... out!"

Brianna wrapped the sheet around her securely and slid off of the bed. "It's very nice to meet you. But this is not a very good time. Maybe you could just give us a few minutes to get dressed and we can chit chat." One tiny woman shooing three men twice her size toward the door was an amusing sight. Amazingly... the men went. "Help yourself to anything in the kitchen," she called as she slammed the bedroom door behind them.

Brianna planted her hands on her hips and raised a brow at Ethan. "I think we need to talk to your brothers about their manners."

"I'm going to kill them all!" He stood and clothed himself in a pair of jeans and a t-shirt with his magic. He dressed Brianna in similar attire.

Brianna wrapped her arms around his waist and rested her head on his shoulder. "You know you aren't going to kill them. They're your brothers."

She felt him shrug. "We try to kill each other all the time. But this time I'm really going to do it. They know better than to do something like that with a vampire who's just found his mate."

She could tell he was calming as she stroked his back. "Maybe we should just talk and get to know each other."

He sighed. "Okay... but then I get to kill them."

"No killing today, Ethan." She shuddered. "I've already seen you in action once today and that's enough." She pulled back to survey his face.

He looked recovered from his injuries, but disappointed that he couldn't kill his brothers and she bit back a smile.

"You're going to be sorry you told them to help themselves." The corners of his mouth turned up in a small, knowing smile.

"Why? I don't mind."

"You will," he told her in an ominous voice as he took her by the hand and led her through the door to meet his brothers.

Ethan stretched as he awoke from his day sleep. He immediately sought his mate but she wasn't sleeping beside him.

It had taken Brianna five days of ingesting his vampire blood to regain her normal strength and to build up the added strength she would need for their mating. His was the blood of an elder and it was powerful, but Brianna had been severely weakened.

His brother Liam was a healer for their brethren and between his magic and Ethan's blood exchanges with Brianna, she had regained her strength. He hadn't touched her sexually since their first exchange. He had come so damn close to losing control that day that he didn't dare.

She said she felt incredibly strong, but Ethan knew it wouldn't last. His mate would start to decline again soon. The mating needed to happen as soon as possible.

Ethan knew he was losing control. His desire to possess his mate was overcoming logic and reason, making it harder and harder to contain his possessiveness, his jealousy.

He couldn't even stand to have his brothers around her. It nearly made him feral with jealousy and possessiveness. Brianna belonged to him and he hated any other male touching her...even his brothers.

Unfortunately, she actually liked his brothers and they, in turn, seemed to adore her. Ethan hated it. He might appreciate it later, but right now he wanted no one near his mate. His brothers knew it... and they taunted him constantly. They popped in often and lingered, eating Brianna out of house and home. She was charmed, and he was pissed. She just laughed and went to the grocery store after their visits. *The bastards!* They were enjoying his agony. He sincerely hoped they all found their mates. *Payback would be hell.*

Ethan leaned back against the headboard of the bed as he grumbled to himself, "I don't like dealing with unknowns."

He acknowledged to himself that the whole situation was an unknown. His friend and fellow Coalition member, Adare, had mated a few months ago. Adare was three hundred years old and *that* situation had been an unknown. Before Adare's mating, no mated vampire had ever crossed the age of one hundred and fifty before finding their mate. There were some who were never called and remained unmated, but the ones who were mated now had been summoned early, soon after they had lost their ability to have sex.

The intensity of Adare's possessiveness and desire had been beyond the normal mating instincts because of his advanced age.

And Ethan was two hundred years older than Adare.

"I'm so screwed." Ethan spoke aloud with quiet resignation. He was already caught up in a web of desire and possessiveness for his mate from which he couldn't escape.

Did he actually want to escape? *Hell, no!* He had waited hundreds of years for Brianna and she was a miracle. But he hated the unknown aspects of the situation. If he had a problem... he solved it. If it was evil... he killed it. His life had been fairly simple... until he had found his mate.

Now he was faced with a "situation unknown" and he didn't like it. The only thing he knew was that his mating instinct was nearly out of control. It grew worse with every day that passed. Every day he spent with Brianna brought another reason to like her... or a dozen reasons to love her.

I love her. I'm not just drawn to her as a mate. I love her.

"Oh hell... I'm totally screwed," he whispered fiercely, knowing his love added fuel to his fire... and he was already a raging inferno.

Had Brianna not been in her weakened state, he would have tried to seduce her. It probably would have taken the edge off of his need to mate, a need that was sitting on a hair-trigger at the moment, just waiting for a tiny nudge to make it explode.

Just as he had decided to roll out of bed, Brianna came breezing into the bedroom.

His heart accelerated and his muscles clenched. She brought light where there was darkness and he desperately needed to be inside her. He needed to consume her. He wanted her so damn badly that he heard a low growl erupt from his throat and he tried to swallow it.

He bit back a groan as his eyes roamed her body. She was wearing a pink night shirt that molded to her curves and stopped mid thigh. It wasn't meant to entice... but it did. Ethan could see her nipples through the thin material and the shirt caressed her beautiful, perfectly formed breasts.

His already stiff cock twitched as he smelled her arousal. His eyes sought and locked with hers. He could see the heat and desire in her gaze as she eyed his naked chest. She was wanting. And he needed to satiate her.

Mine!

She slid into the bed beside him, never taking her eyes from his.

Ethan snapped, sanity deserting him. He needed to possess this woman and he couldn't wait any longer.

CHAPTER 6

Brianna no longer knew if the desire she scented was hers or Ethan's. She heard a low growl from his throat and she knew he needed her as much as she needed him. She had been like a female animal in heat since she had first touched him. As she had regained her normal strength, her desire had grown into a mass of raw need.

Brianna knew that her vampire was an alpha who needed to dominate sexually, especially before they mated, and she wanted to be dominated by him. She wanted him hard and fast and she didn't care if it was rough. She was beginning to think that getting it hot and hard was the only thing that would quench the fire.

Being sexually dominant was part of his vampire nature and she accepted it. Hell...she wanted it. She didn't want to tame him and she knew she couldn't change his dark desire even if she wanted to. And she definitely didn't want to. She wanted him wild, untamed, out of control. She wanted to submit to whatever he needed. They were so connected that she knew satisfying him would satiate her. And right now... right at this moment... he needed to dominate her to reassure himself that she belonged to him.

Brianna reached under the bed and brought out the soft restraints that she had bought a few days ago for just this occasion. She dangled them in her fingers in front of Ethan. "You might like these."

Ethan groaned, "Yes. I want to tie you down so that you can never get away. Mine."

"Then take me, Ethan. I want it, too," she whispered softly as she attached the restraints to her wrists, her voice heavy with passion.

"Need to fuck you. Take you. Make sure that you belong to me." He tore her nightshirt straight down the middle, baring her breasts to his hot, hungry gaze. He pulled it roughly off her body. He didn't have the control to use magic; he was being ruled by mating instincts. He grabbed the end of the restraints and attached them to the headboard.

His words had ramped up her desire, her need to have him take her. She pulled at the restraints, feeling the resistance. She would be his to possess in any way he wanted to, needed to.

Brianna gasped as his mouth took hers, devouring it. It was a kiss born of desperation and scorching hot, raw need. His mouth clamped down on hers, his tongue sweeping into her mouth, searching for hers.

Brianna opened her mouth, welcoming him. Their tongues mated, entwined, and dueled against each other. His hands reached for her breasts, running over them possessively, roughly. His fingers pinched her nipples, sending a shock through her system and saturating her panties.

He ripped his mouth from hers and began tonguing her breasts. His mouth both bit and soothed, arousing her almost to climax. His tongue licked every inch of her breasts as though he didn't want any part of her skin untouched, no area unclaimed.

His hands moved down the curves of her body until they reached her hips. He reached out and ripped her panties down the front, throwing them to the floor. His fingers invaded her moist heat aggressively, and she moaned at his invasion, loving the feel of his strong fingers running over her clit.

"You're so wet. For me. Mine. Tell me it's for me," he demanded in a graveled voice.

Brianna gazed at him, adoring his fierce look of passion and desire. He was a ferocious, breathtaking man in spite of all of his darkness and intensity. *Or maybe because of it.* Her vampire. Her eternal mate.

"Yes, Ethan. Only for you," she whispered, soothing her savage beast.

Brianna whimpered as he buried his head between her thighs. He was conquering her and he proceeded in a "take no prisoners" attack. His tongue invaded her wet folds in one long slide, destroying her control. She bit back a moan as his tongue spiraled around her clit. The bud was swollen and needy, begging for his caress.

She arched her back, reaching for his mouth with her hips. She needed his total possession, needed his tongue sending her over the edge.

Brianna was consumed in erotic pleasure, mindless of anything but Ethan. "Please, Ethan. Please," she pleaded as her hips rotated wildly, seeking the heat of his tongue.

When his fiery tongue landed on her begging nub, she moaned. He laved and nipped until she was wild and lost, helpless to do anything but let herself feel. He played her body like a master musician, knowing exactly how to touch. How hard… how fast… how long.

Brianna felt her climax approaching with a shudder. It started deep in her belly and scorched her to her toes. She came with a loud cry that burst from her lungs involuntarily. It was a screech that extended into a moan as Ethan lapped at her, extending the wild pleasure. He licked the cream that erupted from her in frenzied abandon, as if it were his favorite dessert.

As Ethan slid up her body sensually, Brianna gasped. Ethan's body felt like it was on fire. He covered her, his skin blazing and his eyes fierce. Those fiery eyes raked her as he buried his head in her neck with a groan. She thought he was going to bite her… but he didn't.

She could feel Ethan panting, his breath hot, hitting her neck sporadically as he gulped for air. "I love you," he choked out between his staccato breaths. "I love you so damn much I can't bear it."

Brianna froze, stunned by his revelation. Her heart was pounding so hard that she was breathless. He loved her. "Oh Ethan, I love you, too, with all of my heart." She melted as she felt him trembling against her. "Take me, Ethan." He needed and she wanted nothing more than to provide. "Please."

He trailed his lips from her neck to her mouth, kissing her with a ferocity that would be terrifying if she had any reason to fear him. But she wasn't afraid. She met his embrace, their passionate movements clashing against each other and merging, intensifying their desire.

His hot mouth left her defenseless, unable to think of anything except her need for him. As he broke for air she pleaded, "Fuck me, Ethan. I need you. I need you inside me."

She could feel his member, hot, heavy, and hard, against her thigh. She squirmed, desperate for him to join them together.

Ethan took her mouth again while he slid his hand down to grasp his swollen cock. He brought the head between her legs, sliding his engorged flesh against her liquid heat.

He was large, but she was ready. There wasn't anything he had that she wasn't ready to accept. She removed her mouth from Ethan's, her breath leaving her body as he slid into her burning channel, his member gripped tightly by her inner walls. She felt herself stretch to accept him, lifting her hips to take him completely inside her. The feel of him was extraordinary. Her muscles clenched and relaxed on his cock, getting used to the feel of the large phallus. They moaned together as he became completely imbedded.

"You're so tight. Have to fuck you. Make you mine," Ethan rasped as he began to move.

"I'm yours, Ethan, all yours." She breathed the words, knowing it eased him.

Brianna's body seized as he began to stroke; long, hard thrusts that seemed to burn her to her core.

"Need you, Brianna." His voice broke as he knelt, pulling her legs up to his shoulders and grasping her hips hard.

"Yes, Ethan, Yes!" She knew she was screaming now… but she didn't care. His increasingly hard and fast pumping was making her crazy and she had to climax, taking Ethan along with her. They needed to find release before they incinerated together.

Finding that release was their driving force as they strained together, her hips moving to meet his pummeling cock. His strength was incredible, but he was a vampire and Brianna had ingested his blood. It made her strong enough to take his rough passion. *Strong enough to wallow happily in it.*

Ethan threw his head back, releasing a sound somewhere between a snarl and a grunt. Her leg was on his shoulder and he turned his head and buried his fangs into her thigh. He suckled hard against her skin as he pounded his cock into her aching channel.

His erotic bite made her fly apart. Brianna's climax erupted with a power and intensity that rocked her body. She came in a wild wave that had her crashing in a turbulent sea of erotic bliss.

Her spasms grasped Ethan's cock and caressed it with a forceful grip-and- release. Over and over. Again and again. She felt him release his teeth from her thigh to heave and plunge deep inside of her. He released a deep, reverberating sound as he came, his cock exploding in rhythmic contractions. His hot release flooded deep inside her as he let out a tortured and relieved groan.

Brianna felt her hands being released as he pulled her tightly into his waiting embrace. They panted together, trying to recover their senses.

He urged her mouth toward his chest where he had opened a vein for her to drink. She took the nourishment along with Ethan's essence, ignoring the sexual rush. She couldn't take any more of that right at the moment. She fed, just enjoying the intimacy. When she had finished, he reached up a hand and stopped the bleeding with a swipe of his finger.

She wasn't sure how long they laid like that, lost in post-climactic bliss.

She lifted her head off of Ethan's shoulder to look at him. God… he was an incredible man. His looks took her breath away. He was physically perfect, but she knew that the thing that struck her right in the heart was the man himself. The way he looked at her, his smile, made her heart sing and dance like a Broadway musical. He hadn't said a word but he was grinning at her.

Brianna pulled his head to hers, capturing the smile with her mouth just because she couldn't resist. Ethan was an unholy temptation, especially when he smiled.

Brianna sighed into the long, leisurely kiss. She hadn't seen Ethan smile much because of the mating instinct, but the man had a wicked sense of humor that popped up on occasion. She could only imagine what he would be like after the mating. He would settle down and lose some of the insanity once his soul had been transferred to him and found its resting place.

Okay… half of her soul and half of his that would become his permanent soul. The vampire mating thing brought a whole new meaning to the term "soulmate."

Her mouth left Ethan's reluctantly and she rested her head on his shoulder. She longed to give Ethan his soul and end his torment. She didn't fear the mating ceremony. If it would bring Ethan peace, she embraced it.

Soon. I'll make sure it happens soon.

Her eyes fluttered closed. She let herself fall into sleep, knowing she would always be safe in Ethan's arms.

CHAPTER 7

The following day, Ethan found himself in the male preparation room for the mating ceremony, which would take place that night.

The vampire headquarters was a centuries-old castle in Europe. It was beautifully restored, opulent, and luxurious, with all of the modern conveniences. Vampires might get old, but they loved every fancy new technology that came along. They probably appreciated advances all the more because they were so ancient. Ethan was old enough to remember what the sanitation and living conditions had been like in the sixteenth century. He shuddered. Maybe he'd rather not remember it and just be grateful that he was now living in the twenty-first century.

He had transported himself and Brianna here to the headquarters in Europe from the U.S. soon after having dinner with her mom last night, arriving just before sunrise because of the time difference. He had fallen into his day sleep, and hadn't seen his mate since then. The ritual for human mates was much more complicated than for the vampire male. She would be involved with the preparation until the ceremony began.

He was currently biding his time with his three brothers and Adare. Adare's wife Kristin, having just gone through this experience a few months ago, had opted to be one of the three women who attended Brianna.

"Shit! Will this agony ever end?" Ethan whispered to himself as his need to see Brianna ripped through him. His need to possess her was getting excruciatingly painful and he couldn't stand to be without her, even for a few hours.

Adare chuckled. "Soon, Ethan. Believe me… it gets better."

At the moment, Adare's blissful happiness was incredibly annoying. Ethan's insides were so torn up that he couldn't imagine being as relaxed and content as Adare seemed to be. However, he did remember Adare's courtship and pain when he was suffering through the mating instincts. He wished he had been more sympathetic.

"And the possessiveness, the insanity… do they really go away?" Ethan asked him, agony showing in his eyes.

Adare shrugged. "It does. It won't be as painful afterwards. Separation will always hurt. The yearning never stops. The possessiveness and a driving need to protect will always remain. But the need to dominate does lighten up quite a bit." He gave Ethan an evil grin. "You'll even let her be on top and in control on occasion. And find it very enjoyable."

"What? It isn't enjoyable now?" Rory asked with curiosity.

Ethan rolled his eyes and exchanged a knowing look with Adare.

Adare laughed and commented, "He's clueless."

"Are you sure I won't hurt her?" Ethan's anxiety was getting the better of him. He was the oldest vampire ever to go through the mating ceremony and nothing was certain. Fuck! He hated the unknown, especially when it came to the well-being of his mate.

"I can guarantee she will be sore when she wakes, but you won't hurt her, Ethan. You're mates. You're connected. Kristin told me that my needs were also her needs. She felt some of what I felt. It will be okay." Adare tried to reassure Ethan, giving him a slap on the back.

Ethan wasn't completely reassured. "But I'm older. Damn it! I don't want to be uncontrolled. And I don't want this witnessed. I don't want anyone seeing my mate except me."

Adare sighed. "You won't care once that time comes. You will be out of your mind to possess her. You'll actually like having people watch you making her yours. It's hard to explain but it's like staking your claim, warning everyone away."

Ethan sighed. The waiting was the worst. Time seemed to creep by, each minute seeming like hours. "I just want her to be mine."

Rory looked at Ethan with a perplexed expression. "She is yours. She's your mate."

Adare and Ethan exchanged another look. Rory truly was clueless. All of his brothers were. It had been way too long since they had experienced any physical desire, and none of them would understand until they mated. If they mated.

If there is any fairness in this world… they will find their mates. Then Ethan could torment them as they had tormented him. Although they weren't torturing him at the moment, they had made sure they added fuel to the fire whenever possible. He was pretty sure they realized if they started anything today it would be like pulling a tiger by the tail. He was edgy and even his brothers weren't willing to tangle with him at the moment.

"How was the dinner with her mom?" Adare asked, trying to distract Ethan.

Ethan rolled his eyes. "Brianna insisted on taking my brothers along. They ate like it was an Olympic competitive event. I'm not sure who won, but the table didn't have a scrap of food left."

"Hey… she liked us. She said she loved feeding men with healthy appetites," Nathan protested. "She was charmed. How could she not be?" *Ego is never a problem with Nathan. His is as big as the solar system.* But it was true that his brothers *had* been charming and Brianna's mother had nothing but nice things to say about his brothers.

Ethan turned to address Adare. "She's a very nice woman. She put up with the four of us."

Liam commented quietly. "Ethan's rich, charming, and handsome. What's not to like?"

Ethan scowled. "Maybe, the fact that I'm a vampire and about to make her daughter my eternal mate. I'm not quite sure how she would feel about that little fact."

"I take it she wasn't invited to the witness ceremony." Nathan raised a brow, throwing Ethan a wicked grin.

Ethan showed him his middle finger. Nathan knew Brianna's mom didn't know. They were planning a human wedding ceremony to be married in the human tradition.

Ethan didn't mind having a wedding in addition to mating. He had gotten Brianna the finest engagement ring he could find that would still suit her tastes for something simple and classy. He was finding out that just about anything that branded her as his made him ecstatic.

"I already told Brianna that you would be more than happy to be my groomsmen for the wedding," Ethan informed his brother wickedly. "She has a maid of honor and two bridesmaids, so it works out perfectly."

Ethan grinned, flashing them an evil look, as all of his brothers' faces registered horror and dismay. None of them were laughing now.

"When is it? I think I already have plans," Nathan grumbled.

"Me too." Rory agreed.

"And me." Liam said softly.

"Oh, no. If you can't make it…you can explain to Brianna why you can't attend one of the most important days of her life. I'm not doing it." Ethan broke into a small smile as they all frowned. His brothers really did adore Brianna and somehow she could get away with getting them to do her bidding. It amused the hell out of him. Like it or not, he knew they would all be there.

There might be a few bumps along the road while integrating their families, but it wouldn't be that difficult. Brianna had a human life and family. He respected that. Although she would be a vampire's mate after the ceremony, she would never be completely vampire.

She would need blood and she would have to avoid the sun, but she wouldn't have magic. Any aging would freeze and she would keep her increased strength, but she would be between two worlds. She would be more vampire than human, but she was raised as a human and he didn't expect her to leave that totally behind.

Ethan was startled when a firm rap on the door broke into his thoughts.

"It's time, Ethan," Adare informed him quietly.

His brothers all slapped him on the back. They were leaving. Brianna might adore them, but she really didn't want them to witness. She had come to care for them like family and she insisted she would rather have strangers at this particular mating ritual than for her future brothers-in-law to see her naked.

Adare was leaving too. Now that he was mated, he could no longer watch the ceremonies like a eunuch. He and Kristin would leave as soon as Kristin had finished her duties as an attendant.

His brothers disappeared. Adare stood at his side, ready to escort him to the mating chamber. Adare would await Kristin outside of the door where she would exit and they would depart together.

Ethan tried to get control of himself, but the closer he came to the mating chamber, the more his control seemed to slip away. He was ready to begin an ancient vampire ritual and the magic involved in the upcoming ceremony seemed to be building.

Adare opened the door and motioned him to enter, stopping and leaving Ethan to continue alone.

As Ethan entered the chamber, he felt a powerful surge of magic, but it wasn't coming from him. This was ancient magic, strong and powerful.

His clothing dissolved and he was suddenly dressed in only a scrap of leather to confine his cock, held in place with only a few strings. His member was already protesting by trying to burst the seams.

His skin gleamed from the ancient mating oils.

He could feel that magic swirling around him, heightening his arousal to an almost feral need. He could only imagine what would happen once their marks touched and the ancient words were said.

He gritted his teeth, trying not to lose complete control while he waited for his mate to arrive.

CHAPTER 8

Brianna approached the mating chamber with two women in front of her and Kristin at her side. Kristin was newly mated and Brianna appreciated the fact that she had just been through what Brianna was going through now. She had helped calm some of Brianna's nervousness.

Brianna wasn't afraid. Hell…she had been close to dying by the time that Ethan had entered her life. Now she was ready to live. She would live a glorious life with Ethan by her side.

She was dressed in the traditional, full, transparent, ankle-length gown and it trailed along behind her as she walked down the narrow hallway. She had chosen a scarlet red that matched her mood today. Her hair had grown quickly, restored to its normal shoulder length and she had left it down over her shoulders.

Brianna had been bathed in sensual, exotic oils. Her skin was still slick from the scented oil that had been applied after the bath.

The women all stopped at the mating chamber door and Kristin moved forward to pull the heavy ornate door open, moving to the side to let Brianna enter.

Brianna stopped, her eyes sweeping the room. Ethan stood on the platform in front of a huge, elevated bed. The bed was covered in black silk, a few black silk pillows scattered over the massive surface.

Brianna smiled. The chamber preparation was Ethan's choice. She guessed he was in a "dark" sort of mood today.

As Brianna entered the room she noticed that it was just as Kristin had described. A circular, small room with darkened windows all around the upper walls. They were for the observers. The witnesses. Everything was lit with candles that were placed on a ledge that circled the windows. She was guessing that the witnesses would get a hell of a good view.

She locked eyes with Ethan. His were almost completely black and intense. She longed to speak with him telepathically, but she didn't. She knew it only made things worse for him when he heard her voice and couldn't yet touch her.

Brianna could feel the electric vibrations in the room and her hair lifted like it was blowing in the wind.

It's ancient magic, Brianna. I've never heard of this happening before. It's probably because of my age. But it's not evil. Don't be afraid.

She started as she heard Ethan growling in her mind, surprised he could still use his magic to speak to her this way. She could feel his need and her body responded. Her body jerked as she was assaulted with his mating instincts. She wanted to lay on those black sheets and satiate this vampire any way he wanted it.

She nodded at Ethan, her eyes never leaving his, to let him know she understood.

"Strip her." Ethan ordered, his voice low and commanding.

Kristin came to her side, frowning as she saw that everything was moving. The gown swirled and Brianna's flowing hair fluttered as though the wind were carrying it.

Kristin hesitated, perplexed.

"It's okay, Kristin. Do it." Brianna whispered to her softly.

Kristin lifted her hands to the ties of Brianna's gown. "Do you agree to this mating with Ethan Hale?"

"I do." Brianna answered, her eyes burning into Ethan's.

Kristin released the gown and it shimmered to the floor. She picked it up and draped it over her arm.

"Leave us." Ethan choked out the demand.

Kristin left, Brianna's gown still fluttering over her arm. She closed the door and locked it behind her. The loud click of the lock on the door should have sounded ominous, but Brianna felt exhilarated. She was finally going to mate with Ethan.

"Come to me." Ethan instructed, his eyes leaving Brianna's to sweep over her body with hunger and desire.

Brianna eagerly responded, climbing the few steps to arrive in front of Ethan next to the elevated bed.

Ethan didn't touch her, but his eyes burned over her naked body as he started reciting the ritual words of the bonding in his native language. She didn't understand, but she loved the lyrical flow of the ancient language, the syllables rising and falling. As the last word trailed off Ethan's tongue, he lowered his forearm to her hip and sealed their markings. She could see his arm trembling right before he joined the marks and pressed them firmly together.

Brianna's body jerked. Ethan grasped her around the waist with his other arm as the flames shot through her body, incinerating her internally. It was incredibly painful…but erotic. She closed her eyes and leaned against Ethan for support, his burning body supporting hers.

She rested that way until Ethan's soul broke free from hers and separated, her own soul then tearing and fusing with half of Ethan's. Their joined marks continued to burn as Ethan's new, completed soul entered him through the conjoined marks, a soul that was half hers, half his, but complete.

Brianna's newly-mated soul settled quickly, finding its old resting place. She was still hot, but the heat was now completely sexual. She needed her mate.

Ethan's soul did not settle so easily. He had never had a soul before and it wandered his body restlessly, looking for a resting place.

She watched his eyes turn red, glowing with an unholy light. Magic swirled around them both, burning like a blue flame.

Ethan's need and desire seized Brianna, clenching her gut as if she were experiencing the feelings herself.

I need to sate him. I need to take away his anguished need to possess. I need his possession as much as he needs to possess me. I need to help him settle his wandering soul.

"Free my cock, Brianna. Now!" The harsh baritone undid her.

Her needs were wild and she reached down and started ripping at the leather ties, needing the swollen, straining member free from its confinement. It spilled into her hands, hard and engorged. She wrapped her hands around him, stroking the hard, silky length.

Ethan grabbed her wrist, preventing her from touching him. He wrapped his arms around her with almost smothering tightness and claimed her mouth in a white hot embrace. It was a kiss of ownership, a branding. Rough and hard. She wrapped her arms around his neck, meeting his conquering tongue with her own. He swept every inch of her mouth and tongue with his, claiming her. Then he picked her up and dropped her in the middle of the silk-clad bed.

He was on her before she had a chance to take a breath. He tied her hands to the headboard with the dangling restraints. He bound her legs, spread wide apart, with restraints on both sides of the bottom of the bed. They had some slack, but very little. She was completely helpless, open wide for his desires.

He circled the bed, his red, glowing eyes burning across her body.

"Mine. Mine. Mine." He was grunting, as though it was too difficult to speak, but she understood him. He seemed to find some satisfaction just by looking at her, knowing she was his to satisfy as he pleased.

"Yours, Ethan. All yours," she whispered softly, breathless with her own desires. She pulled at the restraints holding her in place, loving the feel of being restrained for his pleasures.

Her pussy was drenched and she could feel droplets sliding down her thighs. She squirmed in her restraints, desperate for him to take her. "Please, Ethan. I need you."

He moved between her legs, roughly stuffing a pillow beneath her hips. "Have to make you come," he growled.

"Oh, God, yes. Make me, Ethan. I need it." She writhed against her bindings. Her body was on fire. She was consumed with heat, ready to combust.

He attacked between her legs, licking her juices from her thighs and thrusting his tongue into her vulnerable pussy. She could hear the sound of his tongue lapping roughly, moving in the drenched opening. She screamed as his tongue laved her clit forcefully, moving fast and hard over the swollen bud.

His fingers slammed inside of her channel, his index and middle finger buried in the opening.

"Oh, Ethan. Yes. Yes. Yes." She was out of control, consumed with the need to climax.

"Come for me," he snarled into her pussy, not pausing in his relentless attack on her clit, his fingers pumping wildly, hard and deep, into her hot, slippery channel.

As if responding to his command, her stomach hardened, seized with spasms that spread directly to her core. Had she not been restrained, she probably would have curled into the climax. Her whole body trembled as the force of it shook her body like a rag doll. She fell over the edge, flying apart in a massive explosion.

She jerked against her restraints as she rode out the waves that were hitting her relentlessly. Ethan didn't cease, but continued his attack as she writhed and burned. He was a man possessed and not nearly satisfied with her long, explosive orgasm.

He turned his body and suddenly his massive cock was over her face. "Take it in your mouth."

Oh, yes. She opened as he lowered his massive member into her moist, eager mouth. Her lips sealed as best they could around the gigantic, swollen phallus. She could feel him groan into her mound as his hips started pumping, fucking her mouth.

He was riding her mouth hard, shoving his cock into her throat. She could barely breathe, but she rejoiced in his tortured groans as she tried to swallow him.

He was working her like an insane man. His hands gripped her thighs and spread her as much as possible. He was still flicking over her clit in hot, wet licks as he invaded her opening with an extra finger, plunging into her with three large digits. She jerked as she felt the fullness and moaned around his cock as he continued to fuck her mouth with furious strokes.

Ethan slid his other hand through her wet folds, drenching his fingers. He slid the moisture over her anus, wetting it with her own cream.

"Mine. Mine. Mine." She could make out his smothered exclamation.

His cock was pounding into her mouth now, hitting the back of her throat. She was in a passion-induced trance and didn't care. She wanted him to release his passion into her. She tightened the grip of her mouth and brought her tongue hard against his sliding member.

She felt his wet finger slide into her virgin ass. It was tight and it hurt, but the erotic pleasure of it overcame the pain. He was fucking her from every angle. Every motion was in sync. The laving of his tongue, his three aggressive fingers in her channel and the fast and furious one pumping into her ass.

It was so much… too much… too fast… too much feeling. Her body was on erotic sensation overload.

She felt the magic swirl around them like a high force gale.

And then it struck. Her climax gripped her body like never before. She was moaning around Ethan's cock as he pounded her mouth.

She felt him tense as he emptied his violent release into the back of her throat. It shot with such force that she never even tasted him. It spurted deep into her throat in forceful spasms, causing him to grunt and growl into her pulsating pussy.

He sounded like a wild animal.

And she felt like a caged lioness.

Her fingernails curled into her palms, drawing blood, as her orgasm continued to rock her body. She thrashed against her restraints as Ethan continued to slam into her from all angles.

Too much… too much.

He pulled his cock from her mouth and she screamed, crying his name over and over. She was completely undone.

No more… more… no more… how much could she take?

Just as she was sure she was going to lose her mind, Ethan swung around and covered her.

Their bodies slid together, both slick with sweat and oils. She locked her passion glazed eyes with his, which were still glowing red.

She was exhausted and spent, but her body still craved his possession.

"Mine." he gasped as he brought his mouth to hers. His hands slid over her breasts as his tongue captured hers. Their essences flowed together as tongue met tongue. The fluids of their orgasms combined together to make a unique taste that was an aphrodisiac to them both.

Brianna's desire was instantly rekindled. Ethan's had never died. She felt his cock, hot and hard, against her thigh.

His hands worked her breasts with just the right amount of pain and pleasure, plucking and stroking her nipples with erotic, passion-inducing strokes.

"I have to fuck you, Brianna. I need my cock buried deep inside you," he panted in her ear, his breath hitting the side of her neck forcefully as he tore his mouth from hers.

The words spiked her need. "Yes, Ethan. Take me." She was nearly choking on her words, her need to have him inside her leaving her breathless.

"Everyone will see us joining. I have to take you hard so that they know you are mine." One hand left her breast to slide down and grasp his burgeoning member. He slid the head along her clit, making her moan from the friction on the hypersensitive bud. Her whole body felt erotically overwhelmed, her senses on overload.

Erotic images floated through her mind, brought on by the knowledge that many were watching Ethan claim her. She wanted them to see him take possession of her body. Watch him claim her.

"Yes, Ethan. Make me yours." Her breath was coming hard and she was mindless with wanting.

He placed the head of his cock against her aching opening and thrust, completely burying himself inside of her. They groaned together, the fusion of their bodies blissful to them both.

Ethan didn't start slow. He fucked her like a man undone, stroking fast and furiously.

Their bodies slid together, burning skin to burning skin, the oil and sweat making their movements an erotic slide. Ethan cupped her buttocks and brought her hips up to slap against his forceful moves.

She was helpless, completely lost in his possession. Her head thrashed, her hands curling in a death grip against her palms and the restraints.

"You're mine, Brianna. Mine. Always mine." Ethan was panting against her neck. She could feel his mindlessness, his driving desire to merge them completely.

His body slammed into hers roughly, his cock buried completely with every hard stroke. Faster... stronger... faster. His hips were jerking hard, pulling her to meet him. They met with such force that every coming together was a loud slap of skin against skin.

Ethan bent his head and buried it into her neck, sinking his fangs into her tender flesh. She felt a flash of pain before the erotic, sensual sensations swamped her.

Although she knew it was going to happen, the eruption of her fangs from her gums startled her. It brought a feral hunger for Ethan that had her burying her newly sprung fangs into his shoulder with an almost violent strike.

Ethan jolted, but she knew it wasn't from pain. He was overwhelmed with the same feelings she was experiencing, the drawing of each other's essence intoxicating to them both. It was carnal and wild and they continued to feed voraciously as they strained toward climax.

When they detached their fangs, they were completely lost. Ethan stopped her bleeding with a swipe of his finger. It took him a moment to remember to stop his own. She licked the drops that had escaped.

Brianna was dizzy, senseless. She knew her climax was coming, building in intensity, the clenching sensation in her gut warning her that it was going to hit her violently.

It battered her with spasms so deep that she tried to arch her back. She threw her head back and screamed as it buffeted her. "Ethan, Oh God. Ethan!"

Ethan did arch his back, strong and hard, as he buried himself deep and was held there by her constricting walls. Her spasms enfolded his cock, constricting and releasing, forcing him to orgasm.

"Mine." He growled and snarled as he released himself furiously into her hot depths.

She was drowning in pleasure, nearly paralyzed by the pulsating of her body. The pressure lightened, but her body was trembling, and she felt like she was floating.

She felt Ethan's body relax as he released her from her bonds. He gathered Brianna into his arms, wrapped himself around her.

His soul had settled and found its place.

They trembled together as they held each other tightly. Ethan scooped her into his lap, looking at her anxiously. He took her palms into his hands and swiped his fingers over the bleeding punctures that she had caused with her nails. When he was done, she wrapped her arms around his back.

"It's over." Ethan panted, sounding relieved.

"It was incredible," she mumbled, spent and exhausted.

Her vampire smiled and her heart melted. "You're mine forever."

She gave him a weak, exhausted smile. "You know... that should be terrifying... but it's not."

"My brave mate." He kissed the top of her head.

Her senses returning, she looked around the room. "The magic is gone." The swirling magic she had felt throughout the room had diminished, leaving only a contented peace.

Ethan gave her a wicked grin. "My love, the magic is just beginning."

She knew that he knew exactly what she had meant, but she smiled. She could never resist that naughty grin.

"I do believe you're right." She lowered her head and gave him a tender kiss.

Ethan arranged the pillows and they stretched out side by side, Ethan spooning her close to him, his face buried in her hair.

He covered them with a blanket, conjured with his own magic.

They both fell into an exhausted sleep, deeply content that they were finally mates, finding their real home in each other for eternity.

EPILOGUE

I t was, of course, an evening wedding, and it was spectacular. Ethan made it a fairy tale affair that would fulfill every dream a woman could ever have about the perfect wedding.

The bride was radiant in ivory and lace. She walked down the aisle on scattered rosebuds in a huge cathedral that housed all of her friends and relatives and half of the vampire population.

The happiness of the bride and groom and their obvious love for each other made every guest sigh.

The bridesmaids were beautiful in gowns of pale blue, decorated with accents of pink.

The Hale brothers were there, much to their dismay, resplendent in their black tuxedos that matched the groom's. No one really noticed--much--that they tugged at the necks of the confining outfits once in a while or that they didn't look entirely comfortable.

They did, however, enjoy the reception. As humans and vampires mingled and laughed, the Hale brothers cleaned the food tables. Ethan had ordered plenty of food, knowing that his brothers would eat at least half of it. He had also ordered an extra cake. One for his brothers… one for the other guests.

To Brianna's delight, her maid of honor and best friend Callie caught the bouquet.

Rory caught her red garter, even though he wasn't even trying. It seemed to gravitate to him and somehow caught on the button of his jacket. He held it out like it was a poisonous snake.

Brianna and Ethan smiled at each other as they watched his reaction. Brianna gave Ethan a curious look as his smile turned wicked and devious.

Ethan continued to eye his brother and the red garter Rory held as he mumbled to himself in a sinful whisper, "Oh... I hope so, brother... I really hope so."

Brianna caught her new husband's devious thoughts and whacked him on the shoulder. "Ethan... you're terrible. I really want all of your brothers to find their mates."

He gave her an innocent expression as he answered, "Oh... me too, love. You have no idea how I look forward to it."

And he really did look forward to it, in more ways than one. He loved his brothers, even though they annoyed the hell out of him. He didn't want them miserable--much.

But payback really would be hell.

His wife gave him an exasperated look and he smiled, beaming at her. She couldn't help but smile back. Ethan smiled so often these days and it still made Brianna's heart skip a beat. It probably always would.

Even though the Hale brothers were mostly good... every one of them had just a little bit of the devil in them.

Brianna sighed. Her husband was probably more than just a little bit wicked.

Ethan scooped her into a warm embrace and as he lowered his lips to hers he told her softly, "Sometimes you like my wicked ways, wife."

As his lips met hers Brianna admitted to herself that she probably did.

In fact, she enjoyed them for her whole wedding night... and beyond.

THE END

of Book One: Ethan's Mate

RORY'S MATE

BOOK TWO

THE VAMPIRE COALITION

CHAPTER 1

Callie Marks sighed as she looked at the wedding cake on the table next to her. She really wanted a piece. It was from one of the best pastry kitchens in the city of Denver. Chocolate marbled with a mousse filling and chocolate frosting.

No. No cake. She had already eaten enough from the incredible gourmet buffet at this reception to feed an army. The last thing she needed was a piece of that cake with enough calories to add a little more jiggle to her ass.

Callie had always been what one of her nicer foster mothers had called "curvy" when she was a teenager. Callie called it what it was… she was plump. She was constantly battling an extra fifteen pounds that she didn't need on her body and was generally defeated by the call of delicious chocolate, rich foods and scrumptious appetizers.

I certainly went into one of the best fields to keep my weight down. I just had to be a chef.

She was head chef for a very highly regarded restaurant. Quite an accomplishment for a woman who was only twenty-seven years old. She loved her job. She loved to feed people. There was nothing better than creating a new gastronomical delight.

Callie pushed her plate away from her. It was completely empty. She sat back in her chair at the bride's table to watch the bride and groom dance.

Brianna Cole was her best friend. She had just gotten married after a whirlwind courtship to Ethan Hale, a rich, gorgeous, and charming man. They looked so incredibly happy. Ethan looked entirely enchanted with his beautiful, slender, blonde-haired bride.

Callie let out a long breath and tried not to feel a twinge of envy. She loved Brianna like a sister and wanted her happiness more than anything. Bri had been suffering from a rare form of leukemia that seemed to be in remission. Callie prayed it wouldn't return. She still had nightmares about the dark days of Brianna's illness and trying to come to terms with losing the only person she had who was like family to her, even though they weren't blood-related.

Being even the slightest bit jealous is just selfish after what Brianna has been through. She deserves this fairy tale wedding and the man of her dreams.

Callie acknowledged that she was a *tiny* bit selfish. She just couldn't help it. But she genuinely was extremely happy to have her best friend happy and healthy.

She smoothed down the skirts of her blue maid of honor dress. It was a lovely pale blue with shimmering accents of pink. Brianna had let her pick the style, a fact for which Callie was highly grateful. She had chosen a high waisted, elbow length style that would hide her plump figure. Callie loved the dress. Too bad she would probably never wear it again.

She frowned at the thought, reaching up to tug at a stray curl of her dark, wayward hair. She had swept it up in a chignon, but it was curly and long. Tendrils escaped and curled around her face. She hadn't looked in the mirror, but she was pretty sure her hair was a disaster.

With her dark brown eyes, hair and fair skin it was hard to detect what her origins were. Callie really didn't know because she was a foundling. Abandoned in a local park and never claimed, she was turned over to children's services and had gone the rounds of foster parents. She had never been adopted.

Callie jumped as a large, dark hand slid a plate across the table that stopped directly in front of her. She had been so engrossed in her thoughts that she hadn't seen the man even approach the table.

Her eyes lifted to see Rory Hale sit down directly across from her, a piece of cake big enough to feed ten people sitting in front of him. He slid a smaller piece, maybe only big enough to feed five people, closer to her.

"I don't want that," she told him, irritated now that she had to actually stare at the pastry in front of her.

"Why not?" Rory cocked his head and shot her an I'm-so-confused smile as he started eating his piece with obvious enjoyment. "It's fantastic."

Callie rolled her eyes, trying not to be charmed by the incredibly gorgeous specimen of manhood. For God's sake, did the man have to look so damn perfect? He had eaten more in one evening than any normal man ate in a month, and he still didn't look like he held one ounce of fat on his body. It was disgusting. Still…she tried to be polite. He was Brianna's new brother-in-law. "I'm trying not to eat sweets, Rory. I have to watch what I eat."

Rory continued to grin as he consumed his giant-sized piece of cake. "Why watch it when you can eat it?" He paused to shoot her a curious look. "How do you know that I'm Rory? Liam was sitting here earlier."

"Who else would you be? We were introduced at the rehears-al." She shoved the piece of cake to the middle of the table as she answered.

"Liam and I are twins. We're identical," he answered, polishing off the mammoth pastry and setting his fork on the plate. He stared at her curiously.

They weren't identical, Callie mused. Not really. Although they were both incredibly handsome with midnight black hair that just touched the back of their collar and very dark eyes, Rory was just…

different. Yeah…they were dressed in matching tuxedos and they looked very much alike…but she would never mistake one for the other.

She shook her head as she answered, "You aren't really exactly alike."

Rory looked perplexed. "Most people can't tell us apart."

Really? Liam was attractive, as was his brother Nathan, but Rory… was a walking temptation. She looked around for Liam, but didn't see him in the crowd. She didn't have anything for comparison but she was doubtful she would ever confuse the two. Liam didn't make her edgy and nervous. Rory definitely did. It was like she could feel the male hormones coming across the table, making her want to leap across the table and attack.

Callie crossed her arms in front of her and answered defensively, "I just don't think you're alike, that's all."

"Does that mean I'm the handsome one?" he asked hopefully, smiling brightly.

It was strange, but he wasn't flirting. It was almost as if he wanted validation. Callie refused to give it to him. His head was probably already fat enough. "No comment."

Rory's face fell. "I guess that means I'm not."

Callie searched his face for signs of conceit, but she didn't see anything except raw honesty. As she took in his perfect features, and glanced at his wavy mass of dark hair, she noticed one little stray strand that seemed to separate from the others and wanted to reach out and brush it back into place.

Come on, Callie. Get real. The guy has to know he's incredibly gorgeous. Don't feel sorry for him.

"I guess not," she answered, feeling even guiltier when he looked even more dejected. Wanting to see him smile again she offered, "Have my cake." She pushed it in front of him.

He pushed it back. "I know you want it."

"I don't," she answered firmly.

"You do." He started to smile again.

"Don't," she insisted.

"Come on, Callie. You were looking at the cake table like a tiger looks at raw meat. You wanted it. That's why I brought it."

Oh, shit. She groaned inwardly. Was she really that obvious? "I'm a chef. I was just checking out the competition."

"You wanted to *taste* the competition. Admit it." He took the plate from her and set it in front of him. Grabbing a clean fork, he scooped up a bite of the irresistible confection, reached over the table and held it to her mouth. She opened automatically and he dropped it gently between her lips.

Callie closed her eyes as the silky chocolate slid over her taste buds. She nearly groaned. It was perfection. She opened her eyes to see him holding out another bite. She slid her chair back. "No, Rory. I can't."

He looked perplexed. "Why?"

Callie was getting pissed. Did she need to spell it out for him? "In case you didn't notice, I can't afford the calories."

Rory sat back in his chair, dropping the fork back onto the plate. "I didn't notice. You look fine to me."

If I looked so fine, you would be asking me for my phone number. You would ask me to dance. Why did you have to say that with nothing but confusion and detached interest?

It wasn't his fault. He just wasn't interested. Callie couldn't even blame it on the fact that he was attached. Brianna had said all of the brothers were single and unattached. Rory just didn't want *her.*

She grabbed the plate of cake and pulled it in front of her. What the hell! She would be careful tomorrow.

Rory picked up a clean flute glass and filled it with champagne, saluting her before he raised it to his mouth. He didn't quite smile, but his lips were twitching.

God, he was irresistible. Rory may not be interested, but he was sweet. Her instincts were telling her he was completely genuine and he was certainly unusual. She could see a certain insecurity in him that spoke to her and she knew what that was like. It didn't matter that he was outrageously attractive, charming, genuinely kind. He just didn't believe he was anything special.

"Rory?" She queried softly between her luscious bites of cake.

"Yes," he answered in a low voice as he refilled his champagne and topped off hers.

She leaned slightly across the table, as if she were about to give away a huge secret. He leaned in slightly.

"You *are* the best looking of all the Hale brothers," she whispered softly, just loud enough for him to hear.

His smile started with his lips and moved to his eyes. His whole face lit up and his eyes sparkled mischievously as he leaned over and she leaned in to hear his secret.

"Callie…you don't need to lose weight. You are the most ravishingly beautiful woman here." Still no interest, but his voice was sincere. He might have said it matter-of-factly, but he truly meant it. He hadn't said it in a suave, artificial way that she would have doubted. He stared her directly in the eye, his gaze almost bashful, but straightforward.

She blushed and tried to look in another direction, embarrassed that she was flushing like an adolescent teenager.

When her face cooled down, she sneaked a look in his direction. He was watching her. Rory lifted his champagne flute and she raised her glass to his in an unspoken salute, a silent agreement.

With the clink of the glasses, a tentative friendship was born.

CHAPTER 2

Three Weeks Later…

Rory Hale awoke from his day sleep in a very good mood, knowing he wasn't going to be alone for the evening. He sat up and stretched, flexing his stagnant muscles to start his blood circulating.

Although vampires didn't sleep like the dead, day sleep was almost like hibernation. Their breathing and heart rate were almost non-existent and nothing and no one could rouse them except for their mate. It was a vulnerable time for any of his brethren and Rory had ultra high security around his home. He lived outside of the city and owned the five hundred acres of land surrounding the spacious, brick two-storey home. His land was surrounded by tall metal fences with only one entry gate and guarded with magic. Metal shutters plunged the house into total darkness at daybreak.

He rolled out of bed completely naked, his cock totally flaccid. He hadn't had to worry about a morning erection for three hundred years, losing all sexual function after he passed the age of one hundred. He was four hundred now and he didn't even remember what it felt like to have a stiff dick in the morning.

He used his magic to trigger the metal shutters open, taking in the tranquility of the night.

It was a perfect late spring evening, unseasonably warm, and he could smell the profusion of flowers that surrounded his house and garden. The crickets were chirping merrily and loudly. God, how he loved the sounds of the night.

He was tempted to linger at the large window, but he stepped into the bathroom and flipped on his large walk-in shower. He tipped his head back, letting the massaging jet flow over his body.

Vampires could clean themselves magically, but Rory loved the feel of water. As he soaped his muscular body his hand ran over his mating mark. He covered it with magic most of the time and didn't see it very often, but now he stared at it, wondering what had ever become of his mate.

The mark was an intricate dragon, no larger than a half dollar. His brothers had similar marks, as the dragon was their family marking, but each one had some subtle variations, making it unique to each brother. As he surveyed the mark he was hit by a twinge of loneliness, wishing he knew why his mate had never called him.

Ethan had warned *all* of his brothers to not give up hope. Rory's brother suspected that the reason he was so late getting to his mate Brianna was because he was no longer open to listening for her. Ethan had thrown in the towel and become resigned to the fact that his mating possibilities were gone. Fortunately, Ethan had been wrong and he had found his mate, now his wife, Brianna, before she died.

Rory covered the marking with his magic, sighing as he rinsed the soap from his body. He didn't want to give up hope. He tried to stay open to possibilities. But it was highly unlikely that his mate would show up after all of these years.

As he stepped out of the shower and toweled himself off, he remembered the agony Ethan had gone through after he had found Brianna. Did he really want to go through *that?*

Hell yeah...he would. Finding his mate would be extraordinary. The one who was born for him. The guardian of his soul. What would it be like to be that connected to a woman?

He was lonely. That was probably why he was so happy to be going to Brianna and Ethan's for dinner tonight. He loved seeing Brianna. And he would see Callie. Ethan was doing barbecue, but Callie was making all of the side dishes, and nobody could cook better than Callie. The woman was a gourmet goddess.

Rory adored Ethan's mate, Brianna. She fussed over all of the brothers, and that was something his brother Nathan hadn't known since their parents' demise four hundred years ago. He and Liam had never known that feeling at all; they had been babies, but Ethan and Nathan remembered the *fallen* attack that had taken their parents. Their mother and father had sacrificed their own lives for their children.

When the group of *fallen* had gotten past the magic protecting their childhood home, their parents had transported the four of them away to confront the *fallen*. Their actions had bought enough time that the *fallen* couldn't follow their trail straight to the children. Nathan still hated his father's friends to this day for not letting him return to help his parents, to enter the fight with the *fallen*.

Rory was grateful. Had Nathan returned he would have been dead along with his parents. It had taken a gathering of ten Ancients to destroy the band of *fallen*…and not without casualties. They had lost three Ancients in that fight.

Nathan had gladly joined The Coalition when he grew older, and Rory knew he took great pleasure in destroying the *fallen*. Nathan's hatred for the *fallen* was nearly an obsession.

Rory paused in the middle of his bedroom, debating how to dress himself.

He frowned, wondering why he cared. His usual attire was jeans, a t-shirt and black leather boots. He'd never really thought about whether or not they were attractive.

But Callie would be there. Rory grudgingly admitted that he liked her. He liked *her*. He couldn't feel physical desire for any women, but he wanted to impress *her*. There was just…something about her. They had only run into each other a few times at Ethan's, but they had somehow become friends. He saw her…and she saw him. They were like kindred spirits who understood each other. He wanted her to like him, to trust him.

She looks at me like I'm someone special.

Rory had never been special. His twin was a healer with extraordinary powers. And Rory…was just the twin. He didn't envy his brother. Being a healer took enormous dedication and it was a huge weight on Liam's shoulders. But Liam was special and sometimes Rory wished that he could be seen for himself, instead of just being the other twin.

He was proud of Liam. He admired him. They were extremely close because they were twins. But sometimes…just sometimes… he felt eclipsed by Liam.

Maybe that was why he valued Callie's friendship. She never looked at Liam the way she looked at him. She didn't talk to Liam or Nathan in the same way.

He clothed himself in an expensive suit.

Nope. Looks like I'm trying too hard.

He tried casual pants and a silk shirt with a thick gold chain.

Christ! I look like a pimp.

Okay…nice black designer jeans. Armani polo shirt. Italian-leather casual shoes. Rolex watch.

Not bad. Better than my usual.

Rory laughed at himself as he grabbed his car keys and let himself into the garage. He could hardly transport himself into Ethan's house with Callie there. Besides, he liked driving. He slid into his loaded Navigator, loving the smell and feel of the custom leather seats. The big four wheel drive was appropriate for winter in the Rocky Mountains and Rory liked the space. He needed it to comfortably accommodate his body.

He pulled out of the garage and secured the house as he exited the front gate. As he drove along the private road that would take him to the main highway, he started whistling a current tune.

Callie's favorite song.

He pushed the accelerator. Ethan's home was a twenty-five minute drive. Maybe he could make it in fifteen.

Callie had arrived at Brianna and Ethan's sprawling ranch home over an hour ago. She had brought some side dishes with her and some she was currently rushing around Bri's kitchen trying to complete.

She had made the banana cream pies in advance and they were currently chilling in the fridge.

Rory's favorite.

Shit! Could she stop thinking about Rory? He was not for her. He was too handsome, too compelling…too everything. He had no interest in her…but she liked him. And she knew he liked her. They could talk. He had no sexual interest in her, but there was… something. Some kind of connection. They hadn't really seen each other all that much, but when they did, they were able to talk like old friends. He gave her his undivided attention and he seemed to hang on her every word.

But the sexual attraction was missing. *On his side anyway.* Personally, she would like to jump his bones and have him a million different ways. Unfortunately, the feeling wasn't mutual. She didn't sense that desire on his part, and he seemed totally oblivious to hers.

She sighed as she finished off her special chef's salad. The man didn't have any vanity, and she couldn't figure out how he had never acquired at least a little. He could act cocky at times, but it was a facade. She felt the insecurity hiding deep within the man, and it was really bizarre for a man that looked like every woman's secret sexual fantasy.

Brianna came breezing into the kitchen looking breathless. *Ethan had caught her again.* She had that glassy-eyed, kiss-swollen lips look of a woman that had just been kissed senseless. She and Ethan couldn't seem to keep their hands off each other.

"How's it coming?" Brianna asked brightly. *Too brightly.*

"Fine, Bri. Ethan catch you again?" Callie laughed lightly as she watched Bri's face flush.

"He's wicked sometimes. But I have to admit I don't try very hard to get away." Bri winked at her and opened the refrigerator, taking out a pitcher of margaritas. She pulled three glasses from the freezer. "I think its cocktail time."

"Can I ask you something, Bri?" Callie questioned hesitantly.

"Ask away," Bri answered as she filled the glasses with frozen margaritas.

"I was wondering…is Rory gay?"

Bri was just starting to take a sip of her drink and nearly choked on it. "Rory? Oh God, no. Why do you ask?"

Callie picked up her drink and took a swallow, savoring the fruity taste. "Nothing. I just wondered."

Scratch that thought. He's perfectly straight and just not interested.

"Callie, are you interested in Rory?" Bri cocked her head and gave her a curious look.

"No, no. Not at all. I was just curious. I mean…I like him. He's really nice. But I know there's no interest there for him," she answered. She tried to hide her blushing cheeks from Bri.

Bri studied Callie for a moment before replying carefully. "Listen hon…things are complicated with Rory. With all of the brothers. It isn't you."

"You don't have to make excuses, Bri. This is me. Your BFF. You don't have to sugarcoat the excuses. I'm used to men not being interested," Callie answered, her arms crossing in front of her.

Bri grabbed her shoulders and shook her gently. "You're a beautiful woman, Callie. Inside and out. I wish you would realize that. Any man would be lucky to have you." Bri looked her straight in the eye before adding, "I repeat…it is *not* you."

"It's nothing, Bri. Don't worry about it. It was just curiosity." Callie broke away from Bri as she spoke, turning back to her vegetables on the stove.

"He does like you, Callie. He asks about you all the time. It isn't lack of interest…it's just…" Bri paused as if looking for the right words. "Shit, Callie. It's really complicated," Bri finished, sounding exasperated and frustrated.

Callie was relieved when the conversation was interrupted by a booming voice. "Did you make my pies?"

Rory. She turned from the stove to watch him enter the kitchen. Oh Lord, he looked good enough to eat for dinner. She'd gladly give up the food if she could have a piece of him. Swallowing the lump in her throat, she answered lightly. "Of course. I got your message from Bri."

He smiled brightly, making her heart flip flop. He grabbed a frozen glass and helped himself to the drinks. "How are you, Callie?" he asked with genuine interest as Bri went forward and hugged him hard and unhesitatingly, giving him a loud smack on the cheek.

"Good. Except I spent the morning in the kitchen making your banana cream pies from scratch. It's supposed to be my day off," she teased him lightly.

He shrugged and raised his brow, pinning her with his eyes. "It's your fault. You brought them last time and now I'm going through withdrawal."

Bri released Rory and gave him the once over. "You look nice tonight, Rory."

Rory blew off the comment by replying. "Not as nice as you two."

Bri did look stunning in her red capri pants and a bright red and blue patterned spaghetti strap top. She had on a pair of strappy sandals that showcased her slim calves.

Callie had tried hard. She had on a yellow sundress with capped sleeves and a pair of white sandals, however, most of her was currently covered by a full apron that she wore while she was cooking. Her long, thick hair was pulled back with a yellow hair tie that left the mass of dark brown curls trailing down her neck. She quickly took the apron off. She was almost done and it looked horrible with her yellow sundress. Callie put it gently on the kitchen chair, trying not to be obvious about wanting to look better.

"Charmer!" Bri picked up her drink and grabbed an extra one in her other hand. "I guess I should go give my husband his drink. He's slaving over the barbecue. Are you coming out to see Ethan?" Bri asked Rory as she made her way across the kitchen.

"I'll be out in a few minutes, Bri."

"Okay. Take your time. We'll be on the patio." Bri's voice trailed off as she exited the kitchen.

Rory picked up his drink again and came to lean against the counter, a few feet from Callie. "Do you need any help?"

Oh, God. She could smell him, and his scent was so damn…male. She wasn't sure what cologne he used, but it drove her crazy. She tried to keep her distance as much as possible. "Nope, everything is under control. If Ethan doesn't burn the steaks, everything will be perfect."

"Everything will be perfect regardless. You're here. I've really missed talking to you." His voice was casual but genuine.

Damn it. I hate it when he says things like that.

Flustered, Callie dropped the spoon into a pan of sauce and went to retrieve it without thinking. She hissed as the hot liquid burned her hand. She quickly pulled the sauce off the heat and went around Rory to get to the sink. She turned on the cold water and let it run over her fingers. It burned, but she was used to worse. It was a just a minor scald to her two fingers.

"Callie, are you okay? Did you burn yourself?" Rory's voice was full of concern.

"I'm fine. It was a stupid thing to do. It's just a tiny burn. It happens a lot in my profession. Occupational hazard." She left the water running over her fingers, the burn already easing.

Rory came to the sink, his eyes full of distress, as she looked up at him.

And then it happened.

He reached out to lift her hand out of the water to look at it… *and all hell broke loose.*

CHAPTER 3

Rory never knew what hit him. One moment he was reaching for Callie's hand and the next thing he knew his whole body was on fire.

Mine!

His mating mark burned as he held Callie's small hand in his larger one. He looked at her and saw his destiny. *His mate. His woman.* His body burned and his cock was rock hard, ready to claim her…now!

She was so beautiful. So…his.

He pulled her into his arms and brought her warm, feminine body flush with his. He claimed her mouth, swooping down, needing to brand her, needing to possess her.

Her mouth was warm, opening under his persistent embrace. His primitive instincts rejoiced in her surrender. He put his hand behind her head and pulled her mouth tighter against his. He captured her tongue and started a slide in, slide out motion, mimicking what he wanted to do with his cock.

He didn't know how long he kissed her. He kept moving position, conquering her mouth from every angle. His hands moved possessively over her body, grasping her rear and pulling her hard against his hot, throbbing member.

I need to be inside her. I need to have her. She's mine. I need to make her moan with pleasure. I need her to want me.

His thoughts were fractured, his actions instinctive. He pulled up her light sundress, needing to feel her moist center. She felt so perfect, so warm, so female.

His hands slid over her panties, cupping her ass. He lifted her and sat her on the kitchen table, his mouth never stopping his relentless assault.

Callie was moaning into his mouth, her arms wrapped around his neck. He demanded and she responded.

Rory could sense her desire, her need. He needed to satiate her.

His need. Her need. They both pounded into him hard. He ran one of his hands along her thighs, stroking her soft skin. His other hand went to her generous, perfect breasts. He needed to feel her soft skin. He grabbed the neck of the dress and pulled. The buttons gave way and the dress opened down the front. He didn't bother to look for a clasp for her bra. It wasn't that tight so he yanked it up to free her breasts.

His hand roamed over both breasts, touching every inch of the soft flesh. His fingers pinched and caressed her nipples.

His other hand slid to her hot core, delving under her panties.

Fuck! She's hot and wet. Ready to be taken. For me. Just for me. Mine.

He pulled his mouth from hers. "Open," he demanded, needing to touch her. She responded by spreading her legs, responding to his dominance, and it nearly drove him mad. His fingers immediately dipped into her soft, moist core.

He laid her back on the table and brought his mouth to her breasts.

"Rory." She moaned his name with passion and it sent him into a frenzy. He needed to satisfy her needs. He wanted to watch her climax. For him. Only for him.

He yanked her panties down her legs and they fell to her ankles. He lifted her dress to her waist, baring her to his gaze. He spread her legs wider and buried his fingers into her slick, wet heat. He continued to lave and nip her breasts as his fingers worked her pussy. He slipped two fingers into her needy channel, filling her. He used his other hand to roughly slide along her clit.

He knew he was sweating. The droplets were pouring from his face and dropping onto her breasts. But he didn't give a shit; all he wanted was to watch her come.

She was groaning, her head thrashing back and forth. *So close. So close.*

He panted as one hand worked her channel, the other sliding along her clit. She was so slick that his fingers glided easily and he picked up the pace, her need becoming his. His fingers were coordinated, slamming into her aching opening and working her sensitive bud in sync.

Rory could feel her entire body trembling, her climax beginning. He lifted his mouth from her breasts as he watched her.

Christ…she was beautiful. Some of her hair had worked itself free and silky strands tangled around her face. She was biting her lip, her eyes closed. She was laid out on the table, open for him to give her pleasure and she looked like the finest feast he had ever seen.

He felt her climax start. It pulsed over his fingers, clenching the two in her channel tightly. She arched her back as she murmured his name over and over.

Elation that he had satisfied his mate washed over him in waves. He could feel her climax almost as if it was his own.

He was tempted to cover her and fuck her just like this, but he was mesmerized, watching and feeling her find her release.

He didn't stop his persistent fingers from their assault and she continued to climax, helpless to stop it, completely at his mercy. And Rory wanted to prolong her pleasure, stretch it out as much as possible.

As he felt the contractions subside, he pulled her up and into his arms. Her arms clasped around him like a vise. She panted, "Rory, Oh God. That's never happened before. Not like that."

He held her tightly, fighting with his instincts. He wanted to beat on his chest with primitive satisfaction. He was the only one to make her come this hard, this good.

Mine!

He continued to hold her trembling body, feeling her hot breath against his neck as she recovered.

Rory fought his instincts to take her. He needed her, wanted her soft and warm beneath him. He wanted that moist heat accepting his hard cock until both of them were breathless. This woman was his. His mate. And he needed to stake his claim on her.

"Rory, what the hell happened?" she asked him softly, her voice shaky as she pulled away from him.

He knew his eyes were burning with desire and longing. Making no effort to hide his gaze, he watched her become aware of his need, his wants, and when she pulled away he nearly growled.

Callie slid off the table and pulled her panties back up. She smoothed down her dress and pulled her bra down, frowning at the ripped buttons of her dress. She held the top together with one hand.

She was afraid. Rory could feel it, sense it and he could see the fear in her eyes.

Her eyes raked over him, her expression horrified. Shit, he knew he looked wild, and she was obviously scared. He struggled for control, barely able to keep from reaching out and taking her again.

But he didn't like seeing her afraid.

Don't be scared. Please don't be scared. He reached for her with his mind. He knew she could hear him. They had already touched. The mental intimacy would be there.

She didn't answer. Her hands shook as her eyes landed on his mating mark. As soon as he had touched her the mark had been revealed and his magic could no longer cover it.

She stared at it, terror in her eyes.

She took one last frightened look at him and fled, grabbing her purse and her keys and started running for the door like her life depended on it.

"No! Callie!" His voice was loud and desperate.

She was running from him. He couldn't ever let her get away.

Rory sprinted after her, nearly catching her at the door. He would have caught her…if he hadn't been restrained by three sets of strong hands holding him back.

Nathan, Liam and Ethan tugged at him. He snarled at them, but they held him fast as he struggled to get away. He needed to get to Callie. She couldn't go.

Callie was already out the door like her ass was on fire, leaving the door wide open. She ran to her car, never looking back.

Rory struggled to get out of his siblings' hold as he watched her drive away.

"Callie! Come back." His voice was anguished and he almost broke away from the restraining hands, so desperate was his need for her.

He dropped to his knees but his brothers retained their hold on him. Everything inside of him needed to find her, needed to possess her, needed to explain and comfort her.

His brothers dragged him bodily to the couch, dropping him, but never releasing their hold.

"Rory," Ethan barked sharply. "You can't chase the woman down like a hound after a rabbit. What the hell happened?"

He sat on the couch, his breath still coming hard and fast. "Mine. My mate."

"Oh, shit. Callie?" Ethan frowned as he loosened his hold and looked up at Bri who had just entered the room, a concerned look on her face.

Rory knew that Bri and Ethan were conversing silently…but he didn't care.

"Calm down, Rory. We need to talk about this. If you flee…I'll catch you," Nathan threatened.

Rory knew Nathan *could* and he *would*. He was two hundred years older and more powerful. Rory took some deep breaths, feeling his brothers release their hold. He still wanted to go after Callie, but he was regaining some common sense. Ethan was right. She was already scared. He couldn't go after her like a maniac stalker.

"Rory, you found your mate." Liam spoke, his voice full of happiness and awe.

As he calmed down, Rory was rather in awe himself. Callie was his mate. *Callie. A woman I already care about, a woman that's probably much too good for me.*

Brianna came to sit beside him on the couch, nudging her husband out of her way. Ethan moved so that Brianna could sit between them. The other two brothers flopped into two of the living room chairs.

"Callie looked upset. What happened, Rory?" Brianna's soft voice calmed him. She brushed back a stray lock of his hair, an affectionate gesture that further soothed him.

He had lost control and attacked her best friend, but he could hardly tell her that and felt ashamed. Not only was Callie his mate, but he'd failed to respect her. He answered cautiously, "She burned herself. I took her hand to look at it and I...lost it." His voice was hoarse. "I've never touched her before. I didn't realize."

Brianna sighed. "She'll understand, Rory...eventually. But Callie lives in the real world. It won't be easy for her to accept that there is another world apart from the one she lives in. She's had a hard life."

"What do you mean?" Rory was curious now. He pushed his mating instincts down, interested in knowing everything about Callie, needing to really know her.

Brianna looked hesitant. After a moment she replied, "It really isn't my place to tell you much about Callie. But there are a few things you should know. She'll have to tell you the details herself once she trusts you. Her childhood and teen years were tough. She was abandoned as a baby. She never knew her parents. She was transferred from foster home to foster home. She wants security. She needs security."

"I'll give her security. I'll give her a home that she can be in forever. Anything she needs or wants is hers." Rory answered firmly. He would wrap her in stability.

"She has other needs than just financial security, Rory. She has abandoned child syndrome. She's suffered with it for years. She's done her best to overcome it...and she's getting there. But she needs people around her who care about her. She thinks nobody wants her. She doesn't feel desirable or attractive. She blames herself for the fact that she was never adopted." Brianna finished, obviously done revealing all of the information she felt comfortable disclosing about her best friend.

Rory gaped at Brianna as she finished. His sweet, adorable Callie. How could she think that nobody wanted her? He had wanted to be around her even before he had found out she was his mate. It wasn't that he doubted what Brianna said was true. Brianna had been a social worker before she had mated with Ethan. She knew about these things, and she had been friends with Callie since childhood.

His heart ached for her. He knew what it was like to want to be special. It was difficult to hear that his mate had suffered so much, had her confidence been eroded by years of rejection?

"You need to be careful, Rory. She's vulnerable, even though she may not act like it. She's become a master at hiding her emotions," Brianna warned him with a frown. "I know your mating instincts are strong but you are going to have to go slow. She's not going to believe you at first."

Rory nodded his head, "I know."

"But you need to convince her, Rory. I can't see her go through what I did. I love her. She's like the sister I never had." Brianna voice choked with tears. Ethan reached for Brianna's hand, comforting her silently.

"You don't have to worry about him pushing things too far. It won't happen unless she calls him to her." Nathan's baritone cut through the silence, powerful and filled with a slight bit of amusement.

"What are you talking about?" Rory demanded, irritated at his brother's knowing smirk.

"He means you can touch her as long as she is enjoying it, but you can't have intercourse unless she calls you to her." Liam answered, talking in a clinical voice.

"It's true. The woman has the ultimate choice. She has to ask you to come. Literally." Ethan choked back a laugh as he answered. Brianna smacked Ethan on the arm with a frown, obviously not appreciating her mate's humor.

"But we almost did. I almost did." Rory answered, confused.

"If you had come close enough to initiating it…" Nathan held his index finger straight up and let it droop down with an evil smile.

Damn. He had been clueless to *that* mating fact.

Ethan took pity on him. Probably because he had been through it himself.

"Before the act can be completed, she has to call you to her. She will call with her subconscious mind while she is asleep." Ethan grinned wickedly. "In the meantime…you'll think you're in hell. You won't want any other men around her, talking to her, touching her."

Okay…maybe Ethan wasn't *that* sympathetic. Rory cursed himself for the way he had pulled Ethan's chain with Brianna when Ethan had been ruled by mating instincts.

"What should I do now?" Rory was talking to himself, but spoke out loud.

Brianna put a hand on his shoulder and suggested softly. "Go home, Rory. I'll talk to her. Just don't push too hard."

He got up from the couch and pulled his keys from his pocket. His body burned and his cock was still hard. Every instinct he had was commanding him to go to Callie, but he didn't. He wanted more than to fuck her. He wanted her as a real mate.

He left without a word. He swung into the seat of his SUV with only one subject on his mind.

Driving home was one of the hardest things he had ever done.

CHAPTER 4

He sent flowers until she could open her own shop. He called her on her cell phone. He called her with his mind, speaking to her although she never answered.

Thank God Rory hadn't come to her door. She might have let him in. He was hard enough to resist when she couldn't see him; she wasn't sure she could ignore him if he was standing in front of her.

Callie stirred the soup she was making on the stove and let it continue to simmer. She had been cooking for days. She cooked after work, on her days off and any time she was feeling confused. That was pretty much continuously, unless she was sleeping. Every Tupperware container she owned was full of food. Her freezer was full, but her mind was still in turmoil.

She could clean…but she had already done that too. Her small one bedroom apartment was so immaculate that she didn't think she could find a speck of dust.

God…she was a mess.

She flopped onto her couch and picked up a novel she had been anxious to read before the scene with Rory. Now, she couldn't keep her mind focused on it.

It had been two weeks since the incident with Rory at the barbecue. The only person she had seen outside of work was Bri. Her best friend had been over to talk to Callie a few times and she still couldn't believe the fantastic stories Bri told her about the brothers and their origins.

Vampires? Really? Bri had been so matter-of-fact and she hated to doubt her words. They had been best friends since they were in grade school. It all seemed too unbelievable. She had seen Bri's marking and nearly caved in. It was so similar to the one on her left buttock. Callie was born with the marking as far as she knew. She had gotten her name because of the mark that had covered her entire butt cheek when she was a baby.

Callista Marks. She wasn't sure what fanciful person suggested that name, but it fit. The marking was beautiful.

Could she really believe that she held Rory's soul, that she had been the guardian of his soul since her birth?

The whole story was inconceivable and incredible. Yet, it was not.

She didn't have any rationalization for what was happening. The matching marks, the mind-speak. How could she explain it? How did one explain the unexplainable?

Damn it. She dealt in facts. However, so much of what Brianna told her *did* make sense in a weird sort of way. Bri explained her mysterious leukemia and what was really the cause of her condition. The doctors certainly couldn't explain Bri's quick remission, and truly, Callie wanted to believe Bri's version. That would mean her best friend would never have to fear the disease returning.

Callie shuddered. If the fantastic explanation was true, it meant that Callie would suffer the same fate very soon. She was a year and a half younger than Bri, but it wouldn't be long.

She closed the book and put it on the side table next to the couch. She couldn't read. Her mind wouldn't focus.

She laid on the couch. Waiting. The sun was setting and Rory would start talking soon. He never gave up, speaking to her in her mind, like she was there. He told her about his life, about the vampire culture. Whatever was on his mind…he shared with her. She never answered, but she heard him. The only time he closed his mind was when he was doing his work with The Coalition because he didn't want her tainted by the violence.

Just the sound of his voice in her mind made her long for him. She could feel his desire. His longing. She had already wanted him, but now she needed him with a yearning that almost tore her apart.

Tears flowed down her cheeks. She never had anyone who saw her as special except for Bri, but she realized Rory always had. She had thought he hadn't felt physical desire for her, when instead, the truth was that he just wasn't capable. Every other action had showed her that he liked her. Truly liked her as a person.

Could it be true that she was his mate? That she belonged with him? She almost believed it, actually wanted to believe it. If she did, that would mean she belonged somewhere, she belonged with Rory, the most incredible man, or vampire, she had ever met.

Her mind wandered often to the night of the barbecue. Her body heated and she groaned inwardly. She couldn't think about that night without touching herself, imagining it was Rory mastering her body. He had given her more pleasure without even making love to her than she had ever felt in her few experiences with sexual relations. What would it be like to make love with such a man?

She could see the vulnerabilities that Rory tried to hide from others, but he was still a dominant alpha male. He had no insecurities in the love-making department. He had been wild with desire and knew exactly how to make her mindless. It had been exciting and a little terrifying all at once.

It was her own overwhelming emotions that had made her run. The identical marking that he had to hers, his voice in her head, the sudden and overwhelming sexual encounter. Everything had shocked and confused her so badly that she had needed to retreat, figure out what all of it meant.

Good evening, Callie.

Rory. He was awake and his low baritone voice flowed into her mind like fine wine, intoxicating and delicious.

What are you doing tonight, love? It's Friday. You have tomorrow off. I know you're probably awake. I'm getting into the shower.

Callie knew he always got into the shower after he awoke. She imagined him naked, hot water caressing his incredible body and she couldn't stand it. She was wearing a night shirt that made it easy to slide her hand into her panties.

"I wish I was there." She answered him aloud but she knew he could hear her in her mind. She was weak and she needed him so badly. She had missed him, ached for him with an intensity that was painful.

Total silence greeted her as she slid her fingers along her wet folds, teasing herself.

Callie, are you all right? His voice was husky and full of alarm.

No, she wasn't all right. She was burning hot and out of control. She spread her legs and delved into her pussy, sliding her fingers the entire length of her aching mound, circling her clit. "I'm touching myself. Imagining you in the shower. I can't help myself. I'm thinking about the night of the barbecue." She answered him, unable to stop now that she had started.

She heard him growl, a low tortured sound that she felt roll through her entire body.

Let me come sate you, Callie. Please. I need to. You're my mate. I can feel your need. And you are feeling some of mine. I'm sorry, Callie. I try to contain it. I woke up hard. I was thinking of you. I was palming my cock. I wasn't thinking.

Callie wasn't sure anything could sate her. She felt like she was in perpetual heat. She rolled her hips up and her fingers caressed her clit.

"Oh God. Come to me naked, Rory. I need to see you."

She had no more said the words and Rory was there. He was dry but gloriously nude. The breath left her body as she saw him standing beside the couch, watching her. His eyes were wild and needy as he watched her touching herself, trying to relieve her burning body. She knew she was looking at him exactly the same way.

His body was perfect, all rippling muscle and golden skin. His cock was hard and…enormous.

He scooped her up, taking her hand away, stopping her from touching herself.

"No," she cried out, needing the stimulation to her clit, as he started walking toward her bedroom. He found the bathroom first and detoured.

"I satisfy my mate. You have no need to do it yourself." He sounded demanding and possessive as he pulled her nightshirt over her head.

He pulled it off and dropped it to the floor, leaving her only in her tiny panties.

He groaned as he put her hands over her head and pushed her against the bathroom wall. He held her wrists with one hand over her head while his head dipped down to tease her breasts. "You are so beautiful, Callie." His comment was muffled as he devoured her, biting and stroking her nipple with his tongue and teeth. His other hand slipped to her other breast, pinching and stroking until Callie nearly screamed in frustration.

She writhed as he toyed with her breasts, his touch making her more out of control.

He stopped and kneeled, jerking her panties down her legs.

She stepped out of them, leaving her completely naked. She didn't have a chance to worry about her body being exposed. Being plump most of her life had left her shy about being nude in front of anyone, but the burning, intense look in Rory's eyes made her sizzle.

"You're fucking perfect," his voice was husky, dripping with need.

He lifted her like she was petite, turned the shower on with his magic and brought her inside. He lowered her to her feet and wrapped her tightly in his arms. His mouth covered hers in a kiss that sucked the breath from her body. He pinned her to the wall, his body covering her, pressing her against the tile, now warm from the hot water. His mouth took hers with intensity. It was a kiss of desperation, of possession, and his tongue stroked hers roughly as his hands molded her body, touching her everywhere.

She groaned into his mouth, needing him, needing more.

As though he sensed her need he brought his hands to her breasts and kneaded them, sending a jolt straight to her core.

His mouth left hers and wandered down her body in an erotic slide, making sure their bodies touched as he made his descent. He lifted her leg to the ledge, forcing her to spread her legs wide. As he lowered his body so that he was kneeling before her, she could feel the hot spray of water caressing her skin.

He filled his hands with her creamy body wash and ran the silky fluid over the inside of her thighs as he dipped his head between her legs.

Sensation overwhelmed her and she moaned his name while his mouth covered her aching pussy, his tongue invading her. He had perfect access with her leg hitched high on the ledge and she was open and exposed. His hands continued gliding over her thighs, the lather making it a continuous erotic slide. His tongue lapped, sliding through her folds, spearing into her hot channel. He buried his face, his tongue fucking her, his teeth abrading her clit as he tipped his head back for full access.

Her hands slapped against the tile, trying to gain purchase as sensation whirled through her body. It was so much...too much. "Rory," she panted his name, her senses out of control.

His lathered hands slid up to her ass, stroking the globes roughly as his tongue slid to her sensitive clit, laving and nipping. He gripped her ass and pulled her snug against his mouth, his tongue tight against her aching bud. He flicked and laved, hard and fast.

She felt like she was whirling, vertigo making her grab for something solid. Her hands landed on Rory's shoulders, clutching him to keep from falling. "Yes, Rory, Yes. Make me come. Please." She was screaming as she threw her head back. She knew she was begging, but she didn't care. This man had total possession of her body and she needed him to give her release.

He took one of his hands off her ass, holding her securely with the other. He slid two of his large fingers into her empty channel, sliding smoothly into her begging entrance. His fingers filled her, starting a furious rhythm that matched the movements of his tongue.

Faster and faster. Harder and harder. So much stimulation. Too much stimulation. The pounding of the hot water on her breasts. Rory's tongue attacking her clit, Rory's fingers fucking her hard.

Her climax pounded over her. She arched her back and screamed as the pulsations exploded through her entire body.

Rory didn't stop. He continued his perpetual pleasure, drawing her orgasm out, making her body blow apart.

When he finally rose, she was shaking from head to toe. He positioned her in front of him, letting her feel the full force of the water flowing over her body. He held her tightly to him, her back to his front. She could feel his ragged breathing, coming hard and fast, and his chest heaving.

He lifted her out of the shower and grabbed a big, fluffy towel from the rack beside the shower. The water shut off without anyone touching the handles of the shower.

She was dazed and a little dizzy. He held her up with an arm around her waist as he dried her.

As he picked her up and carried her to the bedroom Callie could feel him trembling. He was breathing hard, but it wasn't from exertion. She knew he was trying to gain control. She had learned much from Bri and she knew how he was feeling. She could feel some of his tension, his wanting, although she had just been completely sated.

He tucked her into bed, kissing her tenderly. "I have to go, Callie," he rasped as he turned from the bed.

Callie's heart ached. She knew he was feeling tortured, but she didn't want him to go.

"Stay with me," she whispered. It was selfish, but she wanted him here. She would feel so lonely without him.

His expression tortured, Rory turned back toward the bed.

CHAPTER 5

Ethan was right...Rory did feel like he was in hell. He had felt that way since he had first touched his mate, but this situation was the worst.

He couldn't deny his mate. If she wanted him, he would stay. He wanted to stay. His heart felt like it was being ripped out of his chest.

His intense loneliness and desire to be at her side consumed him when he was without her.

His burning desire to possess her nearly killed him when he was with her.

He was completely fucked either way.

Pleasing his mate was a compulsion. He didn't want to leave her. He wanted to be with her.

"If you don't want to...I understand, Rory. I'm sorry."

She was biting her lip and the look of raw vulnerability in her eyes made his chest ache. He slid into the bed, pulling her naked, warm body against him. "It isn't that I don't want to, Callie. I want to be with you every minute. It nearly killed me not to hear your voice for the last few weeks. It's just..." his voice trailed off, low and soft.

"I know we can't have sex. Bri explained it. I haven't called you to me." She snuggled up against his powerful chest.

"You will, Callie." She had to…or he would go insane.

She went silent and Rory could feel her slow, even breathing against his neck.

He needed to feed. Satisfying Callie had taken a slight edge off of his insanity because her need wasn't pounding at him, but he had come to her before he had fed. It would help to be at full strength.

Mature vampires could go a week without feeding, but being in the mating process and not being able to claim his mate had taken a lot of energy. He fed at least once a day to keep his beast at bay.

He slid slowly from the bed, hating the loss of her warm, silky body against his.

He heard her moan lightly, reaching for him. He slid a fluffy pillow into her arms and she clutched it and settled back into sleep.

He took one last look of longing at her sleeping peacefully before he removed himself to a darker area of Denver. It was a place where creatures, human and immortal, roamed the night with no good intentions.

He found his source quickly, feeding from the drug dealer without remorse. He wiped the man's mind clean, leaving him with nothing but a dazed look.

He flashed back to Callie's apartment. As he stood at the side of the bed he felt a familiar sensation.

Fallen!

The evil was nearly palpable. There had to be more than one.

Nathan!

He called for his older brother. Nathan would get the distress signal. He didn't call Ethan or Liam. He didn't want Ethan to leave his mate and Liam was healing. They were twins and he could feel the faint buzz of Liam's power when he was at work, which was almost every hour that Liam was awake.

Rory tried to sense the evil, pin down the location. It wasn't inside the apartment, but it was close. He transferred to the outside of the building and sensed a stronger presence.

He cursed himself for not surrounding the building with magic. He had nearly failed to protect Callie.

He barely had time to raise his arm to manufacture his sword before the *fallen* were upon him.

Three ugly, sunken faces appeared before him. They could sense him just as he could feel their evil.

The three attacked together, probably thinking they could dispose of him quickly to get him out of the way.

Rory spun around to get out of the reach of their razor-sharp claws, but he caught slashes in the back and to his chest as he moved. He swung his sword toward one of the *fallen,* slicing its chest open. Black fluid flowed from the *fallen's* wound, but that didn't stop it.

The attackers circled Rory, slashing at him with their claws, trying to drain him of his blood. Rory gave as good as he got. Both black fluid and blood flowed to the ground.

He wasn't about to lose. His mate was near and he would never let them get any closer to her.

He transported, taking himself out of their circle. He appeared behind one of the *fallen,* spearing the enemy in the chest. His aim was perfect. The heart of the *fallen* ruptured. The creature fell to the ground writhing. It would soon be nothing but dust.

Rory would have taken a swipe to the neck that probably would have ripped his head off, if not for Nathan.

His brother appeared, completely armed and furious. With unrestrained violence and rage, Nathan cut through the *fallen* about to attack his brother. He sliced the head from his prey and plunged his sword into its heart.

Rory turned to the last *fallen,* determined to extinguish it. The bastard needed to die. Rory was seeing red. Literally. His mind was volatile at the threat to his mate. He stepped close enough for the *fallen* to take a few swipes at him, but Rory didn't even feel it.

Destroy. Kill. Remove the threat from my mate.

He and Nathan struck at the same time. Rory from the front, Nathan from the back, their swords meeting with a force so hard that it sent vibrations through Rory's body. Rory swayed and hit the ground. He heard Nathan curse.

"Why the hell didn't you arm yourself," Nathan asked in a loud, irate voice. "You could have ended up headless."

"No time. They took me off guard," Rory replied weakly.

"You should have fucking made time," Nathan grumbled as he knelt at Rory's side and started stemming the bleeding from his wounds. "You lost a lot of blood."

Rory already knew that. He could feel the pain and weakness now that the adrenaline had dissipated.

Nathan removed what was left of Rory's t-shirt and worked on all of the wounds, stopping the bleeding, but the slashes were deep. Rory needed blood and day sleep.

Nathan had gotten away without a scratch. He was dressed in their fighting attire which included a black shirt and gloves designed by Liam to repel some injuries from the *fallen's* claws. It was a long sleeved, turtle neck of stretchy, lightweight material. Nathan's lower body was encased in jeans, thick boots and a belt that held a wide variety of weapons.

"Are you okay?" Rory questioned his brother.

"Of course I'm all right. I was smart enough to come armed and I didn't fling myself into the direct path of the *fallen's* claws. What the hell were you thinking, Rory?" Nathan's fingers were on Rory's face, stemming the bleeding.

"Protecting Callie," he answered, as though that should explain his bizarre behavior.

"Next time prepare to protect her." Nathan shook his head, still angry. "You're a trained warrior for Christ's sake. You know better."

"Didn't matter. I needed to get them away from her." Rory's voice was growing weaker. He knew the blood loss was getting to him.

"It does matter? Shit! Can't any of you keep your head on straight when you find your mate?" Nathan muttered vehemently.

Rory looked at Nathan's ferocious expression and gave him a weak smile. "No," he said simply.

He couldn't think of anything except Callie.

Rory. Come to me.

The soft, feminine voice drifted through his mind. He jerked as he felt her gentle voice compelling him.

I need you to come to me.

He knew instinctively that it was the mating call. It beckoned him. Seduced him. It was her unconscious mind and it was hypnotic.

"Take me to Callie," Rory commanded his brother, knowing he was too weak to transport. He needed Nathan's help.

Nathan rolled his eyes, exasperated. "You need blood. Now."

"She's calling. I have to go to her." Rory's voice was desperate.

Nathan looked like he was going to argue, but he touched his brother's arm and transported him to Callie.

Rory appeared beside the bed, Nathan holding him up. Rory's legs wouldn't hold him. He sank to sit on the side of the bed with Nathan supporting him.

Callie woke, her voice heavy with sleep, "Rory?"

Nathan bathed the room with light, turning on the bedside lamp. Then he used his magic to clean the excess blood from Rory and clothed him in clean jeans. He left him shirtless because of his un-healed injuries. Callie sat up and gasped as she saw Rory.

"Oh my God, what happened?" Callie eyed his torso and gently touched her fingers to his face.

Rory knew he was torn up and probably a pretty ugly sight. He would have waited…but Callie had called…and the urge to go to her was irresistible.

"He had a little run in with a few of the *fallen*. If you think he looks bad…the *fallen* lost." Nathan answered casually. "He needs blood."

He pulled a knife from his belt and slit his own wrist without hesitation. He held it out to Rory.

Rory took it gratefully, knowing he was weak. He took as much from Nathan as he could without weakening him and stopped the cut from bleeding with a swipe of his finger.

Rory felt the roar of Nathan's powerful blood flow through his veins. He wasn't at full strength, but it made him significant-ly stronger. The large gashes hurt less and he could move without much effort.

He turned to Callie and informed her softly, "You called me. Do you remember?"

She paused for a moment and then shook her head.

He put his hand to her cheek, looking into her eyes. "Remember, Callie." It was a command, a subtle jolt to her subconscious.

She nodded slowly before answering, "I remember. I could sense that you needed me. I needed to see you. I did call to you." She frowned as she looked over his injuries. "Do you need more blood? Can you take it from me?"

Before he could open his mouth Nathan answered, "He could use it." Nathan and Callie exchanged a look, a silent communication. Nathan looked satisfied that Callie would take care of his brother. "I have to go do damage control and clean up duty. I'm pretty sure a few people noticed the fight. They need to forget it."

"My injuries are closing from your blood. I'll finish healing during day sleep," Rory told Nathan.

Nathan's eyes evaluated the gashes. He nodded his agreement. "You will heal. Next time try arming yourself before you take on three *fallen* at a time, brother." He gave Rory a mocking expression before he disappeared.

Nathan was gone before Rory could even thank him. Not that Nathan would acknowledge it. "He always has to have the last word," he grumbled to himself as he turned back to Callie.

"Lay down, Rory. Can you take off your jeans?" Callie started fussing, stroking his hair, her expression concerned.

He raised his eyebrows and gave her a mischievous smile. "If I say that I can't, will you do it for me?"

Callie gave him a scolding expression. "This is no time for jokes, Rory. You were badly hurt."

She was unbuttoning his jeans and pulling down his zipper before Rory had the chance to remove them. He was perfectly able to do it now, but her fingers were brushing against his cock and he rather liked the feeling. His mating instincts flared. His cock was hard and ready and Callie was struggling to move the zipper over his enlarged member.

He lay back on the bed, resting his hands behind his head and let her fuss over him.

His injuries hurt…but he had suffered much worse injuries with his work in The Coalition. This was nothing more than a temporary annoyance.

His mating instincts were another issue. As he watched Callie get his zipper down and start to gently pull his jeans off, his body was on fire.

Mine. Need to take her. Fuck her senseless.

Rory watched her eyes grow large as she shucked off his jeans. He wore no underwear and his cock was standing fully erect. She licked her lips and he almost groaned. He could feel her desire and he knew she was trying not to look at his cock, her concern for him coming before her desire. But it was there.

She shimmied back up his body, examining his injuries as she went.

Need to have her.

When she reached the head of the bed she kissed him softly and held her arm over his lips, telling him anxiously, "Here, Rory. Take my blood. You need it."

Rory started to smile at her earnest expression, and at her trembling wrist dangling in front of his face.

He pulled her body against his and rolled, pinning her beneath him, telling her in a low, wicked voice, "No sweetheart, that isn't exactly what I had in mind."

CHAPTER 6

R ory had moved so fast that he was on Callie before she could blink, the movement happening in a blur. His body felt so good on top of her, strong, warm, and seductive.

"No, Rory. You're hurt. You can't do this." She squirmed under him, trying to get away. She wanted him, but not when he could aggravate his wounds.

His mouth took hers, hard and demanding. His hands held her head, holding it still to accept his possessive claim. His tongue demanded entry and she gave it, helpless to fight him. She accepted the wet, erotic intrusion of his tongue, her body on fire. One touch, one kiss…and she was lost to him.

"It's not my injuries hurting, love. It's my need to fuck you," he told her in a low, husky voice as he pulled his mouth from hers and put it near her ear. "I have to have you."

He laved her ear and the side of her neck, his mouth moving over the large vein. She felt a sharp pain and then her body ignited.

She was flooded with erotic, sensual heat, her hips rocking up against him as he drew from her neck. Her desire escalated and her need for him pounded through her body. She held his head, ran her hands through his wavy, silky hair.

She groaned. "Fuck me, Rory. I need you."

He reached down between their bodies, stroking between her thighs. He finished suckling and stopped her blood flow with his finger, while two fingers from his other hand slid into her warm, wet core. She was slick and sensitive, her body jerking as his finger slid over her clit.

"You're so hot and wet. I need to be inside of you." His voice was tortured and raspy. He pinned her arms over her head easily, taking her wrists in one hand. His hot breath panted in her ear, "Tell me you want me. Beg me to fuck you."

His primal instincts had taken over…and so had hers. She wanted to sob with need. She wanted to submit to him as much as he wanted to conquer her. "Please, Rory. I need you. Take me."

He took his massive cock in hand, teasing her drenched flesh with the head. He slid it along her clit, wetting himself with her abundant juices.

She thrashed her head, needing him to fill her. "Please, Rory. I feel so empty."

"Mine," he breathed in her ear with a growl.

"Yes. Yours. Always yours." Her mind was in turmoil, focused only on her emptiness and the need for him to possess her.

He slid his cock into her in one smooth glide, breaching her completely in one hard thrust.

It burned. He stretched her, opened her. She had never been filled like this before, but she rejoiced at the feeling of their joining. Her walls squeezed him and she heard him make a strangled sound.

"So tight. So wet. So mine. Put your legs around my waist," he choked out as his mouth moved to claim hers.

She wrapped her legs around him, locking them around his hips. He started to move as his tongue thrust into her mouth.

The silky friction drove her wild. He wasn't slow or gentle. He mastered her, taking her hard, pumping into her with deep, fast strokes. His tongue fucked her mouth as his cock invaded her core.

His hands held her wrists firmly. She tried to pull them away so that she could touch him, but he had her captive. Her hips rose to meet him, colliding with his groin with ferocious intensity.

Skin slapped skin and she could hear the wet meeting.

Faster…harder…deeper.

He pulled his mouth from hers, his breathing shallow and rapid.

She could feel her climax approaching, her body trembling and her muscles contracting. "Rory!" She screamed his name, her body beginning to spasm.

"Yes, Callie, come. Come for me." His chest was heaving as he continued to drive his cock home, his voice demanding.

She ruptured as the orgasm took control, seizing her body. Her muscles squeezed his cock and he threw his head back. "Mine." He let out a tortured groan.

Rory buried himself deep inside her, releasing himself in a hot stream as Callie milked him with her contractions.

He fell on top her, his body sweaty and hot. He released her wrists and rolled immediately off her.

Callie missed his heat. She was breathless and spent as she lay beside him. He took her hand in his, pulling it to his mouth to kiss her palm.

They didn't speak as they tried to recover.

Rory raised his head and looked at her, raking his eyes over her body. "Did I hurt you?" He sounded anxious.

She smiled weakly as she met his nervous gaze. "I'll be sore in muscles that I haven't used for a while."

He frowned and cursed. "I shouldn't have taken you. We haven't exchanged blood. You aren't strong enough to deal with a vampire's sexual urges. I tried to hold back once I thought about it, but I was too far gone. I tried not to hurt you." His voice was remorseful, almost agonized.

"Rory, you didn't hurt me. For God's sake, I've never orgasmed like that. I wanted you so much." She stroked his cheek lightly, avoiding any of his injuries. "I'm worried about you."

He smiled. His bright, wonderful smile that made her heart accelerate and skip a beat. This man was so extraordinary, and he was hers.

She felt the tears leak from her eyes as she watched his smiling, but still concerned, face. He had gashes from his waist up that would have anyone screaming in pain, yet his only concern was for her.

He reached up gently and wiped away the tears, but they continued to fall.

"Callie? Baby, what's the matter. Please don't cry. I did hurt you. I'm so sorry." His entire face expressed sorrow and guilt.

"No, Rory. It isn't that." She hiccupped as she tried to find words to explain.

"I love you, Rory. I probably have almost since the day we met at the wedding. You've been someone special since that day." It wasn't what she had meant to say, but it had come from her heart.

He buried his face in the side of her neck, his body trembling. "I love you too, Callie. My mind and heart adored you even though my body couldn't respond. I am in awe that you are actually my mate." His voice was completely sincere.

He loved her. The tears flowed harder. This wonderful, sensational man really loved her. "All my life, all I've ever wanted was someone who wanted me."

He growled as he pulled her against him. "I want you, Callie. You're my mate, and I want *you*. I always have. You're everything to me now. I'll never stop needing you, or loving you. You fill the emptiness inside of me. I feel like someone special because you love me."

He was all she really needed. All of the lonely, sad days seemed to slip into the past, unable to hurt her anymore. The love of one good man…or one good vampire…was better than the adoration of many. Maybe she had intentionally closed herself off, looking for excuses, waiting for this man.

"Oh, Rory. I don't understand how you could not know how special you are." She stroked his hair as she wiped her tears. Her crying days were over.

He pulled back and looked at her. "I'm a twin. The twin of a very powerful healer. I love Liam. I would die for him. But sometimes I've felt like I walk in his shadow. I've never had a talent of my own that made me stand out. He was always special. I was just… his twin."

Her heart ached and she suddenly understood that Liam had gotten a lot of attention because he was a powerful healer and Rory was left in the background. Kind, sweet Rory, who brought sunshine to everyone's day with his smile. The man who liked to make other people happy just because it pleased him. Maybe to him that was nothing special, but Callie knew it was, she knew he was an uncommon man.

She put her arms around his neck and kissed him tenderly. When she finished she looked him in the eye and told him solemnly, "You have your own talents and your own personality, Rory. You have traits that Liam doesn't. You're twins…but very different. You're separate, each having your own strengths. You are very special. I could never have fallen in love with Liam."

He tightened his grip, pulling her tighter against him as he answered in a possessive tone, "It's a good thing you didn't or I would have had to commit fratricide. And I actually would rather keep Liam around."

She laughed. She couldn't help it. Rory made her happier than she had ever been in her life. He took away the pain of her past and made her realize that she hadn't really been rejected. She just hadn't let herself live a life free of guilt, self-blame and depression. She had closed herself off from the world because she *felt* rejected.

"It wasn't you, Callie. It was your parents. I don't know why they left you, but it was their problem, not yours." Rory spoke to her as though he had heard her thoughts. Maybe he had.

"I know. Although my life was unstable, it was better than living with drug addicts or worse. I can see that. It could have been worse." She answered sincerely. She was starting to believe in fate. Some things happened for a reason.

"It could have been a hell of a lot better, too. I'll make it up to you, Callie. I'll give you everything you need and more. You are mating with a very rich vampire thanks to Nathan and his hobby of building all of our investments." He shot her a wicked grin. "I'm loaded. And I'm a vampire. I can buy or make anything that you want."

She burst into laughter. He might have insecurities at times, but he still had a touch of the Hale arrogance. "You forgot handsome and very well endowed."

He puffed his chest out. "That too. I have it on very good authority that I'm the best looking of the Hale brothers."

She couldn't argue with that. "Yes, you are, Rory. You definitely are," she told him with laughter still in her voice.

His face changed, becoming serious and intense. He lifted his hand, making a fist and closed his eyes. When he opened them he asked in a hopeful voice, "Does that mean you'll have me, Callie? Will you mate with me? Will you marry me?"

Her eyes filled with tears again. Damn it. Rory could make her laugh and cry in the same breath. She guessed her crying days weren't quite over…but at least they were tears of joy. "I wouldn't have anyone else."

He opened his fist and in his hand was a beautiful ring. He moved back to slide it onto her finger. It fit perfectly. She knew he had made it for her, visualizing in his mind what he wanted and what she might like. It was gorgeous, everything she would have wanted in a ring given with love. Two tiny hearts entwined, decorated with perfect diamonds. One large stone in the middle bringing the hearts together and other smaller ones around and in the middle of the hearts. It was enchanting.

"It's beautiful," she breathed out softly.

"Never as beautiful as the woman wearing it." He quipped back, smiling broadly.

"If you keep saying those things I'm going to have to make you a banana cream pie." She told him, smiling up at him, her eyes still glistening with tears.

His smile turned seductive and he breathed into her ear, "I could think of something better than a banana cream pie. Would you like to swap a little blood?"

She shivered as his warm words caressed her ear. She could think of all kinds of things she would like to do for this man. "Absolutely not, Rory. You need to heal."

He licked her ear and traveled slowly to her neck. Damn it. She had to toughen her resolve. "Rory, we are not doing this right now."

"I feel fine, Callie." His voice was like velvet, sliding over her body and making her shiver.

Yeah…he felt fabulous. She could feel his warm, hard member pressing against her thigh.

She protested.

He seduced.

He won her over to his way of thinking, making her forget all about the banana cream pie.

CHAPTER 7

One Week Later...

Rory woke from his day sleep, reaching for his mate. He sat up, recognition dawning that this was his mating night. He had taken Callie to the vamp headquarters before returning home and collapsing into his day sleep.

The shudders opened, letting in the smells and sounds of the night.

His and Callie's time had finally come. They would be joined eternally after tonight.

The last week had been the happiest of his life. He could only imagine what life would be like, spending eternity with Callie. His mate had taken a leave of absence from her job, telling him she would eventually go back part-time. She couldn't imagine not being a chef. They had traveled the world and he had watched her excitement as he showed her places like the Taj Mahal in India and the Pyramids of Egypt. She had shown such childlike delight that he had enjoyed sharing her emotions. It was almost like seeing those things for the first time himself. No...it was even better. He was sharing them with his mate.

His brothers teased him without mercy. Ethan was the worst, paying Rory back twofold for Rory's needling when he was mating with Brianna. Rory hated anyone touching his mate right now and his brothers knew it. They hugged her, bussed her on the cheek, put an arm around her every chance they could. They smirked when Rory frowned or his face became volatile. Rory had no doubt that they adored Callie as much as they did Brianna, but they also loved to torment him. *The bastards!*

Rory rolled out of bed, wanting to reach for Callie, but knowing he should not. Both his friend Adare and Ethan had warned him not to mind-speak. It made his desire to possess her even greater.

As Rory looked down at his rock hard cock he wondered how his desire could be greater. He could have her several times a day and still need her constantly.

They had exchanged blood at least once a day and Callie was strong. Strong enough to get through a rough mating ceremony.

Rory chuckled as he made his way to the shower. Callie still complained about her curvy figure. She thought if she was in top physical condition that she should be more slender. To Rory, she was perfection. He told her that every day and she complained about it less and less.

His need to make her his was getting relentless and he was damn glad they were mating tonight. His animal instincts were strong and nearly overwhelming. He knew he couldn't wait much longer.

As the hot water of the shower beat over his chest he palmed his cock. Would that make it worse or better? With a groan he pictured his mate, being disrobed for his pleasure, freeing his cock. He wanted to satisfy her every need until she could think of nothing except him.

No longer thinking of the benefits or problems of getting himself off, he stroked his shaft harder. He leaned his head back and closed his eyes, resting himself against the tile of the shower as his hand pumped furiously.

Rory, are you okay? Callie's voice came to him hesitantly. She was reaching out to him because she was feeling his need.

Shit! He shouldn't be doing this, but he was helpless to stop. "I'm…trying…to…calm myself. I'm in the shower." He knew he was groaning his answer, his hand still stroking his cock furiously.

You're masturbating. I can feel you. Relieve yourself, Rory, before you drive me mad. I can't because I'm surrounded by women.

"I'm sorry, love," he groaned, unable to stop jerking his own cock. Her soft voice escalated his need and he needed to come.

Don't be sorry, Rory. Imagine my lips around you. I love sucking your cock, licking it up and down. You're so big, so hard.

Oh, Christ! The visualization almost killed him. He pictured her on her knees, wrapping her lips around him, sucking his member like her favorite lollipop.

You taste so good, Rory. Orgasm for me. Release into my mouth. I'm dying to taste you.

Her words sent him over the edge. Between her words, his imagination and the furious strokes to his cock…he exploded. He came with a loud groan as he came with an intensity so strong that his stream hit the tiled wall of the shower.

He leaned back against the wall, his breathing rough.

Okay now, my love?

Her voice came to him and his heart ached. "I love you, Callie." His voice was raw and coarse.

I love you too. Soon, Rory. I'm almost ready.

"I'm beyond ready." He answered dryly as he stepped from the shower and dried himself off.

He heard a trail of light laughter as their communication faded.

It better be damned soon! He tossed the towel into the hamper near the shower and clothed himself. Then he transported himself to the vampire headquarters.

Callie met Rory's fierce eyes as she stood before him naked. Her attendants had departed. Rory's brothers and Brianna had left. The ceremony was starting.

He had ordered her to him and she had gone willing. She had consented. He would be hers.

His eyes never left hers as his low, rugged voice began reciting the mating vows in his native language. Even though she didn't understand, the words flowed over her and she felt the force, the power in the vows.

It was as though the entire room was pulsating, powerful magic surrounding them. Callie shivered even though the room was not cold.

Rory's voice trailed off and he wrapped his arms around her. One around her back and the other along her butt cheek…meeting their identical marks.

She knew it would hurt. She was prepared for the burning sensation of the joined marks. Both Brianna and Kristin had warned her. What she wasn't ready for was the erotic heat. She threw her head back as she felt their souls unfurl, Rory's breaking free of her protection. As their souls separated and reconnected her entire body was set aflame. She felt Rory's recreated soul pass from her and slip into his body through their touching mating marks.

He jerked as his soul entered his body. Hers settled back into place. She looked up and saw his haunted, glowing eyes as his soul fought for purchase in his body. It was unsettled and it would be that way until he joined with his mate.

"Mine!" His voice was ragged. His glowing eyes revealed the hunger of a predator.

Callie quivered as he took her mouth, his arms like steel around her body. She could feel his need to possess, to take her. He brought his hand roughly behind her head, controlling the embrace, demanding her submission. He grunted as he pulled his mouth from hers.

"Free my cock." His demanding voice set her on fire. Their needs were combined; there was no way of knowing which were hers and which were his. She only knew that she needed him. She reached down and felt for the strings that would liberate his member. Her fingers brushed over his swollen cock, hard and demanding to be free from its confinement.

As she tossed away the cloth he scooped her up and brought her to the silken bed, decorated in a black and white leopard pattern.

Rory pushed a button on the headboard and she saw something lowering from the high ceiling. He set her on her feet beside the bed and brought her arms up above her head. She felt the restraints tighten around her wrists and groaned. He had her on her feet and secured with restraints from above.

"Mine." His scarlet eyes blazed, surveying her in her vulnerable position.

Callie yanked on the restraints. They were metal poles except for the wrist fastenings and they had very little give. They were tight and she was his prisoner. Her already moist pussy flooded.

His hands roamed her body possessively. She gasped as his hands pinched at her erect nipples, the sensation rocketing straight between her thighs.

"Rory…I need you to fuck me." Her body burned to feel his cock slamming into her.

He ignored her. His mouth joined his fingers in tormenting her breasts, his tongue laving and nipping. His hand found its way between her legs, gliding into her moist center where she was already slick and wet.

"Wet. Hot. Have to taste you." Rory grunted as he moved down her body. "Spread your legs. Now."

She opened her legs, but he pulled them further apart still. He attacked her mound with his mouth, teeth and lips, sending her into a spiral of need and desire. She pulled against the restraints, wanting to pull his head into her aching pussy. "Rory, please, make me come." Her every thought was focused on relieving this agony from her fiery body.

His masterful tongue slipped along her lower lips. His thumbs separated her and plundered her sensitive clit, making her body quake. She had to climax. She couldn't stand it anymore. With a tortured moan she tried to grind against his mouth, needing more so she could climax.

His hand came down on her ass with a smack. It was firm and sent a jolt to her core. He slapped the other cheek and she whimpered, completely out of control. Over the edge, his domination was driving her insane, feeding her erotic need.

He lifted one of her legs to the bed, opening her completely. He grabbed her ass and buried his face between her legs, eating her like a man famished. His tongue flicked roughly over her clit. Faster. Then faster still. And she could feel her climax building.

Unconsciously, she shoved her hips toward his devouring mouth. He smacked her ass again several times, sending her into a powerful orgasm. She threw her head back and screamed his name, unable to control herself while she was in the grip of his powerful possession. She rode the waves of her orgasm while Rory stretched it out with his merciless tongue.

She wasn't yet recovered before she felt the restraint poles lowering. Rory rose and pushed her to her knees. She went willingly, her legs weak.

"Suck me." His voice was harsh and feral.

She knew he was completely consumed by the mating instincts and so was she. She was starving for the taste of his cock. Although she had just climaxed, her need…or was it his?…pounded her.

Her hands still confined above her head, she opened her mouth and caught his rock hard cock in her mouth, swirling her tongue around the head.

Rory grabbed her head from both sides, impaling her mouth with his rod. He demanded, "Hard. Fast." His hands gripped her head and he fucked her mouth furiously. Her eyes watered as she tried to swallow his massive cock. She could hear his tortured moans as he slipped in and out of her mouth. She wanted to make him come. His need? Her need? She didn't care. She needed to make him orgasm.

His hips jerked hard as she tightened her lips and flattened her tongue snug against his cock. He held her face tightly against him as he found his release, shooting hot fluid down her throat. She swallowed him eagerly, loving the warm release on her tongue.

He released her hands and pulled her up, only to drop her in the middle of the bed, coming down on top of her. His body covered hers. "Mine, Callie. Mine. Need to fuck you."

Oh, God, yes. Her channel was clenching at the thought of his huge cock filling her. She needed him. "Yes, Rory. Fuck me. Please," she pleaded.

He pinned her with his body, holding her hands to the side of her face. "Don't move your hands," he barked. She looked at his ravaged face, his eyes still glinting. He was so fierce. And she wanted his savage need quenched and her feral desire satisfied. Her wanting body was begging for his tempestuous mating.

He spread her legs wide and claimed her channel in one hard stroke. She clenched the silk at the side of her head, needing to touch him, but also needing to obey his commands. She gripped it hard as Rory started to fuck her. He pushed deep and the two of them groaned together as he started a demanding pace.

"Need you to be mine." His face and body were pouring sweat as the statement was torn from his throat.

Callie lifted her hips to meet his frenzied thrusts. Everything about their joining was elemental and primal, nothing existed except their heated bodies straining for release. She rolled her head, gripping the silk hard with her hands. Oh, God. Her body was in flames, seared with erotic flames.

Rory leaned down and licked her neck. She knew what was coming and she knew it would throw her over the edge. His teeth sank into her with almost no pain, the erotic pull of his mouth working in tandem with his cock.

Fangs erupted from her gums and she jerked. Her thirst for him beat at her and she sank her fangs into his shoulder. Her body was flooded with scorching heat. They sucked at each other, drowning in erotic sensations.

He pulled his fangs from her neck and swiped his finger over it. She reluctantly let go of his shoulder and he flicked a finger carelessly over the punctures.

As their blood mingled, Callie was submerged in her desire.

Rory gripped her ass firmly and stroked his cock into her hard, pulling her to meet his pummeling thrusts. He felt so…incredible. He pulled her legs to his shoulders, getting deeper access.

"Yes, Rory, Yes. Fuck me hard." She was caught up in her urgency to climax. She could feel it building as he hammered without slowing. Her stomach clenched as her orgasm overwhelmed her. Her channel squeezed, as her body rocked under his.

"Rory, Rory, Rory," she chanted his name in a scream as her hips bucked and her body shook.

She could feel Rory tense as he pulled her ass hard against his groin. He let out something in between a growl and a moan as he buried himself deep inside of her, releasing himself into her depths.

They were both breathless, both unable to move. Rory collapsed and rolled, pulling her on top of him as his body vibrated and he struggled hard to get his breathing under control.

She could hear his heart racing as she rested her head on his chest, her body quivering.

"It's done." Rory's chest was still rising and falling fast, but his voice was back to normal. She looked into his dark eyes, no longer laced with red.

"Are you all right, Callie?"

"I'm more than all right. I'm yours." She gave him a tremulous smile. "That was…intense. How do you feel?"

He gave her a broad smile. "Content. Incredibly happy…and like I could sleep for a week."

They were both spent. Rory pulled a light sheet over them and she slid to his side, curling into his body.

She tried to keep her eyes open, but her eyelids drifted shut. She could feel the tug of sleep beckoning her.

"That was incredible. I think I owe you a gourmet dinner with pie," Callie mumbled softly as she floated into the darkness.

His light laughter was the last thing she heard before letting the darkness take her under.

Rory followed shortly after.

EPILOGUE

Another day. Another wedding. But this time it was different for Callie. She was having the fairy tale wedding and she was the beautiful bride. She had chosen a waist-hugging, white silk gown with pale blue accents. There were some similarities to Bri's wedding, though. The bride was radiant, and her groom was impossibly handsome.

Callie smiled broadly at her husband, still in awe of the fact that Rory was hers. It had all started with a wedding…Brianna's wedding. Callie felt like she had gone full circle.

Every day was an adventure with Rory. He was the most thoughtful man she had ever known. There was rarely a day that he didn't do something so amazingly sweet that it brought tears of joy to her eyes.

She had gone back to work part-time, although she really didn't need to. When Rory had said he was loaded…he wasn't joking. But she enjoyed working and it filled the evenings when Rory was doing his work with The Coalition.

She looked around the bride and groom's table where she sat beside Rory. Liam, Nathan, Ethan and Bri. Kristin and Adare were also there. They had all been part of the wedding party and they were like the family she had never had.

She eyed Liam and Nathan, wishing they could find their mates. She had come to care about all of Rory's brothers and wanted their happiness.

Hmmm…maybe Nathan. He was oldest. She loved Nathan like a brother but he would be a hard man to crack. He was an elder. He would be volatile. It would take a special woman.

It would take a saint, love. She heard Rory's wry comment in her mind.

Rory. Would she ever get used to the fact that they could communicate without speaking?

He doesn't need a saint. He needs a woman who will stand up to him. Shake him up a bit. She answered with certainty. Nathan Hale needed a strong woman.

"He wouldn't like it," Rory mused aloud.

"But it would be good for him. He'd secretly love it," she insisted.

Rory looked at her doubtfully and she smiled. "I guess we'll just have to wait and see what's fated for him."

"He's certain he won't mate," Rory warned her.

"I think he will. Just call it women's intuition, but I do think Nathan will have a mate." She told him with confidence.

"That would be something I wouldn't want to miss," Rory answered with laughter in his voice.

"Sometimes…it just takes the right woman." Callie sipped her champagne thoughtfully.

"Yes it does, love. I know I was a lucky bastard." Rory turned her face to his and kissed her gently.

Her heart melted as she looked into the eyes of her destiny.

He reached out and filled his champagne flute and then refilled hers.

They had already had an official toast, but this was theirs alone.

He raised his glass and she raised hers to touch his.

With the clink of glasses, a love that would last forever was sealed.

THE END

OF BOOK TWO: RORY'S MATE

NATHAN'S MATE

BOOK THREE

THE VAMPIRE COALITION

CHAPTER 1

He came to her in the dark as he always did. She couldn't see his face, but he was tall and dark, his shadowy presence casting off no illumination. She waited for him impatiently, her body burning for his possession and her mind consumed by need.

He slipped into her bed completely nude. Her hands ran over his massive, muscular chest, needing to feel his body and know that he was really here in her bed. She gasped as his strong arms pulled her into his body, leaving no space between them. It was exactly what she wanted. Her body was bare and they touched, skin to skin, nothing between them.

He took her mouth as though he owned it. She welcomed him like a flower seeking the sunlight. His masterful touch set her body and soul aflame, his seeking hands over her naked body eliciting a small moan that was muffled by his mouth. Her hands roamed, running over his broad, sinewy shoulders and back as she continued to lose herself in his embrace.

His powerful, muscular leg parted her thighs and she could feel her dewy, wet core slam hard against his sturdy limb. Grinding her mound against the steely surface, she hungered for release.

She didn't know if the need was hers, his or a combination of the two… but it didn't matter. They were both caught in a web of desire that they couldn't escape. She started rotating her hips against his leg, breaking away from his mouth with a whimper to pant against his shoulder.

"Please. I need you," she whispered achingly, needing him to take her.

He stroked and teased her breasts, lightly pinching her pebble hard nipples with expert fingers. His tongue traced her earlobe and the side of her neck, finding every sensitive area of her skin.

She reached between them, trying desperately to grasp his cock and place it near her empty channel. He snatched her seeking hands by the wrists, pinning them above her head. He held them tightly with one large hand while the other snaked between her legs. She wanted to protest. She needed to keep moving against his leg like a bitch in heat until she came, but he pulled it back, denying her satisfaction.

His hand traced her wet folds lightly as she arched her back, begging silently for more significant contact, pleading for his touch in the place that would send her over the edge.

"So hot. So wet. So needy. Call for me and I'll make you come until you're begging for mercy," his gruff, low baritone murmured in her ear. "Let me sate you."

She groaned, the sound of his erotic voice making her pussy flood with even more heat. Her head turned from side to side, frustration threatening to take her sanity.

She yanked at her hands to free herself even as her hips rose to his teasing touch between her thighs. He held her snuggly by her wrists as his other hand circled her clit, teasing her, driving her mad.

She jerked as his finger toyed with the protective hood of her bud, lifting it, brushing lightly over the exposed nub.

Yes. Yes. Right there. More. Please, more.

His scorching mouth descended on her right nipple and she shuddered from the contact.

She had to climax before she went insane.

Before she could orgasm, the touch of her lover faded. Her mind screamed in protest even as he faded away and her mind became alert and...she woke up.

Sasha Taylor woke slowly, coming out of her foggy, erotic dream in a frustrated stupor.

Shit! She sat up, her body drenched with sweat and her heart pounding so hard she could hear it drumming in her ears. These damn horny dreams were going to kill her. This was the second one she had experienced in the last four days. They were coming more often, more vivid, keeping her in an almost constant state of arousal.

Her whole body was soaked, including her dripping mound. She flopped back against the pillow and considered trying to satisfy herself, but she already knew it was a quick fix that wouldn't last. All it would take was one thought of her dream lover and she would be right back in the same state of frustrated lust.

Unfortunately, she couldn't stop thinking about him. He seemed to be with her constantly, both irritating and stimulating her.

Sasha knew instinctively that it was her vampire mate. She had known she was the mate of a vampire since the mark had appeared on her hip around her eighteenth birthday, which had been ten years ago.

Shocked, appalled, and disgusted, she had never mentioned it to anyone.

A mage with a vampire? It was a taboo. The mage hated the vampires and to mate with one would get her nothing but ostracized from her fellow mages forever. Her parents were both mage as was her sister, Regan. Vampires were blood drinkers, barbarians that took their mates by force. None of her family or mage friends would accept her vampire mate. Hell...she didn't want a vampire mate. Who wanted to be mated with a domineering, overbearing savage?

Sasha rolled out of bed and grabbed some clean clothes as she headed toward the shower. She would shake this off and get to work. She and her sister Regan were business partners in their jewelry business. Sasha did the designs and Regan did most of the intricate work of putting everything together. Their pieces were sought after and it kept them both very busy and brought in a good income.

Call for me and I will make you come until you beg for mercy.

Sasha shivered as she pulled her soaked nightshirt over her head in the bathroom. She could still hear his "pure sex" baritone whispering to her.

If the man in her wet dreams was her mate...he had a body made for sin and a voice that could almost arouse a woman to climax with just his words.

Disgusted with herself, Sasha turned on the water, making it as cold as it could get without causing her hypothermia.

Nathan Hale had woken from his day sleep in a bad mood that had just seemed to continue through the rest of the evening as he roamed the city. His rest had been disturbed by images and dreams that rarely invaded the day sleep of vampires. It made him edgy and uneasy.

His brother Liam was busy with a healing and Nathan had left his other two brothers behind, using the excuse that there wasn't much to do but patrol for the *fallen*. There had been no reported sightings.

He was hunting alone tonight and although he didn't mind roaming for fallen vampires to kill by himself, his brother's "love fest" was getting on his nerves. Ethan and Rory were getting careless, so engrossed with their love and lust for their mates that they missed the little things that could get them killed. He wasn't sure he wanted either of them on the streets right now. Maybe once they got over their rapture honeymoon phase they could finally go back out with him to dust the *fallen*. In the meantime...they were acting just plain stupid.

Nathan shook his head as he cruised one of the lower class areas of Denver, wondering how any vampire could act so witless over a woman. He liked Brianna and Callie well enough, but it was as if finding their mates had lowered Ethan and Rory's IQ by at least forty points. If finding a mate made a vampire into a total idiot, he was damn glad he had never found his own mate.

Chances were that he never would. At over six hundred years old, his time had passed. He hadn't felt sexual desire for over five hundred years and probably wouldn't know what to do anymore if he did. He wasn't sure if the loneliness and yearning ever went away, but he tried to bury it.

Most of it was covered by hatred for the *fallen*. His main mission in his eternal life was to grind every *fallen* into dust that would blow harmlessly away in a strong breeze. They had killed his parents while Nathan had been made to stand by helplessly and wait for news of their demise.

But...no longer. He was an elder now and at the helm of The Vampire Coalition. He spent almost every waking moment burning with hostility and loathing for the creatures that had taken his parents away from him and his brothers. He wanted vengeance, no matter how long it took or how many fallen that he had slay to feel a sense of peace again.

Nathan slipped around the corner of an alley, entering the street. Two gang members, that appeared to be looking for trouble, eyed him with sleazy smiles. He scowled, daring them to approach, almost looking for a fight. He had already fed, but he'd enjoy thrashing the two punks just trolling for innocent victims to rob...or worse. Unfortunately, they averted their eyes and walked on. He was just cursing his bad luck that they had avoided him when he felt it.

Fallen.

They were close, and the evil sense of their presence sent an electric wave down Nathan's spine. He started moving quicker than the human eye could see, tracing the feeling of malice and mayhem. What were the bastards up to now?

He halted abruptly as he took in the scene before him. He had found the *fallen*...and they weren't alone. His temper flared and his eyes were nearly black with rage as he saw that they were tearing at a young woman who struggled between them. The fuckers had shredded her shoulders from holding her with their razor sharp claws. She had slashes all over her body, leaking blood that left a ruby puddle at her feet, but the woman still was kicking and fighting, yelling obscenities that Nathan had rarely heard come out of the mouth of a female.

Nathan yanked a short blade from his belt, unwilling to use anything longer that might hit the woman between the two monsters. The woman saw him appear behind the *fallen* who was torturing her, but he held a hand up in a silent signal. She quieted as he drove the knife into her tormenter's heart. The *fallen* crumpled to the ground, squirming like a worm on a fisherman's hook.

The creature who was holding the woman let go of her body, and she too crumpled to the ground.

Nathan's eyes flashed with enmity as he met the red-eyed stare of the *fallen*. He knew he had to dispatch the bastard quickly and get help for the female...if there was still even a slim chance that she could be saved.

He dodged an aggressive attack of slashing claws as the two of them did the death dance. It was one he planned on winning. Fury and adrenaline fueled his attack on the hairless, sunken-featured monster, waiting for an opening.

Nathan stepped close and brought his arm under the *fallen's* wrists, deflecting his claws as he simultaneously drove the knife into the freak's chest, rupturing his heart. The *fallen* hit the ground. Nathan withdrew his knife as he fell. He'd be damned if he'd lose a perfectly good knife. He cleaned it with his magic as he re-sheathed the blade at his waist.

Both of the *fallen* disappeared, leaving only a pile of dust where they had once stood, tormenting a defenseless woman to death.

Crouching next to the unknown woman, he assessed her injuries.

"Fuck!" he uttered sharply as he surveyed the slashes and severe loss of blood. She was breathing shallow and her heart was still beating in a fast, thready rhythm.

Nathan scooped up her body in his arms.

Mage!

He could feel the magic zinging through her body. If she was mage, she was a little stronger than the average human, but she wasn't immortal. He scowled, knowing she couldn't go to a human hospital. The mage had their own healers and their physiology was a little different than a human's.

Liam. I need you.

Nathan sent the urgent call out for his healer brother before gathering the unconscious female close to him and dissolved into the night.

CHAPTER 2

Nathan transported himself to the master bedroom of his home and laid the injured woman on his bed. He knew without a shred of doubt that this was the female who had haunted his dreams. Her long, blonde hair fell in waves that reached nearly to her waist. Her eyes were closed, but he already knew that they were an unusual violet color that wasn't produced by artificial lenses.

Had he dreamt of her because she was in danger? The dreams had been anything but a warning. They had contained acts that were long forgotten and something that was only possible for him to experience in dreams. This woman had been his lover.

He stripped the clothes from her body with his magic and tried to stop as much of the bleeding as he could. He wasn't a damned healer and he couldn't heal the deep gashes in her shoulders and arms. Grimacing as he checked the rest of her body, he also noticed that she had deep slashes on her hips where the claws of the *fallen* had landed when they were assaulting her.

Where in holy hell is Liam?

He knelt next to her naked body, wishing that he knew more about the mage. Mage and vampires didn't mix, so he knew only the bare minimum of information about the magical species.

They were not immortal. They lived a little longer than humans, but their existence was finite. Born with magic, they could cast spells and bend magic to do their bidding. Mage were stronger than humans, but not as strong as an immortal.

Oh hell...that was about all he knew. He had never even come in contact with a mage since they seemed to have an aversion to vampires.

Nathan jerked backwards, landing on his ass in shock as his fingers moved over her left hip to slow the bleeding on a deep slash in her skin.

My mark!

"Christ!" he whispered harshly as he levered himself back to his knees and lightly touched the dragon symbol on her hip with trembling fingers. He brushed it gently, tracing the lines of the small marking.

Not possible.

He made his mark appear on his right arm to confirm that it really wasn't his marking. Nathan hadn't even looked at his mating mark for so long that he couldn't remember the exact design.

They were identical matches.

The dreams.

The marks.

My mate.

"You don't have to keep staring at it, brother. She's definitely your mate." Nathan jerked his head around to see his brother Liam with an arm propped casually against the doorframe and a smile on his face.

He hid his marking as he asked hotly, "Where in the hell were you? This girl is bleeding to death."

Liam's smile only grew broader as he nudged Nathan aside and assessed her injuries. "She's hardly a girl. And I was busy. I got here as soon as I could." His hand moved quickly over her body, using his healing ability to completely stop her bleeding. "She's mage and she needs a mage healer. There's only so much I can do. She'll end up scarred."

"I don't give a damn about the scars," Nathan answered fiercely. "Just don't let her..." his voice softened as he choked out the last word. "die."

"Back away from my sister or I'll fill you both full of silver bullets."

Nathan and Liam's heads both snapped up to stare at the woman in the doorway. She was blonde, her hair not quite as long as her sister's, and her hands were shaking as she held a handgun trained on the two men.

"I think you have your myths confused. Silver bullets are for lycanthropes and they don't really work on them. That's a more modern myth," Liam told the woman casually as he stood.

"Yeah...well...I could certainly make you miserable." Her voice sounded shaky and unsure.

It would be painful, Nathan thought, but all it would do was really piss him off.

"I'm a vampire healer. I was trying to help your sister. We weren't going to hurt her. We want to help her." Liam told her reasonably.

"It was vampires that attacked her." The woman replied defensively, still waving the gun in their direction with shaking hands.

"Fallen vampires. They're the bad guys. We aren't fallen. We try to contain them. It's my guess that my brother Nathan saved your sister's life." Liam's voice was soothing as he spoke quietly to the obviously nervous woman.

"Oh, thank God! I was afraid I'd have to shoot you." The blonde blew out a pent- up breath and lowered the gun. "I'm a healer...not a killer."

Liam gave her a sympathetic smile. "I've done all I can do. Perhaps you can take over."

"Yes. Of course." Dropping the gun in a chair she rushed to the bedside.

"How in the hell did you get in here?" Nathan demanded. "I have more security than Fort Knox."

"I spelled myself in. I can't transport, but I can gain entry with spells. You aren't mage protected," she answered distractedly as she took Liam's place that he had vacated at the bedside. "Oh, Sasha," she whispered as she looked at the nasty gashes. "Has she been unconscious like this for a while?"

"Since I killed her attackers. Is that bad?" Nathan asked anxiously.

"No. It's our way of conserving energy until we can be healed." She opened a bag she had brought with her and began to apply a paste to her sister's injuries.

"Is that her name? Sasha?" Nathan questioned, breathing her name softly.

"Sasha Taylor. I'm her sister, Regan."

"This is Nathan Hale." Liam waved his hand toward his brother. "And I'm his brother, Liam. I'm a vampire healer. Can I help in any way? I don't know much about the mage, but I'll do whatever I can to help."

"I'm going to do a healing spell. If you can send me any healing energy, it might help." She crinkled her brow in concentration.

Sasha. My mate's name is Sasha.

While Regan chanted her healing spell and Liam closed his eyes to send healing energy, Nathan stared at the vulnerable woman on the bed with awe and confusion. Hundreds of years of waiting...and she was finally here. He had given up hope, and he wasn't sure if he should rejoice or mourn. He didn't want a mate. Did he?

Sasha started thrashing, her long lashes flickering. Nathan went to the opposite side of the bed and crawled over the empty space of the enormous structure to get to his mate. He held her hand and put a comforting hand on her forehead.

She was healing, her injuries closing before his eyes to leave nothing but smooth skin. Nathan looked from her to her sister. Regan's face looked strained and contorted as she continued the healing spell. Liam's head was thrown back in concentration, his eyes closed. Nathan wasn't a healer but he could feel the combined energy swirling through the bedroom. It was all directed toward Sasha, making her thrash and moan as her body healed.

Nathan stared fixedly at his mate, his displeasure at the whole situation evident. She was in pain and he didn't like it. He stroked her cheek and she quieted.

Her eyes fluttered open, confusion and pain mingling in her panicked eyes.

"Don't be afraid. You're being healed. You were injured. Stay still." Nathan tried to reassure her.

Her gaze flew straight to his face and she started, her face frightened and alarmed. "You're *him*. I recognize your voice. The man from my dreams."

Nathan realized he was still stroking her cheek and she was *awake*. He scrambled back on the bed, but he wasn't fast enough.

His face grew feral and his body shook with reaction. The mating instinct had kicked in and it seized his entire being, infusing him with possessiveness and lust. His cock hardened like a diamond and heat rushed through every artery, vein and capillary in his body.

"Mine!"

With the healing completed, his fierce, loud growl brought every eye in the room to him with shock and alarm.

CHAPTER 3

Sasha couldn't do much more than stare at her dream lover who had suddenly come alive in much too graphic detail. Holy hell...the man was enormous and there was no veil or shadow this time to make him less scarier. Nostrils flaring and eyes burning, the man pinned her with his black stare but said nothing more. He seemed to be struggling...with himself. His eyes raked over her body and face hotly.

Sasha scrambled for cover, pulling back the sheet and blankets to cover herself from chin to toes. She flushed as she realized she had been as naked as the day she was born, exposed to every eye in the room. Had they seen her mark of the vampire?

Liam was the only one brave enough to approach Nathan. He walked calmly around the bed and dragged his brother to his feet, yanking hard with both arms around his shoulders. Nathan was two hundred years older than Liam, but Liam had his own elevated degree of power as a healer and Nathan didn't really resist. He was too busy trying to control his animal instincts.

"You okay, Nathan?" Liam slapped him on the back as Nathan stood, stumbling a little as he gained his balance.

Nathan held up his hand. "I'm fine. I'm six hundred years old for Christ's sake. I can control myself."

Liam gave him a doubtful look as he returned to Sasha. He introduced himself and his brother as Regan looked on curiously.

"What's wrong with him? He doesn't look so good," Regan probed quietly, as she continued gaping at Nathan.

"Let's go get something to eat, Regan. The healing was draining. I'll explain everything." Liam nodded his head toward the door, indicating that they should leave Sasha and Nathan alone.

"Are you sure it's safe?" Regan didn't sound so sure that leaving them alone was a good idea.

"They'll be quite safe, Regan. Come along and I'll explain. They have a few...issues to work out." Liam coughed to cover his laugh as he motioned Regan out the door.

Regan moved behind him slowly, shooting her sister one last, perplexed look as she followed Liam.

Sasha watched as the pair disappeared, her mind whirling. She remembered the monsters that attacked her and seeing a brief glimpse of the vampire that Liam had introduced as Nathan before she lost consciousness. She also remembered sending out a calling spell to Regan. She had obviously received it. She was here, and she must have healed her.

"You saved my life," Sasha whispered, knowing that he must have destroyed the creatures attacking her.

Nathan walked around the bed and sat on the floor beside the bed before replying, "I almost didn't make it fast enough." His eyes never left her face, Sasha could see the fear and concern in his expression.

She lifted a hand to his cheek, unable to stop herself from comforting him. "You made it. I would have been dead had you not shown up. What were they?"

"Fallen vampires."

Sasha shuddered. She didn't know that vampires could fall and become such hideous creatures. "And you hunt them?"

"Yes." Nathan answered simply. "They prey on the innocent."

"And you don't?" She couldn't stop herself from asking the question. Weren't all vampires evil? The mage shunned all vampires, never mentioning that there were good and bad among them.

A volatile look crossed his face as he answered roughly. "No. I do not. Vampires may survive on blood but we take from those who aren't so innocent and we don't kill to do it."

She believed him. His insulted look was definitely not false. He looked like she had slapped him. Remorse stabbed at her sharply as she replied, "I'm sorry. I know very little about vampires."

"Probably about as much as I know about the mage." His voice was rough and low. "Do you know that we're mates?"

Sasha flinched. "I knew I was the mate of a vampire because I have the mark. I didn't know who he was. But I have dreams..." Her voice shook. "I never see a face...but I dream. I recognized your voice."

"I dream the same dreams. But I could see you very clearly." Nathan willed his mark to appear and held his forearm out to her. "We are definitely mates. I can feel the mating instinct even now."

Sasha stared at Nathan's mark, a twin to her own. She could feel the mating instinct too, and it wasn't comfortable. She wanted to pull Nathan into the bed and have him at least a million different ways. The only difficult part would be where to start.

You cannot mate with a vampire...no matter how handsome and compelling he may be. You are mage.

"Mage and vampires don't mate," Sasha said, speaking as much to herself as to Nathan, trying to convince herself that she could never have this man who was already turning her inside out.

"Make no mistake, little one...we will mate. The process has begun and it will end with us being mated." His stare was intense and his voice rumbled. "I understand that you don't know all there is to know about vampire mates. I'll explain. But we will be mates."

Sasha felt her temper rising. He may have saved her life, but no man was going to tell her what to do or what was going to happen with her life. She made her own destiny. She opened her mouth to tell him exactly that, but he had started explaining the nature of mates.

Curiosity overruled her anger...and she listened as he explained exactly what being the mate of a vampire really meant.

Sasha smiled as she woke one week later in an array of silken rose petals. She stretched in her bed, inhaling the fragrant smell that surrounded her. As she opened her eyes she ran hand a through more than an inch of soft, red petals, piled high around her. She laughed as she tossed a handful in the air and watched them waft slowly back to the bed.

His courting is bewitching me.

When Nathan decided something...he was immovable. He had decided he was going to court her...and she had been spoiled rotten for the last week. All she had to do is wish or want for something and it appeared.

This was the seventh day she had woken up in a bed of rose petals. Sasha knew from experience that once she exited the bed, the petals would disappear and her bedroom would be filled with several vases of roses, covering every available surface of the room.

Nathan's power was terrifying, but strangely enough, Sasha had never feared him. She got in his face often enough when he pissed her off, but he showed nothing but patience with her. His control was nearly as scary as his power. The vampire might vibrate with power, but the strength contained, just waiting to explode.

She hopped out of the bed, shaking off petals as she went, yawning as she glanced at the window, realizing it was twilight. Although she had never been an early riser, her nights had gotten longer and she slept the day away.

Coffee.

She made her way sleepily toward the kitchen to put on the coffee pot only to find a large, steaming mug of latte waiting for her. Extra milk, extra sugar. Just the way she liked it.

Exasperating man! He probably had not even woken from his day sleep yet and he was able to cater to her wants. Ah…the benefits of having a six hundred year old vampire mate.

Sasha blew on the steaming mug and took a small sip of the much needed caffeine. *Perfect. As usual.* Sighing softly, she carried the mug back to the bedroom. The rose petals were gone and the vases were arranged around the room. How in the hell did he do that? Did he arrange it with magic before he slept or was he so powerful that he could do all this while he slept? She had asked him before and he had just shot her a deliciously wicked look.

She sat on her bed and cradled her coffee, sipping at it leisurely as she wondered what she should do this evening. She could go to the homeless shelter and help out as she had been doing the night she had met with the two *fallen*, but she had promised Nathan that she wouldn't go there without his escort.

It was Saturday night. She and Regan never worked on the weekends. They had been working in her basement workshop all week with Nathan, his brothers, and their mates as frequent visitors. She had even met Adare and Kristin, friends of the brothers. They were all so…likeable. Even Regan, shy and quiet as she was, laughed and joked along with the brothers and their mates, enjoying their company. They all teased each other mercilessly, but Sasha could also see the bond between the brothers, ties of respect and love in addition to just blood.

So different from the mage, Sasha thought. Mages were serious creatures that rarely laughed or showed their emotions to one another. Their main concern was the survival of the species and keeping the purity of their mage heritage.

She shuddered, her coffee nearly spilling as she thought of her parent's reactions to her revelation that she was a vampire mate.

They were disappointed in her and they showed it. She was treated as a dirty outcast by everyone except Regan, who treated her no differently than she always did. Her parents had told Sasha, in no uncertain terms, that she was an aristocratic mage and she would be mated to another of her kind.

Sasha had refused. She may not end up mated to Nathan, but she could not mate with another mage knowing that she was the keeper of Nathan's soul. She couldn't do it. She would end up an old maid before she mated with a mage simply for bloodlines.

You will be mated with me, love.

Nathan's voice floated through her mind like a caress, making her shiver in reaction. All she needed was to hear that sultry voice to make her heart race and her soul fill with yearning. Her body reacted, her panties dampening and her nipples hardening.

"So sure of yourself, vampire?" she whispered as she smiled into her coffee mug.

He was infuriatingly arrogant and smug. He could also be kind, tender, and thoughtful. It was almost an irresistible mix. She longed for him as she had never wanted another man.

I have no doubt, Sasha. You belong to me.

His voice was low and possessive. How it could anger her and arouse her at the same time was a mystery. "I belong to no man, vampire," she answered stubbornly.

She heard his chuckle as he murmured back in her mind. *We shall see, little one.*

Sasha's spine stiffened in indignation. Tall for a woman, she was hardly little. Just because Nathan was a giant of a man didn't make her small. "Don't call me that. I'm not a child."

"I am well aware of that, love. You are well developed in all the right areas." His voice was husky and full of desire.

Her panties flooded as she imagined him exploring all those areas, every place that she wanted him desperately to explore. Her lust for him was undeniable. Although he had done nothing more than kiss her forehead, she longed for him to take her to bed and claim her.

The thought had no more crossed her mind when Nathan appeared in front of her, dressed only in a pair of body hugging jeans and a slight smile. Her breath caught as she took in his muscular, hard body in the flesh. He was gloriously handsome with his dark hair and eyes that were shooting her a look of intense lust.

"Tell me you want it as much as I do, Sasha. I'm not sure how much longer I can fight it," he growled as he held out his hand to her.

CHAPTER 4

Sasha trembled as she set her empty coffee cup on her bedside table. Oh...she wanted it. She had wanted Nathan since he had appeared in her dreams. Now that she knew him in reality, her desire had intensified to an unbearable level. To let him take her was dangerous; to be without him was unendurable.

She met his intense gaze, returning it with a look of longing and vulnerability that she knew he could see in her eyes.

"Come with me, Sasha. I can feel your need and it claws at me." His hand stayed extended, palm up as he took a step closer.

She wasn't the least bit afraid of *him*. She was afraid of her own reactions. He called to a part of her that she never knew existed and on a level that was painful in its intensity.

She reached out and placed her palm in his. Within moments he had scooped her into his arms and teleported them to his bedroom.

As he laid her in the middle of his bed, he murmured roughly, "I need to see you here in my bed. Mine. I've imagined it so many times in my mind."

She was still in her little short pink nightshirt and little else. Her hair was braided and he sat beside her and started unraveling the braid. She sat up while he worked. His ragged breath was hot on her neck and her heart was pounding. "Nathan...I have to tell you something."

He stroked her cheek as his hand loosened her hair, letting it fall in waves over her back. "What is it, Sasha? There is nothing you can't tell me."

"I haven't...I've never...the mage don't have sex before they are mated." She choked out the embarrassing fact before she lost her nerve.

"Sasha?" He tilted her face to his, those burning eyes bright with concern. "Are you trying to tell me that you're a virgin?"

She nodded, unable to answer.

"Mine. Completely mine." His voice was hoarse with emotion. "I'll try my best to be gentle, Sasha, although knowing I am the first and last man to possess you will likely drive me insane."

"Don't be gentle, Nathan. I need you." She reached out boldly and stroked the large bulge through his jeans. She wanted him as he was...hard, possessive, demanding.

He yanked her short nightie over her head, baring her breasts to him. His hands cupped them both, stroking over them, teasing the nipples with his thumbs. His intimate touch on her body made her squirm as his mouth crashed down on hers. His tongue demanded entrance as he licked at her lips and swept into her mouth. She met him tongue to tongue, moaning into his mouth as his fingers continued his assault on her sensitive breasts.

Her hands crept to his shoulders, relishing the burgeoning muscles and sifted into his silky, dark locks of hair. She could barely breathe as his embrace sucked the air from her lungs. He pulled his lips from hers and trailed his hot tongue along her ear. She could hear him panting, trying to gain control. She shivered as he trailed his mouth along her neck and to her breasts. He replaced his hand with his mouth on her nipple as his fingers descended to her barely-there, pink thong.

"Mine." His hand ripped away her panties as he uttered the word harshly against her breast.

His fingers invaded her already dripping mound, toying with tender folds and sliding smoothly into her pussy.

She clasped his head as he suckled and stroked her nipples with his rough tongue, abrading the flesh. "Oh, God. Nathan."

His fingers caressed, seeking her bud of pleasure. They were bold as they stroked over her clit.

"Yes. Please. More." She was begging as her fingers stroked his back.

"Can't touch me anymore, love. Not now. I can't take it." His voice was strangled.

Sasha gasped as her arms flew over her head and were held there by his power. Invisible ties held her as surely as bindings. She jerked, but her hands were pinned above her head. She was helpless, his to command.

His mouth trailed down her stomach and she squirmed, her body burning with need. She needed him. Sasha could feel his need to dominate her as well as her own to be taken and possessed.

She whimpered as his mouth moved south, licking closer to her wet core. She closed her legs in reaction, not sure she could endure the sensation. Moving between her legs, he spread them open wide, exposing her vulnerable pussy. Her legs were locked in position. She fought to close them instinctively, but they were held open as surely as her arms were pinned above her head.

Her body trembled as his mouth clamped onto her pussy without mercy. His scorching tongue laved her folds before delving into her inner depths. His thumbs held her folds open as he lapped at her juices.

"Nathan. I can't stand it. Please." She couldn't move, couldn't think.

She felt him snarl into her flesh as he nipped at her clit, lifting the covering to get at the naked pearl. He flicked and tortured the tiny bud as her hips lifted for satisfaction.

She was shivering with need as he inserted his finger in her empty channel. She clenched around it, hungry to capture him inside her. He growled as he inserted a second finger.

She was slick, but tight, and his fingers stretched her as he continued a fast pace on her throbbing clit with his tongue.

Her body burned with the need for release, and she strained against his magic bindings. They didn't give an inch and she groaned her frustration, her need to climax nearly killing her.

His fingers stroked inside of her, deep but slow.

"Hurry, Nathan, please. I can't bear it," she whimpered as he started pumping faster.

She raised her hips as much as she could, trying desperately to make him take her harder. His fingers were sliding smoothly over her sweet spot and his continual stimulation of her clit made her belly clench.

Her release started with a creamy rush, her channel spasming over Nathan's fingers. She cried out as he lapped at her orgasm, stretching it out by vibrating his tongue over her naked clit hard and fast.

"Nathan!" She screamed his name as her hips jerked and her body trembled.

She panted in the aftermath. She had never experienced an orgasm like that. It rocked her world and she wasn't sure if she would ever recover.

She watched as Nathan rose and shucked his jeans. He was commando and his cock sprang forward, hard and huge.

"I'm not sure it will fit," she whispered as she gawked at his member.

She heard him make a sound that was half laugh and half groan as he covered her. "It will fit, my love. Don't be afraid. We were made for each other." He stroked her hair as he continued. "I can't promise it won't hurt a little. You're so tight that I may go mad. I can't believe you're mine."

She didn't argue. His words were so reverent, his tone so in awe of her...how could she quibble with him?

Her heart was thundering as she looked into his eyes and saw forever. She could never live without this man. She might be the keeper of his soul, but he was stealing her heart.

He grasped his cock, his expression pained. She knew he was struggling for control. For her. Because of her. At that moment she didn't care if it hurt like the very devil. She needed to be joined with him, filled by him, consumed by him.

"Fuck me, Nathan. I feel like I've waited forever," she told him softly.

He coated his cock with the cream from her hungry pussy, teasing her bud with the tip.

"Mine. My mate. My woman." His cries were hoarse as he inserted the tip of his penis against her tight opening. He pressed forward, his body shaking. "So tight. So hot."

Sasha could see the veins in the side of his neck bulging as he slowly pressed his cock inside her. She lifted her hips, desperate for him. "Take me, Nathan. I'm yours."

His control slipped and he buried himself inside her completely. She felt a pinch of pain, but it was quickly gone and all she could feel was Nathan. Her walls expanded and clenched, unused to being filled with a cock, much less a cock like Nathan's. The fullness left her breathless, eager to have him possess her completely.

"Yes," she hissed, her channel rejoicing at his taking. "Fuck me, Nathan."

"Mine. I'll make you come until you beg for mercy." His voice was wild, his control lost.

She moaned at his familiar words from her dreams and his uncontrollable lust as he pulled out and thrust back in.

Finally...he had made good on that promise. The reality of him was so much better than the dream.

He released her legs from his power and pulled them around his waist. His hands went under her ass and pulled her hips to meet his thrusting cock.

He hissed as he pumped into her tight, hot depths. "Need you. Have to fuck you hard."

"Yes, Nathan. Please." Her pussy throbbed as she begged for rough possession. She could feel his need and she wanted it as much as he did.

He pumped into her forcefully, staking his claim as his cock pummeled her. She wanted to touch him but her hands were still held tight above her head. Her back arched at the incredible friction and the force of his member filling her.

Sasha knew she was going to come. She felt it building as waves of ecstasy started to roll mercilessly over her body. She threw her head back as her body exploded, her muscles grabbing and clenching at Nathan's cock.

He continued pistoning his hips as she screamed, milking him with her clenching walls. He leaned his body into hers and licked at the vein in her neck. She stiffened as she felt the initial prick of his fangs and then was flooded with complete erotic pleasure. She felt another orgasm gathering and she let it take her. Although she didn't think it was possible, it was stronger than the last one, making her come apart. When Nathan pressed her mouth to his shoulder, she didn't resist. She lapped at his blood, taken from a slash he had opened, her body convulsing from the sheer ecstasy of being part of each other in another way. She was shocked by the intimacy of sharing blood and the erotic delight that accompanied it. As the second climax rolled over her, she released his shoulder and he stopped the bleeding on her neck and his small wound.

"Mine." He groaned as he buried himself in her depths and released his hot stream, his spine arching in agony and bliss.

Her arms came loose and she wrapped them around Nathan as he dropped onto her welcoming body, holding him tightly, with tears streaming down her face.

He rolled, taking her with him as they lay on their sides, panting, their hearts pounding against each other.

"What is this, little one?" He swiped lightly at her tears with his thumbs.

Her cheeks flooded pink with embarrassment. Mages didn't let their emotions overwhelm them. "It's nothing. Really" She blew it off as she swiped the rest of the tears away.

"Tell me, love. I'll make it go away," he insisted, his eyes full of confusion.

Sasha burst out laughing. He was so very serious and so very sure that he could make any of her problems go away...take care of her every need. She knew he would always try. He was the eldest brother, the protector. It was part of his very nature. A part that she was learning to love about him.

She loved him. That's why she was crying. Emotions welled up in her throat and she tried to swallow them, afraid of revealing her feelings. He felt the mating instincts as she did, but could he also care for her? She wanted him to love her. Her. Sasha. She wanted more than just the mating bond.

"I'm fine, Nathan. Really. That was incredible. I always cry over a good orgasm." She snuggled into him and rested her head on his bulky shoulder.

"I'm rather afraid that I will make you cry often then." His voice was disgruntled. "Are you sure I didn't hurt you?" he asked anxiously.

"It was so good. I'm ready to cry again." She pulled back and gave him a mischievous grin.

He returned a wicked smile but he rose from the bed and scooped her up into his arms. "I think you could use a hot soak in the tub. You'll be sore."

She pouted, her lower lip poking out as she gave him a disappointed look.

"It's a very large tub, big enough for two." He chuckled as he bounced her up in the air as she squealed and grabbed his shoulders.

"Can I...explore you, Nathan. I never really got to...touch you." And she wanted to. Badly.

"You'll kill me, woman," he muttered, but carried her happily to the hot tub and let her satisfy her curiosity until she was quite content.

CHAPTER 5

Nathan knew he was a goner, acting as stupid, or possibly worse, than his brothers acted over Brianna and Callie. He understood now what it was like to be completely captivated by a mate.

Sasha.

His cock went stiff just thinking about her in his bed, with her long blonde hair flowing over his pillows, and those needy moans of hers that drove him to sate her every desire.

He stretched as he shook off his day sleep. He could smell her scent on his sheets and his chest ached. He missed her already and they had just been together last night. He wished she had stayed with him to sleep at his side. It would be bliss to see her smile every night when he awakened. He felt...lonely.

He didn't just miss her body. It was...Sasha. She was the delight of his life. She would stand toe to toe with him when she got in one of her stubborn moods, arguing with a man twice her size without ever flinching. He smiled, knowing she was one of the bravest, smartest women he knew. When she wasn't near...he missed her.

He reached for her with his mind, but couldn't reach out to her. Knowing she was probably sleeping, he sighed.

He loved everything about Sasha, even her stubborn determination that mage and vampires didn't mate. His lips curved into a smile. She wouldn't win that argument. No matter how hard she resisted, he would make her call him to her somehow and they would be mates. Not only was she destined for him, but he loved her nearly to the point of insanity.

Nathan's security gate buzzed just as he was rolling out of bed. He hit the intercom button. "State your business."

He stiffened as he heard the breathless female voice on the other end. "Nathan, let me in. It's important. I don't have time to spell myself in right now."

Regan. What was she doing here? Nathan quickly hit the button to open the gate and dressed himself magically as he ran down the stairs to the front door.

Regan's sporty little blue vehicle came to halt with screaming tires as she scrambled out of the car. Nathan frowned as he saw the look of terror on the usually calm and sedate woman's face.

He grabbed Regan by the shoulders gently. "What is it?"

She started to cry, tears rolling down her cheeks. "They took her, Nathan. Our parents went to the mage elders. The council decided she needed to be mated with a mage and they took her. They said they would beat the vampire devil from her and mate her with a mage."

"Sasha?" he breathed softly but dangerously.

Regan nodded. "We were working and they just invaded her house and took her away. We both fought them with our magic, but there were too many elders. They drugged her and took her away in chains. She was still fighting." Regan finished with a sob. "She loves you, Nathan. She'll be miserable, and I'm afraid they'll have to hurt her badly because I know she won't accept the mating. Please help her."

Fury rose up inside of him, anguish ripping and tearing at his insides. Death to anyone who dared to lay a hand on his mate. He stared at her sister, willing himself to be calm. Regan was hysterical and she needed reassurance. "Do you know where they are?"

"I'm...not sure, probably at the mating grounds." Regan choked back her sobs. "I can't believe that our parents betrayed her."

She quickly gave Nathan directions to the mage mating grounds.

Liam. Rory. Ethan. I need you.

He sent a call to his brothers and every one of them appeared almost instantly. He explained quickly that his mate had been kidnapped.

"Regan, I want you to stay here. Sasha would want you to be safe. Liam, please stay and watch over her. She's upset." Nathan looked at the serious faces of Ethan and Rory. "I might need help."

"We've got your back. Lead on." Ethan replied instantly as Rory nodded.

Nathan?

Chills fluttered down his spine as he heard his mate's weak, defeated voice in his head.

Please come to me, Nathan. I need you.

"I'm coming, love. Are you at the mating grounds?" His heart racing, he spoke aloud. His brothers waited tensely as he spoke to his mate. Regan looked perplexed, but watched anxiously.

Yes. I can't fight, Nathan. I'm drugged. I can't wake up. Every time I start to wake, they hit me with more drugs.

His heart flip-flopped as rage infused him. He forced his voice to gentle. "Don't fight it, sweetheart. Don't make them drug you anymore. If you wake, pretend to sleep. We will be there soon."

Please hurry. They are choosing my mate even now. I can't bear the thought of any other man touching me.

Over his dead body! No one touched his mate. He didn't know her exact location so he started to follow her essence, his brothers Ethan and Rory close on his heels. They moved through the night in a blur, Nathan tracking Sasha like a desperate man...which he was.

"Did they hurt you, sweetheart?" Nathan dreaded the answer, but he had to keep her from slipping out of his mind and back into a normal sleep. He had to keep the connection open. She was calling him to her and they could connect right now even though she slept.

I'm okay, Nathan. I just need you.

The bastards had hurt her. If they hadn't, she would have told him so. Fuck! His heart hammered in his ears as violence and wrath flooded through him. "I'm here, love. I just arrived."

I love you, Nathan. Her soft sigh washed over him. *Please don't kill anyone. My parents are here. And my kin.*

His mind was reeling from her declaration and it took a while for her request to register. "You're asking a lot of me, love. I want to nail every one of them that took part in your kidnapping."

Please, Nathan.

Her voice was weak and pleading. He could deny her nothing. "Only because I love you, Sasha. If I loved you less, they would all be dead."

As Nathan and his brothers broke into a clearing and he saw his beloved chained naked to a post, her face and body littered with bruises, he almost took back his words. Fuck! He wanted to dust every one of them...painfully.

Ethan grasped Nathan's shoulder as he spoke, "Take care of your mate. Rory and I will handle the others."

Six mages sat around a small table only feet from Sasha, arguing over how they would rid her body of her vampire mark. Even though he wanted to gut every one of them, his heart was crying out for him to go to his mate. "She wants them alive. They are her parents and kin," he muttered to his brothers.

Ethan's face crumpled. "Damn. She takes all of the fun out of revenge." He brightened. "But she didn't say we couldn't rough them up?"

Rory and Ethan both looked at him expectantly, an evil look on their faces. "She just said don't kill them."

"Right. We'll leave them breathing. Barely." His brothers strode toward the council as Nathan arrived beside Sasha.

He didn't give his brothers another thought. They would have no problem taking care of six mages. They were no match for the power of two vampires.

He ripped off the chains that kept her upright and manufactured a blanket to wrap her nude body.

Christ! And they call us vampires barbarians! A vampire would never do something like this to a woman.

He picked her up gently. "Sasha?"

Her head slumped against his chest and she didn't answer. She had fallen back into a drug-induced sleep. His face was stormy as he glared at her family. He wasn't sure which two were her parents, but he really didn't care. He hated every one of them.

Their faces were all filled with fear as Rory and Ethan descended on them. Nathan got a twisted sense of delight knowing they would suffer. Ethan and Rory wanted justice for their brother's mate and they would get what they had given to his mate...and more.

He disappeared into the night, his life and love cradled in his arms.

CHAPTER 6

Sasha knew that Nathan was none too happy to be staring at her across the mating chamber the following night. He said it was too soon, the night before being too difficult for her.

But here he was...catering to her desires once again. Her heart raced as she watched him, his eyes intense on her nude body. She had been stripped and consented to the mating. She was eager to belong to him. After what had happened last night they couldn't be mated fast enough for her. She needed to give Nathan his soul and she desperately wanted to be his forever.

I won't bind you, Sasha. Not after yesterday.

His fervent statement flowed through her mind and she smiled at him as she approached him. "Do what you must, my love. It doesn't matter," she whispered to him softly. "As long as the end result is that I belong to you and you have your soul."

She was aware of the eyes that watched the ritual mating from the darkened windows. She thought it would unnerve her, but she found it strangely arousing. Those vampires, unknown strangers, would watch as Nathan made her his. She knew the ritual by heart, so it startled her as Nathan reached down and freed his own cock, ripping off the leather covering and tossing it on the floor. "If you want this done today...I will do it my way," he told her fiercely as he scooped up her naked body and climbed the steps to the silk covered bed.

Nathan had chosen a violet color for the bed that matched her eyes exactly. As he laid her on the smooth, cool covering, he slid onto the bed and they faced each other. His eyes were intense as he spoke the binding words in his native language.

Sasha quivered as she felt the magic swirl through the room. Her emotions mirrored Nathan's and she could feel him trying to hold himself in check. He kept his eyes frozen with hers as he murmured the words that she couldn't understand, but that moved her with their power.

His mating mark glowed as he brought it to her hip to match their marks. It burned like the fires of hell as Nathan's soul escaped her grasp and their souls parted and split...and then melded together again. She gasped as his soul passed into him through their joined marks.

She started murmuring her own spell as Nathan's eyes glowed red and his body jerked. She didn't have his enormous power, but she could help him.

"Mine." Nathan growled as he reached for her. He took her mouth roughly and grasped her head to keep her from moving as he devoured her with his tongue. Her already damp pussy flooded as his tongue swept into her mouth, branding her. She gave as good as she got, aggressively seeking his out of control tongue with her own. He broke off the kiss, panting for breath, trying desperately not to control her.

Before he had a chance to make any demands, she reached for his rock hard cock and wrapped her lips around the engorged member. She pushed him onto his back as she licked the tip, savoring the taste of him. She heard a growl, and then groan as she slid her mouth over him boldly, satisfying his need. She stayed with him, acting before he could, sensing every desire that he had.

Crawling over his body, she swung her hips around until she straddled his face.

"Mine." He snarled before he attacked her mound as she continued to suck his cock, her cheeks puffing in and out as she took him as deeply as she could. She took the rest of him in her hand and worked his cock over and over as he groaned into her pussy.

She moaned around his member as his mouth invaded her, hot and unrelenting, making her squirm against his face. His tongue was like fire licking over her clit, arousing her to a fevered pitch.

She fingered his balls gently as she sucked him as hard and fast as she could. He was groaning against her and her body writhed against him as she felt him tense. He came with an intensity that made his whole body shake. His scorching release exploded in the back of her throat and she swallowed, eager for every drop of his explosion.

He tongued her hard, moving her folds and zeroing in on her clit. She stiffened as she knew what he wanted next. He wanted to invade every orifice on her body. His slippery finger slid into her back hole and his other hand slipped two fingers into her empty channel.

Sasha levered herself on her arms as she felt his attack from every angle. She threw her head back as he fucked both holes with his fingers as his tongue continued laving her clit.

"Oh, God. Nathan. It's too much," she sobbed as his fingers worked furiously, and his tongue was relentless.

Over and over. Again and again. She was on overload and ready to come apart. He was working his fingers opposite, so that he was withdrawing from her anus as he pumped into her soaking channel.

Her heart was ready to fly out of her body from pumping so hard and she screamed as she came, flooding Nathan's mouth with hot, creamy liquid that he lapped at voraciously.

Dizziness overwhelmed her and she had to fight for consciousness as she nearly passed out from ecstasy. Nathan was holding her hips upright as her limp body tried to sink. He continued swallowing her juices as she gasped for oxygen.

His strong arms swung her leg over his face and he pulled her on top of him. He wrapped an arm around her neck and kissed her. She could taste their sex mingling together as their tongues met and their sweat-soaked bodies slid together.

Sasha could feel his hard cock against her ass cheeks as he scooted her back and broke off the erotic embrace. "Mine." His eyes were still sparking red and his face looked pained. "Ride me. Ride my cock."

She slid further back and grasped his steely, massive member. She was spent, but need was driving her...and she needed to feel Nathan inside her.

They were both slick and wet. Sasha tried to relax her muscles as she slid her aching pussy over his cock until it was buried deep inside her. *Oh, God.* She felt so full. He penetrated deep in this position and she clenched around him hard.

He grasped her hips. "Fuck me. Ride me hard."

She let him set the pace and got carried away by his needs and desires that were also hers. He was demanding, lifting his hips up to meet her descending flesh. She was lost in the slapping of skin against skin and his cock filling her again and again. Faster and faster. He lifted one hand and brought her hand to her breast. She knew what he wanted and she unashamedly fingered her nipples, pulling and tugging as she rode his cock at a furious pace.

Her eyes met his red gaze, but she could still see Nathan beneath the red glare. He was watching her hotly, taking in every sound that escaped her throat.

"Mine. My Sasha." He snarled as he slammed into her, pulling her hips hard against him as he penetrated her deep and strong. Her body quaked as she began to climax. She moaned as she rocked her hips frantically against Nathan's.

He reached up his arm and curled it around her neck, bringing her down to him. His lips licked erotically over her vein before his fangs punctured her. She felt the moment of pleasure/pain before she was flooded with complete erotic pleasure. The tiny fangs that sprang from her own gums startled her, even though she knew it was coming. It wasn't so much the fangs appearing as the intense hunger that she had for Nathan. She sunk her fangs into his shoulder, ravenous for the taste of him. He jerked and tensed, burying his cock to the hilt. She came, milking his cock at the same time as he spilt deep into her womb.

They detached their fangs and Nathan quickly stopped the bleeding before wrapping her against him. The orgasm seemed to last forever, sucking every bit of energy she had as she lay breathlessly on top of Nathan.

She tried to roll off him, knowing he was taking every bit of her weight, but he held her there. "Stay." His voice was hoarse as he held her tightly on top of him. She felt a thin sheet cover them and she turned her head to look into his beautiful brown eyes.

She saw eternity in that adoring, loving gaze.

"Did you use your magic on me?" he mumbled sleepily.

"Just a little spell to help me hear your urges quickly, feel them as they were coming to you." She told him innocently. "I knew you didn't want to lose control. I thought it would help if I could... anticipate your needs."

"It helped. It wasn't too rough, was it?" he sounded anxious.

She sighed. "I would say it was just perfect. We belong to each other now."

"Sweetheart, we always have," he whispered softly to her. "Now it's just official."

She kissed him softly and laid her head on his shoulder as darkness took her in its loving embrace.

EPILOGUE

The mage didn't have wedding ceremonies...but the Hale brothers insisted on a party...with lots of food.

Sasha smiled as she watched the Hale brothers and Adare devour more food than most people could eat in a month. Staring fondly at her mate who was currently involved in the eating and back slapping male bonding, she let out a long, deep breath.

Nathan looked up and their eyes met. He excused himself abruptly and came to her side muttering, "When you look at me like that I want to take you to bed."

She rolled her eyes. "Any look I give you makes you want that. I can give you the evil eye and you want to go to bed." She laughed softly as he pulled her against him.

"You don't even have to look at me. All I have to do is think about you and I want you." He gave her a wicked grin as he continued, "Which is pretty much all the time. I could probably keep you in bed forever and it still wouldn't be enough."

She could feel his hard cock against her belly and her body quickened. Her mate's sexual appetite secretly delighted her, although she teased him about it. In the last week since they had mated, they had spent more time in bed than out of it. His brothers razzed him constantly about being enchanted by his mate...but he didn't seem to mind very much and it didn't change his behavior one bit. He continued to drool over his mate daily...much to his brother's delight. It gave them a reason to hand back all of the words he had spoken to them when they had their heads up their asses because they were beguiled by their females.

She smiled as saw the gold and precious stones glint from the ring on her finger. Regan had crafted the jewelry for her and Nathan, a beautiful matching set of mating rings as a gift. The workmanship was beautiful and the matching gold dragons glittered with tiny rubies, sapphires and diamonds that almost brought the creatures to life. She and Nathan both wore them with pride. Regan had given them to her in a private moment that had revealed a rather shocking revelation.

"What are you thinking about now, my love?" Nathan drew her closer and she laid her head on his shoulder.

"Liam needs his mate. He's the only brother left." Sasha smiled as she told him.

"Liam swears he's a healer and he won't find his mate. No healer has found their mate in over a millennium. He says his mate is his work." Nathan frowned as he looked at his brother, standing off to one side, chatting with Regan.

"Oh...I'm pretty certain he's wrong," she told him with confidence.

Nathan pulled back and met her eyes. "Why do you think that? Do you know something I don't know?"

"Maybe...but I won't tell," she rubbed up against his erection, trying to distract him. *It's not my secret to tell.* She would tell Nathan someday...but not just yet. He wasn't exactly subtle and to tell him right now would be a disaster.

"Rub against me like that again and we're leaving." He gave her a look filled with desire and longing.

"Promise?" she asked him in a low, sultry voice.

"You'll find yourself in bed, flat on your back and naked in less than five seconds," he warned in a voice daring her to do it.

It was a threat she couldn't resist. Her panties moistened at his commanding, dominate tone. She squirmed and wriggled against him, leaving him in no doubt about the fact that she was calling his bluff.

He scooped her into his arms and they disappeared, leaving the guests to continue the party without them.

THE END

of Book Three: Nathan's Mate

LIAM'S MATE

BOOK FOUR

THE VAMPIRE COALITION

CHAPTER 1

Excerpts From The Book Of Vampire Healer:

An intimate act with your chosen mate will release the mating instincts of the vampire healer...

And so, the vampire healer is a subspecies, classified as vampire, but with definite differences in power and mating habits...

You are vampire and this book was not written to make you feel different from your brethren, brothers and sisters. It is merely a reference to help you better understand your purpose, obligations and the rules that come with the great privilege that was bestowed upon you at your birth...

Regan Taylor slammed the monstrous leather-bound tome closed with a loud *bang* and a disgusted snort. "Surely you don't believe all of this garbage, Liam?"

Liam Hale tried desperately not to smile as he eyed the fierce look on Regan's face and reached for the soy sauce in the middle of the low, round table that was practically groaning from the weight of the massive spread of Chinese food. It was his night to pick what they had for dinner. He had called for Chinese to be delivered to his house because he had been working late. Maybe he had gotten a little carried away while he was ordering. "It's our only reference book," he answered casually as he shifted off of his knees and into a sitting position on his living room floor.

Regan pushed the book from her lap and let it slide to the carpeted floor as she scooted up to the table and lifted her spoon. "It isn't a very good reference. It doesn't even tell you how to mate," she replied indignantly as she spooned a small amount of rice into her mouth.

Liam paused with his fork half way to his mouth and answered with a smirk, "I actually already know how to do that extremely well. I had plenty of practice in my first hundred years." Too much practice, Liam thought. He had essentially been a man-whore because he knew he was almost certainly never going to be able to have sex again after he crossed the age of one hundred. And he hadn't. Not in three hundred years.

Regan's cheeks were flushed as she answered, "Don't try to embarrass me, Liam. You know what I mean." She waved her empty spoon toward the book and frowned, "I think they deliberately make it difficult for vampire healers to mate. Not only do you have to find your mate, but then you have to perform an intimate act of some sort before you are really able to be intimate? It makes no sense. Why the mystery? Why can't they just tell you what to do?" Regan swallowed a bite of kung pao chicken before continuing, "And going on and on about the great honor you are given as a healer...blah, blah, blah." She rolled her eyes before adding, "Being a healer is more like being a prisoner for you. You work almost every moment you're awake."

Liam shrugged as he watched the residual blush fade from Regan's animated face. God, she was pretty, and maybe he shouldn't pretend to misunderstand her meaning just to see her rosy cheeks, but he couldn't help it. Problem was...she was pretty much onto him. They had been in each other's company almost every day for eight months and she rarely got flustered anymore. "I doubt that it matters," he replied as he picked up another egg roll and devoured it. "No vampire healer has ever found their mate in the last thousand years. And

I've only heard tales of it happening in the long distant past. I'm not certain if it's truth or myth."

"Whoever created those stupid rules make it impossible. A regular vampire will at least get a chance when his mate calls him to her. Vampire healers don't even get that opportunity. You can't even recognize your mate, much less know what to do to initiate the mating instinct."

She was right. He was basically screwed, but Liam had pretty much accepted that hundreds of years ago.

Regan was still vehemently contesting his lack of rights as a vampire healer, but Liam couldn't be anything but happy as he watched her, delighted by her changing expressions and unusual show of emotions. He had been in a state of happiness for the last eight months, since the day that he and Regan had met and become friends. Granted, she had been pointing a gun at him and his brother Nathan at the time, but that could be easily forgiven since she had thought they were trying to kill her sister, Sasha.

Okay, maybe she hadn't taken to *him* right away, but Liam had adored Regan since the day she had so bravely stormed Nathan's house, without a single thought to her own safety, to protect her sister.

Maybe his cock wasn't hard, but what he felt for Regan went way beyond infatuation and physical desire. He had come to depend on seeing her every day. It made life as a vampire healer a hell of a lot more bearable and a whole lot less lonely.

"Vampire healers don't have a life of their own, Regan. You know that," he answered her calmly as he continued to watch her and consume enormous amounts of food at the same time. It was a skill he had perfected since he and Regan had started having dinner together every night.

Regan sighed as she put down her spoon and stopped eating to look at him. "You work too hard, Liam. You need to have some of the other healers work more. You deserve some sort of life."

It was strange that he had never really cared about how much he worked, which was why he answered most of the healing calls. He was re-thinking that now that he wanted to spend more time with

Regan. She made him want to do more than work. It wasn't easy to change habits that had formed over hundreds of years and the other healers still grumbled about taking their share of calls sometimes, but he was starting to kick their asses into gear. He had spoiled them over the last few hundred years.

"I'm working on it." At least he had some time every day to do something other than work and fall into an exhausted day sleep. His friendship with Regan had made him reconsider a lot of things that he had never even thought about before.

Regan pushed her plate away as she added, "And you need to tell your brothers about the backlash."

Oh, hell no. "I can't do that. If they get into trouble they would never call me." *Time to change the subject.* "Are you going to eat any more of the pot stickers?"

Regan laughed lightly and shoved the container of pan fried dumplings toward Liam. "I'm full. They're all yours. I don't know how you manage to put away so much food."

He grinned as he grabbed up the container. "Vampire metabolism."

"Did you feed today?"

"Nope. Worked too late."

There it was, the little crinkle that formed between her eyebrows when she was concerned. Liam wanted to lean over the low table and kiss it from her forehead.

"You're a healer. You expend a lot of energy and you need to feed every day. Human food won't cut it," she informed him, probably for the millionth time in the last eight months.

"Tomorrow," he promised.

"You always say that."

"I always do it," he reminded her, grumbling the reply. Was there anything he wouldn't do for Regan?

Liam hated feeding, but he always did it once he promised Regan that he would. Otherwise, he avoided it as long as possible, disliking the fact that he had to find human donors and take their blood without consent. He knew he had to do it to continue to thrive and serve his people, but he received no pleasure from the act. It was simply a necessity.

Regan always sounded like a concerned mate, worrying about him like he really meant something to her...and Liam ate it up. Had any woman ever cared about him in that way? Probably not. He had lost count of how many women he had screwed in his early days, but none of them had ever given a shit about *him*. They had wanted sexual satisfaction from an able male, and he had given it to them.

He released a tired breath as he finished off the last fried dumpling and dropped the empty container on the table. How did he ever get lucky enough to find a friend like Regan? Hell yes, she fussed sometimes. But he actually enjoyed it. He found himself wanting to humor her, make her happy. She didn't exactly have it easy herself as a mage healer, and he was obsessed with keeping her happy, keeping her safe.

"You're the most frustrating vampire I know," she mumbled as she crossed her arms.

He quirked a brow at her and tried not to laugh. "And exactly how many vampires are you personally acquainted with?" Since mage and vampire didn't mix, Liam was willing to bet that the only ones she knew were his brothers.

She shot him an irritated don't-go-there look and huffed, "You're frustrating, Liam Hale."

"You're beautiful." It popped out of Liam's mouth without a thought and he said it with complete honesty. She was beautiful, and he wasn't referring to just her gorgeous baby blues and silky blonde hair that brushed her shoulders in cute, fat curls. He loved those twisted locks. They made him want to reach out and straighten them to see if they would bounce right back into place.

Regan radiated a quiet strength and compassion that drew him to her with an intensity that he couldn't seem to fight...and didn't want to fight. While he had always had his brothers for companions, he had still been incredibly lonely before he had met Regan. He loved his brothers and would give his life for any one of them, but there were certain things that he couldn't talk to them about, forcing him to keep them at a distance.

Maybe his brothers had never felt the distance - but Liam felt it, especially with his twin, Rory.

All of his brothers were now mated and although Liam was happy for them, it had made the loneliness that much more acute. Until he had met Regan. She eased the ache, made the loneliness fade while she was near him. A mage healer, Regan understood him, sometimes better than he understood himself.

"Don't think that compliments will get you out of feeding." Regan still had her arms crossed and now her eyebrows were raised as she glared at him, but Liam could see the underlying amusement in her expression.

"Do they ever?" he quipped, his tone wry, as he shot her a questioning gaze.

"Nope," she tossed back at him. "I'm completely immune to your charm."

Damn. Something inside of Liam flinched as he wondered why that comment scored a hit. For some perverse reason he really didn't want her to be immune to him, but he certainly couldn't seduce her. His mind was more than willing...but his body wasn't capable. "I'll feed tomorrow, Regan. I've never broken a promise to you."

Her face softened and she smiled, a smile that lit up Liam's whole world and nearly knocked him on his ass. "I know you haven't and I know you wouldn't," she murmured softly.

Liam's felt a pang in his chest and barely stopped himself from rubbing it. There were moments when Regan could make him feel like the most powerful creature on earth just because of her trust and faith in him. God help him, but he never wanted to lose that.

"My council has chosen a mate for me," Regan said quietly, almost as if she was talking to herself.

"Oh, Christ! Again?" *Shit!* Liam noted to himself that he'd have to take care of that problem for longer than a few months this time. This was the third mate they had chosen for Regan in the last eight months. He was so fucking tired of the mage council trying to sell

Regan off to the highest bidder with the best bloodline as if she was a damn prize cow. "I'll take care of it, Regan."

"No, Liam. You've always refused to tell me how you got me out of the other matches, but I can make a good guess. You can't keep doing this. This man doesn't sound so bad," she said hesitantly.

"Over my dead body," Liam growled.

Regan started twirling a lock of her hair, something that Liam knew she only did when she was nervous. "I have to mate eventually."

"No...you don't. Not until you find the right one. You don't love him."

"Love isn't part of our mating process," she answered quietly.

"It will be for you. You deserve to be loved and cherished." Liam tried to get a grip on his irritation. Love *wasn't* a part of the mage mating process. It wasn't really part of a vampire mating either, but all of his brothers had gotten lucky and he didn't want to see anything less for Regan. He'd buy off a thousand potential mage mates for Regan before he saw her mated to some jerk who didn't appreciate her. The mage might value blue blood, but the snobby assholes were severely lacking in funds. Luckily, money was something Liam had in an almost unlimited supply. He wouldn't miss a million...or three, and wouldn't hesitate to part with the money again to save Regan the heartache of mating with a male who would make her life miserable.

Personally, Liam thought the mages needed a serious infusion of new blood. Their gene pool was obviously screwed up from too much inbreeding. Well...with a few exceptions. Sasha was great...and Regan was damn near perfect. If he could have chosen the perfect mate for himself...

Don't go there, buddy. It isn't happening!

Liam jerked himself back to reality as he listened to Regan speak. "Fine. I'll get to know him first this time. He's closer to my age and maybe I'll fall madly in love, but I don't want you to interfere. I'll handle it. You can't fight my battles for me, Liam." Regan was up on her knees now and glaring down at Liam, who still had his ass flat on the floor. Liam tried not to let his amusement show on his face. It wasn't like she had gained much height on him, even in her elevated position. She was a compact spitfire, but then, her strength and power had nothing to do with her physical size.

"Of course I can." He rose to his knees and crossed his arms over his chest as they glowered at each other. Despite his delight at her little flash of temper, this wasn't a battle that Liam intended to lose. "I'm your friend…I'm male…and I'm a vampire," he told her seriously, like that explained everything that she needed to know.

Regan tossed her head and broke his gaze as she flopped onto her back, rolling with laughter. "Oh my God, Liam! You can be so arrogant and chauvinistic sometimes." She rolled onto her side to look up at him as she continued to chortle and choked out, "Just when I think you're coming into the twenty-first century, you go all knight-in-shining-armor on me."

His arms stayed crossed and he gave her a dark look as he replied, "I'm not that old. And I don't see women as inferior, but they are not as physically strong and sometimes require protection." And damn it, he'd be more than willing to slay dragons for her if she had any stalking her.

"Tarzan?" she suggested, still giggling.

"Completely fictional," he answered in denial.

"Tyrant?"

He seemed to consider that for a moment and replied, "Possibly."

Regan propped herself on her elbows, tears of mirth flowing down her cheeks, and said lightly, "Come back to the twenty-first century, Grandpa. We need to discuss this rationally."

Liam took a deep breath to tell her there was no way he was letting her mate with someone who wasn't good enough for her when his phone started vibrating on the table.

Nathan. "Yeah, Nathan," he ground out irritably.

"Liam? Can you meet us all downtown? We have a fallen situation."

Since Nathan was all business, Liam took the location of the meeting, promising he would get there as soon as he could.

"I have to go help my brothers…but this discussion isn't over," Liam warned her ominously as he ended the phone call abruptly.

Regan frowned and stood up as Liam rose to his feet. "Please tell me you aren't going out to destroy fallen vampires." Her voice was trembling, all traces of amusement gone.

"I'll just assist. Don't worry." Liam couldn't resist and bent down to try to kiss away the worry lines between her eyes. They didn't disappear, but he had that brief, fleeting moment of feeling her soft skin beneath his lips and breathing in the light sent of lilacs before he started to fade.

He knew his brothers were waiting for him so he started summoning the power to teleport himself to the designated meeting place.

"Please be careful."

That sweet, feminine voice and the sight of her lightly touching the spot where he had pressed a butterfly kiss were the last things he heard and saw before he was abruptly transported to his brothers.

And all hell broke loose.

CHAPTER 2

Was Liam a complete masochist, or just a vampire healer with a constant death wish?

Regan had been contemplating the same question for the last two hours as she paced Liam's large, tastefully decorated living room. She had long since cleaned up any remnants of their Chinese meal even though Liam could have done it with a wave of his hand. The task had occupied her body, but it didn't stop her mind from racing with fear for his safety.

Damn it! When would the stubborn vampire admit that, as a vampire healer, he was different? He couldn't fight battles with the *fallen* and come out unscathed. She had watched him suffer way too often not to feel outraged over the entire situation. His brothers needed to know, but Liam certainly wasn't going to be the one to enlighten them.

Liam was her friend, she reminded herself as she stopped pacing before she wore a hole in the plush carpeting and flopped onto a comfortable leather sofa. When he was hurting, it nearly killed her.

Because Liam is your mate!

Regan wanted to shake her head in denial, but it wouldn't help. Liam *was* her mate, but he could never know the truth. How many times had she wanted to tell him to see if they could solve the mystery of the intimacy clause in the Book Of The Vampire Healer?

You love him.

God help her, but she did love Liam Hale with every breath in her body, which is why he could never know that she was his chosen mate. She couldn't pinpoint the exact moment when she had known that she loved him, but his safety had become her number one priority.

Regan had known the truth about being his mate since her sister had mated with his brother Nathan eight months ago. It hadn't been difficult to figure out who the mark that was imprinted on her hip belonged to after she had seen Sasha's marking and her sister had revealed its meaning. Liam had been the last unmated brother and his mark was very similar to Nathan's. The mark of the dragon.

Regan curled her body into the corner of the sofa and shivered as she remembered the horror of the night the mage council had come to her home, shortly after Sasha had mated with Nathan, and stripped her naked to look for the mating mark of the vampire on her body. Her own mother had ratted Regan out, remembering that her youngest daughter had the strange birthmark. While Sasha's mark had appeared on her eighteenth birthday, Regan had been born with hers. After slowly and painfully altering the mark, the council had given her a choice - mate with the mage of their choice or see Liam killed by the mage league of assassins.

Tears leaked from Regan's eyes as she rubbed the altered mark on her hip. While the pain of the alteration had been excruciating, the fact that Liam would never be hers hurt even more. She could never risk him, never tell him that they were destined mates. And oh...how she wanted to blurt out the truth and try every intimate act that she could think of to fire his mating instinct.

But would Liam even want me?

He was fond of her. Regan knew that. What she didn't know is if he would really want her as a mate. He treated her like a buddy or a sister, and while she knew he wanted her company, would he ever want her as she wanted him? Yeah...he threw her an occasional compliment, but she suspected it was more out of sympathy than any other emotion.

Maybe she should just mate with the mage council's choice and get it over with. She would be forcefully separated from Liam's company and possibly get over her raging desire for Liam. Getting over it would be good since he would never be hers. Why prolong the agony?

Liam insisted that being a healer kept him too busy and that he would never mate because he couldn't be a good partner. Did he mean that, or was he only saying it to make himself feel better about the slim possibility of finding his mate?

It doesn't matter. You'll never have the opportunity to find out.

Only Sasha and the council knew that she was Liam's destined mate and she had begged Sasha not to share the truth with Nathan. Nathan would certainly tell Liam and then Liam...would be dead. Somehow, at some point, the league of mage assassins would take him out. Sasha had been hesitant to hold back the truth from Nathan, but Regan's sister also knew the power of the league of mage assassins. That knowledge had been enough to keep Sasha silent on the subject of Liam and Regan.

Regan wiped the tears from her cheeks in swipes of angry resignation. Why did she torture herself by spending nearly every day in Liam's company?

Because you can't stay away. You love him, you feel his loneliness, feel his need for companionship.

It was true. She couldn't stay away from him and although their time together was both bliss and torture, she ached to be near him.

She was drawn to him, compelled to try to take care of him. Liam had been conditioned almost from birth to sacrifice...and he needed a friend to save him from himself. He gave too much, kept too many secrets, and never gave a second thought to the price he had to pay for keeping those secrets or making those sacrifices.

"Oh, Liam," she sighed softly as she remembered how he had pursued her friendship in the beginning even though she had tried to brush him off. She had never had a chance against his determination and persistence. Liam Hale could be a total pain in the ass when he wanted to be. A handsome, sexy, caring, and sometimes arrogant pain in the ass, but still, a continual pain in the ass when he wanted something. And for some unknown reason, Liam had wanted Regan's friendship and companionship. Who could ignore those chocolate brown eyes filled with an emptiness that tugged at her heart and that muscular, towering body that was made for sins that Regan hadn't even contemplated committing before she met Liam? Lately, she had been thinking about sex way too much.

Regan felt an irrational ping of jealousy toward all of the women that Liam had ever had in his bed. Those women might be hundreds of years deceased, but she still disliked every one of them for having a part of Liam that she would never see. What would he look like with his dark hair mussed and his eyes filled with desire?

Absolutely terrifying! And completely irresistible.

Crap...the man was already an unholy temptation and he had zero sexual desire, she could only image what those women had felt during the time that they were the object of his desire. No doubt, Liam had satisfied every one of them.

Regan's womb clenched and her nipples hardened at the thought. She had never had a man inside of her because the mage didn't have relations with anyone other than their mate, but she was a healer. It wasn't as if she didn't understand the act, but for the first time she craved it with a man...with Liam.

She wrapped her arms around her body and tried not to feel the pain of longing for something that she could never have. She was mage and had been taught from the time that she was an infant not to display her emotions. Naturally quiet, shy and withdrawn, the way of the mage had come easily to her...until she had met Liam. He fired off a whole barrage of emotions that she wasn't used to handling on a daily basis. It felt good to be alive, to laugh, to have someone that she could talk to other than her sister, Sasha. But being with Liam also brought a certain amount of pain and fear that she had to stuff deep inside of herself or end up suffocated by the emotions.

If you'd just mate with the council's choice, you could go back to being quiet and withdrawn. You could completely hide your emotions again.

Liam would no longer be in danger from the mage. She would mate to protect Liam from the wrath of the mage, even if it meant never seeing Liam again.

"You're still here."

Regan's head jerked to the other side of the room and her heart raced as the deep baritone flowed over her body, flooding it with relief. "Liam," she breathed softly as she came to her feet, wanting to throw her arms around him as she met his dark eyes with a concerned expression. "Are you okay?"

He grinned at her reassuringly. "I'm fine. Which is more than I can say for the *fallen*."

He was hiding something, forcing that smile. Regan had seen his various expressions for long enough to know when he was holding back the truth. "You had to kill?"

"You should go. Get some sleep," he yawned broadly, obviously trying to change the subject.

Regan's eyes shot to the clock. It was still several hours before he would be able to give himself up to day sleep. "Liam Hale, answer my question."

He sighed as he dropped the veil of pretense. "Yes. I had no choice. We were outnumbered. It was either dust a few *fallen* or watch my brothers get beheaded. It wasn't a difficult choice," he finished calmly.

She took his hand and tugged him toward the stairs. "Come to bed."

"Sweetheart, I would have killed to get that offer from you a few hundred years ago," he breathed softly in her wake as she pulled him up the stairs.

Ignoring his innuendo she demanded quietly, "How many?"

"Three."

"Oh God, Liam. It's horrible if you have to dispose of one." She stopped beside the bed. "Undress."

Regan could see the signs of pain registering on his face and he didn't argue. He climbed into bed and pulled the covers up before he evaporated his jeans, t-shirt and every other article of clothing from his body.

Tears flowed freely from her eyes, knowing what was to come. How could she bear to see him suffer...again? And three times worse than she had ever seen it before. Regan took up her usual place on the floor beside his bed for her vigil, closing her eyes briefly to gear herself up for a tense few hours.

"Hey," Liam's husky voice sounded from the edge of the bed as his hand reached out to stroke her cheek softly. "Don't cry for me, Regan. I can take it. I'm used to it."

She didn't answer as she opened her eyes and the tears flowed faster. He might be resigned to what was to come, but Regan didn't think she could ever get used to watching Liam in pain.

"Go home. I want you to. I'll be fine tomorrow." His fingers wiped away her tears, but they continued to stream from her troubled blue eyes.

"No."

"Yes. Go now."

"Absolutely not."

"Stubborn." His voice was starting to slur and he pulled his hand back as he curled inward to absorb the pain.

Backlash!

It was already starting with a vengeance.

"With you...I have to be stubborn." Regan's chin came up and she ground her teeth as she stroked his wayward hair away from his face. She wasn't about to leave him when he needed her.

"Ah...fuck!" Liam shouted as he started to shiver and Regan flinched as his body buckled and thrashed.

Shit. She hated this. Regan had been through this numerous times before with Liam after he had needed to take the life of a *fallen*. He felt backlash pain every time he took a life. Any life. It didn't matter that he was ridding the world of evil. Backlash was guaranteed any time a vampire healer killed. And three? Dear God, it was painful when he had to extinguish one *fallen*. This was going to be bad.

Really bad.

The intensity of the attack kept getting worse over the next ten minutes. Liam was incoherent and writhing on the bed. Regan knew the fact that he hadn't fed wasn't helping and she cursed his disdain for feeding. Damn it. Why did he have to be so...so...moral? Any other time she might have laughed at the thought, but she wasn't rational when it came to Liam being in horrible pain.

Liam was usually coherent during backlash. Hurting, certainly, but nothing like this. He usually talked his way through it while she stayed beside his bed and tried to take his mind off his discomfort until he could fall into the oblivion of day sleep.

I feel so damn powerless! And I'm a mage healer.

A mage healer. She *was* a mage healer, and although healing a vampire wasn't exactly her specialty, Regan wondered if one of her spells might work on him and help relieve some of his misery.

Regan tried to think rationally, her thoughts frantically going over various options. Maybe she could try something to throw him into his day sleep early...and he could drink from her. Her power was nothing compared to Liam's, but her blood was certainly stronger than a human's.

She didn't hesitate as she stood and pulled her pink tank top over her head and shoved her jeans down her legs. Kicking them off, she slid quickly into the bed beside Liam, clad in only a delicate pink bra and panties. Body to body contact might help. She would use any benefit she could get from being close to him. She wasn't sure this would work on a vampire, but she needed her healing magic to connect with him.

Regan chanted the familiar spell without thinking about it as she scooted up against Liam's thrashing, groaning body. *Oh God, please let this work. I can't stand to see him like this.* Her heart was aching as she finished reciting the magical words of the spell, willing her strength and power into his body as she wiggled against him, her back to his front.

Yanking her hair aside, she reached behind her and pulled his face against her neck. "Bite me, Liam." Her command was firm and loud, hoping his instinct would take over. "Take my blood."

She closed her eyes, willing him to strike her neck. His body straightened as his arm encircled her waist and his lips nuzzled the vulnerable skin of her neck.

Yes. Take what you need. Bite. Please.

Regan nudged back and stretched her naked skin against his. She shivered as the light hair on his thighs and chest abraded her smooth skin. His body was blazing hot and now firm against hers, turning them both into a furnace. She pushed against him, willing him to take what she offered, begging him to take it. Cocking her head to one side to allow him better access, she pressed her hand more firmly to the back of his head.

"Regan," she heard his tortured groan as his tongue traced her vein before he sunk his fangs into her exposed skin.

The initial strike was painful and her body tensed with the shock, but the slow suck and draw lulled her into a place of pleasure that she had never experienced before. She squirmed against him and buried her fingers into his hair as she encouraged him to take whatever he needed from her.

She tried to concentrate on her magic, but the experience was so erotic and her body so heated that she wanted to reach her other hand into her panties and find release. Her body arched back into him and she released a hungry moan. "Liam." His name came out soft and breathy.

Regan swallowed a squeak of frustration as she felt him disconnect and close the tiny puncture wounds. His warm palm moved in a soothing, circular motion over her quivering belly as his tongue continued to lap at the punctures, laving over the tiny wound in sensual circles.

He finally buried his face in her hair at the side of her neck, panting wildly. "Did you know?" he asked her in a breathless, husky voice that was coherent but still filled with pain.

Confused but relieved that her idea had worked and he was talking, she replied, "Know what?"

"That we're mates."

His voice was demanding and she couldn't deny it. It wasn't a guess. Somehow, he knew the truth. "Yes," she admitted in a strangled voice, her body quivering.

His other arm came around her like a vise, locking her firmly against him. Her ass was pressed against something intrusive, large... and extremely hard.

Oh, holy shit! Regan knew exactly how he knew she was his mate. The evidence was pressed firmly against the cheeks of her ass.

The mystery was solved and the secret of releasing a healer's mating instincts was no longer an enigma.

"An intimate act with your chosen mate will release the mating instincts of the vampire healer..."

The act of intimacy was the taking of blood from their chosen mate. Was it always like that, or had it been so sensual only because she was his mate?

"Liam, I--"

Regan never got to finish her statement. Liam flipped her to face him and his mouth covered hers with a ravenous hunger and swiftness that took her breath away. Before she could blink, she was engaged in a kiss so hot that any thoughts she had flew from her mind as his desire, and her own, completely consumed her.

CHAPTER 3

Mine!

Liam's blood was pounding so hard through his body that all he could focus on was the roaring in his ears and the primal desire and possessiveness that swamped his entire being.

Regan. Soft. Feminine. Hot. His to possess, his to claim.

My mate!

There was no technique or skill involved as he claimed her mouth with his and forced his powerful thigh between her silky legs. Raw need raged through him as he ravaged her mouth, his hand behind her head to keep her lips accessible. His nostrils flared as he breathed in her feminine, light floral scent, a fragrance that made his already hard cock twitch and his heart hammer.

He devoured her mouth like a starving man, his tongue marauding, conquering, sweeping the warm cavern, demanding her surrender. He growled in satisfaction as her arms crept around his neck and her tongue entangled with his, giving herself to him.

Not enough. Not nearly enough.

He barely gave them both a chance to breathe before he rolled her beneath him, desperate to stake his claim. Groaning with the satisfaction of having her pinned beneath him, he continued to own her lips and mouth, nibbling at her lips and then going back inside to insist she cede to his dominance.

His hands wandered over her body, over her hips, touching every bare inch that he could access. His mind was lost in his need to conquer this woman, make her his in every conceivable way.

His whirling brain tried to process the onset of a humming numbness that slowly crept over his body. Liam snarled, trying to fight the onset of day sleep.

No! Not now. He needed. Had to have...

"Liam?"

He registered Regan's soft, concerned voice as he rolled onto his back so that he wouldn't crush her.

Liam panted, trying to fight the urge to close his eyes, unable to process what was happening because of the unrelenting tug of day sleep.

Damn it. Not now.

But day sleep would wait for no vampire. It beckoned. He responded.

She knew. Regan betrayed me. She knew that she was my mate.

Liam could feel the backlash still beating at his vulnerable body. His mating instinct had taken over, covered the pain for a time, but now that he was being blanketed with the instinct to sleep...it tore through him again with a vengeance.

As the day sleep yanked him toward darkness, Liam's last conscious thought was that the backlash didn't hurt nearly as bad as the thought of Regan's betrayal and rejection.

His heart bled.

And then he slept.

I stayed with Liam too long.

Regan felt panic rise in her body and adrenaline kick into high gear as she stuffed articles of clothing into her suitcase that sat open in a rocking chair beside her bed. It swayed erratically as she shoved each item into the growing pile. She didn't have any idea what she was packing, she simply opened drawers and threw things into the case until it was nearly too full to close.

She should have left Liam to his day sleep immediately after the success of her spell had thrown him into an early slumber and taken her ass straight home, but she hadn't been able to leave his side and had fallen asleep curled into his body, not waking until an hour ago.

Regan shot a nervous glance at her bedroom window and noticed that the sun was setting. She had to get away from here, as far away from Liam as she could possibly get before he woke. He would track her, find her, and she couldn't risk that.

Sitting on the suitcase to close it, she grasped the tab and zipped it closed. *Screw it.* If she didn't have everything she needed, she would buy it when she was away from Colorado, away from Liam.

Regan wanted to throw herself on the bed and weep, but she didn't have time to give in to the sorrow that was trying to devour her soul. To protect Liam, she had to leave and get herself so lost that she could never be found...by anyone.

Her only other option was to try to convince Liam to reject her, release her. It was an alternative mentioned in The Book Of The Vampire Healer, a choice given only to healers. Somehow, Regan highly doubted that Liam would agree. She knew him well enough to be fairly certain that he would see her as a new responsibility... and he would take it seriously, whether he wanted her as a mate or not. The threat of the league of mage assassins wouldn't even budge the judgment of her stubborn vampire. Actually, it would probably cement his decision, claiming that she needed protection.

Regan grunted as she hefted the heavy suitcase off the chair and dropped it in an upright position. Her hands were trembling as she attached the pull strap to the case so that she could wheel it. The mage were strong, stronger than a human, but the suitcase felt like it was filled with lead. Or maybe it was the fact that the task was abhorrent to her and it was her heart that was full of lead. The thought of never seeing Liam again was tearing her apart, but what other option did she have?

"Going somewhere?" The low, growling voice sliced through Regan like a knife and she spun around to see the object of her thoughts leaning against her bedroom door.

His stance was casual as he rested one shoulder against the door frame, but Regan could sense the tension in his hard, muscular body. Her mouth went dry and her whole body froze. Just this morning she had been pinned beneath that enormous, powerful body and kissed to the point of insanity by those perfect lips that were now forming a small, mocking smile.

"I-I-have to go out of town." Lame. Very lame. But it was the truth...sort of. She looked away, unable to meet his angry gaze. She licked her dry lips and stared at the cream colored wall off to his right. *Be strong. Be strong. If he knows the truth he won't let you leave.*

"And what might that truth be, mate of mine?" Liam snarled as he advanced into the room. "That I'm good enough to have as a friend, but not as a mate?"

Oh, shit. She had forgotten the mind communication between acknowledged mates. She shielded her thoughts, slamming a barrier down to contain her rampant emotions as she answered, "That's not true. Get out of my head, Liam. I don't appreciate having my thoughts read and analyzed by anyone but me." Her eyes shot to his face, furious at his invasion. Big. Mistake. Regan had never seen his face so intense, his eyes so stormy. Instinctively, she backed up as he slowly moved forward like a big cat stalking prey.

"Yes, obviously you don't want to share much of anything with a lowly vampire," Liam snarled back as he crowded her, his body stopping as he literally had her back up against the wall. "Sorry to disappoint you, but you aren't going anywhere." His index finger traced her lips and slowly glided down her neck, stroking the lines of her collar bone. "Discovering my mate has put me in desperate need of a fuck, and I plan on getting what I want."

Regan shivered as his tongue replaced his finger and he licked over the places his fingers had just traveled. His denim-clad thigh slid between hers and she was dizzy from the masculine scent that assaulted her senses. Even angry and uninformed, she wanted him.

She should be feeling insulted by his blunt language and his I'm-taking-what-I-want attitude, but honestly, it heated her blood.

No. No. I can't give in to him. Remembering all of the reasons that she had to flee, Regan pushed hard against his chest. "Liam, stop."

It was like an insect swatting at an elephant. Liam grasped her wrists in one of his hands and trapped her hands over her head, leaving her helpless. Her lower body was ensnared by his strong thigh and her hands were confined. She couldn't keep a moan from escaping as his mouth came down on hers, sweeping her into a dark tunnel of desire and need.

Buttons popped as he tore her blouse open while his lips and tongue continued a relentless, volatile assault, demanding her full surrender. He tasted fiercely male, untamed and wild, and Regan's response was unconditional. She needed this. Needed him. She met his marauding tongue with carnal thrusts of her own that had him groaning into the embrace.

He freed the front clasp of her bra and roamed her breasts, cupping the flesh, teasing the sensitive nipples until Regan could only arch into his hand, begging for more.

Liam ripped his mouth from hers and Regan wanted to weep from the loss. "How does it feel to be touched by the lower class, Regan? I wonder if you'll like getting down and dirty with a vampire instead of the polite sex of a blue blooded mage," Liam panted as he pulled the remnants of her shirt and bra from her body. Her wrists were captured again and placed firmly over her head, making her breasts jut out from her body. He clasped her chin between the fingers of his other hand and forced her gaze to his. "There's nowhere to run. No place that I won't find you," he rasped harshly. "Did you really think that you could run away from me?" The question was rhetorical.

"Liam, I wasn't really running from you. I-"

"Save it! Right now I just want to fuck you. I'll have you screaming my name, begging for it, even if I'm not worthy of being your mate," he told her abruptly as he lowered his mouth to her beaded nipples, nipping and laving them with tortuous, erotic strokes that melted her bones and soaked her panties.

Dear God, she had never seen Liam so fierce, so passionate, but it was her undoing. He was angry at what he believed was her rejection and she couldn't blame him, but maybe it was better if he continued to believe that. Maybe he'd eventually release her so that she could protect him.

Her body was burning with unsated lust and desire. His assault on her aching breasts had her thrusting out her chest for harder contact and she ground her wet core against his thigh.

More. She needed more. "Liam, please." If he wanted a fuck, she'd give him one. If he didn't take her soon, she would probably expire from need. She couldn't separate her needs from his, and she knew she was feeling them both, the force of them nearly leveling her.

He scooped her body up easily, but before she could even begin to enjoy being held against him...he dropped her onto the bed. She watched without shame as he pulled his t-shirt over his head and dropped it onto the floor before he joined her, covering her body with the weight and bulk of his own.

Regan sighed, welcoming his scorching hot body that blanketed her smaller form. She ran her hands over smooth skin and bulging muscle and raised her hips, feeling the steely bulge of cock against denim. She rocked up again, begging for him.

Liam evaporated the rest of their clothes and she moaned as she felt his rock-hard shaft between her legs. She squirmed, trying to get it closer to her core and threaded her fingers through his hair.

"Don't. Touch." Liam grabbed her wrists again and stilled her roving hands above her head. "I don't want you to touch me. This is just about scratching an itch. Getting laid." He let go of her hands, but they remained stretched over her head and locked in place with magic. She yanked, but Liam's magic was powerful and her arms were completely immobile.

Regan recoiled, feeling like Liam had slapped her. She felt the tears forming in her eyes and willed them not to fall. She reminded herself that Liam believed that she had betrayed him, repudiated him, and she longed to tell him the truth, but she bit her lip and remained silent. She had to suck it up and take what Liam could give her right now. And she would. Because she loved him, and she wanted this. If a casual screw was all she could have…she'd take it. Damn it, she wanted one time, one moment of intimacy, one experience of being the object of Liam's desire.

Regan bit back a groan as Liam's hot mouth trailed along the side of her neck and back to her breasts. She thrashed her head as his fingers trailed over her stomach and crawled closer and closer to the place where she needed him the most. "Oh, God, Liam."

"Need something, Regan?" his husky voice asked, his question innocent, but his intent evident. He was going to make her pay.

Her legs slammed shut automatically just as he finally reached the soft hair between her thighs, but Liam parted them again easily and locked them into place just as he had her wrists above her head. Regan wanted to sob as he lightly stroked her wet folds, his fingers delving into her moist depths.

Fingers circled around her clit as his hot mouth devoured her nipples, alternating between the two, bringing them to tight peaks. She moaned and strained against her invisible bonds, "Liam, please."

He removed his fingers from her shivering pussy and positioned himself over her. His breath was hot and uneven against her ear and she trembled as he plunged his hands into her hair and rolled his hips, bringing his burgeoning cock in contact with her swollen clit.

"Tell me what you want," Liam demanded in a voice that Regan had never heard from him before.

"You," she answered honestly, squinting in a room illuminated only by the moonlight now that complete darkness had fallen. She longed to see a look of desire, but she couldn't quite see his eyes. His face looked strained and at the moment she could feel the testosterone percolating in his body, seeping through his pores, and it made every inch of female in her body stand up and take notice. "Please."

"You want me to fuck you? Even though I'm a lowly vampire?"

"Yes. Yes," she whimpered, desperate for his possession. She was a female responding to her mate, and she needed him. Now. Badly.

"Then tell me," he growled. "Beg for it."

"Fuck me, Liam. Please." Regan lifted her hips as far as she could strain with the magic restricting the movement of her limbs.

"At least you want me now." With a carnal noise somewhere between a groan and a snarl, Liam positioned the blunt head of his member to her tight opening and buried himself deep inside her, breaching her virginal sheath and forcing himself between her tight walls.

Oh, God. It hurt. It hurt really badly. Regan was caught between pain and the joy of being joined completely with Liam.

Liam's body froze as his cock came to rest inside the hot, tight cavern, his balls resting against Regan's ass. "Virgin?" he rumbled.

Regan tried to relax her body, breathing through the pain that had become a dull ache. One sharp pain that had quickly receded. "Yes," she breathed softly in his ear, ruffling his hair as she breathed in and out again.

"I don't think I can stop," he rasped, his breathing ragged.

"Don't stop." He couldn't stop. Now that the pain was almost gone, she willed him to move, to quench the desire that roared through her body. She arched her back, letting the coarse hair on his chest abrade her nipples and her hips undulate up into his groin. "Fuck me."

She felt her plea jolt his body into action as he pulled his cock almost completely out of her and slowly sunk back in. "Fuck. You're so tight. So hot. Mine."

Yes. Yes. She was his. She had always been his. Regan longed to wrap her arms and legs around him to claim him. The soreness between her legs didn't dampen her desire for Liam to take her completely.

She felt the shift in the air the very moment he lost control and began a relentless rhythm that made her come apart and shatter. His hips hammered in and out of her slick, tight channel, opening her, asserting his dominance and she relished it.

"Mine. All mine. Never try to run from me. I'll find you. Never let you go." The fevered, possessive words that he chanted mindlessly as he lost himself to passion made the storm of tears that Regan had been holding back flow down her face. "Need to see you come. Come for me." Liam reached between their bodies and stroked her clit as he kept slamming himself home in a frenzied joining.

"Bite me, Liam," she told him urgently, craving the additional intimacy.

His tongue licked over her vein in an erotic swirl that nearly put her over the edge before he obeyed her request and his fangs pierced her tender flesh. "Oh, God, yes," she hissed as the same hot, erotic pulse stole over her body as he sucked her life blood and pounded into her body with equal force.

He pulled his finger from her clit and thrust both of his big hands underneath her ass as her body began to spasm and she screamed his name. He buried himself deep inside her and Regan could feel him trembling as he released, grinding his groin against her center, bringing them tightly together.

Regan's heart was still stuttering from her incredible climax as Liam closed the tiny pinpricks at her neck and rolled onto his back.

"Could…could you release me please?" Regan requested breathlessly.

Her limbs jerked loose abruptly. She closed her legs and brought her arms down, her muscles quivering from the strain and the aftermath of the volatile climax. Wanting to cover herself now that embarrassment was creeping in, she started to roll from the bed, but Liam grabbed her upper arm, bringing her back to lay on her side facing him.

"What's this?" he asked quietly as he stroked her mangled hip.

"Nothing." Regan knew it was a stupid thing to say, but she wasn't sure how to respond. Liam knew exactly what it was and he could see it very clearly in the dark.

Her hands shook at the memory as she tried to bat his fingers away.

His fingers did move, but only so that he could place them at her temple. It took her a few moments to understand what was happening, but by the time she comprehended his intentions….it was too late. She cursed her stupidity as she tried to pull away.

Regan's memory was accessed and she was completely exposed.

CHAPTER 4

I t only took Liam a second or two to find the memory of the branding on Regan's hip, but he knew instantly that it was a nightmare vision that would haunt him forever.

Regan naked with his marking completely exposed on her hip. Regan fighting...but losing the battle. Several mage males and one female holding her down on the floor, her hip exposed. The sizzling brand being held to her hip. Burning flesh. A pained scream. Threats.

Liam flinched and pulled his hand away from her temple, unable to continue seeing Regan's pain. *Coward. She lived it.* But he couldn't watch it anymore.

A red haze formed over his vision and his body tensed as he clenched and unclenched his fists to try to gain control of his fury. "They hurt you. Threatened you."

"Yes." Her voice was barely audible.

"I hurt you," he choked out, his anger and rage barely contained.

There was a slight hesitation before she confirmed. "Yes." Liam heard her suck in a breath before continuing, "But Liam-"

"I couldn't even watch the whole thing," he admitted harshly as his finger stroked over the brand covering his mark.

Mage. One word. One ugly brand covering his entire mark until only a few traces of his colorful marking remained around the very edges of the scarred flesh at her hip.

Dear God, what had he done? Rolling to his back, Liam struggled to find the words to express himself, but his emotions were tempestuous and he couldn't clear the red fog that threatened his sanity.

Beads of sweat trickled from his forehead, soaking Regan's pristine pillow.

Kill. Kill.

The word pounded through his head like a jackhammer, and all Liam wanted were the necks of every person who had harmed his mate.

"Liam, I have to answer the door. It might be someone who needs a healing." The feminine voice seemed to filter to him through a long tunnel, the voice of his mate.

No. Protect. Protect. Kill.

He rolled over to keep Regan on the bed, keep her close, protect her from any harm.

He landed on his stomach with only a comforter beneath him.

Regan was gone.

Regan cinched the heavy cotton robe around her waist with shaky fingers. Liam was scaring her. She wasn't afraid of him, she was frightened for him. He wasn't really hearing her or acknowledging her. Had her mangled hip freaked him out so badly that he wasn't responding? It was ugly, but was it really that bad? Or had it been his glimpse of her memories that had him stunned?

She slipped the chain lock and took a deep breath, hoping that it wasn't a healing request. She really couldn't leave Liam. Another healer would have to be called immediately.

A mage male, probably in his early thirties, came into view as she swung the door open. Recognizing the magic but not the face, she inquired politely, "Can I help you?"

He would probably be considered handsome in mage circles. His light blonde hair was cut in a neat, attractive style and he had aristocratic features with high cheekbones and a sculptured nose and mouth. Probably a little over six foot and lean, he had the usual mage build. He wasn't smiling, but then, the mage rarely smiled.

"Regan Taylor?" His voice wasn't a low, pleasing baritone. It was a tenor with a rather impatient tone.

"Yes."

"I'm actually here to help you. I'm Tom Spencer, the council's choice for your mate." He smirked at her as he strolled into her home without waiting for an invitation.

He was coarse, base and she disliked him immediately. A cold chill was running up her spine as she answered sarcastically, "I'm not ready to receive guests at the moment, as you can see. Perhaps we can meet at another location and time." *Or not!* Definitely...not!

He closed the door and turned to face her, backing her up against the wall as she tried to move away from him. "Right now is good for me. What you have on is also good for me. I want to inspect the merchandise before I buy," he stated arrogantly, as he reached for the tie to her bathrobe.

She nearly gagged as she got a whiff of hard alcohol and pungent aftershave. Ewww... "Get the hell away from me." Regan was pissed off now and pushed him hard enough to move sideways and away from his wandering hands. How dare he come into her home and treat her like an object to be bought and inspected?

"Heard you were a vampire whore, but that can be overlooked, as long as you come from the Taylor line. You're attractive enough and probably could be adequate in bed with some training," he told her flatly, moving closer as she backed into her living room to get away from him.

Regan froze, taken aback by his blunt words. Of course he didn't care, as long as they produced a good lineage. She was a Taylor, he was a Spencer. Two prominent families that were both direct descendants of mage royalty. No matter that neither of those so-called aristocratic families had two pennies to rub together; they would make blue-blooded babies.

Her stomach rolling in disgust, Regan put out an urgent calling spell to her sister, hoping Sasha would bring Nathan along with her. She was going to need help getting this repugnant, vile male mage out of her house. For some unknown reason, he already thought he owned her, and he obviously wasn't leaving by request. Tom was older and male, but Regan would be damned if the vile creature would be disrobing her for inspection. She'd already gone through *that* at the hands of the council. No way was some beady-eyed, drunk, male mage pawing her like she was property and nothing more.

Her ass hit the couch and she groped wildly to come up with something, anything to bash him on the head hard enough to stop his progress. Her hand came up with a flower pot of artificial stone. Not as heavy as she would have liked but...

The flower pot stopped in mid-swing as a low, menacing growl came from the other side of the room. Regan's head jerked to the bedroom door to see Liam, dressed in a black t-shirt and jeans, his eyes red, his face nearly unrecognizable, and completely ready to go in for the kill.

"Liam?" *Please hear me. Don't kill the revolting mage. He's not worth the backlash.*

The carnality of the noise rose to a menacing snarl and Regan reacted. She swung the pot with all her strength against the head of the unsuspecting Tom Spencer, and it was hard enough to knock him from his feet. As he sprawled to the floor, Regan threw herself over Tom as she pleaded, screaming, "No, Liam. Don't do it. He's not worth it."

Her fingernails dug into the leather of Tom's jacket as Liam sprung, trying to yank her from Tom's body as he growled, "Kill. Protect."

Just as she was about to give way, the pressure released and she heard several voices screaming curses. She couldn't decipher exactly what voices were hurling what violent oaths, but she relaxed slightly as she recognized Nathan.

Stumbling to her feet, Regan quickly took in the six additional bodies, three male, three female, in her small living room. Nathan, Ethan and Rory had a hold on Liam, while Brianna, Callie and Sasha looked on in horror as Liam suddenly broke his brothers' holds and rushed for Tom.

"Jesus Christ! He's like a vampire on steroids." Nathan grunted as he tried and failed to hold Liam again with the help of his brothers.

Regan's living room was utter and complete chaos as the brothers struggled, trying to keep Liam from getting in any more hits on Tom, who was still sprawled on the carpet in shock.

Regan lunged toward Tom, ready to throw herself on top of him again, but Sasha, Brianna and Callie held her back, away from the flying limbs and thrashing bodies of the Hale brothers.

"He can't kill him. He can't kill him." Regan tugged, trying desperately to break free, but her sister held her back, grasping her tightly around the waist to keep her from running forward.

"Stop, Regan," Sasha told her in her severe, big sister voice. "Let the guys handle this."

It really didn't look like the guys were handling anything. Fists were flying and Liam was coming out on top, repeatedly making his way back to Tom in his furious attempt to snuff out his life.

"ENOUGH!"

The whole room rocked from the booming order and everybody stopped whatever they were doing, including Regan. She tried to move, but she was locked into place, frozen, unable to even twitch her little finger.

Holy hell. What now?

If she could have moved, she would have instinctively stepped back from the form that suddenly appeared in her line of vision, a man who meant business and radiated power that pulsed through the entire room. Shit. He was massive. Strangely enough, he moved his hugely muscled body with the grace of a dancer, strolling casually over to Liam and placing his hand on Liam's shoulder. "Time for you to cool off, my friend." The voice was still powerful, but Regan swore she heard a twinge of empathy in the statement.

Liam vanished without another word, leaving the man to lower his arm back to his side. "I believe it's safe now. You will all stay calm."

"Where's Liam?" Regan demanded the moment she could speak again. "What have you done?"

She stepped in front of the strange male, craning her neck to see his face. His expression was as hard as stone. He didn't look any older than his mid-thirties, but his eyes gave away the fact that he was ancient. Those eyes spoke of knowledge, infinite knowledge and endless wisdom. Definitely vampire, with his signature brown eyes and dark hair that was cut almost military short, making his sharp features appear even more severe than they already were.

The black jeans that molded to his lower body, the black steel-toe biker boots and a black t-shirt just added to his menacing demeanor, but Regan scowled up at him, determined to find Liam.

The big man's lips twitched slightly as he answered, "Your mate is safe, someplace that he can't hurt himself or anyone else."

"I want to see him," she demanded, frantic to find out if Liam was really okay. He hadn't exactly looked normal, sane or safe for that matter. "And who in the hell are you? And why did you move him?"

His lips twitched again as he stared down at her from his elevated height. "So demanding, little one? I will eventually take you to Liam, if you still want to see him. He isn't exactly-" he hesitated before adding, "himself right now." He placed his beefy hand on her shoulder and Regan felt an instant calming sensation. Her pulse slowed and her body relaxed as he continued. "I am known as Daric, Prince Of The Vampire Healers. I was your mate's mentor and teacher in his youth."

Nathan, Ethan and Rory instantly dropped to one knee and bowed their heads as they all uttered in unison, "Your Highness."

"Oh, for God's sake, get up." Daric's booming voice rose as he removed his hand from Regan's shoulder and motioned for the brothers to rise. "I'm not into all that royalty gibberish. You are all fierce warriors and don't need to kneel for anyone. Call me Daric."

Regan nearly smiled. Daric actually looked embarrassed.

"With all due respect, Daric, where is my brother?" Nathan asked as he rose to his feet, Rory and Ethan rising at almost the same time. "And how in the hell did he get that strong?"

"Why are you calling Regan his mate?" Rory inquired in a confused voice.

"She's my intended mate," Tom squawked from his seated position on the floor, finally finding his voice.

"You..," Daric's eyes were intense as he glared at Tom, "are leaving." Daric flipped his hand as though he was batting away a fly and Tom disappeared.

Regan didn't bother to ask where Tom had been sent. She really didn't care. Even for a mage...he was disgusting.

Daric walked slowly towards the Hale brothers, his hands clasped behind his back. "To answer Nathan's question, Liam has always been strong, but his power is usually put into his healing."

"I've never seen him....like that." Rory gulped as he tried to comprehend the fact that Liam had an enormous amount of power. "He's my twin. I should have known."

Daric stopped in front of the three brothers as he remarked, "There are a lot of things that you all should have known, but Liam thought it was in your best interests to remain ignorant of some of the facts of his life." He looked at each brother as he added, "I disagree. I think being informed is the best protection for all of you." He waved his hand in the air. "Watch and learn."

Regan's eyes were riveted to the images that sprang forth. It was almost like watching a big screen television suspended in the air.

Liam's life rolled by, scene after scene, while seven pairs of eyes stayed glued to the images, gaping expressions on all seven faces.

Daric had to explain some of the scenes as they played, but Regan knew about most of them and some, like the backlash experiences, she had actually witnessed up close and personal.

Good or bad, Liam's secrets were being revealed.

CHAPTER 5

The screen disappeared as the last episode of backlash flashed away. Daric eyed Rory as he asked quietly, "Not the grand life that you imagined your twin had, is it?"

Rory shook his head, his expression wistful, "I always thought he was the lucky one. Now I realize he wasn't." Rory sighed as he continued, "I always imagined he went away to a grand adventure when he was gone for long periods of time when we were young. I was jealous."

"In reality, he went away for weeks at a time for healer training. It's not a grand adventure. It's hell. You've seen some of it," Daric replied.

"Yeah...I guess I was really the lucky one. I had a childhood. I had friends. And I had Ethan and Nathan."

"Being a healer is a load of responsibility at a very young age and it's a lonely life. There is nothing grand about it," Daric remarked gravely.

"I still don't understand why he didn't tell us about the backlash," Nathan muttered, obviously irritated.

"Because he feared that if you knew that he would pay with pain for killing a *fallen*, you wouldn't call him when you were in trouble. He didn't want to take the risk of losing one of his brothers," Daric commented quietly. "He was protecting you all in his own way. He never wanted anyone to know about his pain."

Regan squirmed, feeling guilty that she did know, but kept Liam's secret.

"Don't," Daric said sternly as he gave her an understanding look. "You're a good mate and kept Liam's secrets as he requested. You honor him." He crossed his arms over his massive chest. "I, however, am a prince of my people. I have no such qualms about blurting out his life story if I think it's for his benefit."

"Liam's found his mate. He'll get his soul and a partner. He won't be lonely anymore," Callie exclaimed in wonder. Callie and Brianna were both grinning, but Sasha's expression was cautious and subdued.

"Liam has a soul. Mating is different for a healer. It's a blood bond," Regan murmured absently, knowing that Liam could never truly be her mate.

The room erupted with chatter, questions all being asked at the same time. Daric held up his hand and the room quieted, allowing him to explain the basic mating rules of the healer.

"Holy shit!" Rory exclaimed loudly as Daric finished. "So it really is a miracle that Liam and Regan found each other."

"Liam found his mate because it was meant to be," Daric answered with a shrug of his mammoth shoulders. "He's the first deserving healer in a very long time. He put his people first and served long and tirelessly. He deserves his mate if that's what he wants." He shot Regan a stern, knowing glance as he finished.

She fidgeted nervously, her voice nearly inaudible as she admitted, "I can't mate with him. The league of mage assassins will kill him if I do."

"That's bullshit. Liam needs his mate. You can't just abandon him," Nathan snarled. "It's not like we can't protect you."

"Quiet!" Daric shouted abruptly. "Don't judge her." He gave Nathan a sharp glance as he waved his hand. "Watch."

The big screen television returned, but this time the image was of the incident that Regan had gone through with the council. Daric hid her nude body, but he didn't tone down the violence of the attack and subsequent painful branding.

Regan turned her head, trying to block the images and stay deaf to her own tortured screams. She rubbed her hip, still feeling the burn, still smelling the burned flesh. "Please, Daric. Stop," she choked out as she turned pleading eyes to the prince.

The images immediately disappeared, but six sets of eyes watched her.

"Where was Regan's protection during that episode?" Daric asked sarcastically as he turned his gaze to Nathan. He sighed loudly as he shook his head. "You are a brave warrior, Nathan, but your temper and rush to judge can sometimes cloud your common sense. Had you planned better the other night and not rushed in to eradicate the mass of *fallen* while being led by anger, Liam probably wouldn't have needed to kill. You're smart, but rash when it comes to killing the *fallen*."

"But-" Sasha rushed to defend her mate.

"No, Sasha. He's right," Nathan said grimly. "My hatred of the *fallen* consumes me at times. I need to get control of it. I can dust the bastards without being stupid. I should have planned better. I should never let my anger and resentment consume me to the point where I put any of my brothers at risk. It won't happen again."

Daric's mouth turned up slightly in an approving smile. "Well said, warrior. You have reason for your hatred, but let common sense be your guide and you will get the best revenge."

"I'm so sorry, Regan. Sorry we weren't there for you. If I had known, we all would have protected you. I understand you were just trying to protect Liam and I'm sorry we couldn't keep you from suffering." Nathan spoke quietly, his voice vibrating with remorse. "Will you mate with him?"

"I don't know," Regan answered honestly. "I love him. I want to. But I'm afraid of the council's revenge. I couldn't live with myself if anything happened to Liam."

"Why didn't the league of assassins come after me when I mated with Sasha?" Nathan asked curiously.

"I don't know."

"I do," Daric answered. "Regan is a possible weapon against the mage. They need to keep her in the mage circle. For her, the council is willing to risk the wrath of the vampires by sending in the league of assassins."

"What do you mean?" Regan questioned with a perplexed expression.

"If you had looked very closely at your mating mark before it was defiled, you would have noticed a very tiny sword being carried in the claws of the dragon. That sword is a sign of a protector, a very rare mating mark for a vampire. It means if the mating is ever completed, the female mate will become a protector of the vampire, able to protect the vampire against harm from her people. You, my dear Regan, will always have the power to protect yourself or any of your vampire kin against the mage." Daric finished and laid his hands on Regan's shoulders in a gesture of comfort.

"How?" Regan questioned, shocked by Daric's incredible revelation.

"You will be able to spell the jewelry you make with a spell of protection after your mating. Mating will release your power as a protector. You will know how after you are mated."

"Oh, God. I can protect Liam. And my vampire family," she sputtered wildly, hardly daring to believe it was true.

"Yes. You can truly make your choice without any other influence," Daric smiled down at her like he was speaking to a treasured child.

"I choose Liam," she exclaimed excitedly. "I'm just not sure he will want to choose me," she muttered in a more restrained tone. "He still has the option of rejecting me."

Daric's eyebrows raised almost to his hairline as he said wryly, "I don't think that will be a problem. He's in such a desperate state right now because he cares too much. However, it might be hard to convince him, but now that you've made your choice, I hope that you can. He's past the point of no return, Regan. You need to reach him or he will not survive."

Regan's heart stuttered and she could feel the palpitations begin as her gaze shot to Daric's sad eyes, "What do you mean when you say he won't survive?" she asked breathlessly.

"If he can't reject you, which I already know he can't, and if you don't mate within the next few days, he will die. Liam needs to either mate or reject. He can't reject you because he wants you. On the other hand, he thinks he has done you unforgivable harm and doesn't want you to take him as a mate out of pity. It will take some convincing."

Regan felt the fear wrap its icy hands around her heart, but she shoved it away. Failure was not an option. "I don't know all of the details for the mating." She gave Daric a pleading look.

"And I will be glad to explain," he told her patiently. "In private," he added, giving everyone else in the room a get-lost-now look that no one would dare to ignore.

Regan hugged everyone quickly, giving her sister Sasha an extra squeeze. "Don't let him go until he does the deed," Sasha whispered urgently in her ear before she and Nathan transported away, followed by Ethan and Brianna.

"Tell him I'm sorry. Tell him...I love him. Please don't let him die," Rory said in a low, graveled voice filled with remorse as he hugged her tightly.

Regan pulled back and looked into the face that looked so much like Liam's as she answered, "I will. But he knows, Rory. And he loves you. More than you know." In a stronger voice she added, "You can tell him yourself later. That stubborn vampire is going to be mine. Lord help him."

Rory gave her a ghost of a smile as Callie wrapped her arms around him and they faded away.

Regan took a deep breath and turned to Daric. His face was solemn as he looked down at her and put his hand lightly on her hip. Slightly confused by his action, she started to pull away as she felt a mild burning sensation under his fingers. "You're fixing my mark." Understanding dawned and her face lit up as he pulled his hand away.

"It's already fixed," Daric corrected her arrogantly.

"Thank you, Daric. Thank you. I hated the brand. I missed Liam's mark so much." In her excitement, Regan jumped up and threw her arms around his thick neck in gratitude, and planted a loud, smacking kiss to his cheek.

He patted her back gently and Regan could have sworn she saw a slight blush as she pulled away from him. The big guy wasn't such a hard ass after all. "You care about Liam."

Daric shrugged. "I wouldn't be getting involved if I didn't care about the outcome. I don't want him to fuck this up. No vampire healer has gotten this opportunity in the last thousand years."

"You're not mated?"

"No."

Regan sensed that there was more that Daric could add, but she didn't push. "So, tell me what I need to know."

"It's getting close to sunrise, so I will go over it with you quickly. I will take you to him at sunset. Until then, I will make sure you are guarded from the mage," he informed her, his expression and tone telling her not to argue. "This won't be an easy task for you, little one. Liam can be stubborn when it comes to doing the right thing, even if it brings harm or death to him."

Regan didn't need easy, she just needed Liam. "Tell me something I don't know. Believe me, I've dealt with his stubborn butt many times and I can be just as cranky as he can. I'm ready."

Daric cocked his head and he gave her a mysterious smile as he answered, "Yes, I believe you are."

By the time the sun began to rise over the mountains, Daric was gone and Regan was armed and ready with information.

She crawled into her bed and breathed in the residual scent of Liam with a small, happy smile before she fell into an uninterrupted slumber.

CHAPTER 6

Liam's eyes popped open the minute the sun descended behind the surrounding mountains, surprised to find himself in his own bed.

Trapped. Can't get out. Can't kill the mage that tried to harm my mate.

Recognition dawned and Liam remembered the entire incident clearly, remembered his mate throwing herself over the mage to protect her kin.

Daric had confined him to his own bedroom, in his own house. Liam sat back against the headboard. He was still seeing red...literally.

"Good. You're awake." Liam's angry eyes looked up at Daric as he strolled into the room, wanting to kill the prince for confining him.

"Lift the confinement," Liam demanded, fists clenched and body tense.

"After the mating, my friend."

"There will be no mating. Regan will never accept me now and she's been through more than she should have to bear. I practically raped her. She went through hell just because she wears my mark and wanted to protect me. She threw herself on top of the mage to protect him from me while I was in a mating rage. I'm nothing more than an animal to her." Liam's voice shook with anger and resentment.

Liam had no more finished his statement when a large *crack* rang through the air and his head jerked sideways from a powerful blow. What the hell? He rubbed his hand over the side of his face, wincing as he poked at his jaw.

Eyes wide, Liam jerked his head up to his prince, stating with fascinated surprise, "You just bitch slapped me." Daric had always been a stern but wise teacher, and he had never resorted to violence.

"Boy, I'll bitch slap you into next week if you don't change your attitude. Now!" Daric thundered as he towered over Liam with a scowl. "Regan jumped on that slimy mage to keep you from killing him, but not for his benefit. She didn't want you to suffer the backlash."

"No, Liam. He's not worth it."

Liam heard her cry clearly, as if she were standing right next to him. Was it possible that she had been protecting him? He shook his head in denial as he replied flatly, "There's no way she could forgive me. I hurt her. She told me. Hell...I can't even forgive myself. And the torture she went through at the hands of the mage because she wore my mark-"

"She wants to be your mate," Daric interrupted, crossing his arms over his chest. "You will mate."

"No." Liam crossed his arms and glared at Daric. "She hates me. It would make her miserable. It would be better if I were removed from her life permanently."

"Then refuse her."

"I can't." Oh, hell no. Liam loved and wanted Regan so much that he could never force the words from his mouth that would release her. It wasn't physically possible. He could only refuse her if he truly didn't want her.

"You'll die."

"I don't care. That way her problem would be solved."

"Gah...I give up. Stubborn idiot vampire healer," Daric threw his hands in the air and stalked out of the room, easily able to breach the invisible barrier that held Liam prisoner. Of course...

Daric had created it - no surprise that he could walk right through his own magic.

Liam flopped back against the pillows, waiting for the inevitable. There was no way he was going to tie Regan to him and he couldn't refuse her. His fate was sealed. Now all he had to do was wait.

"Liam?"

The soft, gentle voice of his mate surprised Liam enough for him to quickly glance toward the entrance of his bedroom...a move that he instantly regretted. Vampire healer matings did not require witnesses and he understood why as soon he looked at Regan. He would kill any male that looked at his mate in the silvery silk gown that she was wearing. It hugged her body, hiding nothing as she walked slowly toward the bed. Slithering over her body like a second skin, the light silk outlined every incredible inch of her feminine form.

Take. Possess. Mine.

Fuck! Liam jerked his head away. He should demand that she leave, but he deserved the torture after the way he had treated Regan and the pain that she had gone through on his behalf. He would give her a chance to berate him if she needed it. He'd always give her anything she needed.

"Look at me, Liam. Please." Her request was compelling, but he wasn't sure that he could look at her and not jump her like a rampant wild animal. It was difficult enough to just be in the same room, hearing her voice.

"I can't, Regan. I'll want to touch you." Yeah, like he didn't want *that* already?

He felt the bed dip slightly as she replied, "I think it will be difficult to mate if you don't touch me, Liam."

"No mating." Liam clenched his jaw and tightened his fists. "I would think your first experience would have been enough to convince you that you don't want me for a mate."

"My only regret is that I couldn't touch you that time. I want to do that now. Can I touch you, Liam?" Her wistful voice socked Liam in the gut. His mouth as dry as a desert, he couldn't have answered, even if he knew what to say.

Regan was already in the bed and moving slowly toward him. Her tiny hand slid to his bicep and stroked lightly, caressing up and down his tense muscles before moving hesitantly toward his chest.

Oh, fuck. Just shoot me now and get it over with!

As Regan's hand got bolder and her nails lightly trailed through the dusting of hair on his chest, Liam decided right then and there that he would rather deal with the backlash of killing a dozen *fallen* than with the light caresses and incredible scent of this one tiny woman.

He probably wouldn't have to wait to die of the unresolved mating conflict wearing on his body slowly until he expired…because Regan, ah Regan…Liam swore she was slowly edging him toward death by heart attack, and if she didn't take that hot little hand from his body soon, he'd be dead in the next few minutes.

"You're so hard everywhere," Regan whispered as her hand slowly trailed over the broad planes of Liam's chest. Every place she touched was firm, solidly muscled. His body fascinated her and she delighted in the feel of warm skin over tight muscle. She was a healer and had seen male bodies with little or no clothing, but she had never seen a male like Liam.

"Yeah. Hard. Everywhere," Liam strangled a reply, sounding like he was in severe pain.

Regan had to bite her lip to keep from smiling. She knew she was tweaking the tail of the beast. She was no siren or seductress, but she must be doing something right. There was a large tent underneath the sheet and comforter. Extremely large. Pulling the covers back with her other hand, she continued her exploration down his ripped abdomen, following the path of dark hair past his navel.

"Oh, God...no wonder it hurt," Regan blurted out before she could stop herself. His cock had been unveiled and it was standing at full attention. Swollen and erect, the phallus looked like a lethal weapon and she couldn't stop herself from curling her hand around the shaft and noticing that her fingers didn't even meet.

Velvet over steel. Her fingers moved over the bulging veins and reverently stroked the soft skin of the rock hard member.

Liam's hips surged upward as she touched the leaking mushroom shaped head, spreading the moisture over the tip. Regan licked her dry lips, longing to find out how he tasted.

Images flitted through her mind, pictures of her taking him between her lips and sucking, stroking him with her tongue. Regan was startled when she realized that they weren't her thoughts, her ideas. Liam's thoughts, that he had previously been blocking, were bursting into her brain while he was struggling to maintain control.

She mimicked the mental visions and lowered her head, licking the salty tip, before taking him between her lips.

Liam released a feral groan before sinking his hands into her hair and guiding her head so that her mouth moved up and down on his shaft. He pumped his hips up and moved her head down as she swallowed more and more of his cock as his movements became more furious. She lightly fingered his balls as she pressed her tongue tightly against his thrusting cock.

"I can't last. Have to come," Liam cried desperately as his hands tried to guide her head away from his pulsating shaft.

His thoughts didn't show me moving. She saw herself swallowing every drop. She wanted every drop. Just as he started to release, Regan took as much of his massive cock as she could and let the hot fluid flow into her throat, keeping him trapped in the moist, hot cavern of her mouth.

"Oh, fuck!" Liam bucked up and grasped her head, holding her mouth to him as he thrashed in the grips of a powerful orgasm.

Regan's heart hammered and her womb clenched as she tasted every drop, licking the warm fluid from his twitching member. He tasted so good, so very good, and her body was tingling with sensual delight as his body relaxed.

Regan's body was burning with the need for Liam to possess her as she shimmied up beside him. "Mate with me, Liam."

"You need to leave, Regan. Now!" Liam's voice was ragged and hoarse, as though he were fighting for control.

She turned on her back, ready to wait as long as she needed for him to change his mind. "I'm not leaving this room until we're mated or you reject me. Maybe I'm not exactly the woman you wanted, but I would like to think that being with me is a better alternative than death," she huffed, trying not to be hurt by Liam's reluctant attitude.

Actually, she had very little time to think about anything at all. Liam was on her, over her, before she could really process her emotions. He threw one strong thigh over her legs and his torso and chest came down roughly over hers, leaving her only enough space to breathe. With an elbow and arm on each side of her head, he effectively pinned her to the bed with his face only inches from hers.

His eyes were wild, his lips frowning and Regan swore she could feel his thundering heartbeat over her breasts, his breathing erratic, as though he were hungry for oxygen. "Do you want to experience the same thing you had last night, Regan? Do you want to be taken by a man who can't control his obsession for you, because I guarantee it won't be much different today than it was yesterday."

She blinked up at him in wide-eyed fascination, her pussy flooding as she watched his struggle, his desperation for her. It was the hottest thing she had ever seen in her life and being the object of his desire was intoxicating. "Yes, please," she squeaked.

His animalistic gaze met hers and Regan could see the muscles in his jaw twitching as he growled, "This is not a joke. I basically raped you yesterday, took your virginity without any care. I want you with the same intensity today as I did yesterday. Or maybe even worse. I want to dominate and fuck you until you are so sated and weak that you can't move from this bed. And then I'll want to do it all over again."

Regan struggled to maneuver her arm inside of his prison so that she could lay her hand on his rough cheek. His whole body was seething and trembling, a cauldron of testosterone gone wild. "First of all, you didn't rape me, Liam. I wanted what happened. If I didn't, I could have easily put out a call for Sasha just like I did when Tom acted like an ass. It wasn't as if I was helpless."

His smoldering stare met hers and Regan saw a flicker of rational thought as he rasped, "Why didn't you?"

"I just told you, I wanted it. You going all caveman on me was like my most fantastic wet dream or fantasy," she told him honestly. "Just because you haven't felt sexual desire for me until now doesn't mean I haven't felt it for you. I have."

His expression was startled as he questioned softly, "You have?"

"Oh yeah, vampire. I touch myself thinking about you having your way with me," she told him bluntly as she traced the outline of his lips with her index finger. "I've never really wanted a man so desperately until I met you. I love you, Liam. I probably have for some time, even when I thought it was hopeless."

Liam broke her gaze and rested his forehead against her shoulder, his big body shaking as he answered, "This is a lifetime decision, Regan, and it will probably be eternal since you will be bonded to me. Are you sure you really want me for a mate? Don't do this if you don't. I couldn't bear it if you ended up resenting me or hating me."

"You're everything I've ever wanted, Liam." Regan's tone was melancholy as she fondled his hair thoughtfully. "I just hope you never regret it."

Liam's head came up and he speared her with a look so intense, so dark, that Regan's jaw dropped.

"I would never regret having you," his angry voice rumbled. "I love you with every beat of my heart, every breath. Do you think I could ever consider myself anything other than a lucky bastard if I had you for a mate, if you could forgive me for what happened to you and the things I said last night?"

He loves me. He loves me.

Regan's racing heart nearly jumped from her chest at his declaration. Liam's mouth crashed down to hers, sweeping her into a kiss of pure possession and raw need. She moaned into the embrace as his tongue devoured and conquered, demanding that she submit to him. Regan toppled and became pliant under him, relishing his power and desire.

Liam broke off the scorching embrace with a grunt and sat her up to lift off her silky gown, and toss it away. "Mine," he insisted with carnal ownership.

Regan shivered at her fierce, primitive response to his possessiveness. The response of a mate to her partner's dominance. "Yes," she agreed softly, her whole body quivering for him to take her. Lying back against the pillow, Regan sent him a come-take-me look as his eyes met hers and his hands wandered over her body, his fingers zeroing in on his mark.

"My mark," he said, his tone touched with awe as he stroked the colorful pattern of the dragon.

"Daric fixed it. Isn't he awesome?" she breathed softly.

"No. He is not awesome. Not to you. He is a good prince. I am the only man who you think is awesome," he replied, his voice demanding and guttural.

Caveman. Liam had definitely gone caveman. Regan bit her lip as desire fired through her body and shot straight to her pussy. "I need you, Liam," she panted as his hand moved up her inner thigh, stroking the soft, sensitive skin.

"I need to taste you first. The scent of your arousal is driving me mad," he told her urgently as he spread her legs wide, leaving her pussy exposed and vulnerable to him.

Regan squirmed, her body burning with need. Dear God, she needed the feel of him between her thighs before she incinerated.

His fingers trailed over her hips as his head lowered, his hot breath streaming over the tiny blonde curls of her mound. Regan clenched her fists at her side, willing him to stroke her core, to ease the driving ache that was tearing her apart.

She whimpered at the first touch of his tongue against her slippery slit. He lapped gently, laving her from bottom to top, sipping her juices like nectar.

Not enough. Not enough.

Out of her mind with the need to climax, Regan finally grasped his head and pulled it tight against her pussy, grinding her hips against his mouth.

Liam retaliated immediately, throwing her hands above her head and locking them in place with fur-lined shackles that bound her magically to the headboard of the massive bed. She yanked and groaned in protest as he murmured, "I want to enjoy my feast. I will satisfy you, mate."

Now. Now. I need it now.

Regan panted as Liam thoroughly explored her, running his tongue over every inch of her quivering, pink flesh. He circled her swollen bud until Regan was ready to scream in frustration. Her hips rose, undulating, begging for relief.

"Mine," Liam muttered, vibrating her clit as his mouth closed over her and his teeth nipped lightly.

"Oh, God. Liam, please." Regan's head thrashed and she jerked at her wrist restraints.

His hands slid effortlessly beneath her and gripped her ass, bringing her begging core against his face as he flicked his tongue along her exposed clit. Harder and harder. Faster and faster.

Regan cried out, the pleasure almost unbearable. She gripped the restraints and dug her nails into the chain, needing something to ground her, to keep her from flying apart.

Her belly clenched as the spasms struck her hard and fast. Her channel contracted and released as fresh juices flowed with her stunning climax. Liam's mouth closed over her, licking leisurely as she spiraled down from her ecstasy.

"I'm not completely sure I know the precise mating procedure," Liam whispered, his voice hoarse, as he spread open-mouthed kisses along her thighs.

"Just join our marks and speak the mating pledge. Daric said you would know instinctively," Regan replied breathlessly, her legs trembling from his touch and the aftermath of her orgasm.

He rose to his knees between her legs, lightly tracing the mark on her hip. "Beautiful. So beautiful on you, Regan," he choked out in a raw declaration as he turned out his arm and matched the identical markings.

Regan didn't know his native language, but his words were lyrical and sweet. The warmth from their matched marks spread quickly through her body, consuming her with the intensity of her need and desire for Liam to fill her. As he finished his pledge, her back arched as the mating heat took control. She wrapped her legs around his waist, trying to pull him down into her, needing his cock to fill her empty channel.

Their eyes met and Regan knew her eyes mirrored his, exposing the raw need to join. "Fuck me, Liam."

He reached for her, flipping her body over, dissolving the restraints before he rolled her to her stomach. "Need to fill you deep, so deep that you know who you belong to," Liam grunted as his arm came around her waist like a vise, supporting her shaking, fiery body.

He spread her legs wide, leaving her open to him, his to take. He barely paused at the tight entrance as he buried his cock into her wet channel. They groaned together, relieved to be joined. Regan pushed her ass back, wanting every inch even though she was already completely filled. There was no pain, just the intense, tight pressure of his cock opening and stretching her, binding them together.

"Mine!" Liam rumbled as he grasped her hips, keeping her steady. He pulled almost all the way out and slammed into her again. Regan gasped at the forcefulness of his repeated strokes, his body claiming her, owning her. Her arms and head dropped into the pillow, leaving her ass in the air as Liam's strokes became needier, faster, and deeper. Regan dug her fingers into the pillow as her body rocked back into his reflexively, needing his rough claiming.

Liam's body came down to blanket hers and his hands slid to her shoulders to keep her from sliding into the headboard from the pistoning of his hips. Regan shuddered as he lifted her hair, moving it to her other shoulder, his tongue licking the side of her neck in hungry swirls.

"Mine forever, my love," Liam whispered softly as his fangs slid into the side of her neck with a slight pinch, unleashing a huge burst of erotic heat that spread through her body, making her moan as he pulled her head back and fed from her life blood.

Regan shattered, gulping for air as she felt the invisible bonds reach from his body to hers, securing their souls tightly together in ties that could never be broken. Tears flowed from her eyes as her orgasm and the binding made every emotion float close to the surface.

I love you, Liam.

Unable to speak, her mind called out to him.

"As I love you, my precious mate," he answered aloud in a low voice as he pulled his cock from her and rolled her onto her back.

He pulled her legs around his waist and entered her swiftly again, as though he was unable to be outside of her tight heat. Regan tightened her legs around him and he lowered his massive body over hers. Their bodies were both slick with sweat and her nipples abraded against his powerful chest as he took her mouth, his tongue mating hers to the same rhythm as his pounding cock.

Liam's breath was hard and heavy as he broke his mouth away and buried his hands in her hair, looking deep into her eyes as he continued to fill her over and over, his hips pumping urgently. Regan could see forever in his fierce gaze as tiny fangs erupted from her gums.

Hunger seized her and she wrapped her arms around his neck to draw him to her. He came willingly and eagerly, offering the side of his neck, which she nuzzled, breathing in his male scent. Her man. Her mate.

Her tiny razor-sharp teeth cut into his skin like it was butter and she drank of his essence. He tasted hot, succulent and wild. Regan could feel him shudder and he groaned, "Yes, Regan. Take from me. Oh, fuck, it feels good."

She knew he was feeling the same sensations that she had felt and she sensed the unseen threads emanate from her body to entwine his soul with hers.

Bonded.

Regan closed the tiny punctures and threw her head back as Liam lost control, pounding into her with carnal lust, triggering a climax that tore through her body like a violent thunderstorm.

Her spasms gripped Liam's cock and he threw his head back, letting out a low, feral cry as he buried himself deep in a powerful release that made his body shudder.

He rolled to his side, dragging her up against him in a fierce, possessive hold as they rocked together, trying to recover from the explosive joining.

Regan lifted her head a little and gently stroked the small mark on Liam's neck. It was tiny and barely noticeable, but she knew if she had a magnifier she would see a miniature version of their mating mark. To the naked eye it looked like a little birthmark.

"It will never disappear?" Liam questioned softly.

Realizing her mate had picked up her thoughts, Regan replied. "Nope. Always there."

Liam gave a satisfied nod. "Good. I like the thought that every man will see my mark and know you belong to me."

"Caveman," she sighed softly, although she was secretly pleased that he would also have her tiny mark on his neck to signify that he was hers.

"Does it bother you that I'm going to be a little possessive?" he asked thoughtfully as he stroked her hair.

A little? Regan choked back a laugh. "No." It made her feel cherished. "As long as you don't get a club and drag me by my hair to your cave," she teased him softly.

"Mmmm...," he hummed quietly, as though considering the idea.

"Don't even think about it," she warned him sternly before adding, "You wouldn't need it. I'd go with you quite willingly," she teased him lightly as she stroked her hands over his body.

"Be careful what you start, my love," he warned with mock severity. "You're going to be sore."

"Already am. So we might as well go for it." She laughed lightly as she wrapped her arms around his neck and pulled him down for a gentle kiss, barely able to process the fact that Liam was actually hers. *Forever.*

"I love you, Regan. I'm not sure what I ever did to deserve such a mate. You're my best friend and the love of my life. I always knew you were special, right from the start. It may seem strange, but I loved you even before we set off the mating instinct," Liam mused, letting out a long, contented sigh. "What did I ever do to deserve you?"

"You gave your life to your people without a single complaint, Liam. You're almost unnatural in your dedication. You deserved to take one thing that you wanted for yourself."

"You're the only thing I ever truly coveted."

God, how could she not love him when he said things like that? "I guess it will save you my nagging about you feeding every day. Is it so bad feeding from me?" she asked curiously.

He pulled back and gave her a wicked grin. "Sweetheart, I can promise you that I'd be more than happy to devour you daily. Maybe several times a day."

"Are we talking about blood here?" She gave him a dubious look as she asked.

Liam shrugged. "Blood...once. The other times I get to feast on your irresistible body. And feel free to taste me any time you like."

"I don't have to feed very often. Daric said maybe once a week to satisfy the vampire part of me," Regan answered as she snuggled against his warm body, both tired and exhilarated.

"More often would be better," he answered, smiling against her hair.

"Hmmm...we'll see," she answered lethargically, her adrenaline waning, exhaustion taking over.

"Tired, my love?"

"A little," she answered with a yawn.

"Sleep, Regan. From now on I will always have you by my side."

"Thank you. For mating with me," she murmured as she slipped quietly into slumber.

Liam's lips turned up into a smile as he watched her slip into a post mating slumber. "As if I did you a favor? Now you have to put up with me for eternity."

She didn't answer and he didn't expect her to. He was feeling the pull of sleep himself, but he wanted to stay awake as long as possible, savor being able to watch her sleep beside him in his bed.

He shook his head slightly as he finally closed his eyes and started to drift, fatigue taking over his body.

He pulled Regan against him, skin to skin, not even bothering to question the miracle he had been granted. For the first time in his life, he would know what it was like to not be lonely, to have the woman of his heart with him forever.

How had he ever managed to become such a lucky bastard?

Liam joined his mate in sleep with a smile on his lips and his mate clasped protectively in his arms.

EPILOGUE

Two weeks later, Regan sighed softly as she looked around Nathan's living room, satisfied that every member of her vampire family was protected. And they were her family now. All of her ties with the mage had been severed completely, but she didn't regret it. It was actually a relief to be the person she wanted to be and not live in fear of her emotions being exposed.

She had chosen a Celtic cross symbol for protection; the same hung around the neck of every male and their mates in her family. Although the actual meaning of the symbol was a little murky, Regan had always loved the design. She had spelled and fastened each one personally around each recipient's neck and no amount of force could ever remove them. Regan was the only one with the power to remove the symbol of protection and that would never happen.

Regan reached up a finger and traced her own symbol that she had fashioned for herself. It was exactly the same as the ones she had made for Sasha, Callie and Brianna, a smaller, more delicate version of those she had made for the males.

Regan had wanted to give one to Daric, but the prince had gracefully refused, stating that it wouldn't work on him, though he offered no further explanation.

Rory and Liam stood together across the room, their faces beaming with so much joy that Regan's heart stuttered as she watched them. They smiled as if they shared secrets, secrets that should have always been shared between twins.

Regan took a sip of champagne and her lips formed a smile as Nathan and Ethan joined Rory and Liam, emitting roars of laughter and much back slapping for their newly mated brother.

"It's a real Kodak moment, isn't it?" Callie stated softly, as all four of the female mates watched their partners with obvious affection.

"If only we had a camera." Sasha said mournfully.

"I don't think we'll need it." Brianna popped her comment in lightly.

Regan had to agree. She was hopeful that this was the way it would be forever. "I think the brothers will truly be brothers now," Regan nodded absently, her eyes unable to leave her mate.

"I'm just sorry for all the pain you suffered, Regan," Callie murmured quietly with obvious sadness.

Regan shifted her gaze from her mate and looked at the women, all of whom she now considered sisters. "Don't be. As I keep reminding Liam, it was one night of my life. I will have so many others that are filled with happiness that it just doesn't matter. I know any one of you would have done the same for your mate. I would do it all over again if the end result was having Liam as my mate. I'd walk through fire for him."

"As he would for you, my love." Regan shivered as strong, masculine arms slid around her from behind, wrapping her in Liam's protective embrace. His mouth beside her ear, he whispered quietly in a voice meant only for her, "Are you ready to go home? I'm not sure I can continue to see you in that *fuck-me* dress without stripping it from your body and tasting every inch of your skin."

Regan's pulse elevated as she saw images of Liam doing just that in her mind. "Stop that, Liam!" She turned in his arms and smacked him on the shoulder for projecting his erotic images into her head. "This is our mating party. Behave."

He put an innocent expression on his face as he answered, "I've been a model mate all night and I've helped my brothers consume all of the food and drink." He shot her a wicked glance, one that she had a hard time not responding to. "Now I want to devour my mate."

"Get a room, you two," Nathan boomed as he pulled Sasha against him.

All four men had joined them and had their mates firmly at their sides.

Regan pulled Liam's head down and whispered seductively in his ear. "I got a beautiful mating gift from my sister and sister-in-laws."

"Where is it?" Liam asked curiously.

"Underneath this *fuck-me* dress." Regan flashed him an image of herself that she had seen in the mirror before pulling her dress on this evening. The sexy lingerie was sinful and Regan had loved it.

"Christ, Regan," Liam strangled out as he received the images. "If I had known that, we never would have left the house."

"I know. That's why I didn't tell. It was a little...surprise."

Liam's eyes were dark and dangerous as he pulled back and his gaze swept down her body, undressing her with his eyes as though he could see beneath the black silk dress that hugged her curves and showed plenty of cleavage. His breathing was ragged as he leaned forward, his mouth against her ear. "You'll pay for this torture later, my beloved mate," he growled.

Ah...her caveman was here. "I'm counting on it," she answered softly, shivering with anticipation.

Knowing her time was limited, Regan pulled away from Liam and hugged each one of his brothers and their mates, thanking them for the lovely mating party. "Where's Daric?" Regan looked around curiously, wanting to bid the prince farewell.

"He had to go, but he told me to tell you that it's been delightful and he hopes to see you again soon," Liam grumbled, obviously not happy that his prince appeared besotted with his mate.

"He's so awesome," Sasha sighed as she grasped Nathan's hand.

"He is our prince. He is not awesome," Nathan muttered.

Regan laughed lightly as she looked at Liam, Rory and Ethan who were all nodding approvingly at their brother's statement.

Oh Lord...every one of the Hale brothers obviously had a little bit of caveman in him!

Ethan and Brianna faded away, followed by Rory and Callie. Nathan and Sasha looked like they were more than ready for bed. Or a couch. Or a chair. Or any other surface for that matter.

Regan wrapped her arms around Liam's neck and placed her head on his shoulder. "I'm ready, Liam."

"Damn good thing, because I was ready hours ago." Liam gave an exaggerated sigh and wrapped his arms lovingly around Regan's waist.

"Then take me home, caveman," Regan requested in a sultry voice.

"As fast as I can drag you to my dark little cave, my love," Liam agreed in a naughty voice that had Regan laughing as the happy couple faded out of sight.

THE END

of Book Four: Liam's Mate

DARIC'S MATE

BOOK FIVE

THE VAMPIRE COALITION

CHAPTER 1

Daric Carvillius paced his remote Colorado mountain home with a heavy sigh, plagued by overwhelming fatigue. Although he was the Prince of the Vampire Healers, he still had some of the same characteristics of an average vampire healer, and he hated to feed. Unfortunately - due to his royal blood, power, and strength - Daric actually needed blood more often than the average healer, and his feelings of revulsion at performing the necessary function were much more powerful than that of other vampire healers. Recoiling instinctively from the act of taking blood from a human without consent, Daric put off the inevitable as long as possible, delaying until he could barely function.

Plowing his way to the kitchen, Daric rifled through the contents of his refrigerator, hoping to calm his urgency for blood with ordinary human food. It wouldn't entirely work, but it would at least keep him occupied with something pleasurable. After he had left Liam's party, the gnawing emptiness had consumed him, leaving him with nothing to occupy himself, nothing to think about except the pain caused by lack of feeding and the void of loneliness that had haunted him for the last millennium.

He'd interfered in Liam's mating, something that was definitely frowned upon in vampire circles, but who was going to tell *him* to do otherwise? He was a Carvillius, Prince Daric, the last of vampire royalty. He'd stopped giving a shit about what he should and shouldn't do long ago, doing as he damn well pleased…and he had chosen to help Liam. Daric answered to no one but himself, and Liam had needed to be kicked in the ass before the boy did something incredibly stupid.

Had to. The dumbass was about to screw up the first chance that a vampire healer had been given to mate in over a millennium.

Like it or not, Daric had to admit that his healers needed mates.

Scowling as he pawed through old bread, moldy cheese and a few unidentifiable leftovers, Daric conceded that he had helped Liam for reasons other than the fact that a vampire healer finding his mate was a monumental event. Honestly, although the boy could be annoying, Daric liked Liam. He admired the healer's dedication, his willingness to sacrifice for his people. Liam deserved a woman if that was what he wanted, and the boy had gotten a good female in Regan.

Maybe it will help a little with the guilt.

"Fuck! There isn't a damn thing to eat in this house!" His voice boomed through the massive home, echoing back at him, nothing more than a failed attempt to drown out his thoughts.

Hell yeah, he felt guilty. Always had. Always would. He just didn't want to be reminded of it. Part of the reason vampire healers had a difficult time finding a mate rested on Daric's shoulders, his fault for not getting to his father before the ancient vampire healer became mentally unsound and dangerous. If he had just gotten there a few minutes earlier, he might have prevented his grief-stricken father from performing an act that would ultimately harm his people, leaving Daric with a bunch of unhappy vampire healers to deal with on a daily basis. Daric was a second son, an unnecessary and useless prince. His father had never had much use for his second-born, his whole life revolving around his heir, Nolan.

Daric Carvillius was now alone, completely alone, his entire family taken away in moments over a thousand years ago, his people suffering because he had failed to stop his father, because Nolan's intended mate had favored another. There had been a Carvillius as King of the Vampire Healers forever, but *that* tradition was ending. Daric refused to take the title that had belonged to his father, with Nolan next in line as the heir.

I was never meant to be King. I don't want to be King.

As far as Daric was concerned, the title of King of the Vampire Healers could die out, because he wasn't taking that mantle, had refused to do so for the last thousand years. He barely tolerated being a lone prince. He would always watch over his people, do his duty as the last surviving member of the royal family, but he wanted nothing to do with the title of *King* that came with the responsibility. What good was the title? It hadn't protected Nolan, heir to the Kingdom, who had been brought down by a selfish, insane female. And it certainly hadn't saved his father from madness. No, the title of King had belonged to his father and should now be Nolan's. Since they were both dead, the title would die with them.

Daric slammed the door of the refrigerator, irritated that he hadn't stopped for food. Problem was, his duties didn't leave him with time to shop, and the food that he conjured tasted like shit. He was rarely at home except to sleep, spending all of his time trying to protect his fellow healers from their own stupidity. Vampire healers had more power than an average vampire, and they didn't always use it wisely. Daric was forced to intervene whenever one of them stepped over the line, which was far too often. His powers as a prince were no match for the average healer.

Frowning as he dug his cell phone out of the pocket of his jeans, Daric hoped that Liam finding his mate was a sign that more and more of the healers would start finding mates. Most of the unrest among vampire healers was due to a lack of female influence - a realization that they were unlikely to ever be blessed with a mate.

Scrolling through his list of numbers, Daric punched the one he sought, so hard that he nearly broke the phone.

Don't know why anyone would want that sort of blessing. Females are really nothing but trouble. Why my fellow healers think they need one is beyond me.

It had been a very long time since Daric had experienced the pleasures of sex, but he didn't think he really missed it. And he certainly didn't think it would be worth the trouble of having a meddling, whiny female around all the time.

Unfortunately, his vampire healers apparently still remembered the pleasures of the flesh, and seemed to be willing to tolerate the discomfort of having a female around just for the sake of having sex.

Daric shook his head as he waited impatiently for someone to answer his call. If females would help his unruly lot of male vampire healers behave, Daric didn't care if every single one of them found a female.

As long as it doesn't happen to me! The last thing Daric wanted was a goddamn female to add to his list of things that irritated him, which, unfortunately, was a pretty damn long list. Watching over an irksome woman would probably send him over the edge.

Finally, after about the twentieth ring, a female voice answered Daric's call.

"Temple's Pizza, how can I help you?"

"I need a delivery. And I don't want to wait forever." Daric's voice was rough, his intense hunger for something other than food making him cranky. Okay…crabbier than usual, since his normal behavior was less than angelic most of the time.

"I'm sorry, sir, but my delivery person is gone for the evening because of the storm." The female voice sounded weary.

Fuck! He ordered from *Temple's* often, and they had never had a problem delivering, even when it was snowing. If they did, they would never deliver because it snowed all the damn time during the winter in this remote area. His home and the tiny town about three miles away, in a far-flung area of the Rocky Mountains, rarely saw a day without snow in the winter at this elevation.

"I'll pay. Five hundred bucks extra to anybody you can find to deliver. In addition to the cost of the food. And I need a lot of food." Actually, he needed blood, and Daric didn't want to waste energy going to retrieve human food. His reserves were low; he'd waited way too long. After his day sleep, he'd be forced to immediately find an unsuspecting blood donor, his need finally overcoming his revulsion. Until then, he was hoping that gorging on pizza and bread sticks would take the edge off the gnawing hunger that was making his gut burn, his gums ache with stabbing pain, and his fangs want to burst free from confinement.

The phone line was silent, but Daric could hear the woman breathing. He clenched his fingers around the phone, fighting the urge to give the woman a *push*, a slight mental compulsion to obey his demands. As a prince of the vampire healers, there was very little that Daric wasn't capable of doing with his magic. However, doing anything other than feeding, like taking away free will from another being, came with a price. The pain wouldn't be anything like the backlash he suffered whenever he was forced to take the life of a *fallen*, but it wouldn't be pleasant in his weakened state. And, his fucking noble conscience would plague him later, beating at him for doing something that he would definitely have chastised one of his healers for doing. Having royal blood could be a real bitch sometimes.

"I'll find someone." The woman's breathy answer was barely audible. Daric didn't recognize the voice, though he thought he had probably spoken to everyone who worked at *Temple's* . God knew he called there often enough. "I need ten extra-large pizzas with everything. No fish. No fruit." Daric shuddered. There wasn't much he wouldn't eat, but there was something criminal about putting pineapple or tiny fish on a perfectly good pizza.

"Must be some party." The female's comment was muttered in a low voice, too quiet for a human to hear.

But Daric wasn't human, and he grumbled, "No party. I'm hungry."

"Sorry…I…sorry." She sounded distressed, embarrassed that Daric had responded to her personal observation. *"I'll get those out to you*

as soon as possible," the woman answered in a louder, more professional voice.

"I'm not done." Did she think that was all he wanted? He had told her he was *hungry* . "I need ten orders of bread sticks with plenty of dipping sauce." He paused before asking, "And those little chocolate desserts. I want ten of those."

"Is this a joke? Who is this?" The voice on the line sounded exasperated.

A joke? The damn human female was mocking *him?* "I am Daric Carvillius." Who did she think she was messing with? Nobody screwed around with his food.

"Shit! I'm sorry, Mr. Carvillius. I should have known. My name is Hannah. I don't take orders very often." Her answer was immediate and remorseful.

Okay. That was more like it. Daric wasn't so sure that the cursing was appropriate, but at least the woman was properly contrite. "Just get it here. Fast."

"As quickly as possible, Mr. Carvillius."

Daric disconnected the call, shoving his phone back into his pocket with a heavy sigh.

Dragging his depleted body into the living room, he threw his massive bulk onto the couch, trying not to think about how desperately he needed blood. Compulsion and revulsion were constantly at war, revulsion almost always winning, until a vampire healer absolutely had to feed. At that point, compulsion took over and the healer fed, hating the act, but compelled by a force stronger than the foul distaste he felt when taking blood. Eventually, need would always win, forcing the healer to act.

Daric was pushing that fine line, his need growing stronger than his morals.

Fuck! It was going to be a long night.

CHAPTER 2

D   *amn it!*

Hannah Temple slammed the phone back into the cradle on the wall, brushing it absently with the towel in her hand to remove the flour that now coated the entire telephone, a result of her grabbing at it without removing the pizza dough from her hands before answering the call.

"I should have just let it ring," she muttered to herself, glancing out of the window of the empty restaurant, seeing nothing but blowing snow, wondering what had possessed her to agree to this order and the delivery.

Money. You could use the money and Temple's needs the business of Daric Carvillius. You can't afford to turn down that kind of cash or piss off Temple's best customer.

Stripping off her contaminated disposable gloves, she tossed them into the trash with an exhausted sigh, yearning for a hot bath and a good book.

Not happening, Hannah. You have a huge order to fill and deliver.

Walking slowly to the door of the small eatery, Hannah flipped the sign to *Closed*. It was nearly closing time, and she didn't really expect to see another customer, but she might as well make it official.

It was going to take her a very long time to finish this order, and then deliver it outside of town. If she could even make it to the Carvillius home. Her old truck was a workhorse, but it wouldn't matter if the mountain roads were filled with more snow than any vehicle could handle. Hannah wasn't sure how much snow had fallen throughout the day and evening. She had been too busy working the restaurant to notice, most of her staff either out with the flu or unable to make it down the rural roads and into the tiny town of Temple. The small village had been named after one of her ancestors, a man responsible for establishing the community. The pizzeria was nearly a historical landmark, a business that had been started by her grandfather in his youth. Hannah's father had learned from her grandfather, running the business as it had always been run, keeping tradition alive. Now, unfortunately, the business was in the hands of Hannah-the-Clueless, a woman totally unprepared for the challenge of keeping the business efficient and thriving.

I should have closed today, not tried to run the restaurant with almost no help.

It wasn't as if the little pizzeria was incredibly busy, but she had been steadily working since lunch, and her leg was aching.

Hannah sighed as she walked back to the kitchen, pulling dough from the refrigerator and plopping it on the preparation counter, returning a second time as she contemplated the number of pizzas she needed to fill the order. She gathered what she needed, her hand occasionally straying to her right thigh, rubbing the aching muscles, and trying to put most of her weight on her left leg to take the stress from her right knee.

What the hell am I doing here? I don't know how to run a business. I don't belong here. I should have closed Temple's when Dad passed away.

Tears filled her eyes, and she willed them not to fall, swiping the back of her hand across her eyes in frustration. Her father had only been dead for eight months, and *Temple's* was already faltering, slowly losing the character and efficiency it had known under her father's nurturing hand.

I need you, Dad. I miss you so much.

Pain lanced through Hannah's chest, barely dulled by the time that had passed since her father's death from an unexpected fatal heart attack.

Probably caused by my selfishness.

Washing her hands and gloving back up, she started on the crusts for the pizzas, shaking her head at her foolishness. Rationally, she knew her father had been taken from her early by heart disease, but it didn't stop her from hating herself for stressing him more than she should have, by not being here in Temple to help him with his business. Had she been a better daughter, she would have been here instead of Vail, helping her father instead of indulging herself in her love of downhill skiing and catering to a man who would never love her as much as he loved himself.

Her career as a member of the ski patrol and ski instructor had ended a year ago, when her fiancé had crashed his SUV on the freeway early one snowy morning, both of them on their way to the slopes for a day of training. Hannah had never blamed Mark for what had happened. It hadn't been his fault that the impact had occurred on her side of the vehicle, mangling her right leg and requiring multiple surgeries just to get her walking again. However, she couldn't help but hate the bastard for dumping her, dropping her like a hot potato when she was no longer able to ski; no longer capable of hitting the slopes with him to admire his skills and sigh over every expert maneuver he made. Mark was an Olympic hopeful, and he had replaced Hannah with a brainless little blonde ski bunny once Hannah was no longer useful to his image or his massive ego.

Couldn't have a limping woman on his arm, could he? It wouldn't look good on camera.

Hannah pounded the dough harder, wishing it was Mark's face. Oh, she didn't delude herself anymore that she loved him, but it was galling that she hadn't seen through his superficial façade earlier, to chase her own dreams instead of making his dream her own for eight years. When she and Mark had left Temple at the age of eighteen, Hannah had been an expert skier and Valedictorian of their class, capable of doing great things in the future. Instead, she had worked ski patrol and taught skiing courses to support the two of them while Mark chased his dreams, with Hannah as his greatest supporter. Honestly, she had loved her job as a member of the ski patrol, but she could have done so much more, should have been working on an education instead of waiting for Mark to marry her. Like an idiot, she had waited for years, making excuses to her father that Mark was too stressed, too busy, too exhausted to worry about a wedding. *And I was too busy worrying about Mark.*

To his credit, her father had never lectured her about Mark. Instead, he had quietly encouraged her to make a life of her own, pursue her education. Looking back, Hannah wondered if her dad had known how things would end with Mark, but had never wanted to push her. Most likely, he had known Mark's true nature, but it wasn't her father's way to interfere, trusting his daughter to figure it out on her own. Now, at the age of twenty-seven, Hannah wasn't even sure what her dreams were anymore.

After spending eight years living Mark's dreams, it was time for her to find out exactly what Hannah wanted. She had spent the last year in and out of the hospital, losing her father four months after her accident, while she was still recovering from her last surgery.

Hannah hadn't been there when her father had died, needing to be closer to a large medical facility to recover. Dad had stayed with her in Denver, taken care of her, only going back to Temple to check on the business. It was during one of those quick visits to Temple that the heart attack had struck, taking him away within moments, leaving Hannah weak and grieving in Denver, while friends looked after the details of his burial here in Temple. She had come home for his funeral, never leaving again since that dark day eight months ago. The local doctor checked her leg, watching for problems or infection. No doubt Hannah would need another surgery in the future, but right now, she was determined to keep her father's memory alive by running *Temple's*.

Hannah had worked at *Temple's* with her father as a teenager, but she hadn't been involved in the business since she'd left for Vail at the age of eighteen. She had dived in, tried to learn everything she possibly could about the pizzeria, from bookkeeping to making the items on the menu. She had a good manager, and business was just as good as it ever was, but something was…missing. It was as if nothing could fill the gaping hole that was left in the business since her father had died. His laughter, his jokes, his positive attitude and gentle ownership were gone, leaving the pizzeria just…empty, a shell of what it had once been.

Give yourself time, Hannah. It's only been eight months. The darkness will lighten eventually. Get this damn order done and go home. You can't afford to mess this up. Not with Daric Carvillius.

Hannah shivered as she placed the pizzas in the oven, recalling the low, demanding voice of Temple's most notorious resident. Daric Carvillius was beyond wealthy, living in an enormous mansion outside of town. Nobody really knew the man, but everyone in Temple knew who he was, and there wasn't a single person in town who wanted to piss him off. Hannah wasn't sure if they were in awe of the man…or his money. She'd heard he was a giant, a man who would dwarf her own five-foot-nine height. Personally, she'd never seen him, having left Temple before he moved here, but she had heard tales of his monstrous orders from various small businesses in town, especially the food orders. There wasn't much to choose from as far as restaurants in town, but Mr. Carvillius seemed to prefer *Temple's,* and Hannah wanted to keep it that way. The business turned a profit, being one of the few eateries in town, but she couldn't afford to screw up with one of her best customers.

How could any one man consume this much food? And why was he offering so much money just for delivery?

She shrugged, preparing the massive orders of breadsticks for the oven, reminding herself to add plenty of sauce to the order. She knew the man was eccentric from the information she had gathered over the months. He placed massive orders like this frequently. And he paid. What did it matter *why* he did it?

Hannah picked up her pace, working as quickly as she could on her battered leg. Mr. Carvillius had not sounded happy on the phone and she had definitely offended him. She needed to move her ass, try to stay in his good graces.

Obviously, the man was bossy, used to getting his own way. He might have reminded her of Mark…but he didn't. Not in the slightest. Mark was whiny, getting his way by manipulation and guilt. Hannah didn't think that was really Mr. Carvillius's style. He sounded like a man who got his way by complete domination rather than manipulation.

God, his voice was sexy.

He had a low, commanding baritone that had sent tingles of heat throughout her entire body, a voice that meant business, expecting to be obeyed whenever he spoke.

He probably looks like a sumo wrestler if he eats like this!

Slamming one of the ovens closed with her hip, she turned and began to start boxing up food. Somehow, she just couldn't match that voice with the body of a sumo wrestler.

That's because his voice made your panties wet.

Yeah, his voice was most definitely hot. But it wasn't just his voice; it was the strength she sensed behind the voice.

Shaking herself slightly, Hannah forced herself to stop fantasizing about her best customer. Seriously, it was ridiculous to read so much into a sexy voice and domineering tone. The man could be an eighty year old bald guy for all she knew.

Smiling, she began to wrap up the order, her mind more at ease as she pictured a large, sweet old man with a husky voice, waiting for his enormous delivery.

Yeah. Better.

It was so much easier to picture Daric Carvillius in a non-threatening way. *And so much safer.*

Wiping the memory of that compelling voice from her head, she kept her attention on getting the order correct and keeping Mr. Carvillius's business in the future.

Daric heard the crash over an hour later, the unmistakable sound of twisting metal. He probably shouldn't have noticed it, wouldn't have noticed it if he had been human, the howling wind so loud that it drowned out every other sound. But he was vampire, and he had no problem discerning the disturbing noise that filtered through the battering wind.

He'd been cursing the fact that he had actually called someone to drive through the raging blizzard, an epic storm that he had gleaned information about only after turning on the television to wait for his food. Finally, he had concluded that there was no way someone was coming to deliver. He had basically been waiting for a call from *Temple's* telling him that they couldn't fill his order or they just wouldn't show.

The area had been pounded with snow throughout the day and evening, visibility almost nil.

Barefoot, dressed in nothing more than a ragged pair of jeans, Daric crashed out his front door, letting loose a string of profanities as he plowed down his front porch.

"Fuck!" He waded through waist-deep snow, disparaging himself for not feeding. He was so fucking weak, so depleted. If he had fed, he could have been to the car right now, teleporting himself there in less than a heartbeat.

"I can't believe someone actually attempted to come way the hell out here. What kind of fool human actually drove the three miles from town to deliver pizza?" he growled, propelling his massive body through the snowdrifts.

Once Daric arrived at his long, winding driveway, the snow was lighter, the wind blowing the powdery flakes toward the accumulations already present in his front yard, forming massive drifts. Still, there was plenty of the white stuff in his driveway, way too much for anyone to be on the roads that were certain to be exactly the same way.

He found the disabled truck in the gully. It looked like the vehicle had slid off his driveway, plunging down about thirty feet head-on into a tree.

Starting the descent on his feet, he ended up on his ass, sliding down the incline until he reached the battered vehicle. He wrenched open the door, hoping the delivery boy was safe, unharmed.

Except, the delivery person was *definitely* not a boy, and *she* was out cold. The woman's head was against the steering wheel, her body unmoving. The truck was old, too ancient to have airbags, and the woman had been virtually unprotected except for her seatbelt, which was securely fastened.

Daric unlatched the belt, examining her quickly, finding a gash on the left side of her head, obviously a *head versus window* impact.

For the first time in his life, Daric felt like a goddamn human, helpless in his weakness, and the feeling infuriated him. What good was he to this woman in his current condition? He put a hand to her wound, resting his palm lightly on her head, using what pathetically small amount of power he had at the moment to assess the damage.

Pain. Loss. Betrayal. Grief. Sorrow.

Her emotions and memories pounded him, causing him to grit his teeth to try to control the bombardment.

"I fucking hate this," he growled, furious that he had very little control over himself at the moment, his weakness making him unable to focus his magic only on her injuries.

Relaxing, he let all of her emotions and memories flow over him, stopped trying to fight them. Strangely, her emotions felt familiar. Only hers were more recent, fresher, and much rawer.

After the initial surge ended, Daric closed his eyes, focusing on her brain, trying to find the cause of her unconsciousness. He saw the crash as it happened, her head flying sideways with the impact, cracking against the window. She had a concussion and a tiny bleed in her brain, just enough that it could become serious. Time was not this woman's friend right now. She needed care.

I brought her out here. I did this to her. I should have called Temple's again. Told them not to send anyone. I just assumed they wouldn't after I heard the weather.

Running his hands over her body, he checked for any other life-threatening injuries, running a hand down her spine to make sure she hadn't suffered any spinal injuries. Humans were so fragile, their lives so finite and short. He didn't want to do anything that could make her injuries worse.

Smoothing the long, dark hair back from her face, Daric noted that the woman was pretty. And young. Probably no older than her mid-twenties. Shoving his hands under her body, he lifted her from the truck, cradling her against his chest, strangely wanting to protect the fragile, human female after experiencing her sorrow, her loneliness and a barrage of other emotions that made her vulnerable.

Daric stood in the snow for a moment, not feeling the cold even though his chest and feet were bare, his legs protected only by denim, a fierce look on his face.

Snow swirled around the two of them, beating at Daric's massive body, but he ignored it, turning his back to the wind to protect the woman in his arms. He lifted a hand and unzipped her pink ski jacket to her breasts, shoving it aside with a grunt.

I have to do it. No choice.

Daric didn't think about his actions any longer than he had to, knowing that he was doing what he had to do to heal her, his compulsion to heal greater than his repugnance. Letting her head tilt to the side, he lowered his mouth to her delicate neck and let his fangs slide into the soft skin, preparing himself for his initial negative reaction to taking blood.

His body tense, he drank, trying to be as gentle as possible with the injured woman. As he drew her essence, he waited…

And waited…

And waited…

But the revulsion never came. Instead, her warm blood slid over his tongue like the finest wine, making him suck harder, faster, unable to get enough of this woman's taste. She was intoxicating, and his muscles bunched and released, his power surged, building until he was at full-strength, yet still wanting more.

Mine!

Every nerve in his body on fire, Daric closed the punctures on the woman's neck with his tongue, savoring the last drop of blood that lingered on her skin.

Mine!

His heart ready to pound out of his chest, Daric teleported to his bedroom, laying the woman on his bed. One mental command removed her damp clothing and dried her body, replacing the garments with sheets and a heavy quilt to keep her warm. Vanishing his soaked jeans and underwear with his magic, he crawled under the covers, pulling her body against his while his chest heaved in shock and mortification.

His large body shuddered as placed his hand on the female's head. Closing his eyes, he forced himself to concentrate, his palm growing heated as he healed the woman's head injuries in moments.

Opening his eyes, his gaze landed possessively on the woman in his arms. He groaned as she began to stir, her bare thigh rubbing lightly against his engorged cock. His dick was fucking sensitive, but he pushed the sensations aside, his main concern the health of his woman.

My woman. Mine. Fucking Mine.

The woman squirmed, moaning as her eyelids fluttered. The quilt slipped, revealing a mark that Daric already knew existed somewhere on her creamy skin. He just hadn't been sure exactly where it was positioned on her body. There, on her left upper arm, was the royal mark, *his* royal mark. It was small, no larger than the size of a half dollar, but it was vibrant against her ivory skin, a Celtic knot in a perfect circle that had the Carvillius royal sword over the top of the marking. He turned his arm, looking at the exact same marking on his right forearm. It was vibrant, just like hers, glowing with a brilliance he had never seen before.

This woman belongs to me.

Momentarily forgetting that he never wanted a mate, Daric was swamped with fierce possessiveness, an emotion he had never truly experienced, and it nailed him right in the gut.

He froze as his gaze was compelled back to her face, finding her eyes open and looking at him in complete confusion. *Green.* Her eyes were the color of the sweeping pastures of the Emerald Isle, and just as stunning, keeping Daric prisoner, completely mesmerized.

Finally, he blinked, only to open his eyes to the same beguiling face, the same ferocious need rolling over his massive body.

Holy Shit!

Like it or not, whether he wanted it or not, Daric Carvillius, Prince of the Vampire Healers, had just found his mate.

CHAPTER 3

Hannah stared at the formidable male face before her eyes in fascinated horror.

What the hell?

She shook her head slowly, blinking to try to clear her mind. The last thing she remembered was trying to plow her ancient truck through the snow-covered roads to get to Daric Carvillius's place.

I made it. I turned into his driveway.

Barely. She remembered the turn. Her heart started to race as she remembered losing control of the truck on a slippery patch of ice, her panic as she realized there was nothing she could do to stop her truck from plunging down the incline on the right side of the driveway, and then…nothing.

Until she had opened her eyes a few moments ago, seeing this dark-haired male, this dark-eyed savage face in front of her, a face that frankly scared the hell out of her.

Realizing that she was in a bed that was definitely not her own, Hannah started moving backward, trying to scoot away from the man who had her clutched against his massive - *really massive* - chest. "Where am I?" She tried again to move away, but his enormous, muscular arms tightened around her, not allowing her to move away from him. "What happened?" She knew her voice sounded panicked, but hell, she was panicked, and working on hysterical. A rare occurrence for her, since she'd never been the hysterical type.

I'm naked!

Her bare body rubbed against his, skin to skin, one of his massive legs between hers.

He's naked!

Struggling in earnest, Hannah pushed against his muscular chest, feeling like a fly swatting at an elephant. The man was pure muscle and strength, and she was no match for him, even if she wasn't exactly petite. "Let go. What the hell happened? Why are we naked?" *Why are you so aroused?* Really, she was more interested in the answer to the last question, the one that she hadn't spoken aloud.

His rock hard member rubbed against her pelvis as she wriggled, trying to get out of his grip.

"Stop!" His command was issued in a harsh voice that obviously expected to be obeyed. "You'll hurt yourself. You were injured. I brought you here. I'm not trying to hurt you, woman."

Oh, God. It was *him*, the owner of the panty-melting baritone. "Mr. Carvillius?"

"Daric," he replied with a low grunt.

Relief flooded her body and she stopped struggling. "Why are we in bed naked? You can let go of me now. I think I'm all right." She didn't know why in the hell she was here, but she felt fine. Maybe she had been hypothermic and he had needed to get her warm. Obviously he had rescued her. "What happened?"

Hannah pulled away slowly, as the bunched muscles in Daric's arms relaxed. He still looked fierce, and dangerous.

The man behind the voice was just as sexy as his baritone. Daric Carvillius was huge, but he was all muscle, his bulk a mountain of raw power. Hannah nearly salivated as the quilt slipped away from his body, stopping at his hips, uncovering a set of ripped abs like she had never seen before. Her eyes devoured him, drank him in, as she moved slowly away from him on the massive bed.

Definitely not an old man. And he looked anything but sweet.

Mid thirties...maybe, and everything about him was menacing. His black hair was so short it nearly spiked and he had a serious five o'clock shadow, tantalizing dark whiskers that made her want to reach out to stroke his face just to feel the abrasive stubble against her palm.

Clenching her fingers into a fist to overcome the temptation to touch him, Hannah backed away a little more, swearing she could almost feel a pulsating power coming from his body.

"You had a head injury. I healed you." His tone was husky, his eyes never leaving her as they wandered over her face.

Lord, this man is intense. Really intense.

Her nipples tightened painfully into tiny pebbles, a reaction that had nothing to do with being cold. In fact, she had the sudden compulsion to fan herself. "Are you a doctor?" she questioned, knowing enough from her training for ski patrol that healing a head injury wasn't exactly simple.

"No. I'm a healer." His eyes grew liquid, heated.

Hannah started to pull the sheet from the bed to cover her body. While Daric didn't seem to have any modesty about revealing that hunky form of his, she wasn't comfortable with flashing her body to a stranger. "What sort of healer?" Getting the sheet loose, she wiggled under the quilt, trying to wrap the cotton under her arms and around her body so she could stand.

"I'm a vampire healer. Actually, the Prince of the Vampire Healers," he answered, his tone slightly arrogant, as though he totally believed the insane statement that had popped out of his mouth.

Holy crap!

Hannah sprang out of the bed and turned to gape at him, the sheet completely covering her body. Seriously? Was the guy a little touched? Okay...maybe more than a little...obviously he was completely whacked. A vampire? Oh hell, it was just her luck to end up imprisoned with a lunatic. "Um...that's...uh...nice." Shit. She didn't want to piss him off. He might come unglued. *Humor him, Hannah.*

His eyes roamed her body, as though he could see beneath the heavy cotton of her hastily-fashioned covering.

"I can. But I'll stop if you want me to," he remarked quietly.

"Stop what?" She shifted uncomfortably, frantically wondering how to deal with an insane man of his incredible size.

"I can see beneath the sheet. But I have to stop if you tell me to. I can't invade your privacy if you ask me to stop. Not without paying the price for doing so. And I'm not crazy. Much." Daric sat up, and the covers slid precariously lower, stopping just short of his groin. "I didn't realize you still suffered from your previous accident. Your leg still pains you." It was a statement rather than a question.

Hannah gasped and turned her back to him.

"That's a nice view too." His voice held a trace of laughter.

Surreal thoughts ran around in her head, fantasy ideas that Mr. Massive really could see her naked body. "Stop. Stop it. You can't convince me that you can actually see me. But if you can, stop it right now. I don't like it. It's intrusive." Had she really just said that? For God's sake, she was going to be losing her mind along with him in a moment.

He took your clothes off. He saw your leg. He absolutely cannot see your body through this heavy cotton.

"Actually, I can. But I've stopped. You're correct. It's rude."

She turned, giving him the *evil eye* . "Are you trying to convince me that you can read my mind now?" Hannah wasn't sure what other parlor tricks the man was capable of, and she wasn't sure she wanted to know. This was all getting just a little too strange for her. "Where are my clothes?" *I need to get the hell out of here!*

Hannah limped around the bed, her leg aching more than usual, probably from the stress of the accident. *Damn it!* Ignoring Daric, she looked under the bed, nearly groaning from the pain as she stretched the muscles in her thigh.

Daric stood, his movement so fast that his form was momentarily blurred.

"I'm a vampire prince. I can read the mind of any being with less power than I have, and since I have more power than any other life form on earth, I can read the thoughts of any living individual, mortal or immortal." He spoke with such command, such confidence, that it made Hannah pause.

Admittedly, the guy emanated power, an enormous amount of strength. She peered up at him, knowing she should be terrified, but she wasn't. Her core flooded with heat as she sighed inwardly at his sharp features and implacable expression, a man so strong that he made her want to sink into his body, be safe in his embrace.

He's a lunatic. He could hurt you. Have some sense of self-preservation, Hannah. Run. Get away.

"I would never harm you, Hannah. You're my mate." His voice was low, seductive, and gentle for a man who could crush her dead with very little effort. Daric cupped her cheek in one of his enormous hands, his dark eyes glowing with an almost eerie light.

Hannah shivered as his hand ran down her neck and to her exposed left arm. She knew she should move, leave, but she couldn't. Her body was momentarily paralyzed, hypnotized by the feel of his fiery hand on her skin.

Caressing her rather large birthmark, he said in a graveled voice, "You wear my mark." He ran his right index finger over her left upper arm, an area that she had always tried to hide because of the blotch marring her skin that had been present since her birth. "It's beautiful."

"It's a birthmark," she whispered, her voice failing her because she was caught up in some sort of magic, some kind of enthrallment.

"It is my marking. You belong to me." He put his left arm around her hips, pulling back enough to hold his right arm out from his body.

Hannah gasped, starring fixedly at his forearm. Dear God! He had the same birthmark. Exactly the same. Except his was sharper, and...glowing.

"Yours looks exactly the same as mine now. It glows and shimmers, the image more pronounced."

She backed away from him, tugging to get free. Stumbling slightly, she escaped because he allowed it, moving until she hit the wall near the door, her face an expression of both horror and astonishment.

This is not possible. He can't be reading my mind. We can't have the exact same mark. He isn't a vampire. Vampires don't exist. They don't. They're a damn myth. Dracula exists only in fiction, movies and books.

Daric prowled after her, moving like a tiger stalking prey. For a large man, he was graceful, stealthy.

"Gah…of course there's no Dracula. Ridiculous legend, and the books and movies are an insult to all vampires. So much fucking drama that it's nauseating. You're in pain. Let me help you."

"Stay away from me." She lifted a hand, trying to keep him at arm's length as he moved closer.

"I can't," he replied, moving close enough to take her extended hand in his and place it on his chest as he pinned her against the wall.

Hannah was enveloped in his heat, surrounded by his strength. Involuntarily, her palm opened over his chest, stroking the hot skin that stretched over his massive chest. "I don't understand what's happening to me," she whispered in a shaky voice, her whole world turned upside down by her reaction to this man, a man who should have had her running from the house screaming, even though they were in the middle of a blizzard.

"You will. I know you're confused right now." His lips nuzzled her temple, and slowly moved lower, savoring the sensitive skin of her neck.

Her neck arched, giving him access, letting him have anything that he wanted. It was as if her body had completely disconnected from her mind, from her common sense. *What if he wants my blood? He thinks he's a vampire.*

"I've already sampled, and although it's a tempting thought, it's too soon. And I *am* a vampire healer," he rumbled against her skin, his voice amused.

Kiss me. Touch me. Take me. Please. The simple contact of Daric's warm lips against Hannah's flesh heated her entire body. "How in the hell do you do that?" *How is he getting into my thoughts?*

As he moved lower, his mouth sliding sensually over the swell of her breasts, she stopped really caring about anything except those roving lips and his pulsating heat surrounding her.

She shivered as his left hand snaked into the sheet, searching for the opening. Quickly finding what he was seeking, his left hand slipped between the folds of fabric, moving possessively over her right hip. He dropped to one knee in front of her.

Hannah looked down at him through a sensual fog, her body vibrating with need. Daric's eyes were closed, his hand moving over her leg, causing heat to rush through every nerve, muscle and bone in her thigh and knee.

It was over in seconds. Daric rose gracefully to his feet, leaned into her body and murmured into her ear in a husky voice, "I couldn't decide whether to kiss you or heal you. My healing instinct, the compulsion to heal my mate was stronger. But now I can finally do this."

Hannah decided, as his mouth claimed hers, that no one would ever claim Daric Carvillius was timid. He seized exactly what he wanted, and, at that moment, he apparently wanted her. Desperately.

He commanded…and she surrendered, unable to resist him, unable to deny him anything as he swooped down on her like a conquering hero, his kiss branding her, owning her. His tongue didn't explore…it demanded she yield, sweeping through her mouth with so much surging power that he stole her breath along with her will.

Hannah's arms curled around his neck, trying to get closer, melting into his powerful body as he mastered her with his mouth. Again and again. Over and over. Until she was nearly as insane as he, her body shaking like a lone leaf fluttering in a strong breeze.

Daric ended the scorching embrace abruptly, wrenching his mouth from hers as though the separation was painful. Hannah was panting, her breath sawing in and out of her lungs as she looked up at his face.

Sweat coated his skin, and his chest was heaving. He speared her with a hot, possessive look that made her respond instantaneously, every atom in her body reaching out for him, needing him with an intensity that was tormenting.

"I feel the same, Hannah. But you aren't ready." His voice was gruff, and filled with longing.

She wanted to scream that she *was* ready, that she needed him. But was it the truth, or just her body's reaction to him? She was so overwhelmed that she didn't know. "I don't know what's happening to me. I don't understand any of this." She sounded lost, and she felt the same way.

Daric stepped back clothing them both in jeans and a t-shirt. Hannah jumped in fright as the apparel appeared magically on her body. "Cripes. Could you warn me before you do something like that?" Her body was trembling, a delayed reaction from the entire day.

The accident. Clothes appearing out of nowhere. The matching marks. A man professing that he was a vampire. And worst of all, the sense that he really *could* read her thoughts, see through her clothing. Everything that was happening was all so…not normal.

He grinned, a small smile that lit up his rugged face. "Sorry. It's normal for me."

Hannah felt refreshed as she looked down on her casual attire. "I feel like I just showered and dressed."

His smile grew broader. "You did."

She pushed on his chest, needing to move away from his beckoning heat, the temptation of that seductive smile. "Do you know how hard this is to believe? Vampires are myth. They aren't real, Daric." Frustrated, she started pacing the room.

He shrugged his massive shoulders. "We are very real. Humans are on a need-to-know awareness of our existence. And almost all of them don't need to know the truth. Could you imagine the reaction and outright hysteria that would occur if they did?" He emitted a heavy sigh and leaned against the wall, watching her.

Hannah stopped abruptly, realizing that her leg had stopped aching. Gingerly, she tested the limb, stretching it more and more in the absence of pain. *What the hell?* Clenching her thigh, she couldn't feel the ridges of her scars. Frantically, she moved her hand over her knee…feeling…absolutely nothing. She bent her leg up, kicked it back, and it reacted perfectly. "Oh, my God. You did heal me." She hopped up and down in delight, cautiously at first, and then dancing in circles as her leg responded to her every command. "I can move. I can bend. I don't limp." *This isn't possible. Daric couldn't have done this.* But, he obviously had. There was no other explanation.

"Don't even think about going back to that asshole again," he growled, coming toward her with purpose.

"Who?" she asked, genuinely confused as she watched his approach. He was scowling at her, his fierce expression making him look like a barbarian in human clothing.

"Your asshole of an ex-boyfriend, Mark," he grumbled as he stopped in front of her.

"How do you know about him?" Hannah looked up at him in startled surprise.

"There's nothing I don't know about you, Hannah. Nothing I haven't experienced. I accidentally absorbed your memories while I was trying to heal your head injury."

Hannah gawked at him. "How?" Her brain on overload, she added quickly, "Never mind. I don't think I want to know right now." Hell, she was still trying to absorb the fact the he had apparently healed an injury that wasn't completely reversible by any human physician.

"You won't go back to him now that I've healed you," Daric stated bluntly, his dark eyes boring into hers. "He wasn't worthy of you."

"I wasn't planning on it. And I agree. He is an asshole," she answered, distracted by the way he was championing her, defending her. It had been so long since anyone had come to her defense. "What did you mean when you said you had sampled me?" she asked, suddenly remembering his strange comment.

"I took your blood in order to heal you. I had to. I had no choice." For the first time, he looked uncomfortable. "All vampire healers hate to feed, to take blood. I shouldn't have let my distaste interfere with my common sense. I was too weak to heal you without feeding."

Hannah's hand flew to her neck. "You took my blood?" She ran her hand over her neck, feeling for any evidence that he had punctured her skin.

"You really think I would leave a mark unless I wanted to?" He lifted an eyebrow, giving her a haughty glance.

Pulling her hand from her neck, she rolled her eyes. Of course he wouldn't. If he was capable of healing head injuries and miracle healing, he wasn't going to leave simple puncture marks behind.

"Oh hell. I need a drink. Maybe more than one." *Or maybe a bottle of whiskey without the glass.* She wasn't really much of a drinker, but this night wasn't exactly ordinary, and the thought of something to calm her unsteady nerves was becoming a very welcome idea.

"Come. You will eat first. And then I'll let you sample some of my wine collection," he held his hand out to her, palm up, waiting for her to accept it.

Hannah knew it was more than a simple gesture; it was an entreaty of sorts, his way of asking her to trust him.

The space around them was electric, the air vibrating with energy. And Hannah knew it was *him*, his vitality, his power.

Taking a deep, steadying breath, she lifted a trembling hand, placing it into the warmth of his palm. His fingers closed around it immediately, securely, enveloping her cold fingers, warming them almost instantly.

Hell, he hasn't killed me yet. I don't suppose it's on his agenda.

Daric smirked, shooting her an amused glance that roamed her entire body. "It's not on my schedule for tonight, no."

Thank God!

He closed his eyes briefly, his brows drawing together as though he were in pain.

"Are you all right?" she asked him anxiously, moving closer and placing a hand on his cheek.

Daric grimaced, bringing his hand up to cover hers. "Fine," he grunted, opening his eyes, the pain seemingly gone.

"What happened? Are you sick?" Scanning his face, Hannah looked for signs of illness, concerned that he might be getting the flu or some other virus that seemed to be running rampant at this time of year.

"No. I was paying for a little indiscretion," he told her unhappily, his voice disgruntled.

"You were trying to strip me again, weren't you? Wow. That's a pretty awesome control system. So if I don't like something, all I have to do is say so?" Maybe she could just mention the fact that she didn't want him reading her thoughts.

"Don't even try it. As your mate I'm entitled to read your thoughts. And I did strip you and took a very long look. If I'm going to pay for it, I might as well make it worth it. I wanted to see the lingerie I conjured for you." He shot her a wolfish grin, looking totally remorseless.

Hannah had no doubt that at least the panties were scandalous. And damn uncomfortable. She could feel the butt floss up her rear, letting her know, without seeing the underwear, that she was wearing a thong.

Daric laughed…a low, throaty, sexy sound that sent a jolt of happiness through Hannah. Instinctively, she knew it wasn't something Daric did often.

Squeezing her hand, he pulled her body into his and the two of them disappeared, leaving the room abandoned in a heartbeat.

Hannah squealed in alarm.

And Daric laughed harder.

Then, the room was silent.

CHAPTER 4

eject her. Do it. Reject her right fucking now, before you aren't able to do it.

Daric watched his mate as she consumed one of the chocolate desserts from her own restaurant, nearly groaning as her tongue snaked out of her mouth to catch a drop of chocolate that had landed on her luscious lips instead of inside her mouth. Christ! He could think of a lot of things he could do with that mouth, places he was obsessed with having her tongue lick over, all of them located on his overheated, eager body.

Reject. Now.

He watched her eyes close with enjoyment, a look of pleasure on her face that made him envious, wishing it had been he who had put such a look on her beautiful face.

It's been hours. Refuse her and get it over with.

Jerking his eyes away from her, he stared at the wall behind her, trying not to let his gaze stray back to Hannah, who was sitting in front of the fireplace, her face flushed and pink from the warmth of the mammoth fire he had started several hours ago.

He'd rescued his food order from her truck with a mental command, heating it to the appropriate temperature, trying to stuff food in his face in an effort to stop himself from nibbling on *her*. They had been talking for hours, and Daric believed she was finally convinced of the truth. He hadn't held back, knowing time was short, and that she needed to know all of the facts.

Not if you're going to reject her, asshole. Just do it.

He shook his head, his gaze straying back to her face.

Mine.

It wasn't that he didn't know that he needed to reject her, or even that he didn't want a mate. Hannah deserved better. He had felt her emotions, relived her life experiences. Hell, he was an asshole, a prince who hadn't really had any significant communication with a female in over a thousand years. He was a cantankerous, irritable, ancient bastard who didn't know a thing about tenderness or the gentle nature of a female. What in the hell would he even do with a woman of Hannah's kind nature?

Keep her. Brand her as mine. Keep her safe forever.

Daric's cock pulsated at the thought of taking Hannah as his, making her moan with pleasure as he took her. Both of them were experiencing the mating compulsion, the need to join as one, his need, his desire feeding hers. The response of her body was merely a small reaction in comparison to his raging desire, his need so strong that it was all he could do to stop himself from touching her. He had seated himself away from her, on the other side of the fireplace, the massive pile of food between them. Not that the paltry distance would stop him from falling on her like a wild animal that needed its mate, but it did give him an instant to think about it. The problem was, his need would only get stronger. As a royal, he was given time to court a woman before the full mating force hit him. A week. Maybe a little more, maybe slightly less. Much depended on how connected he became to Hannah.

Fuck! If this is the prelude, I sure as hell don't want the full experience. It sucks!

"So how does this rejection happen?" Hannah questioned in a hesitant voice, as she stared down at the glass of wine that she held cradled between her delicate hands.

Daric felt a tiny crack form in the heavy ice that encased his heart. Hannah looked so vulnerable, her hair a curtain now hiding her face as she continued to stare at her wine, swirling it around aimlessly. Goddamnit! He wanted to be the one to protect her, to make sure she was never hurt again. Her grief and loneliness beat at him, demanding he comfort her and make sure she was never alone again.

Don't fool yourself. She also soothes your soul, fills the empty places inside of you. You covet her. You want her.

"I speak the ancient words and it will be so." Rejection was pretty straightforward.

She looked up at him, her forest-green eyes piercing him. "Will I remember this after it's over?"

Daric clenched his jaw, the thought of Hannah going about her normal life, not remembering who she belonged to, wasn't sitting well with him. "No. Our ties will be broken and you won't be attracted to me, won't remember even meeting me." *Fuck. That thought nearly killed him.*

"If I meet you in the future, I'll still find you attractive," she mused, her brow wrinkling in thought.

"You'll feel differently," he answered her gruffly, irritated by that fact and not wanting to think about meeting her in the future. Right now, he could sense her longing, her desire. Although it drove him insane, made him want nothing more than to pleasure her until she was crying out his name in ecstasy, he knew she would feel differently after their ties were broken. And, dammit, it rankled.

"I was attracted to your voice when you called in your order. Something about you made me hot and bothered, even on the phone. Is that why? Because of the mate thing?" She tilted her head to one side, giving him a questioning look.

"No. Not then. I hadn't acknowledged you as my mate."

She shrugged. "Guess it was just your sexy voice that set my panties on fire."

Daric took a healthy sip of his wine, nearly choking on it, as her comment registered. Over the last few hours of discussion between the two of them, Daric had quickly learned that Hannah wasn't coy, saying whatever she was thinking. He didn't respond, knowing if he thought about the sexy lingerie he'd paid the penalty to see, he'd have her pinned to the floor and out of those barely-there panties in seconds.

Thankfully she continued on another subject. "If we're mates, why can't I read your mind, see your thoughts?"

"I'm royal. It doesn't happen naturally. I have to allow you access." Thank God she wasn't going to be his mate or he would *have* to allow her access, and his mind wasn't exactly filled with rainbows and sunshine. *More like violent storms and eternal darkness.*

"You said you were the last surviving royalty. Wouldn't that make you King? And who's the King of the other vampires?" she asked, her voice inquisitive, curious.

"The general population of vampires is regulated by a council of elders. Only the healers have a royal family." He sighed before continuing, "Vampire healers are powerful, requiring someone more powerful than they are to keep them in check at times. There are those who would suffer the pain of backlash or penalty to do things that shouldn't be done by a healer."

"What if the royals are tempted to evil?"

It was an intelligent question, but it still irritated him, "There has been a Carvillius ruling for thousands of years. We are not tempted to evil." He paused before he admitted, "We are ruled by ancient magic. There are some things that even royalty is not allowed to do. That's why my father died. He was King. Should still be King. He died trying to save my brother, Nolan, who was dying of mating conflict. He drained all of his power into Nolan's dying body in his grief and madness, an act that is not allowed without penalty of death."

"Why?" she asked in a hushed voice.

"To keep the rulers in check. Transfer of power or magic is not allowed. I suppose because a ruler could steal power if he were capable, or give away power to another being in exchange for something he desired, making him less capable of ruling. It upsets the balance."

"I don't understand why your brother didn't just reject his mate like you're going to do," Hannah said pensively, her finger tracing the patterns on her wine glass.

"He wanted her. He wasn't capable. But she didn't want him. It left him in mating conflict, one of the few things that can kill a royal vampire healer." Even now, Daric didn't understand why Nolan had wanted Maya, a whiny, and more than a little insane, human female. She had been beautiful, but there had been no character beneath the beauty.

"I'm sorry. You lost your brother and your father at the same time. That must have been awful for you." Her eyes shining with tears, Hannah scooted around the food and crawled next to him, taking his hand in hers. "I lost my father, and the pain of that loss still eats me alive. I don't know how you could bear it."

Daric's heart ached, feeling her loss more acutely than before. "I shouldn't have spoken of it. It reminded you of your loss. You shouldn't feel guilty, Hannah. It wasn't your fault."

She nodded her head. "Logically, I know that. But it's difficult not having regrets."

Ah, yes. Daric knew all about regrets. "I understand. I still wish I could have stopped my father from killing himself, from making his subjects suffer by changing the law of our people before he drained himself of power. My people have suffered for the last thousand years for something that he did in a moment of madness."

Hannah squeezed his hand as she replied, "He was King. Was it even possible for you to stop him?"

"I don't know. But I could have tried. I wasn't there. I should have been there. I was studying the books of the ancients, trying to figure out if there was any way to save Nolan." He hadn't found anything, and his father and brother had died without him being present. "I went as soon as I heard Nolan's cry of distress in my mind, but it was too late." Daric had been greeted by a pile of ashes that had once been his father and brother, able to read the preceding events from their remains. They were images that he had never been able to forget, his father's outrage as his son slipped away, his father's mad act of changing the Book of the Vampire Healer so it was virtually impossible for any healer to find his mate, hoping it might reverse Nolan's death. Then, realizing that his desperate attempt had failed, draining his life energy and magic into Nolan. Nolan had already been gone, so it was an act of suicide, although his father's mind had been so twisted, he probably didn't think of it that way.

"If your father was capable of changing the mating rules, I'm sure you couldn't have stopped him, Daric." Hannah crawled into Daric's lap and rested her head against his chest, wrapping her arms around his neck. "I know he was grieving, but I don't think I like him. He left you alone. I understand it was a horrible loss for him, and I don't blame him for mourning, but he had another son to think about."

If anything or anyone had ever felt as good as the warm, comforting woman in his arms, Daric didn't remember it. He tightened his arms around her, sighing against her hair, losing himself in her softness. "Nolan was his whole world."

Hannah tightened her arms around his neck. "What about you?"

Her tone was defensive, protective and indignant. Daric would have laughed at the thought that *she* was rising to *his* defense if it hadn't touched him so deeply, made his heart ache with tenderness for the small, human female who reacted like a tigress. "I was a second-born prince. Nolan was the heir, the future King."

"You were his son, dammit. It shouldn't matter when you were born." She pulled back to look at him. "Were you and Nolan close?"

He looked at his woman, so fierce, so angry on his behalf, and he felt the ice crack a little more. "Yes. I still miss him to this day. He was patient and kind. We were so different, but we were very close. He would have made a fine King."

She laid her head back on his shoulder as she murmured, "You still haven't explained the King thing."

Unable to stop himself, Daric stroked her silky hair. "It isn't complicated. I didn't want the title. I can watch over my people without the title of King."

"Yes. Obviously you can. You've watched over your people for a thousand years without it." She shook her head against his chest. "Yikes. That sounds odd. Exactly how old are you?"

"I was only two hundred years old when my father died," he muttered in amusement.

"Only? So you're twelve hundred years old? Can a vampire that old even get it up anymore?" She laughed against his chest. "Do you still have your own teeth or do you need…like…denture fangs?"

Daric smiled against her hair, knowing he should be insulted by Hannah's questioning of his manhood, but unable to do anything other than let her laughter surround him, filling him with a peace he hadn't felt in…well…ever. He growled playfully and pulled her ass into his groin. "I'd have no problem satisfying my mate." *And then some!* His cock was straining against his jeans, swelling impossibly large as Hannah's delicious ass wiggled against it.

Mine!

"Hmmm…I guess I'll have to take your word on that one since you're refusing me," she murmured in a sleepy voice.

At that moment, Daric wanted nothing more than to teleport them to his bedroom and show her all of the ways he could pleasure her, sate her until her body was limp and begging for mercy. His need for her was already becoming almost impossible to deny, growing stronger with every touch, every word, every bit of her sweetness that he lapped up like a starving man.

I need to speak the words. Release both of us. This is fucking torture.

Taking a deep breath, he tried to form the words to refuse Hannah, set her free, but they stuck in his throat, clogging him into silence, choking him like dry grains of sand in a sandstorm.

She's my mate. Mine. I'm not giving her up. Never. I want her. I need her.

Cursing himself for being a selfish bastard, he kept trying, but the words wouldn't come.

Fuck!

Hannah stirred in his arms and then settled back in with a feminine sigh, after finding a comfortable spot on his chest.

Daric's arms tightened around her possessively, his heart racing. Who in the hell did he think he was trying to fool? Somewhere deep inside…he had known the truth, had probably known since the first moment he'd realized that this woman was his, that he wouldn't be able to refuse her. He'd been inside her head, seen glimpses of her heart. Maybe his goddamn noble ancestry demanded that he try to do the right thing and let her go, but everything inside him, every vampire instinct he had, told him that this woman belonged to him.

She deserves better.

Oh, fuck no! He might be royalty, but he wasn't feeling particularly noble. The thought of his woman with anyone else nearly sent him over the deep end, making him want to claim her in the most primal way possible. Over and over again, until she could do nothing but moan his name in ecstasy.

Daric rose gracefully to his feet, Hannah cradled in his arms.

She lifted her head slightly, whispering in a drowsy voice, "I'm sorry. I think I dozed off. Is it possible for you to take me home?"

"You will stay here. Sleep." Daric glanced at the clock. It was nearly dawn. No wonder his woman was exhausted. She'd had an exhausting day and the wine had probably added to her desire to sleep.

"The restaurant--"

"Will function just fine without you. You stay here." He had seen the memories of Hannah going home to the empty house her father had lived in, surrounded by sorrow and regrets. She wasn't going back there again. Not until she had healed enough to go without pain.

"For tonight," she agreed in a slumberous voice.

Forever.

Daric's covetous gaze caressed her face, watching her eyes flutter closed as she fell back to sleep. Having already been roasted over the coals by his woman for teleporting her earlier, he made sure she was asleep before he transferred them from the living room to his bedroom.

He dissolved their clothing as they reappeared in his bed, covering them with a quilt and fresh sheets.

Hannah snuggled against him with a trusting sigh, still sleeping the sleep of the innocent.

His cock still throbbed and his body was tense with the need to be inside her, but at the moment he could still contain the beast and enjoy the happiness of having his mate beside him, trusting him to keep her safe.

She'll never be alone again. She'll never suffer again. I'll do everything in my power to keep her happy.

Daric grinned, a cocky smirk that came from knowing that he was the most powerful being that walked the earth. How difficult could it be to make one human woman happy?

The automatic shutters on his windows whispered closed, signaling the coming sunrise. He yawned and closed his eyes, letting himself slip easily into day sleep, a hint of that insolent smile still on his lips as he slept the sleep of a vampire.

CHAPTER 5

"Are you kidding me? I can't do this!" Hannah stood at the top of a deserted mountain, gaping down at the seemingly endless blanket of perfect, untouched snow that seemed to stretch for miles down a never-ending incline. "Where the hell are we?" Her head was still spinning from whatever that thing was that Daric did to get them from one place to another at warp speed.

"We aren't that far from Temple," Daric answered, his voice agitated. "I thought this would make you happy. It's what you wanted. You wanted to be able to ski again. I'm trying to make you happy, woman."

"Well…I'm not." Hannah shot Daric a belligerent look. He'd pulled her out of a perfectly warm bed, plied her with coffee and transported them God-knew- where, to the top of a deserted mountain, and he expected her to ski down unknown territory after being nearly sedentary for a year. "I'm not in shape for this. I'm not ready. I haven't done more than walk at a slow limp for months."

Yesterday, she had been fairly certain that she'd never walk without a limp, and now anything was possible. Overwhelmed, she looked down at her favorite pair of skis with a sigh.

Daric frowned, as though offended. "You think I'd let you get injured?" He crossed his arms in front of him, biceps and triceps rippling beneath a short sleeved t-shirt. Dressed in only jeans, the lightweight shirt and black boots, Daric didn't look the least bit cold, although the temperature had to be nearing the zero mark.

Hannah was appropriately dressed in red ski attire, all of her wardrobe and personal belongings having mysteriously appeared in Daric's home before she had even woken up in his bed earlier in the evening.

"It isn't about getting hurt. Not really. I'm just not sure I'm ready for this right now." Oh, but she wanted to be. As Hannah looked at the moonlit, perfect terrain, she wanted to drive into it, feel the excitement of the cold wind in her face as she flew down the mountain, the first to break the new and perfect snow.

New snow. Deep snow. Avalanche territory!

"Not happening," Daric drawled, raising an eyebrow.

No. Of course it wasn't. Hannah rolled her eyes at his arrogant stance and seemingly endless confidence that there was nothing he couldn't do or accomplish. What she wouldn't give right now for that kind of self-possession. After living most of her adult life taking care of Mark's needs and never acknowledging her own, she no longer knew who she was or what she wanted. She had failed to accomplish much of anything in her life so far. She couldn't even run *Temple's* the way her father did.

"What does Hannah want?" The low, rumbling voice sounded next to her ear as Daric wrapped his arms around her waist from behind.

What do I want? It was the first time in her life any man had ever asked her that question. Even her father had never really asked, only gently encouraged her to reach for her own goals.

"I don't know," she answered honestly.

"I'll take you home right now if this isn't what you want to do." His arms tightened around her, his breath forming a visible cloud of white vapor in front of her face.

No! No turning back. Hannah wanted to find her way, and maybe it started by taking this mountain. "It could get dark once the moon is blocked by the trees," she answered, her eyes scanning her purposed path.

"It won't." Even as he uttered the words, the path lit up with artificial light, even though Hannah couldn't see the source.

Do it, Hannah. You know you're dying to go.

Daric loosened his hold around her waist. "I'll be right behind you. Don't second guess what you want. Your instincts are almost always correct. Trust them."

Trust me. Isn't that what Daric was actually saying? Isn't that what he was asking her to do?

"Yes," he answered, his arms lowering away from her body.

Before she lost her nerve, Hannah struck the snow with her poles, lowered her goggles, and pushed herself off the mountain, plunging into some of the best fresh powder she had ever experienced. She started slowly, her confidence building as she navigated around obstacles, some of them disappearing before she even got to them. *Courtesy of Daric's magic!*

Hannah flew down the mountain, laughing as she tore up the snow, her leg working perfectly. Having Daric behind her, letting her lead the way was novel. She turned her head to the right, catching a glimpse of Daric tearing down the mountain slightly behind her, skiing like an Olympic Gold Medalist.

Exhilarated by her growing speed and confidence, she let herself enjoy the ride. She knew this moment in time, this magical experience, would stay with her forever. For the first time in a very long time, she was flying down a mountain just for the sake of enjoyment, tearing up snow just because she loved to do it. She wasn't on patrol, she wasn't helping Mark train, and for the first time since she had been a teenager, she actually felt free.

As Hannah neared the bottom of the mountain, she felt tears form in her eyes. Coming to a halt, snow spraying around her from her quick maneuver, she pulled her goggles up to swipe at her eyes with a gloved hand. She was panting from exertion, her body no longer in condition to tackle a run that required that much physical strength. She gripped her thighs, laughing, trying to catch her breath. Her head was down, but she saw Daric's feet planted next to hers, his skis gone, replaced with the black boots he had previously been wearing.

Hannah straightened, still breathless but slowly recovering, her heart still pounding. "Thank you for this." She met Daric's eyes, not quite sure how to express what this experience had meant to her or how to tell him that it had a significance far greater than just skiing down a mountain.

"Don't." He speared her with a dark glance. "I already know. Why do you think we're here? You've spent enough time in the shadows of another, never pleasing yourself. What does Hannah want?"

You. The word fluttered through her mind instinctively, automatically. "I didn't really want to leave Temple. I wanted to stay here and learn how to run a business from my father. Vail and Olympic training were Mark's dream. I was never happy there." *I was never happy with him.* It had never truly been the location or her occupation. The problem had been her relationship with Mark.

"He never valued you. Never protected you or loved you. Why did you go if you didn't want to?" Hannah's ski equipment disappeared, and Daric moved closer, pinning her between his body and the trunk of a large tree, his eyes never leaving hers.

"Mark and I grew up together. We were childhood friends. I guess we just gradually became a couple. He was all I knew." Even as she spoke, Hannah realized that even from a very young age, Mark had somehow convinced her that she needed him, and she had believed it. Somewhere along the line of their very long relationship, Hannah had lost herself. "He didn't value me because I stopped valuing myself." Tears flowed from her eyes, blurring Daric's face. "All those years wasted. Time with my father that I can never get back again. I rarely even saw my dad because Mark didn't like him."

Daric wrapped his arms around her, holding her tightly in his embrace as he grumbled, "I'll kill the son of a bitch for you."

Hannah didn't doubt it for a moment, and she smiled through her tears as she buried her face against Daric's warm chest, her heart leaping at his defense and outrage for her sake. "No. He's not worth a moment of your pain. I made the choice and it was the wrong one."

"You won't think about him again." Daric's tone was demanding, as though issuing a royal declaration. "If thoughts of him distress you again, I'll kill him."

Daric's body was fiery hot, even in the bitter cold atmosphere, and Hannah snuggled against him, her heart hammering. No man had ever treated her as though she were precious and cherished, but this man, a male she had only known for a day, treated her like she was everything to him. It was tempting, intoxicating.

"You're my mate, Hannah. There is nothing or no one on this earth more important to me than you." His voice was husky, and radiating with raw emotion.

"I thought you refused me." The words struck Hannah straight in the heart.

"I can't." He grabbed her by the shoulders, his eyes clashing with hers in a volatile meeting. "My fate is in your hands, Hannah. I want you, therefore I can't refuse you."

She shivered as she held his gaze, feeling as if she were drowning in his heated eyes. His loneliness called to her, beckoned her closer with every second that passed. Her heart aching at the thought of leaving this strong, powerful man vulnerable, she whispered, "What do we do?"

"That will be for you to decide. I'm an Ancient. On my good days, I'm just an asshole. On my bad days, I can be a vampire healer's worst nightmare," he replied, his voice as menacing as the scowl on his face.

Hannah knew Daric was arrogant, demanding and probably occasionally harsh, but she couldn't manage to connect the man she was getting to know with his own description. Daric was just… Daric. And there was so much emotion beneath his gruff exterior. He wasn't a man she feared. He was her protector, her champion, the first man who had ever considered her feelings. And Hannah was fairly certain that even without the mating instinct, she would still think him the hottest man, or vampire, to walk the planet. She had always believed that sex was highly overrated, over in minutes and not particularly exciting. Now, she wasn't quite certain she was correct in that assumption.

Taking a deep breath, she asked, "Will I get the asshole, or will you be my nightmare?" She needed to get her mind off the erotic thoughts that were starting to swamp her brain.

He shrugged his massive shoulders. "Depends on how difficult you decide to be."

"I won't follow your every command." Never again would she walk in a man's shadow.

"That isn't what I want. I want you to do whatever makes you happy. But know this…I will be protective, high-handed and I will try to keep you from harm by every means available to me. This is a supposed to be a lull period of mating for me, a time to court you. But my need grows stronger every second, and eventually I will have a difficult time trying to control it. I already consider you mine. I'm just trying to wait for you to make the same decision." He wrapped his arms around her waist. "You're getting cold. Let's go home."

After that speech, Hannah was far from cold. The thought of Daric wanting her so desperately soaked her panties and stole her breath from her lungs. She closed her eyes as he held her tightly against him.

Dizzy from the transport, she opened her eyes to find herself in Daric's kitchen. "I thought you'd take me home."

"You are home," he answered in a low, dangerous voice.

"I meant my home." Exasperated, she stepped away from him and planted her hands on her hips.

"You aren't going back there until you can do so without feeling sad." He shot her a seriously cranky look.

"And you'll decide when that might be?" she retorted.

"I'll know. I can read your emotions and your thoughts."

It wasn't as if Hannah hadn't already known that Daric was in her head, but the significance of it hit her suddenly, wondering what exactly he really could see. "Can you see my past memories, intimate memories?" she asked, wondering if he could see her less than wonderful sexual experiences with Mark.

"You won't think about him anymore," Daric replied, moving forward to wrap his steely arms around her waist. "I don't see those memories. I can't. They are filtered beyond my reach to keep me from going crazy from seeing my mate with another male. I only see them if you visualize them in your current thoughts."

Yeah. Like that was something she actually *wanted* to remember? "Not much likelihood of that happening," she muttered, her arms curling around Daric's neck, longing flooding her entire body as Daric dissolved her outerwear, leaving her clothed in only a t-shirt and jeans. "Crap, I'm back in a thong again," she cursed loudly, annoyed by the thin strip between the cheeks of her ass. "Why do you do that if you can't even look?"

"I torture myself with imagery," he told her, his voice both self-deprecating and amused. "And I might look. It would be more than worth the price." His big hands stroked over her back and down, finally cupping her ass possessively.

"No! You can look. I give you permission. Feel free." Her modesty wasn't worth the price of Daric feeling the pain of penalty. She could change into her own lingerie now that her own possessions were here, modest panties that wouldn't tempt him.

"You tempt me merely by existing, Hannah. It doesn't matter what you're wearing," Daric said huskily, his hands kneading the flesh of her ass, pulling her hot core up and against his pulsating cock. "I'll always want to be deep inside you, surrounded by you, claiming what belongs to me."

Every nerve in Hannah's body went up in flames, her entire being feeling like liquid fire. "Please," she whispered in a needy voice, not even quite sure what she wanted, only certain that whatever it was, she needed it now and no one but Daric could quench the flames. Confused by the intensity of her emotions, Hannah wondered which emotions and wants were her own and which were caused by the mating compulsion, the small portion of those urges that emanated from Daric to her.

"I won't be able to stop." Daric warned ominously as he pulled back, searching her eyes, his face a mask of tortured desire. Placing a hand on each side of her head, he closed his eyes as he growled, "Share my mind. Know what desire is yours and what belongs to me."

Hannah's whole body rocked as his memories, his thoughts flooded her brain. Closing her eyes at the onslaught, she shook her head furiously, overwhelmed. "Oh, God!" Confused, she clenched Daric's shirt, fisting the cotton, desperate to be grounded.

"Relax. Separate my thoughts from yours," Daric commanded, pulling her thrashing head against his chest. "Sort them out in your mind. I'll help you."

His voice penetrated the thick fog in her brain, forcing her to grit her teeth and try to make sense of the massive overload of information that was taxing her senses. Her body relaxed as she sensed Daric in her head, filing away most of the information from his past, leaving only the present thoughts and emotions.

Grimacing, Hannah tried to mentally push his emotions on one side and hers on another, but the dividing line was blurred, intertwined. "Shit. I can't completely separate them," she muttered, frustrated.

"Relax. You'll become accustomed to the sensation. Information will come to you slowly over time. You can't handle twelve hundred years of memories and emotions all at the same time. And the emotions of true mates are always blurred. You will know what emotions originate from me, and you will always sense how I feel, know what I'm thinking," he answered, stroking her hair gently, massaging her scalp.

Calmed by Daric's reassuring touch, Hannah settled, but her body was still aflame, yearning for more, clamoring for *him*. Nothing had changed; her need was her own, except she could sense Daric's emotions and thoughts. And at the moment, every one of them featured the two of them entwined together in shared ecstasy. As much as Daric needed to possess, Hannah needed him to claim her. Lifting her head, she told him softly, "I need you. I need you as much as you need me."

His dark eyes scanned her face as he replied, "If you let me take you, I'll never let you go. Hell, I probably won't anyway. But if I fuck you, have you once, I'll track your ass down until you either mate with me or I die of mating conflict. I don't have Nolan's noble morals that allowed him to die with dignity while his mate left him. Your ass is mine. And I'll chase you until the moment I breathe my last."

Hannah felt a shiver run down her spine at his dominant oath, a promise that she knew that he would fulfill. As if she'd let him die? "Then fuck me, Daric. I need to know what it feels like to truly want and be wanted."

"You'll definitely know what it's like to be wanted. To the point of insanity." His mouth claimed hers roughly, his tongue driving between her lips in a frenzied meeting of mouths, a devouring kiss that left her in no doubt of how much she was needed, wanted.

Daric's hand fisted into her hair, holding her head for the fierce possession of his mouth, as his tongued plundered relentlessly. Frantic to get closer, Hannah lowered her hands, searching for his t-shirt, desperate for skin to skin contact. Finding it, she thrust her hands under his shirt, moaning into his mouth as her fingers touched his fiery skin, wanting to know every inch of his enormous body, feel every ripple of muscle.

Closer. I need to get closer.

Hannah was panting heavily as Daric released her mouth and moved to the sensitive lobe of her ear, nipping gently and then laving it with his tongue. Clothing vanished, leaving Daric nude and Hannah in nothing but the racy underwear he had conjured.

Her fingers sought and found his enormous cock immediately, sliding over the silky skin with trembling fingers. His length and girth made her pussy clench, flooding the already saturated flesh at the apex of her thighs. What would it feel like to have this inside her, claiming her?

"You're going to know very soon," Daric growled. "If you keep touching me, it will be right now."

"Yes," she breathed softly.

"No." He backed her up until her bare ass cheeks collided with the refrigerator. He lifted her hands over her head. "You'll behave before I lose control. It's hanging from a nearly invisible thread right now. And I need to pleasure you."

Hannah shook her head as she glanced at his face, so full of heat and desire. "I need you." Her pleasure would come from having that mammoth cock inside of her. She went to reach for him again, only to find that her hands were unable to move. "Let me loose, dammit." She needed to touch him now.

"There are other pleasures to be had," he said, his mouth vibrating against her skin as his hands explored her body. "You will experience those delights before I take you."

Hannah moaned aloud, not sure if she could take whatever he had in mind. Her need was roaring through her body, demanding to be satiated. She had never thought she would enjoy this kind of complete domination, her body under a man's control. Strangely, she relished it. A wild instinct rose up inside her to greet the alpha male vampire that was Daric, needing to let him sate her body any way he desired. She just wasn't entirely sure how much she could take without screaming from frustration.

She arched her neck as his teeth gripped the flimsy lace of her bra, ripping the garment from her body, freeing her breasts to his gaze. His hands and mouth were there immediately, his large fingers cupping her breasts as his thumbs circled her hard, sensitive nipples. His tongue and teeth teased, alternating from one breast to another, making her core spasm with need, every inch of her body hypersensitive. "Please," Hannah whimpered, desperate for Daric's possession, her body aching to be taken.

"Mine. You're so beautiful," his voice was rough against her breasts.

His touch continued down her body, Daric sliding to his knees as he touched and licked every inch of her skin. "Daric. I can't. I need. I want."

"You may want, but your need could never be as great as mine. You will come for me, Hannah," he grunted, his fingers playing over the lace thong that barely covered her pussy. Hannah shivered from the brush of his fingers on her pink, saturated flesh, as he hooked a finger under the material and tore it from her body, without her feeling even one tiny bit of pain.

His hands roamed over her ass as his tongue licked slowly up each of her thighs, making Hannah's entire body thrash with erotic torture. "I can't take anymore. Please." She yanked at her hands frantically, needing a rough possession to satisfy the untamed desire battering at her body.

"You will take this." Daric gripped her ass at he spoke, holding her in place. "I can smell your need, your arousal. You will come for me." He sounded barely human, an animal wildness making his voice vibrate in something similar to a snarl.

Hannah could feel his hot breath wafting over her quivering pussy. Her muscles tense, she waited, holding her breath.

She released her pent-up breath in something between a whimper and moan as his tongue finally touched her trembling flesh, pushing his way between the folds, seeking and devouring. He showed no mercy, and Hannah didn't want any. Her arms secured, Daric pulled her legs up over his massive shoulders and buried his head between her thighs, his mouth and tongue all over her sensitive clit.

He took her weight like it was nothing, keeping her body support-ed, ensuring no tension on her restrained arms. All Hannah had to do was feel, and her body responded to his dominant, erotic touch with a relieved groan, her climax approaching like a speeding train.

He manipulated her clit with his mouth, his strong arms and hands holding her ass, squeezing it, bringing her core tighter against his mouth, and flicking her tender flesh harder.

"Yes. Please, Daric. Oh God." His whiskers were abrasive against her tender thighs, another erotic sensation that blended with every touch of his tongue, driving her nearly insane.

A deep, reverberating sound left his lips, vibrating against her throbbing bud. Tilting her gaze downward, Hannah could see his dark head buried between her thighs, consuming her, the image so erotic that she pulled her eyes away and arched her back, her climax erupting with a force that made her scream. "Oh, my God. Daric. Daric. Daric." She chanted his name like a mantra, unable to think, her whole body convulsing with the strength of the most incredible orgasm she had ever experienced.

Daric stood, still holding the weight of her body as he wrapped her legs around his waist. He kissed her, stealing whatever breath that was left in her body, but she didn't care. She could taste herself on his lips and her own primal urges rose up to meet his, desperate for him to take her.

Pulling his mouth from hers, he pushed her hair back from her face. "Now you have had a small taste of want and desire," he whispered harshly. "Multiply it by a hundred and you might have an idea of how I feel."

Hair cleared from her face, Hannah looked at Daric, initially startled by the wild, feral look on his face. As her gaze clashed with his, she found herself drowning in carnal need, swamped with erotic heat. "Take me now," she answered, her voice low and trembling with urgency, with the painful ache to feel this man inside her.

"Tell me that you want me," he rumbled, his expression dark and volatile.

Hannah knew he sensed her desperation, but some animalistic part of him wanted to hear it. "I want you, Daric. I ache for you. Only for you." The words came out on a long moan. "Release me. Please."

Her hands came loose and she wrapped them around his massive shoulders. "Now, fuck me. Please."

Daric lifted her ass, pinning her against the cool metal of the refrigerator. With one smooth thrust of his hips, he impaled her.

"Mine!" He released the word in a feral groan, his hands tightening on her ass, fusing them together tightly.

He was massive, but Hannah felt no pain, only a satisfying fullness and the incredible joy of being joined with him. "Yes," she whispered in a husky voice, unable to form any other words.

"You belong to me, Hannah," he grunted as he pulled out and thrust again, as though staking his claim.

Yes. Yes. Yes.

Her mind screamed what her mouth could not. She wrapped her arms around his shoulders, hanging on as he pumped in and out of her slick channel, branding her again and again.

The joining was rough and primal, carnal and needy. Hannah reveled in the elemental fusing of their bodies, heat emanating from both of them in incendiary waves. She was lost in the pounding of Daric's body, the flexing of his muscles as he pummeled into her, the stretching of the walls of her channel as she accepted his cock inside her, over and over.

He caught her lips, his tongue thrusting into her mouth in the same rhythm as the phallus sinking into her repeatedly.

Daric's overwhelming desire to bite her, to sink his fangs into the tender flesh of her neck inflamed her senses. Tearing her mouth from his, she begged, "Do it. I want you to. Please." The carnality of the image of him sinking his teeth into her neck beckoned.

"Mine," he snarled against the smooth flesh of her neck before sinking his fangs into her skin.

Daric's reaction was so intense, so overwhelming, that Hannah didn't even flinch at the initial strike piercing her skin. It was a mere pinch followed by such a surge of erotic pleasure that it had her imploding in his arms, so submerged in Daric that she could do nothing but spasm helplessly as she moaned, "Daric."

He released her neck, licking at the wound, and then groaning fiercely as he buried himself inside her so deeply that Hannah wasn't sure they would ever come apart again. Daric flooded her womb with his hot release, his massive body shuddering against her.

"Fuck!" The curse exploded from his mouth a moment before he teleported them to the bedroom.

Hannah's head was spinning, and she closed her eyes as Daric gently untangled them and laid her on the bed. He joined her immediately, pulling her limp, sated body against his strength, covering them both with the sheet and quilt.

"I didn't know it could ever be like that," she murmured against his chest, her body still humming as she recovered her breath, waiting for the world that Daric had just rocked to settle back into place.

"Neither did I," he answered in a husky, raw voice.

"But you must have had a lot of experience before…" Her voice trailed off, not really wanting to think about this extraordinary man with another woman.

"Never like that," he shook his head, his expression intense. His arms tightened around her before he repeated, "Never anywhere near like that."

Hannah snuggled against Daric's strong chest, feeling sated and completely at peace in a way she had never known. If she had been lost previously, Daric had found her, surrounded her with a sense of belonging. "I was waiting for you. I just didn't know it." Even as the words left her mouth, she knew it was the truth.

"I'm glad you feel that way, love. Because you're stuck with me. Forever," he replied roughly, but his arms protected her, cradled her like she was someone precious.

Forever.

Hannah closed her eyes and smiled, deciding that as long as she had Daric, she could live with that.

CHAPTER 6

Hannah left *Temple's* a week later with a wave to her employees and a broad smile on her face. It was nearly the dinner hour and she knew the little pizzeria would get busy shortly, but she had already done her paperwork and she felt comfortable leaving the place to her capable manager and employees. Taking a deep breath of the frigid air that greeted her as she walked out the door, she stopped to watch the sun setting, the massive fireball slowly sinking behind the enormous snow-covered peaks in the distance, allowing darkness to fall in a spectacular, cloudless sky.

Hugging herself tightly as she walked toward her new SUV, purchased by her mate for its elevated safety rating, Hannah's thoughts drifted. Daric would wake soon, and she wanted to get home. He hated it when she went out while he was in day sleep, and his protective instincts grew worse with every day that passed. Usually, she waited until he woke, going to work in the evening. Sometimes he'd come with her, usually eating his way through the restaurant menu while she was doing paperwork. If he didn't accompany her, it was because he had business to do with his healers, but he always showed up at some point in the evening, making sure she never left *Temple's* by herself in the dark. His presence in the little eatery had chased away the shadows, breathing new life into *Temple's*. Or maybe Daric was breathing new life into her, encouraging her to follow her instincts, supportive of anything she really wanted. Hannah went to the restaurant every day, determined to keep her father's memory alive by keeping *Temple's* open, but she also wanted to make her own mark on the place, something she had been working on by changing some of the outdated décor and adding some new recipes to the menu.

The peace that Daric had surrounded her with a week ago remained, growing stronger every day she spent with him. Oh, not that life itself was actually peaceful living with a vampire prince. Her mate could be a royal pain in the ass when he didn't get his way, most of his complaints revolving around her safety, her happiness. It made it hard for her to argue with him when his main concern in life seemed to be her happiness and well-being, even though he growled commands instead of really discussing issues when it came to safety. But even when he was surly and cantankerous, Hannah was happy, accepting her broody vampire prince exactly as he was, because he accepted her with all her faults. All he seemed to want was her happiness. Like she could not be happy? She was nearly deliriously contented, and Hannah wanted Daric to feel the same joy she felt. It was impossible to put a finger on his feelings, but he was definitely fighting something internally, although he denied it. He was blocking some of his thoughts, and it bothered her, wondering what he was thinking that he couldn't share or didn't want her to know.

She halted at her SUV, pressing the button to open the doors of the vehicle. The lights blinked and the short beep sounded to deactivate the alarm, at the same time that what felt like sharp claws wrapped themselves around Hannah's wrist, preventing her from getting into her vehicle. Hannah backed up in horror, her ass hitting the hood of her vehicle, as a mass of hideous creatures swarmed her, appearing one after the other. Despite her terror, she didn't have to wonder what the ugly things surrounding her were or what they wanted - having seen a few of Daric's darker memories, she already knew. *Fallen* . Vampires that had turned evil.

Hannah tried to break the hold on her wrist, but it only caused the claws digging into her arm to tighten, drawing blood. Despite her terror, thoughts of Daric popped into her mind.

I shouldn't have waited to watch the sun set. I should have listened to Daric.

He had warned her, over and over, about the dangers she faced as the mate of a vampire prince. The *fallen* were preying on mates who hadn't completed the mating process yet, and Daric had cautioned her about the creatures that might be able to sense her, even in a remote community like Temple, simply because she was the mate of a powerful prince.

I'm sorry, Daric. So sorry.

Hannah trembled as the horde grew larger, more aggressive, swarming around her until there were too many to count. With sunken, hairless faces and freakish red eyes, they were worse than anything she had ever imagined, even in her darkest nightmares.

Panicked, Hannah tried to close her thoughts. If these things were awake, then so was Daric. There had to be at least a hundred, maybe more, of the *fallen*. If rescuing her didn't kill him, the backlash from killing so many just might. She had only seen the backlash in his memories, but she knew he had never killed this many *fallen*, and that the resulting backlash would be catastrophic. She'd die before she let these disgusting, ugly things take Daric to his death.

The beast holding her wrist moved closer, its fetid breath nearly causing her to retch. Kicking her legs up, she struck the *fallen* in the groin, twisting to get away, to somehow get out of its grasp. It didn't falter, didn't even seem to feel the pain, but it grabbed her shoulder with its other set of claws, slashing her flesh open.

Shit. These bastards are strong.

Male voices rang out in the night, some panicked and others forceful. Obviously, chaos had begun in the small town of Temple with the arrival of a large number of *fallen*.

Blank your thoughts. Don't think about this. Keep Daric away.

Claws pierced her flesh in other places on her body as she fought to get away, red eyes everywhere she looked. Heart slamming like a jackhammer against her chest, Hannah fought, but was no match for the *fallen* that pierced her skin with every touch.

Screams shattered the night, cries of anguish, pain, fear and panic. One shrieking voice was closest to her, loud enough to nearly pierce her ear drums. It was a voice Hannah recognized as her own as she finally succumbed to darkness.

Where the fuck did she go?

Daric had woken from his day sleep edgy and alone, his only thought to find his mate. It was dark, and Hannah wasn't in the house.

Dammit. He loved his stubborn mate more than he ever thought possible, but there were times when she pushed him too far, tested his patience too greatly. He was nearing the end of his ability to stay in control, the overwhelming instinct to protect and mark Hannah as his, nearly making him insane.

I love her. Goddamit, I love her.

As he stormed into the kitchen, bellowing Hannah's name, he admitted that he loved his mate to the point of derangement, his rational mind leaving his body as primitive instinct pounded him. After having absorbed her memories and emotions from her body, he knew her, probably better than he knew himself. And he fucking wanted her more than anyone he had ever desired, making him fight the flare of the mating instinct that had occurred days ago, the overpowering desire he had to dominate and hold his mate to him.

In the beginning, he had tried to wait, had tried to give Hannah time to adjust, time to love him back, his love for her making him want to have her love in return. However, the time for all that had passed. He didn't have the strength to hold back what destiny intended any longer.

Fucking need her. My mate. Mine.

Daric raked a trembling hand through his hair in frustration, his whole being on fire to find his mate, his rational mind completely slipping away.

Should have taken her earlier. Made her mine earlier. Now it's bad. Really bad.

He had been so cocky about his ability to control the flare - the lunatic desire to brand his mate - even though it had grown worse with every passing day. *I wanted her to love me.* Now, he had pushed himself to the brink, he was more animal than vampire, unable to control any of his actions.

Fuck control! Hannah. Mine. My woman. She's never getting away from me.

As he stomped into the living room, he stopped abruptly, his face turning red with rage, his eyes burning flame as he sought and found his mate's mind.

Fallen! In Temple. Touching my mate, hurting Hannah.

His fury became a towering, overpowering violence as he saw his vulnerable mate in the hands of the *fallen* that were taunting her, injuring her.

Kill. Protect. Rip the bastards apart piece by piece for touching my mate.

Completely crazed, Daric summoned the power to teleport himself to Hannah, his wrath exploding from his body in a powerful howl for vengeance, his urgency to get to his mate nearly incinerating him.

"I'm the fucking King and nobody touches my mate!" he bellowed, his eyes wild, sweat pouring from his muscular body.

He growled, his mind so lost that he couldn't do anything but grasp the sword that suddenly appeared in his hand, not even questioning how it had gotten there or how it had manifested itself into his grip. It was heavy, and it would kill well. That was all that mattered.

Daric disappeared in flames, his maniacal instincts finally consuming him, leaving nothing but a vampire in complete mating fury, ready to destroy anything and anyone that got between him and his mate.

Hannah fought the darkness, trying to push into the light, forcing her eyes open. Large, muscular arms held her immobile, but they weren't Daric's arms, and she fought the imprisonment.

Fallen. Sunken faces. Brutal pain. Claws shredding my skin until my whole body felt like it was on fire.

"Let go of me," she hissed, her arms flailing and her legs pumping to get free.

At that instant, Hannah registered that strangely, she no longer felt any pain. As she tried to free herself from the arms of the unknown man holding her, she realized that she had somehow been healed.

"Shhh…calm down, woman. My name is Liam. I'm here to protect you, not to harm you. Daric left you in my care after he healed you. He'd have my head if anything happened to you," the unknown protector told her gently with a touch of amusement.

Hannah stopped struggling, looking up into a face that was anything but ugly. The vampire had dark hair and dark eyes, and she recognized him from Daric's memories. "You're the healer who recently found your mate?"

"Yes, with the help of our prince," he agreed readily, his voice reverent.

"Where's Daric?" Panicked, Hannah scanned the surrounding area, aware of distant voices and the sounds of battle.

She and Liam were some distance away from the battle, but she could see several unknown warriors in the street, all of them cutting through the horde of *fallen*. Her eyes frantically raked over the violent scene, finally finding her beloved mate. Sword swinging and dressed in nothing but a pair of jeans, he was cutting down *fallen* with dizzying speed. Mesmerized, she watched his muscles rippling as he wielded his blade again and again, his expression that of a man gone completely berserk. At his side, four additional men, dressed all in black, a belt of weapons around their hips, were fighting with skill, as though they had done this many times before, but Daric fought like a man possessed, taking down *fallen* at an alarming rate.

"No!" Hannah broke away from Liam's hold, scrambling off his lap. "He can't do this. The backlash will kill him."

Desperate to stop Daric, she stumbled forward before Liam caught her by her jacket, his iron grip keeping her steady, preventing her from moving forward.

"You will not interfere. Daric made his orders clear and I will follow them. He has my brothers and Adare to help him. The *fallen* nearly killed you, nearly completely drained you of blood. Had I been in his place I would have done the same," Liam told her sternly, his arms tightening around her as she resisted his hold. "Daric healed you and joined the fight. He's my prince and I owe him my life. You will stay here until they have disposed of the *fallen*. I would be fighting myself if I had not been ordered to protect you." Liam sighed heavily. "He needs to do this. Daric knows you're in danger and he needs to eliminate the threat to his mate."

Hannah watched helplessly, tears pouring down her face as she watched Daric kill without a single thought to the pain he would later experience, his expression wild and determined. "He'll suffer, Liam. Terribly," she sobbed, swiping tears impatiently from her face.

"It's his choice. After seeing what the *fallen* had done to you, there was no stopping him. He won't cease until the threat to you is gone. He's a vampire protecting his mate. He won't die, Hannah. But his pain will be great; I won't lie to you," Liam answered gravely.

"I did this to him. I'll never forgive myself," she choked out remorsefully.

"They would have found you. My brothers and I have been watching this group, wondering why they were gathering together to make their way to one particular small town in the middle of nowhere. We waited, hoping we would have the chance to eliminate them all at the same time. We didn't know they were coming after the mate of our prince," Liam muttered, obviously unhappy that he hadn't known that Daric had found his mate.

Hannah listened to Liam, but her eyes never left Daric, flinching every time he took down another *fallen* , his total disregard for his own pain making her want to start sobbing all over again. Was there nothing he wouldn't do for her, to protect her?

No. Nothing. Protect. Kill. Keep you safe.

She started in surprise as she heard Daric's ferocious, guttural voice in her head. In her anxiety about his safety, she had forgotten that their minds were connected.

Please stop. I love you. I don't want to see you suffer. Let the others finish this. Hannah begged, sending her thoughts to him with her mind.

Daric didn't answer; he just kept swinging, sometimes beheading the creatures before he struck a brutal blow to their heart.

Scared for Daric, Hannah's breath came harshly, sawing in and out of her lungs at a frantic pace that matched the hammering of her heart. "Please, Liam. There must be something we can do." Something. Anything but sit here helplessly watching the man she loved seal his fate to suffer excruciating pain just to ensure her safety.

"It's almost finished," Liam answered stoically.

Hannah's eyes finally left Daric to survey the surrounding area of the battle. It was dark, but the streetlights illuminated the street enough to show the horrors of the fight. The pavement held puddles of blood and ash, *fallen* in all stages of death. Some had already faded to dust, some were writhing on the streets and others were oozing black secretions onto the pavement.

Very few *fallen* were left standing.

Hannah searched for bodies of humans, citizens of the town that may have gotten caught in the crossfire, but there were none. "No one in Temple was hurt?" she questioned Liam softly.

"No humans. Their safety was a priority and they were sent back to their homes. We'll have clean-up to do to erase their memories of this night but they're all physically well. But my brothers, Adare and your mate look a little wasted," Liam answered, his voice concerned.

Hannah struggled to move forward as the last *fallen* hit the pavement, Liam releasing his hold on her only after her mate had dispatched the creature.

Oh, God. How will Daric survive this? So many fallen, so much pain.
Tears streamed from her eyes, nearly blinding her as she ran to her mate, oblivious to everything except him, and her need to reach him.

Daric stepped out of the carnage to meet her, catching her fast-moving body around the waist, bringing her to an abrupt halt.

"You will never leave me like that again," he stated with a feral grunt, his eyes boring into hers with a savage expression that took Hannah's breath away.

Before she could formulate an answer, his mouth crashed down on hers, showing no mercy as he pulled her body against his heaving chest and sweat-soaked skin, demanding her surrender. The embrace was rough, a brand of ownership, but Hannah yielded, needing the raw possession, the brutal passion. His tongue swept through her mouth with a carnality that sent a chill down her spine, flooding her panties and making her body weak with need.

Daric yanked his mouth away and sank his fangs into the tender skin of her neck. Hannah moaned, her body flooding with erotic heat as he fed, lifting her hands to spear through his damp hair, cradling his head against her flesh. She could feel his hunger, and there was nothing she wanted more than to meet his need. "Yes," she hissed as he drew deeply from her, sucking ravenously against her skin, taking what he wanted, what he needed. He needed blood after the battle, but Hannah knew that he also took from her to reassure himself that she belonged to him.

Daric sealed the punctures with a coarse sweep of his tongue, his face no less intense after he finished taking her blood. Yanking her to his side, he turned to all the Hale brothers and Adare. Without a word, he closed his eyes, and Hannah could feel the power vibrating from his body as wounds healed and the streets cleared of nasty spots of debris and blood.

Hannah gaped, staring first at her mate and then at the five men in front of them, one dark blond, the others all dark like Daric. In seconds, the scene went from one of post-battle carnage to the usual street in her small town of Temple, the men blending in with the darkness. Not a drop of blood or a single wound remained on any of them.

Yes, she had known that Daric was powerful, but actually seeing that power, feeling it radiate from his huge body was still a shock. And the results were nothing less than staggering.

Completely healed, all five men came forward, dropping to one knee in front of her.

"Your Highness." All five spoke in unison, their voices reverent.

Hannah shook her head in confusion, trying to figure out why these powerful warriors were kneeling in front of her.

"Only Liam is a healer, but they are all pledging their loyalty to you. They are showing respect to their future Princess," Daric answered aloud, his voice graveled.

"No. They are showing respect to their future Queen," a loud, booming voice proclaimed from the shadows.

Hannah's head whipped around, watching apprehensively as a very large man walked out of the darkness and into the glow of the streetlights, her shocked mind not certain if he was friend or foe.

"Father?" Daric's fierce expression turned to one of bewilderment.

Hannah recognized him from Daric's memories. His father was dark, frightening, and so very much like Daric. Stunned, she watched as he approached Daric, hearing her mate's confused thoughts as they joined with her own inside her head.

How? It's not possible. He's dead.

Daric's father didn't look a day over his mid-forties, even though Hannah knew he was many thousands of years old...and supposedly...dead. But here he stood, right in front of her eyes, dressed in a scarlet robe, his hands sparkling with jewels.

"It's a trick. Some sort of illusion," Daric rumbled, his face contorted with agony..., and yet, with hope.

His father approached him with a sad smile, laying a hand on Daric's shoulder as he stood in front of him. "Know the truth, son. Feel it inside me. I was granted this brief visit because you are ready to take your place as King. You proclaimed it and it will be so. You were left without the power or knowledge of a King, and it must be passed on. Now."

Hannah stepped back as the members of The Vampire Coalition rose to their feet, their faces showing their confusion, bodies preparing to defend Daric if needed. Daric caught her hand, keeping her close to him.

"I have no desire to be King," Daric said flatly, his eyes locking with his father's stubbornly, knowing that the man who stood before him was the spirit of his parent.

"You proclaimed yourself King when you manifested the Carvillius Sword. You are King, Daric, as you were always meant to be," his father answered.

"I was never meant to be King. The title was yours and then meant to be Nolan's," Daric answered harshly.

Daric's father shot his son a look of remorse and closed his eyes. Hannah squeezed Daric's hand, her heart breaking as she looked at the agonized and confused look in the eyes of her mate. Light emanated from his father's bejeweled hand, illumination that seemed to be radiating from the older man's palm and into Daric's body. She felt her mate shudder, and moved closer to his body, plastering herself along his side, sending comforting thoughts into his mind. She wasn't entirely sure exactly what was happening, but Daric had his father here, something she knew he needed if he was ever going to completely escape his past.

The glowing light faded and the ancient king slowly removed his hand from Daric's shoulder. "Now you have the ancient knowledge and power to be King. I have merely been waiting for you to declare yourself, as you should have done a thousand years ago."

"I was angry when I said that earlier. I don't want to be ruler. I just want to watch over my people," Daric said, agitated.

His father stopped, his hands behind his back, and stared at Daric. "What do you think a King does? You are doing what you were always meant to do. But you've been doing so without the full power to lead."

"I was not meant to be King!" Daric exploded, his expression fierce.

His father sighed. "Actually, you were. I did wrong by you, Daric. I never loved you any less than I did Nolan, but I knew Nolan's time on the earth was limited and I was losing my mind, so I threw all my energy into him, knowing he was going to leave me just as your mother did. I didn't plan what happened. I regret that I hurt my people, and that I hurt you. I hope that you can forgive me some day."

"I don't understand. Nolan was your heir, the favored son," Daric questioned without rancor.

"Nolan was never destined to be King. He was born without the marking of a Carvillius King, a mark that always bears the Carvillius Sword. I knew he would never live to be King. When you were born with the mark, I should have treated you equally, but the realization that I wouldn't have Nolan with me for long made me focus all my attention on him, because I wasn't well enough to see anything except another loss. The very fact that I knew I would lose him sent me deeper over the edge of madness. It was never that I loved you less, Daric. I should have prepared you to be King." The older man resumed pacing with a long sigh. "I should have passed the title to you after your mother died. I wasn't capable of being King anymore."

Hannah's chest tightened as she watched the older man struggle with his guilt and remorse. She knew Daric's mother had died soon after he was born, a victim of the *fallen*.

"I thought you were grieving for Nolan so desperately that you let yourself go with him. I didn't think I was valuable enough or worthy enough to make you want to stay." Daric answered hoarsely.

The ancient king stopped, shaking his head as he looked at his son. "I was mad long before Nolan died, Daric. I couldn't live without my mate. It doesn't excuse how I behaved or how I treated you, but I hope someday you'll forgive me. It wasn't lack of love for either of my sons, it was the dementia I suffered because of losing my mate."

"Why didn't you tell me then?" Daric asked, his voice tormented.

"I was weak, pathetic, my mind broken. I didn't want Nolan to know his fate before his time. It wasn't fair to you, but I wasn't thinking like a king. I was functioning on the level of a child."

"Nolan had a right to know, and I should have been allowed to know that my brother was going to die," Daric answered, his voice irritated.

"You did have the right to know and I don't blame you for your anger," his father responded immediately. "I just wasn't strong enough or sane enough to deal with it properly. I'm sorry, son. I failed both you and my people."

"Nolan?" Daric asked, his voice choked, unable to utter anything except his brother's name.

His father smiled weakly. "He walks with me among the Ancients, with his true mate. Maya was not the female for him. His female awaited him beyond. He's happy, Daric. His destiny wasn't here on earth. He asked me to tell you that you will always have his love, even though you're not together right now."

Hannah watched Daric's face soften, his precious memories of his brother rolling through his mind and into hers. "Tell him I feel the same," Daric answered hoarsely. "And that I miss him."

"Rule well and long, King Daric," his father answered quietly, his intense eyes focusing lovingly on his son. "Lead without guilt and knowing that I was a broken, weak king who failed my people and my son. All that happened was not under your control. Nothing you could have done would have ended things differently. I walk with your mother just as Nolan walks with his true mate. You have found your true mate here on earth. All was fated before your birth."

Hannah shivered as the elder king's eyes moved to her. "Thank you for loving my son. You will make an excellent Queen."

"I still don't want to be King," Daric grumbled.

His father eyes pierced him sharply. "You are King. Your sons will be princes and all will be as it should be. Don't be so damn stubborn."

My sons.

Hannah caught the whispered thought as it went through Daric's mind and his world finally righted itself. She felt his acceptance and his forgiveness all at once, her heart rejoicing that he was finally at peace with his past and his family. Maybe some good would come from this *fallen* attack after all.

"Oh, God. The *fallen*. The backlash." In all the turmoil of the evening, she had forgotten about the pain that Daric would suffer very shortly.

Daric's father smiled, the first genuine smile Hannah had seen from him. "There will be no backlash. Your mate wields the Carvillius Sword. It's one of the benefits of being King. As long as the sword is used to defeat evil, there will be no backlash. It wouldn't do to have a king out of commission." His smile grew even broader as he added, "And he has a mating that needs to occur very soon. He's pushed himself far enough."

Hannah's tension dissipated, and she returned the ancient king's smile with one of her own. "I'll make certain it does, Your Majesty."

"I'm no longer king, but I'd be honored to call you daughter," he answered, his ancient eyes filled with longing.

Hannah looked at her mate, her eyes filled with tears. Daric's father was asking for forgiveness, for absolution for his actions that had been caused by something out of his control.

He's here now. He loves you, Daric. I don't think he ever meant to hurt anyone. Hannah sent the thoughts to her mate, asking him silently if he forgave his parent.

Her mate's fierce gaze connected with hers as he answered. *I have a mate and I know now how a vampire can lose his mind quite easily because of her.*

Daric shot her an accusing look, a glance of warning that he wasn't done with the issue of her putting herself in harm's way.

Hannah stepped forward, pulling her hand from Daric's as she embraced his father. "Thank you," she whispered quietly as she hugged the ancient ruler.

"No. Thank *you*, daughter," he answered as he hugged her tightly, his voice choked with emotion.

A low growl vibrated through the air as Daric stepped forward and pulled her back against him. "Mine," he grunted, his arms coming possessively around her.

His father released her with a hearty laugh. "If he's jealous of an ancient spirit, you'd best get the mating done." He sobered as he added in a booming voice, "All Hail King Daric Carvillius, King of the Vampire Healers. Heed him, serve him, and you shall be rewarded with your mate."

Hannah watched in fascinated awe as one by one, vampire healers appeared, until the streets were filled with healers kneeling before their newly-appointed King.

"Will they find their mates now?" she asked, desperately hoping that Daric's healers were finally going to be happy.

"They will," Daric's father answered confidently. "The damage I did has finally abated. Liam and Regan started the healing and it will continue from this day on." The ancient king's voice started to lose its power. "Be happy, my son and daughter."

"Father!" Daric let go of Hannah long enough to reach for his father, taking the man into his arms for an emotional hug. "No regrets. No guilt. I understand," Daric told his father in a husky voice.

"I love you, son," his father answered weakly, clinging to Daric.

"I love you," Daric said gruffly, his eyes moist as he clung to the dissipating image of his parent until the elderly king had completely faded away.

Tears spilled from Hannah's eyes as she melted into Daric's shuddering body. Finally, her vampire healer had found peace.

Daric turned, facing the masses with her cradled at his side, cringing as he saw all of the healers, Adare, and the Hale brothers kneeling before him. "Oh, Christ! Get up. I hate that shit." He eyed his subjects, his eyes intense. "Go back to work. Kissing up to me isn't going to get you a mate any faster," he told them in a booming voice that carried his comment to the mass of healers before him.

The healers vanished with a mental command from Daric, leaving only the Hale brothers and Adare before him. The men rose, all of them smirking at Daric.

"You aren't going to insist that we kneel to our King now?" Liam asked curiously.

"Hell, no. This is a new generation of royalty. No kneeling. No scraping and bowing. It irritates me," he grumbled. "You've all shown your respect for my mate. Now leave us."

"So being King makes no difference to you?" Nathan asked in a low voice filled with mischief.

Daric's look was evil as he replied, "Yeah. It means I have a bigger...sword." He manifested the Carvillius Sword and waved it in the direction of the Hale brothers menacingly. "Now leave before I show you the hard way just how powerful I am."

Ethan snickered. "He's got a bad case of the mating compulsion."

"Can I kiss Hannah good-bye before I go?" Rory asked cheerfully.

Hannah's lips curled, knowing the brothers were needling Daric. As she felt his body tense, she wasn't entirely sure that was a good idea at the moment.

"You will go before you leave your mates widowed and alone. Take care of the clean-up with the humans in town before you go home," Daric boomed, his command so forceful that Hannah stepped back in alarm.

One by one, the Hale brothers and Adare took their leave with a knowing smile, each sending Hannah a playful wink before teleporting away without another word. The brothers might like to tease, but they were far from stupid.

The night was suddenly deadly quiet. Hannah watched Daric as he dissolved the Carvillius Sword and focused his intensity on her.

"You, my dearest mate, will answer for disobeying me about your safety!" he snarled as he stalked her.

She stepped back, the fury in his eyes startling her. Never once, after their first meeting, had she truly feared Daric, and she wasn't afraid of him now; however, she'd have to be daft not to be cautious about approaching him when he was in this mood. "I wanted to clear my schedule so we could spend the evening together. I planned to be home before dark. I'm sorry."

"I don't want you to be fucking sorry. I want you to listen to me when I tell you that I won't tolerate you being stubborn when it comes to your safety. Dammit. I need you to be safe," he told her harshly, latching onto her arm as he spoke.

Hannah sighed as Daric pulled her into his body, seeing his mind exploding with thoughts of something happening to her, images of what he had seen when he had arrived at her encounter with the *fallen*. His brain was filled with fury, but it was a frenzied rage entirely manifested by his mating instincts and his fear of losing her.

"I'm safe, Daric," she whispered as he clutched her against his chest so tightly she could barely breathe.

"Damn right you're safe and you're going to stay that way. We mate now," he answered in a blistering tone.

Hannah was nearly panting as she responded to his need to dominate, feeling the effects of the mating instincts grabbing hold of her body, wrapping her in heat. "Now," she agreed with a moan, eager to follow wherever his testosterone overloaded body led. She had been ready to be his mate ever since he had goaded her into flying down that mountain, encouraging her to be free of her past and to look toward her future.

The two of them vanished, Hannah groaning as Daric's mouth covered hers roughly, an early warning that his violent mating need had taken control.

CHAPTER 7

Daric knew he was lost. Somewhere, in the small piece of his rational mind that was left inside his head, he knew that his mating instincts had taken over, wanting to dominate his mate, mark her as his in every way possible, demand her obedience. He was functioning on a visceral level, his instincts would not be denied, and he no longer gave a shit whether he was rational or not.

Mark. Protect. Keep her safe. Make her heed my commands.

He manifested in his bedroom, his mate in his arms, and his desires ruling his body and senses.

Daric stripped Hannah with a mental command, leaving her standing before him nude, her body exposed to his maniacal gaze. His eyes moved over every inch of her body, claiming her with his possessive stare.

Mine. Need to have her moaning, trembling, begging for me, pleading for my cock to be inside her. Only for me.

His hungry gaze landed between her thighs, feeling her arousal, scenting her need. He stripped her pussy bare with his magic, eliminating the short curls, grunting as he saw her bare flesh glistening with moisture, proof of her desire.

If he had previously held a small amount of rational thought, it deserted him at that moment, leaving him with nothing but tortured need that had to be sated before his temporary insanity became permanent.

Hannah's gut clenched as she looked at Daric's face, his expression so feral that her heart kicked into overdrive, wondering exactly what he was planning. His thoughts were hard to read, a tangle of conflicted emotions and needs. Much the same as her own.

"You will obey me from now on," he growled, grasping her arm and pulling her toward the bed.

She went willingly, perplexed as he planted her hands on the wooden post at the corner of the bed, her body bent at the waist.

It wasn't until she felt the first sting of his hand on her ass that she understood his intentions. He was spanking her, actually punishing her for disobeying him, for putting herself in danger. Yanking to pull away automatically, she found her hands immovable, held to the post by Daric's magic. As the second smack landed, she moaned, the jolt going straight between her thighs, flooding her pussy. Her whole body submerged with erotic heat as his big fingers delved into her saturated folds from behind, teasing her, before he slapped her ass again.

"Daric, please," she groaned, her body on fire.

His needs swirled inside her brain, along with her own, swamping her with heat, wanting his domination of her body, needing it.

Hannah writhed with every erotic smack on her ass cheeks, every stroke of his fingers on the sensitive flesh between her legs. Daric alternated, torturing her with her need, while she stayed helplessly in place, his to command.

He kneaded the flesh of her ass, his hands running over the now fiery skin. "Mine," he uttered mindlessly, his big hands cupping her ass in a gesture of pure possession.

He finally released her, pulling her up to face him. "Undress me," he demanded.

Hannah shivered at his dominating tone, a voice that would allow no argument. And she didn't want to argue. She wanted to do whatever he wanted, however he wanted it, her need to please him overwhelming her. Knowing he could make his clothing disappear effortlessly, she recognized his order for what it was...an act of dominance, his need for her to satisfy his pounding desire to control and take.

Dropping to her knees, she wanted nothing more than to liberate that massive cock from his jeans. Her fingers shook as she pulled down the zipper, making her try twice before successfully opening the top button. She tugged down the denim, almost frantic to free the engorged member that was straining against the cotton. Her eyes moved up to Daric's face, his intense stare drilling into her as their eyes met, submerging her in his raw need, opening her senses to the same desire he was experiencing, elemental and completely, utterly primal.

As she returned her attention to divesting him of his jeans, the material disappeared, Daric obviously having lost patience, leaving his cock large, hot, and heavy in front of her face. Licking her lips nervously, the desire to taste him was almost overwhelming.

"Claim my cock with your mouth," he insisted, threading his hands through her hair to bring her mouth to him.

Daric's words jolted her into action, the erotic command inundating Hannah with pleasure, leading to the realization that she was taking what was hers, as much as Daric was demanding what belonged to him. She flicked her tongue over the head of his cock, savoring the salty drop of moisture leaking from the tip.

I'm his mate. I do this to him. Only I can pleasure him this way.

She hummed her satisfaction as her lips consumed him, taking as much of his huge phallus into her mouth as she could handle. Sucking sensually, she bobbed up and down on him, hearing him release a tortured groan as his hands guided her faster, deeper. Every lick, every stroke was vigorous, a rough taking of what was hers to take, hers to pleasure. There wasn't a speck of the silky cock that she didn't want to possess, didn't want to make her own with her tongue and mouth.

Hannah slid her hands along the back of Daric's rock hard thighs until she reached his tight ass. Her hands kneaded the muscles there, feeling them flex as his hips pistoned in and out of her mouth.

Like a woman possessed, she dug her fingers into his ass, swallowing him deeper, deeper than she could ever have imagined she could take him, his cock bumping the back of her throat.

I need to make him come. Need to taste him.

A hoarse, strangled cry left Daric's throat as she felt him tense.

Yes. Come. I need to taste you. Now.

His hands fisted in her hair as he threw his head back and groaned. Hannah watched his face as his hot release poured into her mouth, moaning at the taste of him, watching the raw beauty of his release. So powerful. So commanding. So completely hers.

Heart pounding, Hannah realized she was experiencing just a small portion of Daric's unrelenting possessiveness, and it was consuming her whole. She needed him inside her, claiming her, pounding into her with unbridled strength and brutal ownership.

He was on her immediately, scooping her up and dropping her onto the bed with a savage grunt. "Need to make you come. Make you fucking beg for it."

Oh God, yes.

She was more than ready to beg, and he hadn't even touched her. Her body burning hot, she undulated her hips. "Please."

Kneeling between her thighs, Daric towered above her, emanating a raw strength and power that should have been terrifying to behold. But it wasn't like that. Daric's intensity was smoking hot, and Hannah trembled with eager anticipation as her hands flew above her head, held fast by invisible bonds.

"You will come for me now," he grunted, his sculpted chest heaving.

Shit. I'll probably explode the moment he touches me.

Hannah's body was primed and ready, begging for his masterful touch. She moaned as he cupped her breasts roughly, running his thumbs around her sensitive nipples, bringing them to hardened peaks. He pinched them lightly, sending a jolt of electricity straight to the apex of her thighs. Her back arched, her arms pulling against her bonds as his hot mouth took the place of his fingers, biting gently and licking first one breast and then the other. "Please, Daric. Please," she cried out, her entire body ready to ignite.

"You will tell me what you need." Daric's voice was hoarse as his mouth moved lower, his tongue bathing her with heat as it moved down her body, claiming it.

"You. Inside me. Now," she whimpered, needing his huge, hungry cock inside her, fusing them together, filling the yearning that was ready to consume her.

"No. *You* will come for me," he demanded gutturally against the hot skin of her lower abdomen, as his scorching tongue glided farther south over her bare mound.

Oh, God. Hannah wasn't sure she could live through the torment of Daric mastering her body. She lifted her hips with a strangled, tortured mewl, a sound of complete surrender and desperation as his tongue finally trailed over her wet folds.

"Yes. Yes, please. Now," she pleaded, his tongue meandering over the sensitive, pink flesh, laving her from bottom to top again and again, teasing her sensitive clit with each pass.

He pushed her legs up and open wide, leaving her completely vulnerable to him, entirely at his mercy. "Mine. So wet and ready for me," he growled against her pussy as his mouth claimed her completely.

Daric feasted on Hannah with a wild abandon that nearly made her lose her mind. He was like a man possessed, his focus entirely on making her climax. Her body thrashed within the confines of his bindings, the feel of his mouth on her naked clit more sensation than she could handle, the tiny bundle of nerves throbbing with every touch of his tongue.

"Daric. I can't stand it. I can't," she panted wildly as she closed her eyes, hearing every beat of her stuttering heart in her ears.

"Come for me." The deep, reverberating sound vibrated through her core.

She flew apart with an agonized cry. "Daric."

Molten heat flooded her body as her sheath contracted and released, quaking with the force of her climax.

Panting, her body drenched in sweat, Hannah opened her eyes and watched as Daric crawled up her body with the grace of a large cat stalking its prey.

Her pulse fluttered erratically as she looked at his face when it came level with hers, his eyes as wild as her heartbeat. His need slammed into her body and mind, a jumbled mess of emotions all tied to his urgency to mate.

"Mate with me, Daric. I need you," she whispered in a breathless voice, her eyes pleading with him. He needed to join them, for his sake and for hers.

Pulses of energy emanated from his massive, sculpted body that was blanketing hers, and his eyes were nearly black with desire. She sighed with relief as her hands came loose and she was able to bring her palm to his tortured face, shivering as her hand met the rough stubble of his whiskers and fiery hot skin.

Daric shifted, bringing himself to his knees, every muscle in his body rippling with tension, catching her hand as he moved and placed it at her side. His fingers slid up her arm sensually, leaving a trail of fire as he moved to her upper arm, tracing his mark. "Mine," he said possessively, his voice guttural and primitive.

"Yes," she agreed, her core clenching with need at his caveman tone.

His brows drew together in a pensive, possessive stare as his fingers moved over and over the marking, as though his touch could brand her deeper. Hannah wanted to tell him that he already had her, heart and soul, so deeply that she could never get free.

"You will never be free. You'll belong to me," he said aloud, answering her thoughts as he moved his forearm to match their marks.

Before Hannah could form a reply, heat started to unfurl within her, a fire that scorched her from the inside out, making her release a primal groan. She flexed her hips, her groin grinding wildly against his rock hard cock.

Daric uttered the mating pledge in his native language while her body pulsed in response. Her mind might not understand the lyrical words, but her body responded with total comprehension. Head thrashing, she wrapped her legs around Daric's waist as soon as the words were spoken. "Please. I need you inside me. Now." *Before I die of yearning.*

Her breath hitched as she felt the head of his cock against her moist heat, ready to join them.

Yes. Yes. Yes. Now.

Suddenly, Daric was buried to his balls in one powerful thrust, a forceful stroke that made Hannah gasp, her walls stretching to accept his length and girth, the joining causing so much ecstasy that she could barely breathe. Mindless, she urged him to move, digging her heels into his taut ass. Ignoring her silent plea for faster movement, Daric pulled almost entirely out of her, groaning as he buried himself slowly and deeply again, letting her tight channel close around his huge member.

"Tight, hot, and wet for me," he said forcefully, repeating the action again.

"Oh, God. Please fuck me, Daric." All Hannah wanted was the rough pounding of that mammoth cock inside her.

His hand fisted into her hair at the back of her head, holding her still while his mouth claimed hers, his cock still buried deeply inside her. His tongue pillaged, owning her with urgent sweeps; fast, volatile movements that she desperately needed him to be making with his cock. She whimpered into his mouth, nearly sobbing with the desire for him to move within her, take her with the forceful strokes that he was applying to her mouth with his tongue.

Please, please. I need you.

Daric yanked his mouth from hers. "Fuck!" The curse left his mouth as though he were in pain. "Want you to burn for me like I burn for you. But I can't take it anymore."

He pinned her hands over her head and thrust into her hard and fast, just the way Hannah wanted it. "Yes," she moaned with relief, the friction exquisite. "I already burn, Daric." *So hot I can't take anymore.*

"Need you to feel the way I do. Need me the way I need you," he snarled as his hips flexed, pounding into her with a force that took her breath away.

"I do." They were the only words Hannah could choke out as her hips rose to meet the forceful thrusts of his cock, their carnal mating the only thing that would satisfy her lust, her desire for her mate's big, powerful body to take her over the edge.

Her back arched as what felt like a thousand jolts of electricity battered her body, centering in her core as Daric moved deeper, faster, furiously. Releasing her hands, he grasped her hips, pummeling into her, owning her.

Sensing his urge to taste her, Hannah turned her head, baring the vulnerable curve of her neck. His fangs sunk into her flesh with a carnality that sent her over the edge, her body climaxing violently as Daric drew from her neck in the same fast and furious rhythm that matched the movements of his cock.

"Oh, God. Yes," she hissed as he pulled deep and fast while he pounded into her channel just as ferociously.

She grasped his shoulders, her nails biting into his skin as she searched for purchase, her body floating as erotic heat coursed through her from Daric's bite, as endless invisible threads wound around their souls, bonding them together as one.

Hannah sobbed openly as the powerful contractions of her channel milked Daric's pounding cock and tiny fangs erupted from her gums. As Daric swirled his tongue over the bite in her neck, closing it, Hannah didn't hesitate, burying her hands into his hair as she bit his neck, sinking her fangs into his flesh with a moan.

"Fuck!" Daric groaned as Hannah ran her hands through his hair, feeding sensually from his neck.

She pulled slowly, taking Daric's blood into her body, savoring his essence. He was feeling the same incredible binding of their souls, and he growled as he buried himself deeply inside of her with a feral groan, his warm release flooding her womb. His entire body shuddered as she ran her tongue smoothly over the puncture on his neck, sealing it.

He rolled, keeping his cock deeply imbedded inside her as she sprawled on top of his huge, muscular body. Struggling for breath, Hannah didn't speak as she floated down from her mating high. Daric held her lovingly, possessively, one hand on her lower back and one in her hair.

Still trembling in the aftermath of the most extraordinary experience of her life, she wished she could find the words to express what had just happened, but they escaped her. There wasn't really anything she could say to explain what had just occurred.

I know. I feel the same.

Hannah smiled as she heard Daric's baritone in her mind. His confusion and pain were gone, replaced with a profound peace.

"I love you," she whispered quietly next to his ear, yawning as she rested her head on his shoulder, so tired she couldn't move.

"Don't move," he demanded, covering them both with a sheet and quilt.

"I'll squash you," she answered, trying to disengage their tangled bodies, knowing she was ready to fall asleep, her body completely drained.

Daric quirked an arrogant brow at her and yanked her back against him, urging her head back to his shoulder. "I'm King of the Vampire Healers. I do not...get squashed."

Hannah rolled her eyes. "Am I going to stay here all day? It could get uncomfortable for you."

"Yes," he answered in a husky voice. "And I love you too, Hannah."

Her heart stuttered and skipped a beat. She already knew he loved her, had known it since he'd rushed into the horde of *fallen* without a concern for his own pain, intent on ensuring her safety. But hearing it aloud made her heart sing. Releasing another tired breath, she answered, "Okay. Just don't complain if you hurt when you wake up." And really, she was so very comfortable and felt so incredibly safe.

"Oh, I'll ache. But you'll be exactly where I need you to relieve the pain," he answered in a wicked, wicked voice. "And I'll know if you try to get yourself in trouble," he added, locking his arms around her waist.

Hannah smiled against his shoulder. Honestly, Daric could be such a caveman. "I won't," she answered honestly. "Seeing what you're willing to do to protect me scared me, Daric. I don't want to put you in danger."

"Speaking of that, mate, you will call me whenever you need me, for any reason. Don't ever try to close your thoughts to me again when you need help," he grumbled. "Or for any other reason."

"I was trying to protect you. I was afraid you would die. And it didn't work anyway," Hannah argued, the horrendous memory of being assaulted by the *fallen* making her shiver.

"Don't ever doubt that I can protect you, love. And I will. If anything ever happened to you I'd go insane just like my father. Only it wouldn't happen slowly. Keep that in mind next time you decide to risk yourself. You risk both of us," he told her sternly, but one of his hands moved from her waist to her hair, stroking it soothingly, as though trying to chase away the memories of the *fallen*.

Hannah sighed, thinking it was really too bad that she couldn't do anything worth him punishing her again. Her ass tingled, and her core clenched just thinking about Daric's brand of punishment.

"I could always think of some minor infraction," he suggested in a husky voice, his hand moving down to caress her ass.

"You'd make up something bogus?" she answered, smiling as she felt his cock starting to swell inside her.

"Yes," he replied immediately.

"Your Majesty, that isn't very king-like behavior," she admonished him with a startled laugh.

Daric rolled, trapping her beneath him, his eyes hot with sinful intent. "Never did give a shit about being King," he rumbled, covering her mouth with his.

Hannah's body ignited, all thoughts of sleep slipping away as her desire roared to life.

Ah…was there anything better than royalty behaving badly?

Later, much later, Hannah decided that there really wasn't.

EPILOGUE

Six Months Later…

D aric tugged on the bow tie of the uncomfortable tuxedo he was wearing with a frown, using his magic to make the tie and top button of the shirt looser and more comfortable. *Better.* The starch in the shirt still scraped at his neck, but he'd live with it to make Hannah happy. *Anything for Hannah.*

He looked around the town park, wondering if everyone in Temple was here. It certainly felt like it. The park was overflowing with people…and vampires. Daric smiled, slightly amused as he wondered what the good people of Temple would think if they knew they were celebrating the Carvillius wedding, mingling around the park on a mild early summer evening, with a whole lot of hungry vampires and vampire healers.

His heart tripped, as he thought back to Hannah coming toward him earlier on Liam's arm, looking more radiant than any woman he had ever seen. And, being well over a thousand years old, he had seen a lot of women. But none compared to his bride, his beautiful Hannah. *Not even close.*

Every day, Daric swore he couldn't love Hannah more than he did that day. But the next he loved her more. Finally, he stopped thinking that he couldn't love her more, because he realized that he would be lying to himself. Every single day she would do something that would touch his heart. She always did. And he didn't think she would ever stop.

His eyes roamed the crowd, automatically searching for his bride, happy to see that many of his healers had attended with their new mates. The last several months had seen many healers mated, a fact that delighted Daric as it meant that he had more time to spend with his own mate, and that his healers were behaving. The Hale brothers were at the buffet table. Again. His smile turned evil as he watched the brothers tugging at the neck of their tuxedos, all of them being part of the wedding party. Liam had given Hannah away and had served as Daric's best man, while the rest of the Hale brothers had been groomsmen. Their mates had all stood up for Hannah as bridesmaids.

Daric shoved his hands in his pockets and made his way to the buffet table, ready to get another plate before the Hale men consumed the entire feast.

"Your Majesty, are you sure you don't want me to make you a protective ward?" Regan asked, standing next to Liam at the table, her brows drawn together with a concerned look.

Daric smiled at Regan, looking around briefly to make sure no one human heard Regan call him by his title. But there was nobody swarming the food except the Hale brothers with their mates tucked to their sides, their women watching them fondly as Ethan, Rory, Nathan and Liam wolfed down the food. "It doesn't work on me, Regan. But I thank you for offering again. Royalty has their own wards, a power that keeps us from harm against the mage. And please call me Daric." He bowed and departed to find Hannah.

Regan sighed. "He's so awesome," she whispered to Brianna, Callie and Sasha. The other women nodded their heads in agreement.

"He is not awesome. He is King. He's our ruler. But he is *not* awesome." Liam stopped filling his plate long enough to scowl at his mate.

Daric snickered as he walked away, listening as all of the Hale brothers explained to their mates why they were not allowed to find their King awesome. As though any one of the Hale brothers needed to worry? Their mates were so devoted to them that none of them needed to worry. Daric had a feeling that Regan had said that just to needle her mate and the other women colluded with her for the same reason. *And people think vampires are diabolical. Women can be the very devil when they want to be.* Personally, Daric loved seeing the Hale brothers get their comeuppance from their mates. When he got it from Hannah? -- Not so much.

All thought of food suddenly left him, as he felt Hannah moving inside his mind, solemn for some reason, on what should be the happiest day of her life.

Skirting around groups of people, both vampire and human, Daric followed the trail of his mate, desperate to know why Hannah was less than blissful at her own wedding reception. Whatever it was… he'd fix it. He and Hannah had spent the last six months in complete bliss. What could be the matter with her? Was she having second thoughts about him?

He stepped out of the lights of the reception area to the wooded area beyond, his temper flaring at the sight of Hannah moving into the woods by herself. Frantic, he pushed his way through the thick foliage, stopping abruptly as he saw a soft glow just ahead, the transparent figure of a woman seeming to hover above the water, his bride standing reverently before it, mumbling softly.

"I love him so desperately. I just don't want to shame him or his family. Thank you for the advice, mother." Hannah inclined her head in a gesture of respect as she spoke.

"You're welcome, child," the shimmering image of the woman replied, slowly fading away, leaving the area lit only by moonlight.

"Hannah?" Daric watched his bride turn slowly, radiant as she started to smile.

Daric's breath seized as her smile widened, a glorious look of happiness on her face that she reserved only for him. Every damn time she saw him. And he always reacted the same way. Wonder. Joy. Awe. And a cock as hard as granite.

Picking up the skirt of her ivory wedding gown, Hannah ran to him, throwing herself into his arms. "I love you, Daric. I can't believe you're my husband."

His arms wrapped around her soft, warm body as Daric inhaled the tantalizing scent that belonged uniquely to his mate. "What was that about? Who or what was that? And why are you out here in the dark by yourself? You know better." He tried to be angry, but he nearly groaned as she wrapped her arms around his neck, her breasts rubbing against him and her softer form molding perfectly against his hardness.

"It was your mother, Daric. Did you know that there are areas where the veil between our world and the world of the Ancients is weak enough to speak to your ancestors? She told me to tell you that if you ever needed her, your father, or Nolan, that you could speak to them here or in one of the other places of weakness. Your father didn't have the chance to tell you," Hannah was chattering, her voice excited.

Impossible. He'd never spoken with the Ancients.

"You never tried," Hannah answered aloud. "All you have to do is call to them, ask for advice."

"And how did you come to know about this?" Daric answered, his voice still doubtful.

"I was worried. I guess everything overwhelmed me today. I was so happy, but afraid that I wouldn't make a good Queen. I have a business to run and things to do. I don't know anything about being Queen or even being the mate of a vampire healer. I called out to your mother, saying I wish I could get her advice. I guess I was desperate. She called me here." Hannah shifted in his arms, pulling back to peer up at his face. "You've probably always been strong enough to handle everything yourself, and you weren't King, before. Your mother said it's a power that can only be used by the King and Queen."

Daric gaped at her, still incredulous that it was actually possible to speak to the Ancients. No. Not once had he ever called on his ancestors for help, tried to speak to his family.

"Because you never needed it," Hannah said wistfully. "I did."

Daric looked at his lovely mate with a frown. "You were worried? Why didn't you say something? You're perfect just the way you are."

"I love you, Daric. I want to be a help to you, not a burden that you have to protect."

Once, he had thought that having a woman would be a burden, a complete nuisance that he didn't want to deal with. "You saw my memories," he stated flatly, knowing she had seen his previous attitude at having a mate.

"Yes," she replied, her eyes leaving his face and staring at the buttons on his shirt. "You never really wanted a mate."

"I want you," he growled. "I didn't know what it would be like to have a woman who filled my heart and soul with happiness. I was fucking clueless, Hannah. I saw the worst example of what could happen with Nolan. I wouldn't change a thing about you and I damn well wouldn't do things differently. I didn't know that you would fill all the emptiness inside me. Hell, I didn't even really know it was there until I found you."

"I'm glad you feel that way because I think you're stuck with me," she answered, her laughter spilling over into her words. "I got bridal jitters after I saw your memories of not wanting a mate. But I think I'm over it now."

Damn well better be. If she wasn't over it, he'd take all the time he needed later to convince her of just how much he loved her, wanted her. "What did my mother say?" he asked, curious.

Hannah sighed. "She said to run my business, be happy with you, and everything else would work itself out. She has a very calming nature," she said thoughtfully.

Daric had never known his mother, but he knew she must have been an extraordinary woman for his father to have descended into madness from losing her.

"Would you like to talk to her? We could call her again," Hannah suggested, wrapping her arms around his shoulders and nuzzling her tempting mouth into the side of his neck.

Daric shuddered. He *would* call his family and talk with all of them. Later. He would like to see Nolan again, get to know his mother and share ideas with his father. He was happy that Hannah had discovered that conversing with them was possible, but it wasn't his priority right now. "Later," he answered, pulling his mate snugly against his body. "Right now I want to discuss the fact that you left without telling me or anyone else."

"Your mother called me here, Daric. She said it was safe," she answered, rolling her eyes at him.

Daric had to admit that Hannah *had* been good about not wandering away or doing things to endanger herself since the *fallen* attack. And his mother had called. Still, she *had* disobeyed.

Daric's cock twitched, swelling at the trail his thoughts began to take. "A minor infraction, then," he told her, his voice harsh and coarse with desire.

His heart started beating at a frantic pace as Hannah smiled up at him with that sinful expression that always made him insane, desperate to take her, to remind her that she belonged to him and only him.

What the fuck. It was his wedding night. It was making him possessive.

Hannah tugged on his bow tie, pulling it loose and drawing it from his neck. "Anything makes you possessive," she reminded him as she tossed the tie over her shoulder.

Well, yeah. He couldn't argue that point. He swallowed the lump in his throat as her nimble fingers started unbuttoning his shirt. God, he loved it when she stripped him, even though he could easily divest them of their clothing with just a thought. "About that infraction," he grumbled. "Very naughty, wife."

He groaned as she started to trail her tongue over his chest, skin that she was quickly unveiling by tearing open his unbuttoned shirt. "Vampire, you haven't seen naughty," she answered in low, aroused voice. "Bring it on. I'm willing to obey your *every* command tonight."

Christ! Daric didn't bother to remind her that he was actually a vampire healer, because he didn't give a shit. She could call him any damn thing she wanted as long she claimed him as hers. "Home," he grunted, wrapping his arms around her, one at her waist and the other in her hair as he tilted her head to devour that wicked mouth of hers.

The two them disappeared as Daric swung his bride into his arms, clutching all that really mattered close to him as he teleported them away from their reception, unable to wait another moment to get his wife into his bed.

Hannah's laughter rang out beside the moonlit water as they departed, the couples' happiness and love strong enough to penetrate the barrier between earth and the world of the Ancients.

Somewhere, beyond the barrier, Daric's mother, father, and brother sighed in relief and rejoiced.

THE END

OF BOOK FIVE: DARIC'S MATE

Please continue reading for an excerpt of

A Dangerous Bargain
Book One

Of my latest paranormal series

The Sentinel Demons

If you enjoyed this collection you might also like:

The Billionaire's Obsession
The Complete Collection Boxed Set
(Mine For Tonight, Mine For Now, Mine Forever, Mine Completely)

and

The Pleasure Of His Punishment
The Complete Collection

For Updates:
Please visit me at http://www.facebook.com/authorjsscott
You can write to me at jsscott_author@hotmail.com
You can also tweet @AuthorJSScott

Excerpt of A Dangerous Bargain

A Dangerous Bargain
Book One

The Sentinel Demons

By J. S. Scott

ISBN-10:1939962331

ISBN-13:978-1-939962-33-1

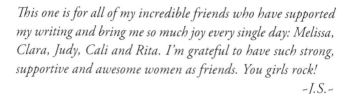

This one is for all of my incredible friends who have supported my writing and bring me so much joy every single day: Melissa, Clara, Judy, Cali and Rita. I'm grateful to have such strong, supportive and awesome women as friends. You girls rock!

-J.S.-

Prologue

"The Sentinel Demons-A History"
AUTHOR-UNKNOWN

Many people believe that demons are evil spirits, possessing humans, taking over their minds and bodies until they are nothing but a shell, a vessel for the evil entity that dwells inside them. What most humans don't know is that there are also other types of demons, physical beings created thousands of years ago, during a period of time when demons came to rule the Earth, having been set loose by careless gods who used them for chaos and revenge. The gods created them in so great a number that they finally had to confine all their creations to a demon realm, a prison that could contain them. Said gods, who are now considered nothing more than myth, and whose vanity was endless, adamantly refused to destroy the demons-to annihilate all of them would be an admission that what the deities had done was actually wrong. All-powerful, all-knowing gods and demigods did not make errors. They themselves declared it impossible. And how could they destroy their own magic, lose creatures that might be needed later? After all, the gods were usually at war, and what if they needed their evil creations for weapons? So instead, the demons stayed confined to the demon realm, a place where no god would venture-a realm of such vile evilness, such toxicity and so malodorous, that no selfish deity could tolerate visiting.

The realm was hidden, situated between Earth and Hades, a place where the demons remained, multiplied, and grew in strength while the gods ignored their existence. Unfortunately, ignoring such heinous immortals eventually created utter chaos, the demons finally gaining enough power to leave the demon realm and create havoc on an Earth that was, by that time, inhabited by a large population of humans. These demons became known as the Evils.

Devastation ruled, humans being taken in large numbers, disappearing in droves. The balance between good and evil tipped, evil ruling the planet, creating a rift that not even the gods themselves could fix. Desperate to restore sanity to an insane world, the gods tried in vain to destroy the vile beasts that upset the equilibrium, finally putting aside their vanity in favor of survival. But it was too late; the demon population was too large, too powerful, and the egotistic gods weren't about to venture near the Evils to destroy them.

Desperate, the deities banded together and created a new breed of demon to fight the Evils; the newcomers' souls would still be dark, but their purpose would be to protect humans from becoming extinct, bringing good and evil back into balance. These newly-created Sentinel demons blended in, appearing human…but they weren't. They were magical beings, although they adapted and took on more facets of humanity as they evolved. Having given the guardian demons the power to recruit humans and thus replace Sentinels lost in the battle between good and evil, the gods no longer needed to be bothered with their "annoying little problem" and went to war with each other once again, losing power as the centuries passed and humans ceased to worship them. However, the Sentinels carried on, striving to protect the human population, governing themselves and growing in magical powers, even though the gods had embedded a set of rules into the Sentinels' magic-supposed fail-safes imposed to keep the guardian demons in check. Still, the Sentinels brought balance back to the planet in spite of the stifling rules, finding ways to bend them or work around them, angry that the only rule imposed on the Evils was that human victims could not initially be taken by force, or coerced via lies. But manipulation was easy for an Evil, and once a human had agreed to an Evil's bargain, there was no end to the torture the heinous demons could impose upon the duped individual in order to increase their own strength.

So…are all demons evil? They are all dark at their core, and have some degree of inherent wickedness…but demons were not all created equal.

Evils and Sentinels are both demons, engaging to this day in a battle of good versus evil that has been going on for thousands of years, a war that most humans are blissfully unaware even exists. However, for the small percentage of individuals who actually have encounters with demons… their lives will never be the same.

Kristoff Agares, king of the Sentinel demons, placed the anonymous papers back into a manila folder with a sigh, dissolving the whole file into thin air with a single mental command. When he had first started getting reports about a human writing about his people, he had blown it off. Most of the sparse information about the Sentinels coming from human origins was mere speculation or myth, not a threat to the existence of his brethren. However, the person writing these accounts was getting too close to the truth for comfort and needed to be stopped. He had a pretty good idea who was authoring the information, and that person had enough dirt about the Sentinels to be dangerous. Fortunately, he knew exactly how to handle the situation, and, if his suspicions were correct, the outcome was bound to be entertaining.

He smiled as he teleported himself from his stately home in Seattle to another equally impressive residence on the Olympic Peninsula, located in an area where humans were few and far between. The residence was more of a palace than a home, hidden from hikers or anyone who might happen to pass by the remote area, by the magic of the gods-or rather, the magic of a goddess, the only one still powerful enough to remain on Earth, while all the others had faded away to the kingdom of the dead. Personally, Kristoff secretly believed the majority of them belonged in Tartarus, rather than Elysian Fields, for creating the Evils and bringing so much suffering to so many humans with their selfishness. As far as he knew, this particular goddess was the only one who had argued against the gods' folly of creating, and then ignoring, the Evils, which had allowed them to eventually overrun the Earth.

What would I do without Athena?

Honestly, Kristoff didn't want to find out. The female deity was his advisor, his confidante, and Athena gave new meaning to the expression of having a "longtime friend" since they had known each other for thousands of years. There were moments when he needed the insight and wisdom of the fragile goddess, and now was one of those times. She had summoned *him*, but he had already sensed that change was coming.

I just wish I had a little more clarity. It really irritated the hell out of him when he didn't have complete information.

"Athena?" he called loudly, his booming voice echoing in the opulent residence. He had materialized in her monument room, a large hall filled with statues of the Greek gods. Scowling as he passed marble statues of Apollo, Artemis, and Zeus, he shook his head, grateful that only Athena remained. The rest of them hadn't been worth a shit, and he couldn't bring himself to regret that they were gone, although he knew that Athena still missed some of her family. Exiting the room, he made his way down a grand spiral staircase. The steps were made of gold, the sparkle glinting from the tiles-probably diamonds and gemstones. The residence was ostentatious, and personally, Kristoff cringed at the gaudy furnishings, from the crystal chandeliers to the heavy forest green draperies, but he knew that Athena didn't decorate this way for show. After all, who came to visit except him? No...Athena did what she thought was pretty and cheerful, money really having no meaning to her. She obviously liked the flashy décor, and was able to manifest anything she damn well pleased to try to brighten her solitary existence.

Kristoff knew Athena was lonely because he knew exactly what it was like to be isolated. Cut off, different…and always alone. But at least he had his Sentinels, even if he couldn't always share everything with them. They were amusing and good company-when he didn't feel like bashing their heads together for doing something stupid.

Athena was sequestered here, her existence known only to him, a prisoner of the grand residence she had created in this isolated area. If she wandered far from her residence, she became sick, confused, and unable to function; thus, she was confined to this area, unable to travel far from her home without some very adverse effects on her body and mind.

Kristoff found her in the solarium, surrounded by lush green plants that she was currently watering with a serene expression that instantly calmed him. Athena was balance and enlightenment, and although she might not always have the answers to his questions, her aura was tranquil and soothing. Not that the goddess didn't have a temper that could be fearsome, but her core essence was peaceful.

"Kristoff!" she exclaimed as she turned, her watering pot disappearing from her hands as her face formed a brilliant smile. "Thank you for coming."

He nearly laughed. Athena had summoned him, and he would have to be a complete idiot to ignore the summons of a goddess, but she greeted him like an unexpected guest. "You called me," he reminded her, making himself at home as he sat down on one of the chairs perched around a small glass table.

She moved toward him gracefully, looking almost fragile. Although there were many depictions and likenesses of the Greek goddess of wisdom-Athena-none of them was totally accurate. She was slight, with her long silvery blonde hair currently in a braid down her back, her slim figure dressed in a flowing silky blue robe that was several shades darker than her ice-blue eyes. Reaching the table, she seated herself elegantly across from him. "Yes. I requested your presence, but I didn't know when to expect you," she answered in her soft, melodic voice. "The time for the Sentinels to increase their magic is coming soon, and it's imperative that they do so because the Evils are growing in power. So you're going to have to move your ass."

Kristoff stifled a chuckle, the words that had just left Athena's lips so out of character and incongruent with her normally serene personality that it was amusing. "Watching too much television again?" he asked, unable to mask a tiny smile.

Athena shrugged. "Not much else to do. Isn't that what humans say when they want someone to take action soon?" She cocked her head and looked at him with an innocent expression.

"Yes," he answered honestly, not wanting to offend her and knowing she was completely cut off from the modern world except for a few electronics. "That's exactly what they'd say." Kristoff didn't add that the words just sounded odd coming from a goddess who was thousands of years old, a deity who had been born an adult with more wisdom and reason than any other creature on Earth. "What did you see?" he asked curiously, wanting to know anything and everything that she had foreseen for the Sentinels.

She sighed, a long beleaguered exhalation, before replying, "Everything and nothing. You know how frustrating it is when you know change is coming, but not everything is revealed." She leaned regally against the back of her chair and folded her delicate hands on top of the table. "The Evils are growing stronger, more powerful. But the Sentinels will also gain advantages. Be watchful, Kristoff. We can't afford to miss an opportunity. It's important for the Sentinels to gain every edge they possibly can."

Leaning back, Kristoff ran a frustrated hand through his hair, leaving some of the blond locks spiked on top of his head. "I've felt it, too. I just don't know exactly *what* is happening." Knowing something was coming, but not knowing exactly what or when it would occur, was exasperating. While his Sentinels thought he was being annoyingly mysterious and evasive, more often than not, he just didn't have specifics until they were revealed to him. Okay… maybe he *did* hide a *few* things, but only information his Sentinels just didn't need to know, or things that would be detrimental for them to find out.

Athena unfolded her hands and laid one of them gently over the fist he held tightly on the table, a gesture of support and comfort. "You will know when it's time for you to know. I just wanted you to be warned and watchful. We've always known the Winston brothers were special. The power will come through them. Soon."

Kristoff had always known those three men were key to the survival of his people. That knowledge had been crystal-clear from the moment he had bargained with them. "But how?" he asked aloud. It was a question he had asked himself many times during the last two centuries, ever since he had converted them from human to Sentinel.

Releasing Kristoff's hand and using her goddess powers, Athena manifested an array of delicacies on the table, and an elaborate tea set. Steam rose from the spout of the teapot as she reached for it. "Let's have tea and share our knowledge. Everything is better with tea."

He nodded automatically, thinking that he'd really rather have a glass of Scotch, or maybe a whole bottle. He might not feel the effects of the alcohol, but the fiery burn caused by the excellent whiskey was much more suited to his present mood than tea.

Like it or not, he was responsible for every Sentinel on the planet, male or female, and the majority of them were more human than demon, and to say that some days he had conflicting emotions about his destiny would be putting it mildly. It was a duty and an honor, a crushing burden and an exhilarating challenge. But mostly...it was just who he was, and he accepted the albatross easily, donned the mantle of king with pride. Because he *was* proud of the Sentinels... most of the time. They had, after all, kept the fight between good and evil in balance since the time of the ancient gods.

Heaving a very masculine sigh, he accepted the dainty cup from Athena, glad he at least had her occasional company to discuss the things that he couldn't share with anyone else. Athena helped center him, and had given him wisdom when he had become a little too hotheaded in his younger years. He'd asked her once why she still remained when all of the other gods had faded from existence. Her reply had been both wistful and pragmatic, telling him that she would remain until she was no longer needed.

As the goddess started talking, telling him about her visions, Kristoff couldn't imagine a time when Athena *wouldn't* be essential to the continued survival of the Sentinels. They spent the next hour in conversation, sharing their ideas and knowledge before he said goodbye, her melancholic face fading as he transported away.

Kristoff left Athena's enormous home with a lot of questions still plaguing his mind, and very few concrete answers. The only thing he knew for certain was that the lives of some of the Sentinels were about to be altered, and he had work to do to ensure that everything turned out the way it was fated. Because sometimes, even if one were on a predetermined course, one could still get lost. The Winston brothers, all three of them, in their own different ways, needed to heal from their past to fulfill their destiny for the future.

As king, he cared for all of the Sentinels, but Zach, Drew, and Hunter were special, more friends than subjects to him, which created a real internal conflict. He couldn't reveal their destiny, but he'd do everything in his power to make sure they fulfilled it.

Kristoff reappeared in Seattle to complete the first of many tasks on his list, determined that, no matter what, he wouldn't fail.

Chapter One

Be careful what you wish for; it might come true.

The oxymoronic saying floated through Zachary Winston's head as he sat with his hands under his chin, listening to the satisfying clack of metal against metal as the two end spheres of his Newton's cradle rose and fell. Kinetic energy, velocity, and scientific explanations were far from his mind at the moment. He simply enjoyed watching the symmetry of the movement, the hypnotic action serving to slightly calm the darkness and bleakness of his demonic soul.

If he had wished more carefully two hundred years ago, his twelve-year-old sister, Sophie, might have actually lived after his bargain with the Sentinel demon king. Zach had agreed to become a Sentinel for eternity in return for fabulous wealth, certain that money could get him the help he needed to save his baby sister from dying of smallpox. It didn't. She had died alone in the squalor of a pest house while he was out trying to steal things to make her more comfortable, and making an eternal bargain that hadn't done a damn thing to help her. The deal had come too late; it wasn't what Sophie needed to save her, and Zach had been left completely alone in the world.

The only person in the universe who had cared about him had been ripped from his grasp, regardless of the fact that he had become one of the richest men in the world because of his demon bargain. Actually, he still was one of the richest men in the world, although money meant little to him now. Not after two centuries of guilt and remorse had been plaguing him every single day, his soul growing darker every year.

I should have made a different wish. Sophie was probably still alive when I struck my bargain with Kristoff.

Zach had made the wrong wish, one that had left him with two hundred years of loneliness, and enough time to curse himself for not thinking harder about Kristoff's offer before agreeing so readily. He would have made a deal with the devil himself to save the sister he had adored, and for whom he had been responsible after the death of his mother.

Zach didn't remember his father. A fisherman, he'd died in a violent storm at sea soon after Sophie was born. His mother had been left in a poor area of London with nothing except two young children to feed and no money. Zach knew his mother had been a prostitute, using the only commodity she had to feed herself and her two children, and he had never condemned her for it. How in the hell else was a woman with two young children going to make money in the early nineteenth century? His mother could have given him and Sophie up, sent them away, but she didn't. Instead, she had become old before her time, developing consumption after years of struggling to take care of them. Before she had breathed her last, she'd made him promise to watch out for his younger sister, and Zach had taken that deathbed promise seriously. Still, he had failed both his mother and his sister. Both of them were dead, his innocent sister Sophie at the tender age of twelve.

Why wasn't it me who died? It should have been me!

"Playing with your balls again, I see." The deep, gravelly voice sounded from the doorway of his plush office. His eyes rose as he glanced at Kristoff Agares, the Sentinel demon king, as he swaggered into Zach's office with a smirk, not waiting for an invitation. Not that he ever did. Kristoff answered to no one as far as Zach knew, and he did exactly as he pleased.

Zach reached out a hand and stopped the clacking executive toy, focusing his scowling attention on the tall blond demon. Although he had gained a grudging respect for Kristoff over the last two centuries, Zach had never quite let go of the fact that the Sentinel demon king hadn't shown up a little earlier, in time to save Sophie instead of him. But he hadn't. Kristoff had intervened when Zach was caught stealing and had made his bargain with him. Later that same day, when Kristoff had come to complete Zach's bargain and transform him into a Sentinel, the demon king had found Zach clawing at Sophie's grave, angry and half crazed because he hadn't even been able to say goodbye, hadn't been there when his sister had perished and been dumped in a mass grave along with other bodies from the pest house. Kristoff had transported him away, taking him into his own home to give him time to get over his grief and anger. Unfortunately, although his anger and grief had lessened over the last two hundred years, his guilt and remorse still remained.

Kristoff lowered his muscular body into the roomy leather chair in front of Zach's desk as he remarked casually, "You need to find your *radiant*. You have absolutely no sense of humor."

"Did it ever occur to you that your stupid comments aren't really all that funny?" Zach muttered as he frowned at Kristoff.

"Nope. I'm hilarious. You're just in desperate need of a *radiant*," Kristoff told him with a grin. "You need to get laid."

His radiant? Oh, hell no.

A *radiant* was the Sentinel equivalent of a mate, the one who would bring light back into his dark soul. All Zach had ever found were women who wanted to lighten his damn wallet...not his soul.

Once...just one time...I'd like to find a woman who wants me and not my money.

Truth was, Zach had given up on taking women to bed just for sex a long time ago. It just seemed to make him darker, and more restless. The emptiness of casual sexual romps just no longer appealed to him. It left him even more lonely and unsatisfied than he'd been prior to the sexual encounters.

"I don't need my *radiant* to get fucked," Zach grumbled defensively, although he hadn't gotten fucked for quite some time.

"Trust me. You need more than a quick, unemotional screw." Kristoff's expression grew serious, his voice concerned.

"I assume you're here for a reason?" Zach shot his superior a glare, wanting to change the subject. He *did* want more, needed more, but it wasn't something he actually wanted to discuss at the moment. He was too restless, too edgy, and he'd been that way for a while now. It was as though he was just waiting, biding his time until some type of mysterious metamorphosis happened, and the uncomfortable, impatient feeling was making his fuse shorter every damn day.

Kristoff shrugged. "Aren't I always?" He leaned forward and shoved a file across the desk toward Zach. "Your next assignment."

Zach actually released a sigh of relief. It had been a few weeks since he had been given a mission. He needed the distraction, the challenge. Boredom wasn't good for him. It gave him too much time to think, and thinking usually led to regrets and guilt. Honestly, he didn't mind being a Sentinel, and he didn't regret that part of his bargain. There was nothing he loved more than letting Evils give him a reason to annihilate the ugly little bastards.

Yeah, I need a mission. I have too much time on my hands right now.

Zach didn't need to worry much about business because there was absolutely no reason why he should. He'd always be wealthy. Winston Industries was worth billions and he knew it always would be. Any decision he made would be the right one to increase his wealth. Being rich was part of the demon bargain he had made two hundred years ago. Demon magic would make it a certainty that he stayed a billionaire, which pretty much took the challenge out of work for him, leaving him with too much time to think, unless he was on assignment.

Zach lifted the file curiously. "A recruitment?"

Kristoff shook his head. "A rescue."

Zach's hand halted before he opened the file, his eyes returning to Kristoff with a startled expression. "The Evils are abducting an innocent? How?" It was a stupid question and he knew it. The bastards had a multitude of trickery and deceit to capture blameless souls. But his surprise over being given a rescue instead of a recruitment disturbed him in a visceral way, an instant denial ringing in his head, telling him that he would suck at rescue. Hadn't he failed in the task of keeping an innocent from harm in the past? *Oh, hell no. Not a rescue.* He was used to recruiting salvageable souls that were straddling the line between good and evil to become Sentinels. He was the last Sentinel that should be left with the care of a blameless soul. More than likely, he'd screw it up; the Evils would take the victim, and he'd end up with another death on his conscience. Whoever the poor unfortunate human might be, that individual deserved a hell of a lot better Sentinel than him as a savior.

Truly evil demons could manipulate humans in any number of ways. Their main goal was to sway as many untainted and unsuspecting humans to the demon realm as possible, using whatever means available. The catch was…the uncorrupt human had to agree, had to give permission to be taken, even when not entirely understanding what the bargain with the Evils entailed, since the assholes weren't exactly into full disclosure. Wallowing in the pain caused by corruption of an unblemished soul was empowerment to an Evil. The purer the soul, the more power the Evil absorbed. And once the vow to go with the Evils was uttered, that was one more soul lost to the Sentinels. And if there was anything a Sentinel really hated, it was to be defeated by an Evil. The instinct to win was strong, the trait imbedded since the creation of the Sentinels and passed on by demon magic whenever a new recruit was changed and indoctrinated.

Kristoff nodded his head to the file that Zach was holding as he replied, "Emotional manipulation. Not uncommon for the Evils, but pretty dirty this time."

Zach opened the folder. His breath *whooshed* out of his lungs as his inspection was met with the blinding smile of a veritable angel. With flame-colored hair that tumbled over her shoulders, Katrina

"Kat" Larson-the name on the file label-was definitely an unholy temptation. Zach viewed all of her pictures slowly, taking in the creamy light skin and curvy, generous figure in every photo. Every picture showed her laughing or smiling and her spirit was almost infectious, even via the glossy images.

No wonder the Evils want her. Her sweetness practically jumps out of the photos.

Kristoff spoke as Zach continued to stare at the woman's pictures. "Twenty-seven-year-old female. Coerced to sacrifice herself to the Evils for a week in exchange for her eight-year-old nephew's life… her twin sister's child. He suffers from leukemia, which is currently in remission. They apparently told her he wouldn't die if she would come with them to the demon realm for a week."

"And will it save him?" Zach asked distractedly as he placed his hand over the smiling face of the woman to absorb her information, rather than wait for it to be revealed on paper. He couldn't read her thoughts unless he was actually close to her, but he could get the general facts faster by absorbing the written words in the file.

Kristoff leaned forward as his voice lowered. "No demon has power over life and death from disease, Zach. Not even me. We can see the outcome sometimes, but we can't interfere. I've told you that. You just choose not to accept it. The Evils can only damage souls or kill a human victim who agreed to bargain. They don't have the power to cure an incurable disease." Kristoff sighed as he leaned his muscular body back into the soft leather of the chair. "They told her that her nephew would live…which is true. What they didn't tell her is that it has nothing to do with any power *they* have. Her nephew's disease will stay in remission whether she goes to the demon realm or not. They've managed to use her fear for her nephew's life to manipulate her without actually lying."

"Bastards! So they led her to believe her nephew would die unless she struck the bargain and went with them?" Zach snarled as he closed the file, his brown eyes starting to glow amber as he looked at Kristoff, his face revealing his frustration and anger. Shit…he hated those ugly little bastards. He'd seen humans who they'd manipulated and taken to the demon realm, souls the Sentinels hadn't been able to save. Sometimes they killed their human victims in the demon realm after absorbing all the power they could get from the individual. Occasionally, they sent the bodies back alive, but drained of their souls, completely lifeless. That particular action was usually done as a taunt to the Sentinels, and it generally worked. His kind had a very hard time not being angry when confronted with the harm done to a human who couldn't be saved.

"Obviously they didn't say that directly," Kristoff answered unhappily. "They just told her that her nephew would live if she gave up a week of her life to live in the demon realm. Not exactly a lie, but definitely an extreme evasion of the truth."

"Dammit. She'll be destroyed, a shell of who she was before leaving…if they even send her back alive. All for nothing." Zach's hands clenched into fists, his knuckles whitening with the pressure. The thought of the smiling, innocent, vivacious redhead being turned into an empty body with none of her spirit left made his guts roll, although he wasn't quite sure why. It wasn't as if he didn't see it happen frequently, but his emotional reaction to this particular case unsettled him. Maybe it was because he didn't normally take these types of assignments.

"Not if you get to her first." Kristoff's eyes were intense as he nailed Zach with an urgent look. "She doesn't understand that they mean to steal the life from her soul and she hasn't given consent. You need to convince her, Zach. She has a soul worth saving." He hesitated before adding, "She's…special." Kristoff sounded like he wanted to add more, but simply shook his head.

"Why me? I'm a recruiter…not a rescuer. Why didn't you give the job to Drew or Hunter?" Drew and Hunter were rescuing Sentinels. Zach…wasn't, and he didn't want to be, although he was reluctant to give this particular assignment to another after seeing the victim and absorbing her general history. Something about her intrigued him, made him want to learn more about her, see her in person.

Zach recruited new Sentinels, humans who had nowhere to go, no one to help them…and who were ready to leap from good to evil because of their circumstances. He offered them the same bargain Kristoff had offered Zach a few centuries ago. *That* was Zach's designation, a demon duty completely different from that of his two partners in Winston Industries. Zach, Drew, and Hunter posed as brothers, all leading Winston Industries together, but they weren't actually blood-related. They had just all wished for the same damn thing, had wanted the same demon bargain. *Money*. And they had gotten it. Drew was the only one of the trio who seemed to be happy with his bargain. Zach was still filled with regret, even after two centuries. And Hunter was downright bitter and angry.

Be careful what you wish for...

"Drew is busy with another mission, Hunter is...unavailable, and I have another urgent situation. It has to be you, or Kat will probably end up in the demon realm," Kristoff replied, his voice neutral, but his eyes were intense as he stared Zach down, forcing him to make a decision.

"How long do I have?" Zach replied, focused on his mission, determined that he wouldn't screw up this time. There was no way the Evils were going to get their claws into *this* one. The woman looked sweet, innocent. Just the thought of her soul being drained of goodness had him half crazed.

No wonder I'm a damn recruiter. How the hell do Drew and Hunter tolerate doing this type of assignment day after day?

"Sundown. They'll appear for her final consent and take her," Kristoff replied without hesitation.

Zach stared at the large glass windows that lined one wall of his office, overlooking the city. As he saw the late afternoon light beginning to fade, he quirked a dark brow at his boss. "Cutting this a little close...don't you think?"

"Not my fault. I didn't discover the situation until this afternoon." As both men stood and Zach stepped out from behind his desk, Kristoff slapped him hard on the back. "It's nothing you're not capable of, Zach."

Zach scowled as he answered, "I may have to bend a few rules if I can't convince her quickly. You didn't exactly give me enough time to do much persuading. "

A smile curved Kristoff's lips as he answered noncommittally, "I think you know how to bend the rules without completely breaking them like Hunter does."

Zach didn't reply. With a curt nod to Kristoff, he allowed himself to fade out until he disappeared completely.

Kristoff's expression turned to one of satisfaction as he watched Zach's form completely disappear before shimmering out of view himself, leaving the plush, high-rise office completely abandoned.

End of Sample.

A Dangerous Bargain

is now available.

Printed in Great Britain
by Amazon